D1462352

· · ·

WILLA SIBERT CATHER

THE WILLA CATHER
READER

an imprint of
RUNNING PRESS
Philadelphia • London

O Pioneers! is reprinted from the first edition, published in 1913 by Houghton
Mifflin Company, Boston. *My Ántonia* is reprinted from the first edition,
published in 1918 by Houghton Mifflin Company, Boston. "The Garden Lodge,"
"Paul's Case," and "The Sculptor's Funeral" are reprinted from the first edition of
The Troll Garden, published in 1905 by McClure, Phillips & Co., New York.
All materials were made available through the courtesy of the Willa Cather
Pioneer Memorial, Red Cloud, Nebraska. All spellings and punctuation
are preserved as they appeared in the original editions, except for
obvious typographical errors.

The interview with Willa Cather is excerpted from "Willa Sibert Cather"
by Archer Latrobe Carroll. It originally appeared in *The Bookman*.

9 8 7 6 5 4 3 2 1
Digit on the right indicates the number of this printing.

Library of Congress Cataloging-in-Publication Number 96-71940

ISBN 0-7624-0175-3

Cover design by Diane Miljat
Edited by Gena M. Pearson
Set in ITC Berkeley Oldstyle

Published by Courage Books, an imprint of
Running Press Book Publishers
125 South Twenty-second Street
Philadelphia, Pennsylvania 19103-4399

CONTENTS

• • •

WILLA SIBERT CATHER

THE WILLA CATHER
READER

PRAIRIE SPRING

Evening and the flat land,
Rich and sombre and always silent;
The miles of fresh-plowed soil,
Heavy and black, full of strength and harshness;
The growing wheat, the growing weeds,
The toiling horses, the tired men;
The long empty roads,
Sullen fires of sunset, fading,
The eternal, unresponsive sky.
Against all this, Youth,
Flaming like the wild roses,
Singing like the larks over the plowed fields,
Flashing like a star out of the twilight;
Youth with its insupportable sweetness,
Its fierce necessity,
Its sharp desire,
Singing and singing,
Out of the lips of silence,
Out of the earthy dusk.

. . .

O PIONEERS!

PART I
THE WILD LAND

I

One January day, thirty years ago, the little town of Hanover, anchored on a windy Nebraska tableland, was trying not to be blown away. A mist of fine snowflakes was curling and eddying about the cluster of low drab buildings huddled on the gray prairie, under a gray sky. The dwelling-houses were set about haphazard on the tough prairie sod; some of them looked as if they had been moved in overnight, and others as if they were straying off by themselves, headed straight for the open plain. None of them had any appearance of permanence, and the howling wind blew under them as well as over them. The main street was a deeply rutted road, now frozen hard, which ran from the squat red railway station and the grain "elevator" at the north end of the town to the lumber yard and the horse pond at the south end. On either side of this road straggled two uneven rows of wooden buildings; the general merchandise stores, the two banks, the drug store, the feed store, the saloon, the post-office. The board sidewalks were gray with trampled snow, but at two o'clock in the afternoon the shopkeepers, having come back from dinner, were keeping well behind their frosty windows. The children were all in school, and there was nobody abroad in the streets but a few rough-looking country-men in coarse overcoats, with their long caps pulled down to their noses. Some of them had brought their wives to town, and now and then a red or a plaid shawl flashed out of one store into the shelter of another. At the hitch-bars along the street a few heavy work-horses, harnessed to farm wagons, shivered under their blankets. About the station everything was quiet, for there would not be another train in until night.

On the sidewalk in front of one of the stores sat a little Swede boy, crying bitterly. He was about five years old. His black cloth coat was much too big for him and made him look like a little old man. His shrunken brown flannel dress had been washed many times and left a long stretch of stocking between the hem of his skirt and the tops of his clumsy, copper-toed shoes. His cap was pulled down over his ears; his nose and his chubby cheeks were chapped and red with cold. He cried quietly, and the few people who hurried by did not notice him. He was afraid to stop any one, afraid to go into the store and ask for help, so he sat wringing his long sleeves and looking up a telegraph pole beside him, whimpering, "My kitten, oh, my kitten! Her will fweeze!" At the top of the pole crouched a shivering gray kitten, mewing faintly and clinging desperately to the wood with her claws. The boy had been left at the store while his sister went to the doctor's office, and in her absence a dog had chased his kitten up the pole. The little creature had never been so high before, and she was too frightened to move. Her master was sunk in despair. He was a little country boy, and this village was to him a very strange and perplexing place, where people wore fine clothes and had hard hearts. He always felt shy and awkward here, and wanted to hide behind things for fear some one might laugh at him. Just now, he was too unhappy to care who laughed. At last he seemed to see a ray of hope: his sister was coming, and he got up and ran toward her in his heavy shoes.

His sister was a tall, strong girl, and she walked rapidly and resolutely, as if she knew exactly where she was going and what she was going to do next. She wore a man's long ulster (not as if it were an affliction, but as if it were very comfortable and belonged to her; carried it like a young soldier), and a round plush cap, tied down with a thick veil. She had a serious, thoughtful face, and her clear, deep blue eyes were fixed intently on the distance, without seeming to see anything, as if she were in trouble. She did not notice the little boy until he pulled her by the coat. Then she stopped short and stooped down to wipe his wet face.

"Why, Emil! I told you to stay in the store and not to come out. What is the matter with you?"

"My kitten, sister, my kitten! A man put her out, and a dog chased her up there." His forefinger, projecting from the sleeve of his coat, pointed up to the wretched little creature on the pole.

"Oh, Emil! Didn't I tell you she'd get us into trouble of some kind, if you brought her? What made you tease me so? But there, I ought to have known better myself." She went to the foot of the pole and held out her arms, crying, "Kitty, kitty, kitty," but the kitten only mewed and faintly waved its tail. Alexandra turned away decidedly. "No, she won't come down. Somebody will have to go up after her. I saw the Linstrums' wagon in town. I'll go and see if I can find Carl. Maybe he can do something. Only you must stop crying, or I won't go a step. Where's your comforter? Did you leave it in the store? Never mind. Hold still, till I put this on you."

She unwound the brown veil from her head and tied it about his throat. A shabby little traveling man, who was just then coming out of the store on his way to the saloon, stopped and gazed stupidly at the shining mass of hair she bared when she took off her veil; two thick braids, pinned about her head in the German way, with a fringe of reddish-yellow curls blowing out from under her cap. He took his cigar out of his mouth and held the wet end between the fingers of his woolen glove. "My God, girl, what a head of hair!" he exclaimed, quite innocently and foolishly. She stabbed him with a glance of Amazonian fierceness and drew in her lower lip—most unnecessary severity. It gave the little clothing drummer such a start that he actually let his cigar fall to the sidewalk and went off weakly in the teeth of the wind to the saloon. His hand was still unsteady when he took his glass from the bartender. His feeble flirtatious instincts had been crushed before, but never so mercilessly. He felt cheap and ill-used, as if some one had taken advantage of him. When a drummer had been knocking about in little drab towns and crawling across the wintry country in dirty smoking-cars, was he to be blamed if, when he chanced upon a fine human creature, he suddenly wished himself more of a man?

While the little drummer was drinking to recover his nerve, Alexandra hurried to the drug store as the most likely place to find Carl Linstrum. There he was, turning over a portfolio of chromo "studies" which the druggist sold to the Hanover women who did china-painting. Alexandra explained her predicament, and the boy followed her to the corner, where Emil still sat by the pole.

"I'll have to go up after her, Alexandra. I think at the depot they have some spikes I can strap on my feet. Wait a minute." Carl thrust his hands into his pockets, lowered his head, and darted up the street against the north wind. He was a tall boy of fifteen, slight and narrow-chested. When he came back with the spikes, Alexandra asked him what he had done with his overcoat.

"I left it in the drug store. I couldn't climb in it, anyhow. Catch me if I fall, Emil," he called back as he began his ascent. Alexandra watched him anxiously; the cold was bitter enough on the ground. The kitten would not budge an inch. Carl had to go to the very top of the pole, and then had some difficulty in tearing her from her hold. When he reached the ground, he handed the cat to her tearful little master. "Now go into the store with her, Emil, and get warm." He opened the door for the child. "Wait a minute, Alexandra. Why can't I drive for you as far as our place? It's getting colder every minute. Have you seen the doctor?"

"Yes. He is coming over to-morrow. But he says father can't get better; can't get well." The girl's lip trembled. She looked fixedly up the bleak street as if she were gathering her strength to face something, as if she were trying with all her might to grasp a situation which, no matter how painful, must be met and dealt with somehow. The wind flapped the skirts of her heavy coat about her.

Carl did not say anything, but she felt his sympathy. He, too, was lonely. He was a thin, frail boy, with brooding dark eyes, very quiet in all his movements. There was a delicate pallor in his thin face, and his mouth was too sensitive for a boy's. The lips had already a little curl of bitterness and skepticism. The two friends stood for a few moments on the windy street corner, not speaking a word, as two travelers, who have lost their way, sometimes stand and admit their perplexity in silence. When Carl turned away he said, "I'll see to your team." Alexandra went into the store to have her purchases packed in the egg-boxes, and to get warm before she set out on her long cold drive.

When she looked for Emil, she found him sitting on a step of the staircase that led up to the clothing and carpet department. He was playing with a little Bohemian girl, Marie Tovesky, who was tying her handkerchief over the kitten's head for a bonnet. Marie was a stranger in the country, having come from Omaha with her mother to visit her uncle, Joe Tovesky. She was a dark child, with brown curly hair, like a brunette doll's, a coaxing little red mouth, and round, yellow-brown eyes. Every one noticed her eyes; the brown iris had golden glints that made them look like gold-stone, or, in softer lights, like that Colorado mineral called tiger-eye.

The country children thereabouts wore their dresses to their shoe-tops, but this city child was dressed in what was then called the "Kate Greenaway" manner, and her red cashmere frock, gathered full from the yoke, came almost to the floor. This, with her poke bonnet, gave her the look of a quaint little woman. She had a white fur tippet about her neck and made no fussy objections when Emil fingered it admiringly. Alexandra had not the heart to take him away from so pretty a playfellow, and she let them tease the kitten together until Joe Tovesky came in noisily and picked up his little niece, setting her on his shoulder for every one to see. His children were all boys, and he adored this little creature. His cronies formed a circle about him, admiring and teasing the little girl, who took their jokes with great good nature. They were all delighted with her, for they seldom saw so pretty and carefully nurtured a child. They told her that she must choose one of them for a sweetheart, and each began pressing his suit and offering her bribes; candy, and little pigs, and spotted calves. She looked archly into the big, brown, mustached faces, smelling of spirits and tobacco, then she ran her tiny forefinger delicately over Joe's bristly chin and said, "Here is my sweetheart."

The Bohemians roared with laughter, and Marie's uncle

hugged her until she cried, "Please don't, Uncle Joe! You hurt me." Each of Joe's friends gave her a bag of candy, and she kissed them all around, though she did not like country candy very well. Perhaps that was why she bethought herself of Emil. "Let me down, Uncle Joe," she said, "I want to give some of my candy to that nice little boy I found." She walked graciously over to Emil, followed by her lusty admirers, who formed a new circle and teased the little boy until he hid his face in his sister's skirts, and she had to scold him for being such a baby.

The farm people were making preparations to start for home. The women were checking over their groceries and pinning their big red shawls about their heads. The men were buying tobacco and candy with what money they had left, were showing each other new boots and gloves and blue flannel shirts. Three big Bohemians were drinking raw alcohol, tinctured with oil of cinnamon. This was said to fortify one effectually against the cold, and they smacked their lips after each pull at the flask. Their volubility drowned every other noise in the place, and the overheated store sounded of their spirited language as it reeked of pipe smoke, damp woolens, and kerosene.

Carl came in, wearing his overcoat and carrying a wooden box with a brass handle. "Come," he said, "I've fed and watered your team, and the wagon is ready." He carried Emil out and tucked him down in the straw in the wagon-box. The heat had made the little boy sleepy, but he still clung to his kitten.

"You were awful good to climb so high and get my kitten, Carl. When I get big I'll climb and get little boys' kittens for them," he murmured drowsily. Before the horses were over the first hill, Emil and his cat were both fast asleep.

Although it was only four o'clock, the winter day was fading. The road led southwest, toward the streak of pale, watery light that glimmered in the leaden sky. The light fell upon the two sad young faces that were turned mutely toward it: upon the eyes of the girl, who seemed to be looking with such anguished perplexity into the future; upon the sombre eyes of the boy, who seemed already to be looking into the past. The little town behind them had vanished as if it had never been, had fallen behind the swell of the prairie, and the stern frozen country received them into its bosom. The homesteads were few and far apart; here and there a windmill gaunt against the sky, a sod house crouching in a hollow. But the great fact was the land itself, which seemed to overwhelm the little beginnings of human society that struggled in its sombre wastes. It was from facing this vast hardness that the boy's mouth had become so bitter; because he felt that men were too weak to make any mark here, that the land wanted to be let alone, to preserve its own fierce strength, its peculiar, savage kind of beauty, its uninterrupted mournfulness.

The wagon jolted along over the frozen road. The two friends had less to say to each other than usual, as if the cold had somehow penetrated to their hearts.

"Did Lou and Oscar go to the Blue to cut wood to-day?" Carl asked.

"Yes. I'm almost sorry I let them go, it's turned so cold. But mother frets if the wood gets low." She stopped and put her hand to her forehead, brushing back her hair. "I don't know what is to become of us, Carl, if father has to die. I don't dare to think about it. I wish we could all go with him and let the grass grow back over everything."

Carl made no reply. Just ahead of them was the Norwegian graveyard, where the grass had, indeed, grown back over everything, shaggy and red, hiding even the wire fence. Carl realized that he was not a very helpful companion, but there was nothing he could say.

"Of course," Alexandra went on, steadying her voice a little, "the boys are strong and work hard, but we've always depended so on father that I don't see how we can go ahead. I almost feel as if there were nothing to go ahead for."

"Does your father know?"

"Yes, I think he does. He lies and counts on his fingers all day. I think he is trying to count up what he is leaving for us. It's a

comfort to him that my chickens are laying right on through the
cold weather and bringing in a little money. I wish we could keep
his mind off such things, but I don't have much time to be with
him now."

"I wonder if he'd like to have me bring my magic lantern over
some evening?"

Alexandra turned her face toward him. "Oh, Carl! Have you
got it?"

"Yes. It's back there in the straw. Didn't you notice the box I
was carrying? I tried it all morning in the drug-store cellar, and it
worked ever so well, makes fine big pictures."

"What are they about?"

"Oh, hunting pictures in Germany, and Robinson Crusoe and
funny pictures about cannibals. I'm going to paint some slides for
it on glass, out of the Hans Andersen book."

Alexandra seemed actually cheered. There is often a good deal
of the child left in people who have had to grow up too soon. "Do
bring it over, Carl. I can hardly wait to see it, and I'm sure it will
please father. Are the pictures colored? Then I know he'll like
them. He likes the calendars I get him in town. I wish I could
get more. You must leave me here, mustn't you? It's been nice to
have company."

Carl stopped the horses and looked dubiously up at the black
sky. "It's pretty dark. Of course the horses will take you home, but
I think I'd better light your lantern, In case you should need it."

He gave her the reins and climbed back into the wagon-box,
where he crouched down and made a tent of his overcoat. After a
dozen trials he succeeded in lighting the lantern, which he placed
in front of Alexandra, half covering it with a blanket so that the
light would not shine in her eyes. "Now, wait until I find my box.
Yes, here it is. Good-night, Alexandra. Try not to worry." Carl
sprang to the ground and ran off across the fields toward the
Linstrum homestead. "Hoo, hoo-o-o-!" he called back as he disappeared over a ridge and dropped into a sand gully. The wind
answered him like an echo, "Hoo, hoo-o-o-o-o!" Alexandra

drove off alone. The rattle of her wagon was lost in the howling of the wind, but her lantern, held firmly between her feet, made a moving point of light along the highway, going deeper and deeper into the black country.

II

On one of the ridges of that wintry waste stood the low log house in which John Bergson was dying. The Bergson homestead was easier to find than many another, because it over-looked Norway Creek, a shallow, muddy stream that sometimes flowed, and sometimes stood still, at the bottom of a winding ravine with steep, shelving sides overgrown with brush and cottonwoods and dwarf ash. This creek gave a sort of identity to the farms that bordered upon it. Of all the bewildering things about a new country, the absence of human landmarks is one of the most depressing and disheartening. The houses on the Divide were small and were usually tucked away in low places; you did not see them until you came directly upon them. Most of them were built of the sod itself, and were only the unescapable ground in another form. The roads were but faint tracks in the grass, and the fields were scarcely noticeable. The record of the plow was insignificant, like the feeble scratches on stone left by prehistoric races, so indeterminate that they may, after all, be only the markings of glaciers, and not a record of human strivings.

In eleven long years John Bergson had made but little impression upon the wild land he had come to tame. It was still a wild thing that had its ugly moods; and no one knew when they were likely to come, or why. Mischance hung over it. Its Genius was unfriendly to man. The sick man was feeling this as he lay looking out of the window, after the doctor had left him, on the day following Alexandra's trip to town. There it lay outside his door, the same land, the same lead-colored miles. He knew every ridge and draw and gully between him and the horizon. To the south, his plowed fields; to the east, the sod stables, the cattle corral, the pond,—and then the grass.

Bergson went over in his mind the things that had held him back. One winter his cattle had perished in a blizzard. The next summer one of his plow horses broke its leg in a prairie-dog hole and had to be shot. Another summer he lost his hogs from cholera, and a valuable stallion died from a rattlesnake bite. Time and again his crops had failed. He had lost two children, boys, that came between Lou and Emil, and there had been the cost of sickness and death. Now, when he had at last struggled out of debt, he was going to die himself. He was only forty-six, and had, of course, counted upon more time.

Bergson had spent his first five years on the Divide getting into debt, and the last six getting out. He had paid off his mortgages and had ended pretty much where he began, with the land. He owned exactly six hundred and forty acres of what stretched outside his door; his own original homestead and timber claim, making three hundred and twenty acres, and the half-section adjoining, the homestead of a younger brother who had given up the fight, gone back to Chicago to work in a fancy bakery and distinguish himself in a Swedish athletic club. So far John had not attempted to cultivate the second half-section, but used it for pasture land, and one of his sons rode herd there in open weather.

John Bergson had the Old-World belief that land, in itself, is desirable. But this land was an enigma. It was like a horse that no one knows how to break to harness, that runs wild and kicks things to pieces. He had an idea that no one understood how to farm it properly, and this he often discussed with Alexandra. Their neighbors, certainly, knew even less about farming than he did. Many of them had never worked on a farm until they took up their homesteads. They had been *handwerkers* at home; tailors, locksmiths, joiners, cigar-makers, etc. Bergson himself had worked in a shipyard.

For weeks, John Bergson had been thinking about these things. His bed stood in the sitting-room, next to the kitchen.

Through the day, while the baking and washing and ironing were going on, the father lay and looked up at the roof beams that he himself had hewn, or out at the cattle in the corral. He counted the cattle over and over. It diverted him to speculate as to how much weight each of the steers would probably put on by spring. He often called his daughter in to talk to her about this. Before Alexandra was twelve years old she had begun to be a help to him, and as she grew older he had come to depend more and more upon her resourcefulness and good judgment. His boys were willing enough to work, but when he talked with them they usually irritated him. It was Alexandra who read the papers and followed the markets, and who learned by the mistakes of their neighbors. It was Alexandra who could always tell about what it had cost to fatten each steer, and who could guess the weight of a hog before it went on the scales closer than John Bergson himself. Lou and Oscar were industrious, but he could never teach them to use their heads about their work.

Alexandra, her father often said to himself, was like her grand-father; which was his way of saying that she was intelligent. John Bergson's father had been a shipbuilder, a man of considerable force and of some fortune. Late in life he married a second time, a Stockholm woman of questionable character, much younger than he, who goaded him into every sort of extravagance. On the ship-builder's part, this marriage was an infatuation, the despairing folly of a powerful man who cannot bear to grow old. In a few years his unprincipled wife warped the probity of a lifetime. He speculated, lost his own fortune and funds entrusted to him by poor seafaring men, and died disgraced, leaving his children nothing. But when all was said, he had come up from the sea himself, had built up a proud little business with no capital but his own skill and foresight, and had proved himself a man. In his daughter, John Bergson recognized the strength of will, and the simple direct way of thinking things out, that had character-ized his father in his better days. He would much rather, of course, have seen this likeness in one of his sons, but it was not a question of choice. As he lay there day after day he had to accept the situation as it was, and to be thankful that there was one among his children to whom he could entrust the future of his family and the possibilities of his hard-won land.

The winter twilight was fading. The sick man heard his wife strike a match in the kitchen, and the light of a lamp glimmered through the cracks of the door. It seemed like a light shining far away. He turned painfully in his bed and looked at his white hands, with all the work gone out of them. He was ready to give up, he felt. He did not know how it had come about, but he was quite willing to go deep under his fields and rest, where the plow could not find him. He was tired of making mistakes. He was content to leave the tangle to other hands; he thought of his Alexandra's strong ones.

"*Dotter*," he called feebly, "*dotter!*" He heard her quick step and saw her tall figure appear in the doorway, with the light of the lamp behind her. He felt her youth and strength, how easily she moved and stooped and lifted. But he would not have had it again if he could, not he! He knew the end too well to wish to begin again. He knew where it all went to, what it all became.

His daughter came and lifted him up on his pillows. She called him by an old Swedish name that she used to call him when she was little and took his dinner to him in the shipyard.

"Tell the boys to come here, daughter. I want to speak to them."

"They are feeding the horses, father. They have just come back from the Blue. Shall I call them?"

He sighed. "No, no. Wait until they come in. Alexandra, you will have to do the best you can for your brothers. Everything will come on you."

"I will do all I can, father."

"Don't let them get discouraged and go off like Uncle Otto. I want them to keep the land."

"We will, father. We will never lose the land."

There was a sound of heavy feet in the kitchen. Alexandra went to the door and beckoned to her brothers, two strapping boys of seventeen and nineteen. They came in and stood at the foot of the bed. Their father looked at them searchingly, though it was too dark to see their faces; they were just the same boys, he told himself, he had not been mistaken in them. The square head and heavy shoulders belonged to Oscar, the elder. The younger boy was quicker, but vacillating.

"Boys," said the father wearily, "I want you to keep the land together and to be guided by your sister. I have talked to her since I have been sick, and she knows all my wishes. I want no quarrels among my children, and so long as there is one house there must be one head. Alexandra is the oldest, and she knows my wishes. She will do the best she can. If she makes mistakes, she will not make so many as I have made. When you marry, and want a house of your own, the land will be divided fairly, according to the courts. But for the next few years you will have it hard, and you must all keep together. Alexandra will manage the best she can."

Oscar, who was usually the last to speak, replied because he was the older, "Yes, father. It would be so anyway, without your speaking. We will all work the place together."

"And you will be guided by your sister, boys, and be good brothers to her, and good sons to your mother? That is good. And Alexandra must not work in the fields any more. There is no necessity now. Hire a man when you need help. She can make much more with her eggs and butter than the wages of a man. It was one of my mistakes that I did not find that out sooner. Try to break a little more land every year; sod corn is good for fodder. Keep turning the land, and always put up more hay than you need. Don't grudge your mother a little time for plowing her garden and setting out fruit trees, even if it comes in a busy season. She has been a good mother to you, and she has always missed the old country."

When they went back to the kitchen the boys sat down silently at the table. Throughout the meal they looked down at their plates and did not lift their red eyes. They did not eat much,

although they had been working in the cold all day, and there was
a rabbit stewed in gravy for supper, and prune pies.

John Bergson had married beneath him, but he had married a
good housewife. Mrs. Bergson was a fair-skinned, corpulent
woman, heavy and placid like her son, Oscar, but there was something comfortable about her; perhaps it was her own love of
comfort. For eleven years she had worthily striven to maintain
some semblance of household order amid conditions that made
order very difficult. Habit was very strong with Mrs. Bergson, and
her unremitting efforts to repeat the routine of her old life among
new surroundings had done a great deal to keep the family from
disintegrating morally and getting careless in their ways. The
Bergsons had a log house, for instance, only because Mrs. Bergson
would not live in a sod house. She missed the fish diet of her own
country, and twice every summer she sent the boys to the river,
twenty miles to the southward, to fish for channel cat. When the
children were little she used to load them all into the wagon, the
baby in its crib, and go fishing herself.

Alexandra often said that if her mother were cast upon a
desert island, she would thank God for her deliverance, make a
garden, and find something to preserve. Preserving was almost
a mania with Mrs. Bergson. Stout as she was, she roamed the
scrubby banks of Norway Creek looking for fox grapes and goose
plums, like a wild creature in search of prey. She made a yellow
jam of the insipid ground-cherries that grew on the prairie, flavor-
ing it with lemon peel; and she made a sticky dark conserve
of garden tomatoes. She had experimented even with the rank
buffalo-pea, and she could not see a fine bronze cluster of them
without shaking her head and murmuring, "What a pity!" When
there was nothing more to preserve, she began to pickle. The
amount of sugar she used in these processes was sometimes a
serious drain upon the family resources. She was a good mother,
but she was glad when her children were old enough not to be
in her way in the kitchen. She had never quite forgiven John
Bergson for bringing her to the end of the earth; but, now that she

was there, she wanted to be let alone to reconstruct her old life in so far as that was possible. She could still take some comfort in the world if she had bacon in the cave, glass jars on the shelves, and sheets in the press. She disapproved of all her neighbors because of their slovenly housekeeping, and the women thought her very proud. Once when Mrs. Bergson, on her way to Norway Creek, stopped to see old Mrs. Lee, the old woman hid in the hay-mow "for fear Mis' Bergson would catch her barefoot."

III

One Sunday afternoon in July, six months after John Bergson's death, Carl was sitting in the doorway of the Linstrum kitchen, dreaming over an illustrated paper, when he heard the rattle of a wagon along the hill road. Looking up he recognized the Bergsons' team, with two seats in the wagon, which meant they were off for a pleasure excursion. Oscar and Lou, on the front seat, wore their cloth hats and coats, never worn except on Sundays, and Emil, on the second seat with Alexandra, sat proudly in his new trousers, made from a pair of his father's, and a pink-striped shirt, with a wide ruffled collar. Oscar stopped the horses and waved to Carl, who caught up his hat and ran through the melon patch to join them.

"Want to go with us?" Lou called. "We're going to Crazy Ivar's to buy a hammock."

"Sure." Carl ran up panting, and clambering over the wheel sat down beside Emil. "I've always wanted to see Ivar's pond. They say it's the biggest in all the country. Aren't you afraid to go to Ivar's in that new shirt, Emil? He might want it and take it right off your back."

Emil grinned. "I'd be awful scared to go," he admitted, "if you big boys weren't along to take care of me. Did you ever hear him howl, Carl? People say sometimes he runs about the country howling at night because he is afraid the Lord will destroy him. Mother thinks he must have done something awful wicked."

Lou looked back and winked at Carl. "What would you do, Emil, if you was out on the prairie by yourself and seen him coming?"

Emil stared. "Maybe I could hide in a badger-hole," he suggested doubtfully.

"But suppose there wasn't any badger-hole," Lou persisted. "Would you run?"

"No, I'd be too scared to run," Emil admitted mournfully, twisting his fingers. "I guess I'd sit right down on the ground and say my prayers."

The big boys laughed, and Oscar brandished his whip over the broad backs of the horses.

"He wouldn't hurt you, Emil," said Carl persuasively. "He came to doctor our mare when she ate green corn and swelled up most as big as the water-tank. He petted her just like you do your cats. I couldn't understand much he said, for he don't talk any English, but he kept patting her and groaning as if he had the pain himself, and saying, "There now, sister, that's easier, that's better!"

Lou and Oscar laughed, and Emil giggled delightedly and looked up at his sister.

"I don't think he knows anything at all about doctoring," said Oscar scornfully. "They say when horses have distemper he takes the medicine himself, and then prays over the horses."

Alexandra spoke up. "That's what the Crows said, but he cured their horses, all the same. Some days his mind is cloudy, like. But if you can get him on a clear day, you can learn a great deal from him. He understands animals. Didn't I see him take the horn off the Berquist's cow when she had torn it loose and went crazy? She was tearing all over the place, knocking herself against things. And at last she ran out on the roof of the old dug-out and her legs went through and there she stuck, bellowing. Ivar came running with his white bag, and the moment he got to her she was quiet and let him saw her horn off and daub the place with tar."

Emil had been watching his sister, his face reflecting the sufferings of the cow. "And then didn't it hurt her any more?" he asked.

Alexandra patted him. "No, not any more. And in two days they could use her milk again."

The road to Ivar's homestead was a very poor one. He had settled in the rough country across the county line, where no one lived but some Russians,—half a dozen families who dwelt together in one long house, divided off like barracks. Ivar had explained his choice by saying that the fewer neighbors he had, the fewer temptations. Nevertheless, when one considered that his chief business was horse-doctoring, it seemed rather short-sighted of him to live in the most inaccessible place he could find. The Bergson wagon lurched along over the rough hummocks and grass banks, followed the bottom of winding draws, or skirted the margin of wide lagoons, where the golden coreopsis grew up out of the clear water and the wild ducks rose with a whirr of wings.

Lou looked after them helplessly. "I wish I'd brought my gun, anyway, Alexandra," he said fretfully. "I could have hidden it under the straw in the bottom of the wagon."

"Then we'd have had to lie to Ivar. Besides, they say he can smell dead birds. And if he knew, we wouldn't get anything out of him, not even a hammock. I want to talk to him, and he won't talk sense if he's angry. It makes him foolish."

Lou sniffed. "Whoever heard of him talking sense, anyhow! I'd rather have ducks for supper than Crazy Ivar's tongue."

Emil was alarmed. "Oh, but, Lou, you don't want to make him mad! He might howl!"

They all laughed again, and Oscar urged the horses up the crumbling side of a clay bank. They had left the lagoons and the red grass behind them. In Crazy Ivar's country the grass was short and gray, the draws deeper than they were in the Bergson's neighborhood, and the land was all broken up into hillocks and clay ridges. The wild flowers disappeared, and only in the bottom of the draws and gullies grew a few of the very toughest and hardiest; shoestring, and ironweed, and snow-on-the-mountain.

"Look, look, Emil, there's Ivar's big pond!" Alexandra pointed to a shining sheet of water that lay at the bottom of a shallow draw. At one end of the pond was an earthen dam, planted with green willow bushes, and above it a door and a single window were set into the hillside. You would not have seen them at all but for the reflection of the sunlight upon the four panes of window-glass. And that was all you saw. Not a shed, not a corral, not a well, not even a path broken in the curly grass. But for the piece of rusty stovepipe sticking up through the sod, you could have walked over the roof of Ivar's dwelling without dreaming that you were near a human habitation. Ivar had lived for three years in the clay bank, without defiling the face of nature any more than the coyote that had lived there before him had done.

When the Bergsons drove over the hill, Ivar was sitting in the doorway of his house, reading the Norwegian Bible. He was a queerly shaped old man, with a thick, powerful body set on short bow-legs. His shaggy white hair, falling in a thick mane about his ruddy cheeks, made him look older than he was. He was barefoot, but he wore a clean shirt of unbleached cotton, open at the neck. He always put on a clean shirt when Sunday morning came round, though he never went to church. He had a peculiar religion of his own and could not get on with any of the denomi-nations. Often he did not see anybody from one week's end to another. He kept a calendar, and every morning he checked off a day, so that he was never in any doubt as to which day of the week it was. Ivar hired himself out in threshing and corn-husking time, and he doctored sick animals when he was sent for. When he was at home, he made hammocks out of twine and committed chapters of the Bible to memory.

Ivar found contentment in the solitude he had sought out for himself. He disliked the litter of human dwellings: the broken food, the bits of broken china, the old wash-boilers and tea-kettles thrown into the sunflower patch. He preferred the cleanness and tidiness of the wild sod. He always said that the badgers had cleaner houses than people, and that when he took a housekeeper her name would be Mrs. Badger. He best expressed his preference for his wild homestead by saying that his Bible seemed truer to him there. If one stood in the doorway of his cave, and looked off at the rough land, the smiling sky, the curly grass white in the hot sunlight; if one listened to the rapturous song of the lark, the drumming of the quail, the burr of the locust against that vast silence, one understood what Ivar meant.

On this Sunday afternoon his face shone with happiness. He closed the book on his knee, keeping the place with his horny finger, and repeated softly:—

> He sendeth the springs into the valleys, which run among the hills;
> They give drink to every beast of the field; the wild asses quench their thirst.
> The trees of the Lord are full of sap; the cedars of Lebanon which he hath planted;
> Where the birds make their nests: as for the stork, the fir trees are her house.
> The high hills are a refuge for the wild goats; and the rocks for the conies.

Before he opened his Bible again, Ivar heard the Bergsons' wagon approaching, and he sprang up and ran toward it.

"No guns, no guns!" he shouted, waving his arms distractedly.

"No, Ivar, no guns," Alexandra called reassuringly.

He dropped his arms and went up to the wagon, smiling amiably and looking at them out of his pale blue eyes.

"We want to buy a hammock, if you have one," Alexandra explained, "and my little brother, here, wants to see your big pond, where so many birds come."

Ivar smiled foolishly, and began rubbing the horses' noses and feeling about their mouths behind the bits. "Not many birds just now. A few ducks this morning; and some snipe come to drink. But there was a crane last week. She spent one night and came back the next evening. I don't know why. It is not her season, of course. Many of them go over in the fall. Then the pond is full of strange voices every night."

Alexandra translated for Carl, who looked thoughtful. "Ask him, Alexandra, if it is true that a sea gull came here once. I have heard so."

She had some difficulty in making the old man understand.

He looked puzzled at first, then smote his hands together as he remembered. "Oh, yes, yes! A big white bird with long wings and pink feet. My! what a voice she had! She came in the afternoon and kept flying about the pond and screaming until dark. She was in trouble of some sort, but I could not understand her. She was going over to the other ocean, maybe, and did not know how far it was. She was afraid of never getting there. She was more mournful than our birds here; she cried in the night. She saw the light from my window and darted up to it. Maybe she thought my house was a boat, she was such a wild thing. Next morning, when the sun rose, I went out to take her food, but she flew up into the sky and went on her way." Ivar ran his fingers through his thick hair. "I have many strange birds stop with me here. They come from very far away and are great company. I hope you boys never shoot wild birds?"

Lou and Oscar grinned, and Ivar shook his bushy head, "Yes, I know boys are thoughtless. But these wild things are God's birds. He watches over them and counts them, as we do our cattle; Christ says so in the New Testament."

"Now, Ivar," Lou asked, "may we water our horses at your pond and give them some feed? It's a bad road to your place."

"Yes, yes, it is." the old man scrambled about and began to loose the tugs. "A bad road, eh, girls? And the bay with a colt at home!"

Oscar brushed the old man aside. "We'll take care of the horses, Ivar. You'll be finding some disease on them. Alexandra wants to see your hammocks."

Ivar led Alexandra and Emil to his little cave house. He had but one room, neatly plastered and whitewashed, and there was a wooden floor. There was a kitchen stove, a table covered with oilcloth, two chairs, a clock, a calendar, a few books on the window-shelf; nothing more. But the place was as clean as a cupboard.

"But where do you sleep, Ivar?" Emil asked, looking about.

Ivar unslung a hammock from a hook on the wall; in it was rolled a buffalo robe. "There, my son. A hammock is a good bed, and in winter I wrap up in this skin. Where I go to work, the beds are not half so easy as this."

By this time Emil had lost all his timidity. He thought a cave a very superior kind of house. There was something pleasantly unusual about it and about Ivar. "Do the birds know you will be kind to them, Ivar? Is that why so many come?" he asked.

Ivar sat down on the floor and tucked his feet under him. "See, little brother, they have come from a long way, and they are very tired. From up there where they are flying, our country looks dark and flat. They must have water to drink and to bathe in before they can go on with their journey. They look this way and that, and far below them they see something shining, like a piece of glass set in the dark earth. That is my pond. They come to it and are not disturbed. Maybe I sprinkle a little corn. They tell the other birds, and next year more come this way. They have their roads up there, as we have down here."

Emil rubbed his knees thoughtfully. "And is that true, Ivar, about the head ducks falling back when they are tired, and the hind ones taking their place?"

"Yes. The point of the wedge gets the worst of it; they cut the wind. They can only stand it there a little while—half an hour, maybe. Then they fall back and the wedge splits a little, while the rear ones come up the middle to the front. Then it closes up and they fly on, with a new edge. They are always changing like that, up in the air. Never any confusion; just like soldiers who have been drilled."

Alexandra had selected her hammock by the time the boys came up from the pond. They would not come in, but sat in the shade of the bank outside while Alexandra and Ivar talked about the birds and about his housekeeping, and why he never ate meat, fresh or salt.

Alexandra was sitting on one of the wooden chairs, her arms resting on the table. Ivar was sitting on the floor at her feet. "Ivar," she said suddenly, beginning to trace the pattern on the oilcloth with her forefinger, "I came to-day more because I wanted to talk to you than because I wanted to buy a hammock."

"Yes?" The old man scraped his bare feet on the plank floor.

"We have a big bunch of hogs, Ivar. I wouldn't sell in the spring, when everybody advised me to, and now so many people are losing their hogs that I am frightened. What can be done?"

Ivar's little eyes began to shine. They lost their vagueness.

"You feed them swill and such stuff? Of course! And sour milk? Oh, yes! And keep them in a stinking pen? I tell you, sister, the hogs of this country are put upon! They become unclean, like the hogs in the Bible. If you kept your chickens like that, what would happen? You have a little sorghum patch, maybe? Put a fence around it, and turn the hogs in. Build a shed to give them shade, a thatch on poles. Let the boys haul water to them in barrels, clean water, and plenty. Get them off the old stinking ground, and do not let them go back there until winter. Give them only grain and clean feed, such as you would give horses or cattle. Hogs do not like to be filthy."

The boys outside the door had been listening. Lou nudged his brother. "Come, the horses are done eating. Let's hitch up and get out of here. He'll fill her full of notions. She'll be for having the pigs sleep with us, next."

Oscar grunted and got up. Carl, who could not understand what Ivar said, saw that the two boys were displeased. They did not mind hard work, but they hated experiments and could never see the use of taking pains. Even Lou, who was more elastic than his older brother, disliked to do anything different from their neighbors. He felt that it made them conspicuous and gave people a chance to talk about them.

Once they were on the homeward road, the boys forgot their

ill-humor and joked about Ivar and his birds. Alexandra did not propose any reforms in the care of the pigs, and they hoped she had forgotten Ivar's talk. They agreed that he was crazier than ever, and would never be able to prove up on his land because he worked it so little. Alexandra privately resolved that she would have a talk with Ivar about this and stir him up. The boys persuaded Carl to stay for supper and go swimming in the pasture pond after dark.

That evening, after she had washed the supper dishes, Alexandra sat down on the kitchen doorstep, while her mother was mixing the bread. It was a still, deep-breathing summer night, full of the smell of the hay fields. Sounds of laughter and splashing came up from the pasture, and when the moon rose rapidly above the bare rim of the prairie, the pond glittered like polished metal, and she could see the flash of white bodies as the boys ran about the edge, or jumped into the water. Alexandra watched the shimmering pool dreamily, but eventually her eyes went back to the sorghum patch south of the barn, where she was planning to make her new pig corral.

IV

For the first three years after John Bergson's death, the affairs of his family prospered. Then came the hard times that brought every one on the Divide to the brink of despair; three years of drouth and failure, the last struggle of a wild soil against the encroaching plowshare. The first of these fruitless summers the Bergson boys bore courageously. The failure of the corn crop made labor cheap. Lou and Oscar hired two men and put in bigger crops than ever before. They lost everything they spent. The whole county was discouraged. Farmers who were already in debt had to give up their land. A few foreclosures demoralized the county. The settlers sat about on the wooden sidewalks in the little town and told each other that the country was never meant for men to live in; the thing to do was to get back to Iowa, to Illinois, to any place that had been proved habitable. The Bergson boys, certainly, would have been happier with their uncle Otto, in the bakery shop in Chicago. Like most of their neighbors, they were meant to follow in paths already marked out for them, not to break trails in a new country. A steady job, a few holidays, nothing to think about, and they would have been very happy. It was no fault of theirs that they had been dragged into the wilderness when they were little boys. A pioneer should have imagination, should be able to enjoy the idea of things more than the things themselves.

The second of these barren summers was passing. One September afternoon Alexandra had gone over to the garden across the draw to dig sweet potatoes—they had been thriving upon the weather that was fatal to everything else. But when Carl Linstrum came up the garden rows to find her, she was not working. She was standing lost in thought, leaning upon her pitchfork, her sunbonnet lying beside her on the ground. The dry garden patch smelled of drying vines and was strewn with yellow seed-cucumbers and pumpkins and citrons. At one end, next the rhubarb, grew feathery asparagus, with red berries. Down the middle of the garden was a row of gooseberry and currant bushes. A few tough zenias and marigolds and a row of scarlet sage bore witness to the buckets of water that Mrs. Bergson had carried there after sundown, against the prohibition of her sons. Carl came quietly and slowly up the garden path, looking intently at Alexandra. She did not hear him. She was standing perfectly still, with that serious ease so characteristic of her. Her thick, reddish braids, twisted about her head, fairly burned in the sunlight. The air was cool enough to make the warm sun pleasant on one's back and shoulders, and so clear that the eye could follow a hawk up and up, into the blazing blue depths of the sky. Even Carl, never a very cheerful boy, was considerably darkened by those last two bitter years, loved the country on days like this, felt something strong and young and wild come out of it, that laughed at care.

"Alexandra," he said as he approached her, "I want to talk to you. Let's sit down by the gooseberry bushes." He picked up her sack of potatoes and they crossed the garden. "Boys gone to town?" he asked as he sank down on the warm, sun-baked earth. "Well, we have made up our minds at last, Alexandra. We are really going away."

She looked at him as if she were a little frightened. "Really, Carl? Is it settled?"

"Yes, father has heard from St. Louis, and they will give him back his old job in the cigar factory. He must be there by the first of November. They are taking on new men then. We will sell the place for whatever we can get, and auction the stock. We haven't enough to ship. I am going to learn engraving with a German engraver there, and then try to get work in Chicago."

Alexandra's hands dropped in her lap. Her eyes became dreamy and filled with tears.

Carl's sensitive lower lip trembled. He scratched in the soft earth beside him with a stick. "That's all I hate about it, Alexandra," he said slowly. "You've stood by us through so much and helped father out so many times, and now it seems as if we were running off and leaving you to face the worst of it. But it isn't as if we could really ever be of any help to you. We are only one more drag, one more thing you look out for and feel responsible for. Father was never meant for a farmer, you know that. And I hate it. We'd only get in deeper and deeper."

"Yes, yes, Carl, I know. You are wasting your life here. You are able to do much better things. You are nearly nineteen now, and I wouldn't have you stay. I've always hoped you would get away. But I can't help feeling scared when I think how I will miss you—more than you will ever know." She brushed the tears from her cheeks, not trying to hide them.

"But, Alexandra," he said sadly and wistfully, "I've never been any real help to you, beyond sometimes trying to keep the boys in a good humor."

Alexandra smiled and shook her head. "Oh, it's not that. Nothing like that. It's by understanding me, and the boys, and mother, that you've helped me. I expect that is the only way one person ever really can help another. I think you are about the only one that ever helped me. Somehow it will take more courage to bear your going than everything that has happened before."

Carl looked at the ground. "You see, we've all depended so on you," he said, "even father. He makes me laugh. When anything comes up he always says, 'I wonder what the Bergsons are going to do about that? I guess I'll go and ask her.' I'll never forget that time, when we first came here, and our horse had the colic, and I ran over to your place—your father was away, and you came home with me and showed father how to let the wind out of the horse. You were only a little girl then, but you knew ever so much more about farm work than poor father. You remember how homesick I used to get, and what long talks we used to have coming from school? We've someway always felt alike about things."

"Yes, that's it; we've liked the same things and we've liked them together, without anybody else knowing. And we've had good times, hunting for Christmas trees and going for ducks and making our plum wine together every year. We've never either of us had any other close friend. And now—" Alexandra wiped her eyes with the corner of her apron, "and now I must remember that you are going where you will have many friends, and will find the work you were meant to do. But you'll write to me, Carl? That will mean a great deal to me here."

"I'll write as long as I live," cried the boy impetuously. "And I'll be working for you as much as for myself, Alexandra. I want to do something you'll like and be proud of. I'm a fool here, but I know I can do something!" He sat up and frowned at the red grass.

Alexandra sighed. "How discouraged the boys will be when they hear. They always come home from town discouraged, anyway. So many people are trying to leave the country, and they talk to our boys and make them low-spirited. I'm afraid they are beginning to feel hard toward me because I won't listen to any talk about going. Sometimes I feel like I'm getting tired of standing up for this country."

"I won't tell the boys yet, if you'd rather not."

"Oh, I'll tell them myself, to-night, when they come home. They'll be talking wild, anyway, and no good comes of keeping bad news. It's all harder on them than it is on me. Lou wants to get married, poor boy, and he can't until times are better. See, there goes the sun, Carl. I must be getting back. Mother will want her potatoes. It's chilly already, the moment the light goes."

Alexandra rose and looked about. A golden afterglow throbbed in the west, but the country already looked empty and mournful. A dark moving mass came over the western hill, the Lee boy was bringing in the herd from the other half-section. Emil ran from the windmill to open the corral gate. From the log house, on the little rise across the draw, the smoke was curling. The cattle lowed and bellowed. In the sky the pale half-moon was slowly silvering. Alexandra and Carl walked together down the potato rows. "I have to keep telling myself what is going to happen," she said softly. "Since you have been here, ten years now, I have never really been lonely. But I can remember what it was like before. Now I shall have nobody but Emil. But he is my boy, and he is tender-hearted."

That night, when the boys were called to supper, they sat down moodily. They had worn their coats to town, but they ate in their striped shirts and suspenders. They were grown men now, and, as Alexandra said, for the last few years they had been growing more and more like themselves. Lou was still the slighter of the two, the quicker and more intelligent, but apt to go off at half-cock. He had a lively blue eye, a thin, fair skin (always burned red to the neckband of his shirt in summer), stiff, yellow hair that would not lie down on his head, and a bristly little yellow mustache; of which he was very proud. Oscar could not grow a mustache; his pale face was as bare as an egg, and his white eyebrows gave it an empty look. He was a man of powerful body and unusual endurance; the sort of man you could attach to a cornsheller as you would an engine. He would turn it all day, without hurrying, without slowing down. But he was as indolent of mind as he was unsparing of his body. His love of routine amounted to a vice. He worked like an insect, always doing the same thing over in the same way, regardless of whether it was best or no. He felt that there was a sovereign virtue in mere bodily toil, and he rather liked to do things in the hardest way. If a field had once been in corn, he couldn't bear to put it into wheat. He liked to begin his corn-planting at the same time every year, whether the season were backward or forward. He seemed to feel that by his own irreproachable regularity he would clear himself of blame and reprove the weather. When the wheat crop failed, he threshed the straw at a dead loss to demonstrate how little grain there was, and thus prove his case against Providence.

Lou, on the other hand, was fussy and flighty; always planned to get through two days' work in one, and often got only the least important things done. He liked to keep the place up, but he never got round to doing odd jobs until he had to neglect more pressing work to attend to them. In the middle of the wheat harvest, when the grain was over-ripe and every hand was needed, he would stop to mend fences or to patch the harness; then dash down to the field and overwork and be laid up in bed for a week. The two boys balanced each other. They had been good friends since they were children. One seldom went anywhere, even to town, without the other.

To-night, after they sat down to supper, Oscar kept looking at Lou as if he expected him to say something, and Lou blinked his eyes and frowned at his plate. It was Alexandra herself who at last opened the discussion.

"The Linstrums," she said calmly, as she put another plate of hot biscuit on the table, "are going back to St. Louis. The old man is going to work in the cigar factory again."

At this Lou plunged in. "You see, Alexandra, everybody who can crawl out is going away. There's no use of us trying to stick it out, just to be stubborn. There's something in knowing when to quit."

"Where do you want to go, Lou?"

"Any place where things will grow," said Oscar grimly.

Lou reached for a potato. "Chris Arnson has traded his half-section for a place down on the river."

"Who did he trade with?"

"Charley Fuller, in town."

"Fuller the real estate man? You see, Lou, that Fuller has a head on him. He's buying and trading for every bit of land he can get up here. It'll make him a rich man, some day."

"He's rich now, that's why he can take a chance."

"Why can't we? We'll live longer than he will. Some day the land itself will be worth more than all we can ever raise on it."

Lou laughed. "It could be worth that, and still not be worth much. Why, Alexandra, you don't know what you're talking about. Our place wouldn't bring now what it would six years ago. The fellows that settled up here just made a mistake. Now they're beginning to see this high land wasn't never meant to grow nothing on, and everybody who ain't fixed to graze cattle is trying to crawl out. It's too high to farm up here. All the Americans are skinning out. That man Percy Adams, north of town, told me that he was going to let Fuller take his land and stuff for four hundred dollars and a ticket to Chicago."

"There's Fuller again!" Alexandra exclaimed. "I wish that man would take me for a partner. He's feathering his nest! If only poor people could learn a little from rich people! But all these fellows who are running off are bad farmers, like poor Mr. Linstrum. They couldn't get ahead even in good years, and they all got into debt while father was getting out. I think we ought to hold on as long as we can on father's account. He was so set on keeping this land. He must have seen harder times than this, here. How was it in the early days, mother?"

Mrs. Bergson was weeping quietly. These family discussions always depressed her, and made her remember all that she had been torn away from. "I don't see why the boys are always taking on about going away," she said, wiping her eyes. "I don't want to move again; out to some raw place, maybe, where we'd be worse off than we are here, and all to do over again. I won't move! If the rest of you go, I will ask some of the neighbors to take me in, and stay and be buried by father. I'm not going to leave him by himself on the prairie, for cattle to run over." She began to cry more bitterly.

The boys looked angry. Alexandra put a soothing hand on her mother's shoulder. "There's no question of that, mother. You don't have to go if you don't want to. A third of the place belongs to you by American law, and we can't sell without your consent. We only want you to advise us. How did it use to be when you and father first came? Was it really as bad as this, or not?"

"Oh, worse! Much worse," moaned Mrs. Bergson. "Drouth, chince-bugs, hail, everything! My garden all cut to pieces like sauerkraut. No grapes on the creek, no nothing. The people all lived just like coyotes."

Oscar got up and tramped out of the kitchen. Lou followed him. They felt that Alexandra had taken an unfair advantage in turning their mother loose on them. The next morning they were silent and reserved. They did not offer to take the women to church, but went down to the barn immediately after breakfast and stayed there all day. When Carl Linstrum came over in the afternoon, Alexandra winked to him and pointed toward the barn. He understood her and went down to play cards with the boys. They believed that a very wicked thing to do on Sunday, and it relieved their feelings.

Alexandra stayed in the house. On Sunday afternoon Mrs. Bergson always took a nap, and Alexandra read. During the week she read only the newspaper, but on Sunday, and in the long evenings of winter, she read a good deal; read a few things over a great many times. She knew long portions of the "Frithjof Saga" by heart, and, like most Swedes who read at all, she was fond of Longfellow's verse,—the ballads and the "Golden Legend" and "The Spanish Student." To-day she sat in the wooden rocking-chair with the Swedish Bible open on her knees, but she was not reading. She was looking thoughtfully away at the point where the upland road disappeared over the rim of the prairie. Her body was in an attitude of perfect repose, such as it was apt to take when she was thinking earnestly. Her mind was slow, truthful, steadfast. She had not the least spark of cleverness.

All afternoon the sitting-room was full of quiet and sunlight. Emil was making rabbit traps in the kitchen shed. The hens were clucking and scratching brown holes in the flower beds, and the wind was teasing the prince's feather by the door.

That evening Carl came in with the boys to supper.

"Emil," said Alexandra, when they were all seated at the table, "how would you like to go traveling? Because I am going to take a trip, and you can go with me if you want to."

The boys looked up in amazement; they were always afraid of Alexandra's schemes. Carl was interested.

"I've been thinking, boys," she went on, "that maybe I am too set against making a change. I'm going to take Brigham and the buckboard to-morrow and drive down to the river country and spend a few days looking over what they've got down there. If I find anything good, you boys can go down and make a trade."

"Nobody down there will trade for anything up here," said Oscar gloomily.

"That's just what I want to find out. Maybe they are just as discontented down there as we are up here. Things away from home often look better than they are. You know what your Hans Andersen book says, Carl, about the Swedes liking to buy Danish bread and the Danes liking to buy Swedish bread, because people always think the bread of another country is better than their own. Anyway, I've heard so much about the river farms, I won't be satisfied till I've seen for myself."

Lou fidgeted. "Look out! Don't agree to anything. Don't let them fool you."

Lou was apt to be fooled himself. He had not yet learned to keep away from the shell-game wagons that followed the circus.

After supper Lou put on a necktie and went across the fields to court Annie Lee, and Carl and Oscar sat down to a game of checkers, while Alexandra read "The Swiss Family Robinson" aloud to her mother and Emil. It was not long before the two boys at the table neglected their game to listen. They were all big children together, and they found the adventures of the family in the tree house so absorbing that they gave them their undivided attention.

V

Alexandra and Emil spent five days down among the river farms, driving up and down the valley. Alexandra talked to the men about their crops and to the women about their poultry. She spent a whole day with one young farmer who had been away at school, and who was experimenting with a new kind of clover hay. She learned a great deal. As they drove along, she and Emil talked and planned. At last, on the sixth day, Alexandra turned Brigham's head northward and left the river behind.

"There's nothing in it for us down there, Emil. There are a few fine farms, but they are owned by the rich men in town, and couldn't be bought. Most of the land is rough and hilly. They can always scrape along down there, but they can never do anything big. Down there they have a little certainty, but up with us there is a big chance. We must have faith in the high land, Emil. I want to hold on harder than ever, and when you're a man you'll thank me." She urged Brigham forward.

When the road began to climb the first long swells of the Divide, Alexandra hummed an old Swedish hymn, and Emil wondered why his sister looked so happy. Her face was so radiant that he felt shy about asking her. For the first time, perhaps, since that land emerged from the waters of geologic ages, a human face was set toward it with love and yearning. It seemed beautiful to her, rich and strong and glorious. Her eyes drank in the breadth of it, until her tears blinded her. Then the Genius of the Divide, the great, free spirit which breathes across it, must have bent lower than it ever bent to a human will before. The history of every country begins in the heart of a man or a woman.

Alexandra reached home in the afternoon. That evening she held a family council and told her brothers all that she had seen and heard.

"I want you boys to go down yourselves and look it over. Nothing will convince you like seeing with your own eyes. The river land was settled before this, and so they are a few years ahead of us, and have learned more about farming. The land sells for three times as much as this, but in five years we will double it. The rich men down there own all the best land, and they are buying all they can get. The thing to do is to sell our cattle and what little old corn we have, and buy the Linstrum place. Then the next thing to do is to take out two loans on our half-sections, and buy Peter Crow's place; raise every dollar we can, and buy every acre we can."

"Mortgage the homestead again?" Lou cried. He sprang up and began to wind the clock furiously. "I won't slave to pay off another mortgage. I'll never do it. You'd just as soon kill us all, Alexandra, to carry out some scheme!"

Oscar rubbed his high, pale forehead. "How do you propose to pay off your mortgages?"

Alexandra looked from one to the other and bit her lip. They had never seen her so nervous. "See here," she brought out at last. "We borrow the money for six years. Well, with the money we buy a half-section from Linstrum and a half from Crow, and a quarter from Struble, maybe. That will give us upwards of fourteen hundred acres, won't it? You won't have to pay off your mortgages for six years. By that time, any of this land will be worth thirty dollars an acre—it will be worth fifty, but we'll say thirty; then you can sell a garden patch anywhere, and pay off a debt of sixteen hundred dollars. It's not the principal I'm worried about, it's the interest and taxes. We'll have to strain to meet the payments. But as sure as we are sitting here to-night, we can sit down here ten years from now independent landowners, not struggling farmers any longer. The chance that father was always looking for has come."

Lou was pacing the floor. "But how do you *know* that land is going to go up enough to pay the mortgages and—"

"And make us rich besides?" Alexandra put in firmly. "I can't explain that, Lou. You'll have to take my word for it. I *know*, that's all. When you drive about over the country you can feel it coming."

Oscar had been sitting with his head lowered, his hands hanging between his knees. "But we can't work so much land," he said dully, as if he were talking to himself. "We can't even try. It would just lie there and we'd work ourselves to death." He sighed, and laid his calloused fist on the table.

Alexandra's eyes filled with tears. She put her hand on his shoulder. "You poor boy, you won't have to work it. The men in town who are buying up other people's land don't try to farm it. They are the men to watch, in a new country. Let's try to do like the shrewd ones, and not like these stupid fellows. I don't want you boys always to have to work like this. I want you to be independent, and Emil to go to school."

Lou held his head as if it were splitting. "Everybody will say we are crazy. It must be crazy, or everybody would be doing it."

"If they were, we wouldn't have much chance. No, Lou, I was talking about that with the smart young man who is raising the new kind of clover. He says the right thing is usually just what everybody don't do. Why are we better fixed than any of our neighbors? Because father had more brains. Our people were better people than these in the old country. We *ought* to do more than they do, and see further ahead. Yes, mother, I'm going to clear the table now."

Alexandra rose. The boys went to the stable to see to the stock, and they were gone a long while. When they came back Lou played on his *dragharmonika* and Oscar sat figuring at his father's secretary all evening. They said nothing more about Alexandra's project, but she felt sure now that they would consent to it. Just before bedtime Oscar went out for a pail of water. When he did not come back, Alexandra threw a shawl over her head and ran down the path to the windmill. She found him sitting there with his head in his hands, and she sat down beside him.

"Don't do anything you don't want to do, Oscar," she whispered. She waited a moment, but he did not stir. "I won't say any more about it, if you'd rather not. What makes you so discouraged?"

"I dread signing my name to them pieces of paper," he said slowly. "All the time I was a boy we had a mortgage hanging over us."

"Then don't sign one. I don't want you to, if you feel that way."

Oscar shook his head. "No, I can see there's a chance that way. I've thought a good while there might be. We're in so deep now, we might as well go deeper. But it's hard work pulling out of debt. Like pulling a threshing-machine out of the mud; breaks your back. Me and Lou's worked hard, and I can't see it's got us ahead much."

"Nobody knows about that as well as I do, Oscar. That's why I want to try an easier way. I don't want you to have to grub for every dollar."

"Yes, I know what you mean. Maybe it'll come out right. But signing papers is signing papers. There ain't no maybe about that." He took his pail and trudged up the path to the house.

Alexandra drew her shawl closer about her and stood leaning against the frame of the mill, looking at the stars which glittered so keenly through the frosty autumn air. She always loved to watch them, to think of their vastness and distance, and of their ordered march. It fortified her to reflect upon the great operations of nature, and when she thought of the law that lay behind them, she felt a sense of personal security. That night she had a new consciousness of the country, felt almost a new relation to it. Even her talk with the boys had not taken away the feeling that had overwhelmed her when she drove back to the Divide that afternoon. She had never known before how much the country meant to her. The chirping of the insects down in the long grass had been like the sweetest music. She had felt as if her heart were hiding down there, somewhere, with the quail and the plover and all the little wild things that crooned or buzzed in the sun. Under the long shaggy ridges, she felt the future stirring.

PART II
NEIGHBORING FIELDS

I

It is sixteen years since John Bergson died. His wife now lies beside him, and the white shaft that marks their graves gleams across the wheat-fields. Could he rise from beneath it, he would not know the country under which he has been asleep. The shaggy coat of the prairie, which they lifted to make him a bed, has vanished forever. From the Norwegian graveyard one looks out over a vast checker-board, marked off in squares of wheat and corn; light and dark, dark and light. Telephone wires hum along the white roads, which always run at right angles. From the graveyard gate one can count a dozen gayly painted farmhouses; the gilded weather-vanes on the big red barns wink at each other across the green and brown and yellow fields. The light steel windmills tremble throughout their frames and tug at their moorings, as they vibrate in the wind that often blows from one week's end to another across that high, active, resolute stretch of country.

The Divide is now thickly populated. The rich soil yields heavy harvests; the dry, bracing climate and the smoothness of the land make labor easy for men and beasts. There are few scenes more gratifying than a spring plowing in that country, where the furrows of a single field often lie a mile in length, and the brown earth, with such a strong, clean smell, and such a power of growth and fertility in it, yields itself eagerly to the plow; rolls away from the shear, not even dimming the brightness of the metal, with a soft, deep sigh of happiness. The wheat-cutting sometimes goes on all night as well as all day, and in good seasons there are scarcely men and horses enough to do the harvesting. The grain is so heavy that it bends toward the blade and cuts like velvet.

There is something frank and joyous and young in the open

face of the country. It gives itself ungrudgingly to the moods of the season, holding nothing back. Like the plains of Lombardy, it seems to rise a little to meet the sun. The air and the earth are curiously mated and intermingled, as if the one were the breath of the other. You feel in the atmosphere the same tonic, puissant quality that is in the tilth, the same strength and resoluteness.

One June morning a young man stood at the gate of the Norwegian graveyard, sharpening his scythe in strokes unconsciously timed to the tune he was whistling. He wore a flannel cap and duck trousers, and the sleeves of his white flannel shirt were rolled back to the elbow. When he was satisfied with the edge of his blade, he slipped the whetstone into his hip pocket and began to swing his scythe, still whistling, but softly, out of respect to the quiet folk about him. Unconscious respect, probably, for he seemed intent upon his own thoughts, and, like the Gladiator's, they were far away. He was a splendid figure of a boy, tall and straight as a young pine tree, with a handsome head, and stormy gray eyes, deeply set under a serious brow. The space between his two front teeth, which were unusually far apart, gave him the proficiency in whistling for which he was distinguished at college. (He also played the cornet in the University band.)

When the grass required his close attention, or when he had to stoop to cut about a headstone, he paused in his lively air,—the "Jewel" song,—taking it up where he had left it when his scythe swung free again. He was not thinking about the tired pioneers over whom his blade glittered. The old wild country, the struggle in which his sister was destined to succeed while so many men broke their hearts and died, he can scarcely remember. That is all among the dim things of childhood and has been forgotten in the brighter pattern life weaves to-day, in the bright facts of being captain of the track team, and holding the interstate record for the high jump, in the all-suffusing brightness of being twenty-one. Yet sometimes, in the pauses of his work, the young man frowned and looked at the ground with an intentness which suggested that even twenty-one might have its problems.

When he had been mowing the better part of an hour, he heard the rattle of a light cart on the road behind him. Supposing that it was his sister coming back from one of her farms, he kept on with his work. The cart stopped at the gate and a merry contralto voice called, "Almost through, Emil?" He dropped his scythe and went toward the fence, wiping his face and neck with his handkerchief. In the cart sat a young woman who wore driving gauntlets and a wide shade hat, trimmed with red poppies. Her face, too, was rather like a poppy, round and brown, with rich color in her cheeks and lips, and her dancing yellow-brown eyes bubbled with gayety. The wind was flapping her big hat and teasing a curl of her chestnut-colored hair. She shook her head at the tall youth.

"What time did you get over here? That's not much of a job for an athlete. Here I've been to town and back. Alexandra lets you sleep late. Oh, I know! Lou's wife was telling me about the way she spoils you. I was going to give you a lift, if you were done." She gathered up her reins.

"But I will be, in a minute. Please wait for me, Marie," Emil coaxed. "Alexandra sent me to mow our lot, but I've done half a dozen others, you see. Just wait till I finish off the Kourdnas'. By the way, they were Bohemians. Why aren't they up in the Catholic graveyard?"

"Free-thinkers," replied the young woman laconically.

"Lots of the Bohemian boys at the University are," said Emil, taking up his scythe again. "What did you ever burn John Huss for, anyway? It's made an awful row. They still jaw about it in history classes."

"We'd do it right over again, most of us," said the young woman hotly. "Don't they ever teach you in your history classes that you'd all be heathen Turks if it hadn't been for the Bohemians?"

Emil had fallen to mowing. "Oh, there's no denying you're a spunky little bunch, you Czechs," he called back over his shoulder.

Marie Shabata settled herself in her seat and watched the rhythmical movement of the young man's long arms, swinging her foot as if in time to some air that was going through her mind. The minutes passed. Emil mowed vigorously and Marie sat sunning herself and watching the long grass fall. She sat with the ease that belongs to persons of an essentially happy nature, who can find a comfortable spot almost anywhere; who are supple, and quick in adapting themselves to circumstances. After a final swish, Emil snapped the gate and sprang into the cart, holding his scythe well out over the wheel. "There," he sighed. "I gave old man Lee a cut or so, too. Lou's wife needn't talk. I never see Lou's scythe over here."

Marie clucked to her horse. "Oh, you know Annie!" She looked at the young man's bare arms. "How brown you've got since you came home. I wish I had an athlete to mow my orchard. I get wet to my knees when I go down to pick cherries."

"You can have one, any time you want him. Better wait until after it rains." Emil squinted off at the horizon as if he were looking for clouds.

"Will you? Oh, there's a good boy!" She turned her head to him with a quick, bright smile. He felt it rather than saw it. Indeed, he had looked away with the purpose of not seeing it. "I've been up looking at Angélique's wedding clothes," Marie went on, "and I'm so excited I can hardly wait until Sunday. Amédée will be a handsome bridegroom. Is anybody but you going to stand up with him? Well, then it will be a handsome wedding party." She made a droll face at Emil, who flushed. "Frank," Marie continued, flicking her horse, "is cranky at me because I loaned his saddle to Jan Smirka, and I'm terribly afraid he won't take me to the dance in the evening. Maybe the supper will tempt him. All Angélique's folks are baking for it, and all Amédée's twenty cousins. There will be barrels of beer. If once I get Frank to the supper, I'll see that I stay for the dance. And by the way, Emil, you mustn't dance with me but once or twice. You must dance with all the French girls. It hurts their feelings if you don't. They think you're proud because you've been away to school or something."

Emil sniffed. "How do you know they think that?"

"Well, you didn't dance with them much at Raoul Marcel's

party, and I could tell how they took it by the way they looked at you—and at me."

"All right," said Emil shortly, studying the glittering blade of his scythe.

They drove westward toward Norway Creek, and toward a big white house that stood on a hill, several miles across the fields. There were so many sheds and outbuildings grouped about it that the place looked not unlike a tiny village. A stranger, approaching it, could not help noticing the beauty and fruitfulness of the outlying fields. There was something individual about the great farm, a most unusual trimness and care for detail. On either side of the road, for a mile before you reached the foot of the hill, stood tall osage orange hedges, their glossy green marking off the yellow fields. South of the hill, in a low, sheltered swale, surrounded by a mulberry hedge, was the orchard, its fruit trees knee-deep in timothy grass. Any one thereabouts would have told you that this was one of the richest farms on the Divide, and that the farmer was a woman, Alexandra Bergson.

If you go up the hill and enter Alexandra's big house, you will find that it is curiously unfinished and uneven in comfort. One room is papered, carpeted, over-furnished; the next is almost bare. The pleasantest rooms in the house are the kitchen—where Alexandra's three young Swedish girls chatter and cook and pickle and preserve all summer long—and the sitting-room, in which Alexandra has brought together the old homely furniture that the Bergsons used in their first log house, the family portraits, and the few things her mother brought from Sweden.

When you go out of the house into the flower garden, there you feel again the order and fine arrangement manifest all over the great farm; in the fencing and hedging, in the windbreaks and sheds, in the symmetrical pasture ponds, planted with scrub willows to give shade to the cattle in fly-time. There is even a white row of beehives in the orchard, under the walnut trees. You feel that, properly, Alexandra's house is the big out-of-doors, and that it is in the soil that she expresses herself best.

II

Emil reached home a little past noon, and when he went into the kitchen Alexandra was already seated at the head of the long table, having dinner with her men, as she always did unless there were visitors. He slipped into his empty place at his sister's right. The three pretty young Swedish girls who did Alexandra's housework were cutting pies, refilling coffee-cups, placing platters of bread and meat and potatoes upon the red tablecloth, and continually getting in each other's way between the table and the stove. To be sure they always wasted a good deal of time getting in each other's way and giggling at each other's mistakes. But, as Alexandra had pointedly told her sisters-in-law, it was to hear them giggle that she kept three young things in her kitchen; the work she could do herself, if it were necessary. These girls, with their long letters from home, their finery, and their love-affairs, afforded her a great deal of entertainment, and they were company for her when Emil was away at school.

Of the youngest girl, Signa, who has a pretty figure, mottled pink cheeks, and yellow hair, Alexandra is very fond, though she keeps a sharp eye upon her. Signa is apt to be skittish at mealtime, when the men are about, and to spill the coffee or upset the cream. It is supposed that Nelse Jensen, one of the six men at the dinner-table, is courting Signa, though he has been so careful not to commit himself that no one in the house, least of all Signa, can tell just how far the matter has progressed. Nelse watches her glumly as she waits upon the table, and in the evening he sits on a bench behind the stove with his *dragharmonika*, playing mournful airs and watching her as she goes about her work. When Alexandra asked Signa whether she thought Nelse was in earnest, the poor child hid her hands under her apron and murmured, "I don't know, ma'm. But he scolds me about everything, like as if he wanted to have me!"

At Alexandra's left sat a very old man, barefoot and wearing a long blue blouse, open at the neck. His shaggy head is scarcely whiter than it was sixteen years ago, but his little blue eyes have become pale and watery, and his ruddy face is withered, like an apple that has clung all winter to the tree. When Ivar lost his land through mismanagement a dozen years ago, Alexandra took him in, and he has been a member of her household ever since. He is too old to work in the fields, but he hitches and unhitches the work-teams and looks after the health of the stock. Sometimes of a winter evening Alexandra calls him into the sitting-room to read the Bible aloud to her, for he still reads very well. He dislikes human habitations, so Alexandra has fitted him up a room in the barn, where he is very comfortable, being near the horses and, as he says, further from temptations. No one has ever found out what his temptations are. In cold weather he sits by the kitchen fire and makes hammocks or mends harness until it is time to go to bed. Then he says his prayers at great length behind the stove, puts on his buffalo-skin coat and goes out to his room in the barn.

Alexandra herself has changed very little. Her figure is fuller, and she has more color. She seems sunnier and more vigorous than she did as a young girl. But she still has the same calmness and deliberation of manner, the same clear eyes, and she still wears her hair in two braids wound round her head. It is so curly that fiery ends escape from the braids and make her head look like one of the big double sunflowers that fringe her vegetable garden. Her face is always tanned in summer, for her sunbonnet is oftener on her arm than on her head. But where her collar falls away from her neck, or where her sleeves are pushed back from her wrist, the skin is of such smoothness and whiteness as none but Swedish women ever possess; skin with the freshness of the snow itself.

Alexandra did not talk much at the table, but she encouraged her men to talk, and she always listened attentively, even when they seemed to be talking foolishly.

To-day Barney Flinn, the big red-headed Irishman who had been with Alexandra for five years and who was actually her foreman, though he had no such title, was grumbling about the new silo she had put up that spring. It happened to be the first silo on the Divide, and Alexandra's neighbors and her men were skeptical about it. "To be sure, if the thing don't work, we'll have plenty of feed without it, indeed," Barney conceded.

Nelse Jensen, Signa's gloomy suitor, had his word. "Lou, he says he wouldn't have no silo on his place if you'd give it to him. He says the feed outen it gives the stock the bloat. He heard of somebody lost four head of horses, feedin' 'em that stuff."

Alexandra looked down the table from one to another. "Well, the only way we can find out is to try. Lou and I have different notions about feeding stock, and that's a good thing. It's bad if all the members of a family think alike. They never get anywhere. Lou can learn by my mistakes and I can learn by his. Isn't that fair, Barney?"

The Irishman laughed. He had no love for Lou, who was always uppish with him and who said that Alexandra paid her hands too much. "I've no thought but to give the thing an honest try, mum. 'T would be only right, after puttin' so much expense into it. Maybe Emil will come out an' have a look at it wid me." He pushed back his chair, took his hat from the nail, and marched out with Emil, who, with his university ideas, was supposed to have instigated the silo. The other hands followed them, all except old Ivar. He had been depressed throughout the meal and had paid no heed to the talk of the men, even when they mentioned cornstalk bloat, upon which he was sure to have opinions.

"Did you want to speak to me, Ivar?" Alexandra asked as she rose from the table. "Come into the sitting-room."

The old man followed Alexandra, but when she motioned him to a chair he shook his head. She took up her workbasket and waited for him to speak. He stood looking at the carpet, his bushy head bowed, his hands clasped in front of him. Ivar's bandy legs seemed to have grown shorter with years, and they were completely misfitted to his broad, thick body and heavy shoulders.

"Well, Ivar, what is it?" Alexandra asked after she had waited longer than usual.

Ivar had never learned to speak English and his Norwegian was quaint and grave, like the speech of the more old-fashioned people. He always addressed Alexandra in terms of the deepest respect, hoping to set a good example to the kitchen girls, whom he thought too familiar in their manners.

"Mistress," he began faintly, without raising his eyes, "the folk have been looking coldly at me of late. You know there has been talk."

"Talk about what, Ivar?"

"About sending me away; to the asylum."

Alexandra put down her sewing-basket. "Nobody has come to me with such talk," she said decidedly. "Why need you listen? You know I would never consent to such a thing."

Ivar lifted his shaggy head and looked at her out of his little eyes. "They say that you cannot prevent it if the folk complain of me, if your brothers complain to the authorities. They say that your brothers are afraid—God forbid!—that I may do you some injury when my spells are on me. Mistress, how can any one think that?—that I could bite the hand that fed me!" The tears trickled down on the old man's beard.

Alexandra frowned. "Ivar, I wonder at you, that you should come bothering me with such nonsense. I am still running my own house, and other people have nothing to do with either you or me. So long as I am suited with you, there is nothing to be said."

Ivar pulled a red handkerchief out of the breast of his blouse and wiped his eyes and beard. "But I should not wish you to keep me if, as they say, it is against your interests, and if it is hard for you to get hands because I am here."

Alexandra made an impatient gesture, but the old man put out his hand and went on earnestly:—

"Listen, mistress, it is right that you should take these things into account. You know that my spells come from God, and that I would not harm any living creature. You believe that every one should worship God in the way revealed to him. But that is not the way of this country. The way here is for all to do alike. I am despised because I do not wear shoes, because I do not cut my hair, and because I have visions. At home, in the old country, there were many like me, who had been touched by God, or who had seen things in the graveyard at night and were different afterward. We thought nothing of it, and let them alone. But here, if a man is different in his feet or in his head, they put him in the asylum. Look at Peter Kralik; when he was a boy, drinking out of a creek, he swallowed a snake, and always after that he could eat only such food as the creature liked, for when he ate anything else, it became enraged and gnawed him. When he felt it whipping about in him, he drank alcohol to stupefy it and get some ease for himself. He could work as good as any man, and his head was clear, but they locked him up for being different in his stomach. That is the way; they have built the asylum for people who are different, and they will not even let us live in the holes with the badgers. Only your great prosperity has protected me so far. If you had had ill-fortune, they would have taken me to Hastings long ago."

As Ivar talked, his gloom lifted. Alexandra had found that she could often break his fasts and long penances by talking to him and letting him pour out the thoughts that troubled him. Sympathy always cleared his mind, and ridicule was poison to him.

"There is a great deal in what you say, Ivar. Like as not they will be wanting to take me to Hastings because I have built a silo; and then I may take you with me. But at present I need you here. Only don't come to me again telling me what people say. Let people go on talking as they like, and we will go on living as we think best. You have been with me now for twelve years, and I have gone to you for advice oftener than I have ever gone to any one. That ought to satisfy you."

Ivar bowed humbly. "Yes, mistress, I shall not trouble you with their talk again. And as for my feet, I have observed your wishes all these years, though you have never questioned me; washing them every night, even in winter."

Alexandra laughed. "Oh, never mind about your feet, Ivar. We can remember when half our neighbors went barefoot in summer. I expect old Mrs. Lee would love to slip her shoes off now sometimes, if she dared. I'm glad I'm not Lou's mother-in-law."

Ivar looked about mysteriously and lowered his voice almost to a whisper. "You know what they have over at Lou's house? A great white tub, like the stone water-troughs in the old country, to wash themselves in. When you sent me over with the strawberries, they were all in town but the old woman Lee and the baby. She took me in and showed me the thing, and she told me it was impossible to wash yourself clean in it, because, in so much water, you could not make a strong suds. So when they fill it up and send her in there, she pretends, and makes a splashing noise. Then, when they are all asleep, she washes herself in a little wooden tub she keeps under her bed."

Alexandra shook with laughter. "Poor old Mrs. Lee! They won't let her wear nightcaps, either. Never mind; when she comes to visit me, she can do all the old things in the old way, and have as much beer as she wants. We'll start an asylum for old-time people, Ivar."

Ivar folded his big handkerchief carefully and thrust it back into his blouse. "This is always the way, mistress. I come to you sorrowing, and you send me away with a light heart. And will you be so good as to tell the Irishman that he is not to work the brown gelding until the sore on its shoulder is healed?"

"That I will. Now go and put Emil's mare to the cart. I am going to drive up to the north quarter to meet the man from town who is to buy my alfalfa hay."

III

Alexandra was to hear more of Ivar's case, however. On Sunday her married brothers came to dinner. She had asked them for that say because Emil, who hated family parties, would be absent, dancing at Amédée Chevalier's wedding, up in the French country. The table was set for company in the dining-room, where highly varnished wood and colored glass and useless pieces of china were conspicuous enough to satisfy the standards of the new prosperity. Alexandra had put herself into the hands of the

Hanover furniture dealer, and he had conscientiously done his best to make her dining-room look like his display window. She said frankly that she knew nothing about such things, and she was willing to be governed by the general conviction that the more useless and utterly unusable objects were, the greater their virtue as ornament. That seemed reasonable enough. Since she liked plain things herself, it was all the more necessary to have jars and punchbowls and candlesticks in the company rooms for people who did appreciate them. Her guests liked to see about them these reassuring emblems of prosperity.

The family party was complete except for Emil, and Oscar's wife who, in the country phrase, "was not going anywhere just now." Oscar sat at the foot of the table and his four tow-headed little boys, aged from twelve to five, were ranged at one side. Neither Oscar nor Lou has changed much; they have simply, as Alexandra said of them long ago, grown to be more and more like themselves. Lou now looks the older of the two; his face is thin and shrewd and wrinkled about the eyes, while Oscar's is thick and dull. For all his dullness, however, Oscar makes more money than his brother, which adds to Lou's sharpness and uneasiness and tempts him to make a show. The trouble with Lou is that he is tricky, and his neighbors have found out that, as Ivar says, he has not a fox's face for nothing. Politics being the natural field for such talents, he neglects his farm to attend conventions and to run for county offices.

Lou's wife, formerly Annie Lee, has grown to look curiously like her husband. Her face has become longer, sharper, more aggressive. She wears her yellow hair in a high pompadour, and is bedecked with rings and chains and "beauty pins." Her tight, high-heeled shoes give her an awkward walk, and she is always more or less preoccupied with her clothes. As she sat at the table, she kept telling her youngest daughter to "be careful now, and not drop anything on mother."

The conversation at the table was all in English. Oscar's wife, from the malaria district of Missouri, was ashamed of marrying a foreigner, and his boys do not understand a word of Swedish. Annie and Lou sometimes speak Swedish at home, but Annie is almost as much afraid of being "caught" at it as ever her mother was of being caught barefoot. Oscar still has a thick accent, but Lou speaks like anybody from Iowa.

"When I was in Hastings to attend the convention," he was saying, "I saw the superintendent of the asylum, and I was telling him about Ivar's symptoms. He says Ivar's case is one of the most dangerous kind, and it's a wonder he hasn't done something violent before this."

Alexandra laughed good-humoredly. "Oh, nonsense, Lou! The doctors would have us all crazy if they could. Ivar's queer, certainly, but he has more sense than half the hands I hire."

Lou flew at his fried chicken. "Oh, I guess the doctor knows his business, Alexandra. He was very much surprised when I told him how you'd put up with Ivar. He says he's likely to set fire to the barn any night, or to take after you and the girls with an axe."

Little Signa, who was waiting on the table, giggled and fled to the kitchen. Alexandra's eyes twinkled. "That was too much for Signa, Lou. We all know that Ivar's perfectly harmless. The girls would as soon expect me to chase them with an axe."

Lou flushed and signaled to his wife. "All the same, the neighbors will be having a say about it before long. He may burn anybody's barn. It's only necessary for one property-owner in the township to make complaint, and he'll be taken up by force. You'd better send him yourself and not have any hard feelings."

Alexandra helped one of her little nephews to gravy. "Well, Lou, if any of the neighbors try that, I'll have myself appointed Ivar's guardian and take the case to court, that's all. I am perfectly satisfied with him."

"Pass the preserves, Lou," said Annie in a warning tone. She had reasons for not wishing her husband to cross Alexandra too openly. "But don't you sort of hate to have people see him around here, Alexandra?" she went on with persuasive smoothness. "He is a disgraceful object, and you're fixed up so nice now. It sort of makes people distant with you, when they never know when they'll hear him scratching about. My girls are afraid as death of him, aren't you, Milly, dear?"

Milly was fifteen, fat and jolly and pompadoured, with a creamy complexion, square white teeth, and a short upper lip. She looked like her grandmother Bergson, and had her comfortable and comfort-loving nature. She grinned at her aunt, with whom she was a great deal more at ease than she was with her mother. Alexandra winked a reply.

"Milly needn't be afraid of Ivar. She's an especial favorite of his. In my opinion Ivar has just as much right to his own way of dressing and thinking as we have. But I'll see that he doesn't bother other people. I'll keep him at home, so don't trouble any more about him, Lou. I've been wanting to ask you about your new bathtub. How does it work?"

Annie came to the fore to give Lou time to recover himself. "Oh, it works something grand! I can't keep him out of it. He washes himself all over three times a week now, and uses all the hot water. I think it's weakening to stay in as long as he does. You ought to have one, Alexandra."

"I'm thinking of it. I might have one put in the barn for Ivar, if it will ease people's minds. But before I get a bathtub, I'm going to get a piano for Milly."

Oscar, at the end of the table, looked up from his plate. "What does Milly want of a pianny? What's the matter with her organ? She can make some use of that, and play in church."

Annie looked flustered. She had begged Alexandra not to say anything about this plan before Oscar, who was apt to be jealous of what his sister did for Lou's children. Alexandra did not get on with Oscar's wife at all. "Milly can play in church just the same, and she'll still play on the organ. But practising on it so much spoils her touch. Her teacher says so," Annie brought out with spirit.

Oscar rolled his eyes. "Well, Milly must have got on pretty good if she's got past the organ. I know plenty of grown folks that ain't," he said bluntly.

Annie threw up her chin. "She has got on good, and she's going to play for her commencement when she graduates in town next year."

"Yes," said Alexandra firmly, "I think Milly deserves a piano. All the girls around here have been taking lessons for years, but Milly is the only one of them who can ever play anything when you ask her. I'll tell you when I first thought I would like to give you a piano, Milly, and that was when you learned that book of old Swedish songs that your grandfather used to sing. He had a sweet tenor voice, and when he was a young man he loved to sing. I can remember hearing him singing with the sailors down in the shipyard, when I was no bigger than Stella here," pointing to Annie's younger daughter.

Milly and Stella both looked through the door into the sitting-room, where a crayon portrait of John Bergson hung on the wall. Alexandra had had it made from a little photograph, taken for his friends just before he left Sweden; a slender man of thirty-five, with soft hair curling about his high forehead, a drooping mustache, and wondering, sad eyes that looked forward into the distance, as if they already beheld the New World.

After dinner Lou and Oscar went to the orchard to pick cherries—they had neither of them had the patience to grow an orchard of their own—and Annie went down to gossip with Alexandra's kitchen girls while they washed the dishes. She could always find out more about Alexandra's domestic economy from the prattling maids than from Alexandra herself, and what she discovered she used to her own advantage with Lou. On the Divide, farmers' daughters no longer went out into service, so Alexandra got her girls from Sweden, by paying their fare over. They stayed with her until they married, and were replaced by sisters or cousins from the old country.

Alexandra took her three nieces into the flower garden. She was fond of the little girls, especially of Milly, who came to spend a week with her aunt now and then, and read aloud to her from the old books about the house, or listened to stories about the early days on the Divide. While they were walking among the flower beds, a buggy drove up the hill and stopped in front of the gate. A man got out and stood talking to the driver. The little girls were delighted at the advent of a stranger, some one from very far away, they knew by his clothes, his gloves, and the sharp, pointed cut of his dark beard. The girls fell behind their aunt and peeped out at him from among the castor beans. The stranger came up to the gate and stood holding his hat in his hand, smiling, while Alexandra advanced slowly to meet him. As she approached he spoke in a low, pleasant voice.

"Don't you know me, Alexandra? I would have known you, anywhere."

Alexandra shaded her eyes with her hand. Suddenly she took a quick step forward. "Can it be!" she exclaimed with feeling; "can it be that it is Carl Linstrum? Why, Carl, it is!" She threw out both her hands and caught his across the gate. "Sadie, Milly, run tell your father and Uncle Oscar that our old friend Carl Linstrum is here. Be quick! Why, Carl, how did it happen? I can't believe this!" Alexandra shook the tears from her eyes and laughed.

The stranger nodded to his driver, dropped his suitcase inside the fence, and opened the gate. "Then you are glad to see me, and you can put me up overnight? I couldn't go through this country without stopping off to have a look at you. How little you have changed! Do you know, I was sure it would be like that. You simply couldn't be different. How fine you are!" He stepped back and looked at her admiringly.

Alexandra blushed and laughed again. "But you yourself, Carl—with that beard—how could I have known you? You went away a little boy." She reached for his suitcase and when he intercepted her she threw up her hands. "You see, I give myself away. I have only women come to visit me, and I do not know how to behave. Where is your trunk?"

"It's in Hanover. I can stay only a few days. I am on my way to the coast."

They started up the path. "A few days? After all these years!"

Alexandra shook her finger at him. "See this, you have walked into a trap. You do not get away so easy." She put her hand affectionately on his shoulder. "You owe me a visit for the sake of old times. Why must you go to the coast at all?"

"Oh, I must! I am a fortune hunter. From Seattle I go on to Alaska."

"Alaska?" She looked at him in astonishment. "Are you going to paint the Indians?"

"Paint?" the young man frowned. "Oh! I'm not a painter, Alexandra. I'm an engraver. I have nothing to do with painting."

"But on my parlor wall I have the paintings—"

He interrupted nervously. "Oh, water-color sketches—done for amusement. I sent them to remind you of me, not because they were good. What a wonderful place you have made of this, Alexandra." He turned and looked back at the wide, map-like prospect of field and hedge and pasture. "I would never have believed it could be done. I'm disappointed in my own eye, in my imagination."

At this moment Lou and Oscar came up the hill from the orchard. They did not quicken their pace when they saw Carl; indeed, they did not openly look in his direction. They advanced distrustfully, and as if they wished the distance were longer.

Alexandra beckoned to them. "They think I am trying to fool them. Come, boys, it's Carl Linstrum, our old Carl!"

Lou gave the visitor a quick, sidelong glance and thrust out his hand. "Glad to see you." Oscar followed with "How d' do." Carl could not tell whether their offishness came from unfriendliness or from embarrassment. He and Alexandra led the way to the porch.

"Carl," Alexandra explained, "is on his way to Seattle. He is going to Alaska."

Oscar studied the visitor's yellow shoes. "Got business there?" he asked.

Carl laughed. "Yes, very pressing business. I'm going there to get rich. Engraving's a very interesting profession, but a man never makes any money at it. So I'm going to try the goldfields."

Alexandra felt that this was a tactful speech, and Lou looked up with some interest. "Ever done anything in that line before?"

"No, but I'm going to join a friend of mine who went out from New York and has done well. He has offered to break me in."

"Turrible cold winters, there, I hear," remarked Oscar. "I thought people went up there in the spring."

"They do. But my friend is going to spend the winter in Seattle and I am to stay with him there and learn something about prospecting before we start north next year."

Lou looked skeptical. "Let's see, how long have you been away from here?"

"Sixteen years. You ought to remember that, Lou, for you were married just after we went away."

"Going to stay with us some time?" Oscar asked.

"A few days, if Alexandra can keep me."

"I expect you'll be wanting to see your old place," Lou observed more cordially. "You won't hardly know it. But there's a few chunks of your old sod house left. Alexandra wouldn't never let Frank Shabata plough over it."

Annie Lee, who, ever since the visitor was announced, had been touching up her hair and settling her lace and wishing she had worn another dress, now emerged with her three daughters and introduced them. She was greatly impressed by Carl's urban appearance, and in her excitement, talked very loud and threw her head about. "And you ain't married yet? At your age, now! Think of that! You'll have to wait for Milly. Yes, we've got a boy, too. The youngest. He's at home with his grandma. You must come over to see mother and hear Milly play. She's the musician of the family. She does pyrography, too. That's burnt wood, you know. You wouldn't believe what she can do with her poker. Yes, she goes to school in town, and she is the youngest in her class by two years."

Milly looked uncomfortable and Carl took her hand again. He liked her creamy skin and happy, innocent eyes, and he could see that her mother's way of talking distressed her. "I'm sure she's a clever little girl," he murmured, looking at her thoughtfully. "Let me see—Ah, it's your mother that she looks like, Alexandra. Mrs.

Bergson must have looked just like this when she was a little girl. Does Milly run about over the country as you and Alexandra used to, Annie?"

Milly's mother protested. "Oh, my, no! Things has changed since we was girls. Milly has it very different. We are going to rent the place and move into town as soon as the girls are old enough to go out into company. A good many are doing that here now. Lou is going into business."

Lou grinned. "That's what she says. You better go get your things on. Ivar's hitching up," he added, turning to Annie.

Young farmers seldom address their wives by name. It is always "you," or "she."

Having got his wife out of the way, Lou sat down on the step and began to whittle. "Well, what do folks in New York think of William Jennings Bryan?" Lou began to bluster, as he always did when he talked politics. "We gave Wall Street a scare in ninety-six, all right, and we're fixing another to hand them. Silver wasn't the only issue," he nodded mysteriously. "There's a good many things got to be changed. The West is going to make itself heard."

Carl laughed. "But surely, it did do that, if nothing else."

Lou's thin face reddened up to the roots of his bristly hair. "Oh, we've only begun. We're waking up to a sense of our responsibilities, out here, and we ain't afraid, neither. You fellows back there must be a tame lot. If you had any nerve you'd get together and march down to Wall Street and blow it up. Dynamite it, I mean," with a threatening nod.

He was so much in earnest that Carl scarcely knew how to answer him. "That would be a waste of powder. The same business would go on in another street. The street doesn't matter. But what have you fellows out here got to kick about? You have the only safe place there is. Morgan himself couldn't touch you. One only has to drive through this country to see that you're all as rich as barons."

"We have a good deal more to say than we had when we were poor," said Lou threateningly. "We're getting on to a whole lot of things."

O PIONEERS!

65

As Ivar drove a double carriage up to the gate, Annie came out in a hat that looked like the model of a battleship. Carl rose and took her down to the carriage, while Lou lingered for a word with his sister.

"What do you suppose he's come for?" he asked, jerking his head toward the gate.

"Why, to pay us a visit. I've been begging him to for years."

Oscar looked at Alexandra. "He didn't let you know he was coming?"

"No. Why should he? I told him to come at any time."

Lou shrugged his shoulders. "He doesn't seem to have done much for himself. Wandering around this way!"

Oscar spoke solemnly, as from the depths of a cavern. "He never was much account."

Alexandra left them and hurried down to the gate where Annie was rattling on to Carl about her new dining-room furniture. "You must bring Mr. Linstrum over real soon, only be sure to telephone me first," she called back, as Carl helped her into the carriage. Old Ivar, his white head bare, stood holding the horses. Lou came down the path and climbed into the front seat, took up the reins, and drove off without saying anything further to any one. Oscar picked up his youngest boy and trudged off down the road, the other three trotting after him. Carl, holding the gate open for Alexandra, began to laugh. "Up and coming on the Divide, eh, Alexandra?" he cried gayly.

IV

Carl had changed, Alexandra felt, much less than one might have expected. He had not become a trim, self-satisfied city man. There was still something homely and wayward and definitely personal about him. Even his clothes, his Norfolk coat and his very high collars, were a little unconventional. He seemed to shrink into himself as he used to do; to hold himself away from things, as if he were afraid of being hurt. In short, he was more self-conscious than a man of thirty-five is expected to be. He looked older than his years and not very strong. His black hair, which still hung in a triangle over his pale forehead, was thin at the crown, and there were fine, relentless lines about his eyes. His back, with its high, sharp shoulders, looked like the back of an overworked German professor off on his holiday. His face was intelligent, sensitive, unhappy.

That evening after supper, Carl and Alexandra were sitting by the clump of castor beans in the middle of the flower garden. The gravel paths glittered in the moonlight, and below them the fields lay white and still.

"Do you know, Alexandra," he was saying, "I've been thinking how strangely things work out. I've been away engraving other men's pictures, and you've stayed at home and made your own." He pointed with his cigar toward the sleeping landscape. "How in the world have you done it? How have your neighbors done it?"

"We hadn't any of us much to do with it, Carl. The land did it. It had its little joke. It pretended to be poor because nobody knew how to work it right, and then, all at once, it worked itself. It woke up out of its sleep and stretched itself, and it was so big, so rich, just from sitting still. As for me, you remember when I began to buy land. For years after that I was always squeezing and borrowing until I was ashamed to show my face in the banks. And then, all at once, men began to come to me offering to lend me money—and I didn't need it! Then I went ahead and built this house. I really built it for Emil. I want you to see Emil, Carl. He is so different from the rest of us!"

"How different?"

"Oh, you'll see! I'm sure it was to have sons like Emil, and to give them a chance, that father left the old country. It's curious, too; on the outside Emil is just like an American boy,—he graduated from the State University in June, you know,—but underneath he is more Swedish than any of us. Sometimes he is so like father that he frightens me; he is so violent in his feelings like that."

"Is he going to farm here with you?"

"He shall do whatever he wants to," Alexandra declared warmly. "He is going to have a chance, a whole chance; that's what I've worked for. Sometimes he talks about studying law, and sometimes, just lately, he's been talking about going out into the sand hills and taking up more land. He has his sad times, like father. But I hope he won't do that. We have land enough, at last!" Alexandra laughed.

"How about Lou and Oscar? They've done well, haven't they?"

"Yes, very well; but they are different, and now that they have farms of their own I do not see so much of them. We divided the land equally when Lou married. They have their own way of doing things, and they do not altogether like my way, I am afraid. Perhaps they think me too independent. But I have had to think for myself a good many years and am not likely to change. On the whole, though, we take as much comfort in each other as most brothers and sisters do. And I am very fond of Lou's oldest daughter."

"I think I liked the old Lou and Oscar better, and they probably feel the same about me. I even, if you can keep a secret," —Carl leaned forward and touched her arm, smiling,—"I even think I liked the old country better. This is all splendid in its way, but there was something about this country when it was a wild old beast that has haunted me all these years. Now, when I come back to all this milk and honey, I feel like the old German song, 'Wo bist du, wo bist du, mein geliebtest Land?'—Do you ever feel like that, I wonder?"

"Yes, sometimes, when I think about father and mother and those who are gone; so many of our old neighbors." Alexandra paused and looked up thoughtfully at the stars. "We can remember the graveyard when it was wild prairie, Carl, and now—"

"And now the old story has begun to write itself over there," said Carl softly. "Isn't it queer: there are only two or three human stories, and they go on repeating themselves as fiercely as if they had never happened before; like the larks in this country, that have been singing the same five notes over for thousands of years."

"Oh, yes! The young people, they live so hard. And yet I sometimes envy them. There is my little neighbor, now; the people who bought your old place. I wouldn't have sold it to any one else, but I was always fond of that girl. You must remember her, little Marie Tovesky, from Omaha, who used to visit here? When she was eighteen she ran away from the convent school and got married, crazy child! She came out here a bride, with her father and husband. He had nothing, and the old man was willing to buy them a place and set them up. Your farm took her fancy, and I was glad to have her so near me. I've never been sorry, either. I even try to get along with Frank on her account."

"Is Frank her husband?"

"Yes. He's one of these wild fellows. Most Bohemians are good-natured, but Frank thinks we don't appreciate him here, I guess. He's jealous about everything, his farm and his horses and his pretty wife. Everybody likes her, just the same as when she was little. Sometimes I go up to the Catholic church with Emil, and it's funny to see Marie standing there laughing and shaking hands with people, looking so excited and gay, with Frank sulking behind her as if he could eat everybody alive. Frank's not a bad neighbor, but to get on with him you've got to make a fuss over him and act as if you thought he was a very important person all the time, and different from other people. I find it hard to keep that up from one year's end to another."

"I shouldn't think you'd be very successful at that kind of thing, Alexandra." Carl seemed to find the idea amusing.

"Well," said Alexandra firmly, "I do the best I can, on Marie's account. She has it hard enough, anyway. She's too young and pretty for this sort of life. We're all ever so much older and slower. But she's the kind that won't be downed easily. She'll work all day and go to a Bohemian wedding and dance all night, and drive the hay wagon for a cross man next morning. I could stay by a job, but I never had the go in me that she has, when I was going my best. I'll have to take you over to see her to-morrow."

Carl dropped the end of his cigar softly among the castor beans and sighed. "Yes, I suppose I must see the old place. I'm cowardly about things that remind me of myself. It took courage to come at all, Alexandra. I wouldn't have, if I hadn't wanted to see you very, very much."

Alexandra looked at him with her calm, deliberate eyes. "Why do you dread things like that, Carl?" she asked earnestly. "Why are you dissatisfied with yourself?"

Her visitor winced. "How direct you are, Alexandra! Just like you used to be. Do I give myself away so quickly? Well, you see, for one thing, there's nothing to look forward to in my profession. Wood-engraving is the only thing I care about, and that had gone out before I began. Everything's cheap metal work nowadays, touching up miserable photographs, forcing up poor drawings, and spoiling good ones. I'm absolutely sick of it all." Carl frowned. "Alexandra, all the way out from New York I've been planning how I could deceive you and make you think me a very enviable fellow, and here I am telling you the truth the first night. I waste a lot of time pretending to people, and the joke of it is, I don't think I ever deceive any one. There are too many of my kind; people know us on sight."

Carl paused. Alexandra pushed her hair back from her brow with a puzzled, thoughtful gesture. "You see," he went on calmly, "measured by your standards here, I'm a failure. I couldn't buy even one of your cornfields. I've enjoyed a great many things, but I've got nothing to show for it all."

"But you show for it yourself, Carl. I'd rather have had your freedom than my land."

Carl shook his head mournfully. "Freedom so often means that one isn't needed anywhere. Here you are an individual, you have a background of your own, you would be missed. But off there in the cities there are thousands of rolling stones like me. We are all alike; we have no ties, we know nobody, we own nothing. When one of us dies, they scarcely know where to bury him. Our landlady and the delicatessen man are our mourners, and we leave nothing behind us but a frock-coat and a fiddle, or an easel, or a typewriter, or whatever tool we got our living by. All we have ever managed to do is to pay our rent, the exorbitant rent that one has to pay for a few square feet of space near the heart of things. We have no house, no place, no people of our own. We live in the streets, in the parks, in the theatres. We sit in restaurants and concert halls and look about at the hundreds of our own kind and shudder."

Alexandra was silent. She sat looking at the silver spot the moon made on the surface of the pond down in the pasture. He knew that she understood what he meant. At last she said slowly, "And yet I would rather have Emil grow up like that than like his two brothers. We pay a high rent, too, though we pay differently. We grow hard and heavy here. We don't move lightly and easily as you do, and our minds get stiff. If the world were no wider than my cornfields, if there were not something beside this, I wouldn't feel that it was much worth while to work. No, I would rather have Emil like you than like them. I felt that as soon as you came."

"I wonder why you feel like that?" Carl mused.

"I don't know. Perhaps I am like Carrie Jensen, the sister of one of my hired men. She had never been out of the cornfields, and a few years ago she got despondent and said life was just the same thing over and over, and she didn't see the use of it. After she had tried to kill herself once or twice, her folks got worried and sent her over to Iowa to visit some relations. Ever since she's come back she's been perfectly cheerful, and she says she's contented to live and work in a world that's so big and interesting. She said that anything as big as the bridges over the Platte and the Missouri reconciled her. And it's what goes on in the world that reconciles me."

V

Alexandra did not find time to go to her neighbor's the next day, nor the next. It was a busy season on the farm, with the corn-plowing going on, and even Emil was in the field with a team and cultivator. Carl went about over the farms with Alexandra in the morning, and in the afternoon and evening they found a great deal to talk about. Emil, for all his track practice, did not stand up under farmwork very well, and by night he was too tired to talk or even to practise on his cornet.

On Wednesday morning Carl got up before it was light, and stole downstairs and out of the kitchen door just as old Ivar was making his morning ablutions at the pump. Carl nodded at him and hurried up the draw, past the garden, and into the pasture where the milking cows used to be kept.

The dawn in the east looked like the light from some great fire that was burning under the edge of the world. The color was reflected in the globules of dew that sheathed the short gray pasture grass. Carl walked rapidly until he came to the crest of the second hill, where the Bergson pasture joined the one that had belonged to his father. There he sat down and waited for the sun to rise. It was just there that he and Alexandra used to do their milking together, he on his side of the fence, she on hers. He could remember exactly how she looked when she came over the close-cropped grass, her skirts pinned up, her head bare, a bright tin pail in either hand, and the milky light of the early morning all about her. Even as a boy he used to feel, when he saw her coming with her free step, her upright head and calm shoulders, that she looked as if she had walked straight out of the morning itself. Since then, when he had happened to see the sun come up in the country or on the water, he had often remembered the young Swedish girl and her milking pails.

Carl sat musing until the sun leaped above the prairie, and in the grass about him all the small creatures of day began to tune their tiny instruments. Birds and insects without number began to chirp, to twitter, to snap and whistle, to make all manner of fresh shrill noises. The pasture was flooded with light; every clump of ironweed and snow-on-the-mountain threw a long shadow, and the golden light seemed to be rippling through the curly grass like the tide racing in.

He crossed the fence into the pasture that was now the Shabatas' and continued his walk toward the pond. He had not gone

far, however, when he discovered that he was not the only person
abroad. In the draw below, his gun in his hands, was Emil, advancing cautiously, with a young woman beside him. They were
moving softly, keeping close together, and Carl knew that they
expected to find ducks on the pond. At the moment when they
came in sight of the bright spot of water, he heard a whirr of wings
and the ducks shot up into the air. There was a sharp crack from
the gun, and five of the birds fell to the ground. Emil and his companion laughed delightedly, and Emil ran to pick them up. When
he came back, dangling the ducks by their feet, Marie held her
apron and he dropped them into it. As she stood looking down at
them, her face changed. She took up one of the birds, a rumpled
ball of feathers with the blood dripping slowly from its mouth, and
looked at the live color that still burned on its plumage.

As she let it fall, she cried in distress, "Oh, Emil, why did you?"

"I like that!" the boy exclaimed indignantly. "Why, Marie, you
asked me to come yourself."

"Yes, yes, I know," she said tearfully, "but I didn't think. I hate
to see them when they are first shot. They were having such a
good time, and we've spoiled it all for them."

Emil gave a rather sore laugh. "I should say we had! I'm not
going hunting with you any more. You're as bad as Ivar. Here, let
me take them." He snatched the ducks out of her apron.

"Don't be cross, Emil. Only—Ivar's right about wild things.
They're too happy to kill. You can tell just how they felt when
they flew up. They were scared, but they didn't really think anything could hurt them. No, we won't do that any more."

"All right," Emil assented. "I'm sorry I made you feel bad." As
he looked down into her tearful eyes, there was a curious, sharp
young bitterness in his own.

Carl watched them as they moved slowly down the draw. They
had not seen him at all. He had not overheard much of their
dialogue, but he felt the import of it. It made him, somehow, unreasonably mournful to find two young things abroad in the pasture
in the early morning. He decided that he needed his breakfast.

VI

At dinner that day Alexandra said she thought they must really manage to go over to the Shabatas' that afternoon. "It's not often I let three days go by without seeing Marie. She will think I have forsaken her, now that my old friend has come back."

After the men had gone back to work, Alexandra put on a white dress and her sun-hat, and she and Carl set forth across the fields. "You see we have kept up the old path, Carl. It has been so nice for me to feel that there was a friend at the other end of it again."

Carl smiled a little ruefully. "All the same, I hope it hasn't been *quite* the same."

Alexandra looked at him with surprise. "Why, no, of course not. Not the same. She could not very well take your place, if that's what you mean. I'm friendly with all my neighbors, I hope. But Marie is really a companion, some one I can talk to quite frankly. You wouldn't want me to be more lonely than I have been, would you?"

Carl laughed and pushed back the triangular lock of hair with the edge of his hat. "Of course I don't. I ought to be thankful that this path hasn't been worn by—well, by friends with more pressing errands than your little Bohemian is likely to have." He paused to give Alexandra his hand as she stepped over the stile. "Are you the least bit disappointed in our coming together again?" he asked abruptly. "Is it the way you hoped it would be?"

Alexandra smiled at this. "Only better. When I've thought about your coming, I've sometimes been a little afraid of it. You have lived where things move so fast, and everything is slow here; the people slowest of all. Our lives are like the years, all made up of weather and crops and cows. How you hated cows!" She shook her head and laughed to herself.

"I didn't when we milked together. I walked up to the pasture corners this morning. I wonder whether I shall ever be able to tell you all that I was thinking about up there. It's a strange thing,

Alexandra; I find it easy to be frank with you about everything under the sun except—yourself!"

"You are afraid of hurting my feelings, perhaps." Alexandra looked at him thoughtfully.

"No, I'm afraid of giving you a shock. You've seen yourself for so long in the dull minds of the people about you, that if I were to tell you how you seem to me, it would startle you. But you must see that you astonish me. You must feel when people admire you."

Alexandra blushed and laughed with some confusion. "I felt that you were pleased with me, if you mean that."

"And you've felt when other people were pleased with you?" he insisted.

"Well, sometimes. The men in town, at the banks and the county offices, seem glad to see me. I think, myself, it is more pleasant to do business with people who are clean and healthy-looking," she admitted blandly.

Carl gave a little chuckle as he opened the Shabatas' gate for her. "Oh, do you?" he asked dryly.

There was no sign of life about the Shabatas' house except a big yellow cat, sunning itself on the kitchen doorstep.

Alexandra took the path that led to the orchard. "She often sits there and sews. I didn't telephone her we were coming, because I didn't want her to go to work and bake cake and freeze ice-cream. She'll always make a party if you give her the least excuse. Do you recognize the apple trees, Carl?"

Linstrum looked about him. "I wish I had a dollar for every bucket of water I've carried for those trees. Poor father, he was an easy man, but he was perfectly merciless when it came to watering the orchard."

"That's one thing I like about Germans; they make an orchard grow if they can't make anything else. I'm so glad these trees belong to some one who takes comfort in them. When I rented this place, the tenants never kept the orchard up, and Emil and I used to come over and take care of it ourselves. It needs mowing now. There she is, down in the corner. Ma-ria-a-a!" she called.

A recumbent figure started up from the grass and came running toward them through the flickering screen of light and shade.

"Look at her! Isn't she like a little brown rabbit?" Alexandra laughed.

Maria ran up panting and threw her arms about Alexandra. "Oh, I had begun to think you were not coming at all, maybe. I knew you were so busy. Yes, Emil told me about Mr. Linstrum being here. Won't you come up to the house?"

"Why not sit down there in your corner? Carl wants to see the orchard. He kept all these trees alive for years, watering them with his own back."

Marie turned to Carl. "Then I'm thankful to you, Mr. Linstrum. We'd never have bought the place if it hadn't been for this orchard, and then I wouldn't have had Alexandra, either." She gave Alexandra's arm a little squeeze as she walked beside her. "How nice your dress smells, Alexandra; you put rosemary leaves in your chest, like I told you."

She led them to the northwest corner of the orchard, sheltered on one side by a thick mulberry hedge and bordered on the other by a wheatfield, just beginning to yellow. In this corner the ground dipped a little, and the blue-grass, which the weeds had driven out in the upper part of the orchard, grew thick and luxuriant. Wild roses were flaming in the tufts of bunchgrass along the fence. Under a white mulberry tree there was an old wagon-seat. Beside it lay a book and a workbasket.

"You must have the seat, Alexandra. The grass would stain your dress," the hostess insisted. She dropped down on the ground at Alexandra's side and tucked her feet under her. Carl sat at a little distance from the two women, his back to the wheatfield, and watched them. Alexandra took off her shade-hat and threw it on the ground. Marie picked it up and played with the white ribbons, twisting them about her brown fingers as she talked. They made a pretty picture in the strong sunlight, the leafy pattern surrounding them like a net; the Swedish woman so white and gold, kindly and amused, but armored in calm, and the alert

brown one, her full lips parted, points of yellow light dancing in
her eyes as she laughed and chattered. Carl had never forgotten
little Marie Tovesky's eyes, and he was glad to have an opportunity
to study them. The brown iris, he found, was curiously slashed
with yellow, the color of sunflower honey, or of old amber. In each
eye one of these streaks must have been larger than the others, for
the effect was that of two dancing points of light, two little yellow
bubbles, such as rise in a glass of champagne. Sometimes they
seemed like the sparks from a forge. She seemed so easily excited,
to kindle with a fierce little flame if one but breathed upon her.
"What a waste," Carl reflected. "She ought to be doing all that for
a sweetheart. How awkwardly things come about!"

It was not very long before Marie sprang up out of the grass
again. "Wait a moment. I want to show you something." She ran
away and disappeared behind the low-growing apple trees.

"What a charming creature," Carl murmured. "I don't wonder that
her husband is jealous. But can't she walk? does she always run?"

Alexandra nodded. "Always. I don't see many people, but I
don't believe there are many like her, anywhere."

Marie came back with a branch she had broken from an
apricot tree, laden with pale-yellow, pink-cheeked fruit. She
dropped it beside Carl. "Did you plant those, too? They are such
beautiful little trees."

Carl fingered the blue-green leaves, porous like blotting paper
and shaped like birch leaves, hung on waxen red stems. "Yes, I
think I did. Are these the circus trees, Alexandra?"

"Shall I tell her about them?" Alexandra asked. "Sit down like a
good girl, Marie, and don't ruin my poor hat, and I'll tell you a story.
A long time ago, when Carl and I were, say, sixteen and twelve, a
circus came to Hanover and we went to town in our wagon, with
Lou and Oscar, to see the parade. We hadn't money enough to go to
the circus grounds and hung around until the show began and the
crowd went inside the tent. Then Lou was afraid we looked foolish
standing outside in the pasture, so we went back to Hanover feeling
very sad. There was a man in the streets selling apricots, and we

had never seen any before. He had driven down from somewhere up in the French country, and he was selling them twenty-five cents a peck. We had a little money our fathers had given us for candy, and I bought two pecks and Carl bought one. They cheered us a good deal, and we saved all the seeds and planted them. Up to the time Carl went away, they hadn't borne at all."

"And now he's come back to eat them," cried Marie, nodding at Carl. "That is a good story. I can remember you a little, Mr. Linstrum. I used to see you in Hanover sometimes, when Uncle Joe took me to town. I remember you because you were always buying pencils and tubes of paint at the drug store. Once, when my uncle left me at the store, you drew a lot of little birds and flowers for me on a piece of wrapping-paper. I kept them for a long while. I thought you were very romantic because you could draw and had such black eyes."

Carl smiled. "Yes, I remember that time. Your uncle bought you some kind of a mechanical toy, a Turkish lady sitting on an ottoman and smoking a hookah, wasn't it? And she turned her head backwards and forwards."

"Oh, yes! Wasn't she splendid! I knew well enough I ought not to tell Uncle Joe I wanted it, for he had just come back from the saloon and was feeling good. You remember how he laughed? She tickled him, too. But when we got home, my aunt scolded him for buying toys when she needed so many things. We wound our lady up every night, and when she began to move her head my aunt used to laugh as hard as any of us. It was a music-box, you know, and the Turkish lady played a tune while she smoked. That was how she made you feel so jolly. As I remember her, she was lovely, and had a gold crescent on her turban."

Half an hour later, as they were leaving the house, Carl and Alexandra were met in the path by a strapping fellow in overalls and a blue shirt. He was breathing hard, as if he had been running, and was muttering to himself.

Marie ran forward, and, taking him by the arm, gave him a little push toward her guests. "Frank, this is Mr. Linstrum."

Frank took off his broad straw hat and nodded to Alexandra. When he spoke to Carl, he showed a fine set of white teeth. He was burned a dull red down to his neckband, and there was a heavy three-days' stubble on his face. Even in his agitation he was handsome, but he looked a rash and violent man.

Barely saluting the callers, he turned at once to his wife and began, in an outraged tone, "I have to leave my team to drive the old woman Hiller's hogs out-a my wheat. I go to take dat old woman to de court if she ain't careful, I tell you!"

His wife spoke soothingly. "But, Frank, she has only her lame boy to help her. She does the best she can."

Alexandra looked at the excited man and offered a suggestion. "Why don't you go over there some afternoon and hog-tight her fences? You'd save time for yourself in the end."

Frank's neck stiffened. "Not-a-much, I won't. I keep my hogs home. Other peoples can do like me. See? If that Louis can mend shoes, he can mend fence."

"Maybe," said Alexandra placidly; "but I've found it sometimes pays to mend other people's fences. Good-bye, Marie. Come to see me soon."

Alexandra walked firmly down the path and Carl followed her.

Frank went into the house and threw himself on the sofa, his face to the wall, his clenched fist on his hip. Marie, having seen her guests off, came in and put her hand coaxingly on his shoulder.

"Poor Frank! You've run until you've made your head ache, now haven't you? Let me make you some coffee."

"What else am I to do?" he cried hotly in Bohemian. "Am I to let any old woman's hogs root up my wheat? Is that what I work myself to death for?"

"Don't worry about it, Frank. I'll speak to Mrs. Hiller again. But, really, she almost cried last time they got out, she was so sorry."

Frank bounded over on his other side. "That's it; you always side with them against me. They all know it. Anybody here feels free to borrow the mower and break it, or turn their hogs in on me. They know you won't care!"

Marie hurried away to make his coffee. When she came back, he was fast asleep. She sat down and looked at him for a long while, very thoughtfully. When the kitchen clock struck six she went out to get supper, closing the door gently behind her. She was always sorry for Frank when he worked himself into one of these rages, and she was sorry to have him rough and quarrelsome with his neighbors. She was perfectly aware that the neighbors had a good deal to put up with, and that they bore with Frank for her sake.

VII

Marie's father, Albert Tovesky, was one of the more intelligent Bohemians who came West in the early seventies. He settled in Omaha and became a leader and adviser among his people there. Marie was his youngest child, by a second wife, and was the apple of his eye. She was barely sixteen, and was in the graduating class of the Omaha High School, when Frank Shabata arrived from the old country and set all the Bohemian girls in a flutter. He was easily the buck of the beer-gardens, and on Sunday he was a sight to see, with his silk hat and tucked shirt and blue frock-coat, wearing gloves and carrying a little wisp of a yellow cane. He was tall and fair, with splendid teeth and close-cropped yellow curls, and he wore a slightly disdainful expression, proper for a young man with high connections, whose mother had a big farm in the Elbe valley. There was often an interesting discontent in his blue eyes, and every Bohemian girl he met imagined herself the cause of that unsatisfied expression. He had a way of drawing out his cambric handkerchief slowly, by one corner, from his breast-pocket, that was melancholy and romantic in the extreme. He took a little flight with each of the more eligible Bohemian girls, but it was when he was with little Marie Tovesky that he drew his handkerchief out most slowly, and, after he had lit a fresh cigar, dropped the match most despairingly. Any one could see, with half an eye, that his proud heart was bleeding for somebody.

One Sunday, late in the summer after Marie's graduation, she met Frank at a Bohemian picnic down the river and went rowing with him all the afternoon. When she got home that evening she went straight to her father's room and told him that she was engaged to Shabata. Old Tovesky was having a comfortable pipe before he went to bed. When he heard his daughter's announcement, he first prudently corked his beer bottle and then leaped to his feet and had a turn of temper. He characterized Frank Shabata by a Bohemian expression which is the equivalent of stuffed shirt.

"Why don't he go to work like the rest of us did? His farm in the Elbe valley, indeed! Ain't he got plenty brothers and sisters? It's his mother's farm, and why don't he stay at home and help her? Haven't I seen his mother out in the morning at five o'clock with her ladle and her big bucket on wheels, putting liquid manure on the cabbages? Don't I know the look of old Eva Shabata's hands. Like an old horse's hoofs they are—and this fellow wearing gloves and rings! Engaged, indeed! You aren't fit to be out of school, and that's what's the matter with you. I will send you off to the Sisters of the Sacred Heart in St. Louis, and they will teach you some sense, I guess!"

Accordingly, the very next week, Albert Tovesky took his daughter, pale and tearful, down the river to the convent. But the way to make Frank want anything was to tell him he couldn't have it. He managed to have an interview with Marie before she went away, and whereas he had been only half in love with her before, he now persuaded himself that he would not stop at anything. Marie took with her to the convent, under the canvas lining of her trunk, the results of a laborious and satisfying morning on Frank's part; no less than a dozen photographs of himself, taken in a dozen different love-lorn attitudes. There was a little round photograph for her watch-case, photographs for her wall and dresser, and even long narrow ones to be used as bookmarks. More than once the handsome gentleman was torn to pieces before the French class by an indignant nun.

Marie pined in the convent for a year, until her eighteenth

birthday was passed. Then she met Frank Shabata in the Union Station in St. Louis and ran away with him. Old Tovesky forgave his daughter because there was nothing else to do, and bought her a farm in the country that she had loved so well as a child. Since then her story had been a part of the history of the Divide. She and Frank had been living there for five years when Carl Linstrum came back to pay his long deferred visit to Alexandra. Frank had, on the whole, done better than one might have expected. He had flung himself at the soil with savage energy. Once a year he went to Hastings or to Omaha, on a spree. He stayed away for a week or two, and then came home and worked like a demon. He did work; if he felt sorry for himself, that was his own affair.

VIII

On the evening of the day of Alexandra's call at the Shabatas', a heavy rain set in. Frank sat up until a late hour reading the Sunday newspapers. One of the Goulds was getting a divorce, and Frank took it as a personal affront. In printing the story of the young man's marital troubles, the knowing editor gave a sufficiently colored account of his career, stating the amount of his income and the manner in which he was supposed to spend it. Frank read English slowly, and the more he read about this divorce case, the angrier he grew. At last he threw down the page with a snort. He turned to his farm-hand who was reading the other half of the paper.

"By God! if I have that young feller in de hayfield once, I show him something. Listen here what he do wit his money." And Frank began the catalogue of the young man's reputed extravagances.

Marie sighed. She thought it hard that the Goulds, for whom she had nothing but good will, should make her so much trouble. She hated to see the Sunday newspapers come into the house. Frank was always reading about the doings of rich people and feeling outraged. He had an inexhaustible stock of stories about

their crimes and follies, how they bribed the courts and shot
down their butlers with impunity whenever they chose. Frank
and Lou Bergson had very similar ideas, and they were two of the
political agitators of the county.

The next morning broke clear and brilliant, but Frank said the
ground was too wet to plough, so he took the cart and drove over
to Sainte-Agnes to spend the day at Moses Marcel's saloon. After
he was gone, Marie went out to the back porch to begin her butter-
making. A brisk wind had come up and was driving puffy white
clouds across the sky. The orchard was sparkling and rippling
in the sun. Marie stood looking toward it wistfully, her hand on
the lid of the churn, when she heard a sharp ring in the air, the
merry sound of the whetstone on the scythe. That invitation
decided her. She ran into the house, put on a short skirt and a
pair of her husband's boots, caught up a tin pail and started for
the orchard. Emil had already begun work and was mowing vigorously. When he saw her coming, he stopped and wiped his
brow. His yellow canvas leggings and kahaki trousers were
splashed to the knees.

"Don't let me disturb you, Emil. I'm going to pick cherries.
Isn't everything beautiful after the rain? Oh, but I'm glad to get
this place mowed! When I heard it raining in the night, I thought
maybe you would come and do it for me to-day. The wind wakened me. Didn't it blow dreadfully? Just smell the wild roses!
They are always so spicy after a rain. We never had so many of
them in here before. I suppose it's the wet season. Will you have
to cut them, too?"

"If I cut the grass, I will," Emil said teasingly. "What's the matter with you? What makes you so flighty?"

"Am I flighty? I suppose that's the wet season, too, then. It's
exciting to see everything growing so fast,—and to get the grass
cut! Please leave the roses till last, if you must cut them. Oh, I
don't mean all of them, I mean the low place down by my tree,
where there are so many. Aren't you splashed! Look at the spider-
webs all over the grass. Good-bye. I'll call you if I see a snake."

She tripped away and Emil stood looking after her. In a few moments he heard the cherries dropping smartly into the pail, and he began to swing his scythe with that long, even stroke that few American boys ever learn. Marie picked cherries and sang softly to herself, stripping one glittering branch after another, shivering when she caught a shower of rain-drops on her neck and hair. And Emil mowed his way slowly down toward the cherry trees.

That summer the rains had been so many and opportune that it was almost more than Shabata and his man could do to keep up with the corn; the orchard was a neglected wilderness. All sorts of weeds and herbs and flowers had grown up there; splotches of wild larkspur, pale green-and-white spikes of hoarhound, plantations of wild cotton, tangles of foxtail and wild wheat. South of the apricot trees, cornering on the wheatfield, was Frank's alfalfa, where myriads of white and yellow butterflies were always fluttering above the purple blossoms. When Emil reached the lower corner by the hedge, Marie was sitting under her white mulberry tree, the pailful of cherries beside her, looking off at the gentle, tireless swelling of the wheat.

"Emil," she said suddenly—he was mowing quietly about under the tree so as not to disturb her—"what religion did the Swedes have away back, before they were Christians?"

Emil paused and straightened his back. "I don't know. About like the Germans', wasn't it?"

Marie went on as if she had not heard him. "The Bohemians, you know, were tree worshipers before the missionaries came. Father says the people in the mountains still do queer things, sometimes,—they believe that trees bring good or bad luck."

Emil looked superior. "Do they? Well, which are the lucky trees? I'd like to know."

"I don't know all of them, but I know lindens are. The old people in the mountains plant lindens to purify the forest, and to do away with the spells that come from the old trees they say have lasted from heathen times. I'm a good Catholic, but I think I could get along with caring for trees, if I hadn't anything else."

"That's a poor saying," said Emil, stooping over to wipe his hands in the wet grass.

"Why is it? If I feel that way, I feel that way. I like trees because they seem more resigned to the way they have to live than other things do. I feel as if this tree knows everything I ever think of when I sit here. When I come back to it, I never have to remind it of anything; I begin just where I left off."

Emil had nothing to say to this. He reached up among the branches and began to pick the sweet, insipid fruit,—long ivory-colored berries, tipped with faint pink, like white coral, that fall to the ground unheeded all summer through. He dropped a handful into her lap.

"Do you like Mr. Linstrum?" Marie asked suddenly.

"Yes. Don't you?"

"Oh, ever so much; only he seems kind of staid and school-teachery. But, of course, he is older than Frank, even. I'm sure I don't want to live to be more than thirty, do you? Do you think Alexandra likes him very much?"

"I suppose so. They were old friends."

"Oh, Emil, you know what I mean!" Marie tossed her head impatiently. "Does she really care about him? When she used to tell me about him, I always wondered whether she wasn't a little in love with him."

"Who, Alexandra?" Emil laughed and thrust his hands into his trousers pockets. "Alexandra's never been in love, you crazy!" He laughed again. "She wouldn't know how to go about it. The idea!"

Marie shrugged her shoulders. "Oh, you don't know Alexandra as well as you think you do! If you had any eyes, you would see that she is very fond of him. It would serve you all right if she walked off with Carl. I like him because he appreciates her more than you do."

Emil frowned. "What are you talking about, Marie? Alexandra's all right. She and I have always been good friends. What more do you want? I like to talk to Carl about New York and what a fellow can do there."

"Oh, Emil! Surely you are not thinking of going off there?"

"Why not? I must go somewhere, mustn't I?" The young man took up his scythe and leaned on it. "Would you rather I went off in the sand hills and lived like Ivar?"

Marie's face fell under his brooding gaze. She looked down at his wet leggings. "I'm sure Alexandra hopes you will stay on here," she murmured.

"Then Alexandra will be disappointed," the young man said roughly. "What do I want to hang around here for? Alexandra can run the farm all right, without me. I don't want to stand around and look on. I want to be doing something on my own account."

"That's so," Marie sighed. "There are so many, many things you can do. Almost anything you choose."

"And there are so many, many things I can't do." Emil echoed her tone sarcastically. "Sometimes I don't want to do anything at all, and sometimes I want to pull the four corners of the Divide together,"—he threw out his arm and brought it back with a jerk,—"so, like a table-cloth. I get tired of seeing men and horses going up and down, up and down."

Marie looked up at his defiant figure and her face clouded. "I wish you weren't so restless, and didn't get so worked up over things," she said sadly.

"Thank you," he returned shortly.

She sighed despondently. "Everything I say makes you cross, don't it? And you never used to be cross to me."

Emil took a step nearer and stood frowning down at her bent head. He stood in an attitude of self-defense, his feet well apart, his hands clenched and drawn up at his sides, so that the cords stood out on his bare arms. "I can't play with you like a little boy any more," he said slowly. "That's what you miss, Marie. You'll have to get some other little boy to play with." He stopped and took a deep breath. Then he went on in a low tone, so intense that it was almost threatening: "Sometimes you seem to understand perfectly, and then sometimes you pretend you don't. You don't help things any by pretending. It's then that I want to pull the corners of the Divide together. If you *won't* understand, you know, I could make you!"

Marie clasped her hands and started up from her seat. She had grown very pale and her eyes were shining with excitement and distress. "But, Emil, if I understand, then all our good times are over, we can never do nice things together any more. We shall have to behave like Mr. Linstrum. And, anyhow, there's nothing to understand!" She struck the ground with her little foot fiercely. "That won't last. It will go away, and things will be just as they used to. I wish you were a Catholic. The Church helps people, indeed it does. I pray for you, but that's not the same as if you prayed yourself."

She spoke rapidly and pleadingly, looked entreatingly into his face. Emil stood defiant, gazing down at her.

"I can't pray to have the things I want," he said slowly, "and I won't pray not to have them, not if I'm damned for it."

Marie turned away, wringing her hands. "Oh, Emil, you won't try! Then all our good times are over."

"Yes; over. I never expect to have any more."

Emil gripped the hand-holds of his scythe and began to mow. Marie took up her cherries and went slowly toward the house, crying bitterly.

IX

On Sunday afternoon, a month after Carl Linstrum's arrival, he rode with Emil up into the French country to attend a Catholic fair. He sat for most of the afternoon in the basement of the church, where the fair was held, talking to Marie Shabata, or strolled about the gravel terrace, thrown up on the hillside in front of the basement doors, where the French boys were jumping and wrestling and throwing the discus. Some of the boys were in their white baseball suits; they had just come up from a Sunday practice gave down in the ball-grounds. Amédée, the newly married,

Emil's best friend, was their pitcher, renowned among the country towns for his dash and skill. Amédée was a little fellow, a year younger than Emil and much more boyish in appearance; very lithe and active and neatly made, with a clear brown and white skin, and flashing white teeth. The Sainte-Agnes boys were to play the Hastings nine in a fortnight, and Amédée's lightning balls were the hope of his team. The little Frenchman seemed to get every ounce there was in him behind the ball as it left his hand.

"You'd have made the battery at the University for sure, 'Médée," Emil said as they were walking from the ball-grounds back to the church on the hill. "You're pitching better than you did in the spring."

Amédée grinned. "Sure! A married man don't lose his head no more." He slapped Emil on the back as he caught step with him. "Oh, Emil, you wanna get married right off quick! It's the greatest thing ever!"

Emil laughed. "How am I going to get married without any girl?"

Amédée took his arm. "Pooh! There are plenty girls will have you. You wanna get some nice French girl, now. She treat you well; always be jolly. See,"—he began checking off on his fingers,—"there is Séverine, and Alphosen, and Joséphine, and Hectorine, and Louise, and Malvina—why, I could love any of them girls! Why don't you get after them? Are you stuck up, Emil, or is anything the matter with you? I never did know a boy twenty-two years old before that didn't have no girl. You wanna be a priest, maybe? Not-a for me!" Amédée swaggered. "I bring many good Catholics into this world, I hope, and that's a way I help the Church."

Emil looked down and patted him on the shoulder. "Now you're windy, 'Médée. You Frenchies like to brag."

But Amédée had the zeal of the newly married, and he was not to be lightly shaken off. "Honest and true, Emil, don't you want *any* girl? Maybe there's some young lady in Lincoln, now, very grand,"— Amédée waved his hand languidly before his face to denote the fan of heartless beauty,—"and you lost your heart up there. Is that it?"

"Maybe," said Emil.

But Amédée saw no appropriate glow in his friend's face. "Bah!" he exclaimed in disgust. "I tell all the French girls to keep 'way from you. You gotta rock in there," thumping Emil on the ribs.

When they reached the terrace at the side of the church, Amédée, who was excited by his success on the ball-grounds, challenged Emil to a jumping-match, though he would be beaten. They belted themselves up, and Raoul Marcel, the choir tenor and Father Duchesne's pet, and Jean Bordelau, held the string over which they vaulted. All the French boys stood round, cheering and humping themselves up when Emil or Amédée went over the wire, as if they were helping in the lift. Emil stopped at five-feet-five, declaring that he would spoil his appetite for supper if he jumped any more.

Angélique, Amédée's pretty bride, as blonde and fair as her name, who had come out to watch the match, tossed her head at Emil and said:—

"'Médée could jump much higher than you if he were as tall. And anyhow, he is much more graceful. He goes over like a bird, and you have to hump yourself all up."

"Oh, I do, do I?" Emil caught her and kissed her saucy mouth squarely, while she laughed and struggled and called, "'Médée! 'Médée!"

"There, you see your 'Médée isn't even big enough to get you away from me. I could run away with you right now and he could only sit down and cry about it. I'll show you whether I have to hump myself!" Laughing and panting, he picked Angélique up in his arms and began running about the rectangle with her. Not until he saw Marie Shabata's tiger eyes flashing from the gloom of the basement doorway did he hand the disheveled bride over to her husband. "There, go to your graceful; I haven't the heart to take you away from him."

Angélique clung to her husband and made faces at Emil over the white shoulder of Amédée's ball-shirt. Emil was greatly amused at her air of proprietorship and at Amédée's shameless submission to it. He was delighted with his friend's good fortune. He liked to see and think about Amédée's sunny, natural, happy love.

He and Amédée had ridden and wrestled and larked together since they were lads of twelve. On Sundays and holidays they were always arm in arm. It seemed strange that now he should have to hide the thing that Amédée was so proud of, that the feeling which gave one of them such happiness should bring the other such despair. It was like that when Alexandra tested her seed-corn in the spring, he mused. From two ears that had grown side by side, the grains of one shot up joyfully into the light, projecting themselves into the future, and the grains from the other lay still in the earth and rotted; and nobody knew why.

X

While Emil and Carl were amusing themselves at the fair, Alexandra was at home, busy with her account-books, which had been neglected of late. She was almost through with her figures when she heard a cart drive up to the gate, and looking out of the window she saw her two older brothers. They had seemed to avoid her ever since Carl Linstrum's arrival, four weeks ago that day, and she hurried to the door to welcome them. She saw at once that they had come with some very definite purpose. They followed her stiffly into the sitting-room. Oscar sat down, but Lou walked over to the window and remained standing, his hands behind him.

"You are by yourself?" he asked, looking toward the doorway into the parlor.

"Yes. Carl and Emil went up to the Catholic fair."

For a few moments neither of the men spoke.

Then Lou came out sharply. "How soon does he intend to go away from here?"

"I don't know, Lou. Not for some time, I hope." Alexandra

spoke in an even, quiet tone that often exasperated her brothers.
They felt that she was trying to be superior with them.

Oscar spoke up grimly. "We thought we ought to tell you that
people have begun to talk," he said meaningly.

Alexandra looked at him. "What about?"

Oscar met her eyes blankly. "About you, keeping him here so
long. It looks bad for him to be hanging on to a woman this way.
People think you're getting taken in."

Alexandra shut her account-book firmly. "Boys," she said seriously, "don't let's go on with this. We won't come out anywhere. I
can't take advice on such a matter. I know you mean well, but you
must not feel responsible for me in things of this sort. If we go on
with this talk it will only make hard feeling."

Lou whipped about from the window. "You ought to think a
little about your family. You're making us all ridiculous."

"How am I?"

"People are beginning to say you want to marry the fellow."

"Well, and what is ridiculous about that?"

Lou and Oscar exchanged outraged looks. "Alexandra! Can't
you see he's just a tramp and he's after your money? He wants to
be taken care of, he does!"

"Well, suppose I want to take care of him? Whose business is
it but my own?"

"Don't you know he'd get hold of your property?"

"He'd get hold of what I wished to give him, certainly."

Oscar sat up suddenly and Lou clutched at his bristly hair.

"Give him?" Lou shouted. "Our property, our homestead?"

"I don't know about the homestead," said Alexandra quietly. "I
know you and Oscar have always expected that it would be left to
your children, and I'm not sure but what you're right. But I'll do
exactly as I please with the rest of my land, boys."

"The rest of your land!" cried Lou, growing more excited
every minute. "Didn't all the land come out of the homestead? It
was bought with money borrowed on the homestead, and Oscar
and me worked ourselves to the bone paying interest on it."

"Yes, you paid the interest. But when you married we made a division of the land, and you were satisfied. I've made more on my farms since I've been alone than when we all worked together."

"Everything you've made has come out of the original land that us boys worked for, hasn't it? The farms and all that comes out of them belongs to us as a family."

Alexandra waved her hand impatiently. "Come now, Lou. Stick to the facts. You are talking nonsense. Go to the county clerk and ask him who owns my land, and whether my titles are good."

Lou turned to his brother. "This is what comes of letting a woman meddle in business," he said bitterly. "We ought to have taken things in our own hands years ago. But she liked to run things, and we humored her. We thought you had good sense, Alexandra. We never thought you'd do anything foolish."

Alexandra rapped impatiently on her desk with her knuckles. "Listen, Lou. Don't talk wild. You say you ought to have taken things into your own hands years ago. I suppose you mean before you left home. But how could you take hold of what wasn't there? I've got most of what I have now since we divided the property; I've built it up myself, and it has nothing to do with you."

Oscar spoke up solemnly. "The property of a family really belongs to the men of the family, no matter about the title. If anything goes wrong, it's the men that are held responsible."

"Yes, of course," Lou broke in. "Everybody knows that. Oscar and me have always been easy-going and we've never made any fuss. We were willing you should hold the land and have the food of it, but you got no right to part with any of it. We worked in the fields to pay for the first land you bought, and whatever's come out of it has got to be kept in the family."

Oscar reinforced his brother, his mind fixed on the one point he could see. "The property of a family belongs to the men of the family, because they are held responsible, and because they do the work."

Alexandra looked from one to the other, her eyes full of

indignation. She had been impatient before, but now she was beginning to feel angry. "And what about my work?" she asked in an unsteady voice.

Lou looked at the carpet. "Oh, now, Alexandra, you always took it pretty easy! Of course we wanted you to. You liked to manage round, and we always humored you. We realize you were a great deal of help to us. There's no woman anywhere around that knows as much about business as you do, and we've always been proud of that, and thought you were pretty smart. But, of course, the real work always fell on us. Good advice is all right, but it don't get the weeds out of the corn."

"Maybe not, but it sometimes puts in the crop, and it sometimes keeps the fields for corn to grow in," said Alexandra dryly. "Why, Lou, I can remember when you and Oscar wanted to sell this homestead and all the improvements to old preacher Ericson for two thousand dollars. If I'd consented, you'd have gone down to the river and scraped along on poor farms for the rest of your lives. When I put in our first field of alfalfa you both opposed me, just because I first heard about it from a young man who had been to the University. You said I was being taken in then, and all the neighbors said so. You know as well as I do that alfalfa has been the salvation of this country. You all laughed at me when I said our land here was about ready for wheat, and I had to raise three big wheat crops before the neighbors quit putting all their land in corn. Why, I remember you cried, Lou, when we put in the first big wheat-planting, and said everybody was laughing at us."

Lou turned to Oscar. "That's the woman of it; if she tells you to put in a crop, she thinks she's put it in. It makes women conceited to meddle in business. I shouldn't think you'd want to remind us how hard you were on us, Alexandra, after the way you baby Emil."

"Hard on you? I never meant to be hard. Conditions were hard. Maybe I would never have been very soft, anyhow; but I certainly didn't choose to be the kind of girl I was. If you take even a vine and cut it back again and again, it grows hard, like a tree."

Lou felt that they were wandering from the point, and that in digression Alexandra might unnerve him. He wiped his forehead with a jerk of his handkerchief. "We never doubted you, Alexandra. We never questioned anything you did. You've always had your own way. But you can't expect us to sit like stumps and see you done out of the property by any loafer who happens along, and making yourself ridiculous into the bargain."

Oscar rose. "Yes," he broke in, "everybody's laughing to see you get took in; at your age, too. Everybody knows he's nearly five years younger than you, and is after your money. Why, Alexandra, you are forty years old!"

"All that doesn't concern anybody but Carl and me. Go to town and ask your lawyers what you can do to restrain me from disposing of my own property. And I advise you to do what they tell you; for the authority you can exert by law is the only influence you will ever have over me again." Alexandra rose. "I think I would rather not have lived to find out what I have to-day," she said quietly, closing her desk.

Lou and Oscar looked at each other questioningly. There seemed to be nothing to do but to go, and they walked out.

"You can't do business with women," Oscar said heavily as he clambered into the cart. "But anyhow, we've had our say, at last."

Lou scratched his head. "Talk of that kind might come too high, you know; but she's apt to be sensible. You hadn't ought to said that about her age, though, Oscar. I'm afraid that hurt her feelings; and the worst thing we can do is to make her sore at us. She'd marry him out of contrariness."

"I only meant," said Oscar, "that she is old enough to know better, and she is. If she was going to marry, she ought to done it long ago, and not go making a fool of herself now."

Lou looked anxious, nevertheless. "Of course," he reflected hopefully and inconsistently, "Alexandra ain't much like other women-folks. Maybe it won't make her sore. Maybe she'd as soon be forty as not!"

XI

Emil came home at about half-past seven o'clock that evening.
Old Ivar met him at the windmill and took his horse, and the
young man went directly into the house. He called to his sister
and she answered from her bedroom, behind the sitting-room,
saying that she was lying down.

Emil went to her door.

"Can I see you for a minute?" he asked. "I want to talk to you
about something before Carl comes."

Alexandra rose quickly and came to the door. "Where is Carl?"

"Lou and Oscar met us and said they wanted to talk to him, so
he rode over to Oscar's with them. Are you coming out?" Emil
asked impatiently.

"Yes, sit down. I'll be dressed in a moment."

Alexandra closed her door, and Emil sank down on the old
slat lounge and sat with his head in his hands. When his sister
came out, he looked up, not knowing whether the interval had
been short or long, and he was surprised to see that the room had
grown quite dark. That was just as well; it would be easier to talk
if he were not under the gaze of those clear, deliberate eyes, that
saw so far in some directions and were so blind in others. Alexandra, too, was glad of the dusk. Her face was swollen from crying.

Emil started up and then sat down again. "Alexandra," he said
slowly, in his deep young baritone, "I don't want to go away to
law school this fall. Let me put it off another year. I want to take a
year off and look around. It's awfully easy to rush into a profession you don't really like, and awfully hard to get out of it.
Linstrum and I have been talking about that."

"Very well, Emil. Only don't go off looking for land." She came
up and put her hand on his shoulder. "I've been wishing you
could stay with me this winter."

"That's just what I don't want to do, Alexandra. I'm restless.
I want to go to a new place. I want to go down to the City of
Mexico to join one of the University fellows who's at the head of

an electrical plant. He wrote me he could give me a little job, enough to pay my way, and I could look around and see what I want to do. I want to go as soon as harvest is over. I guess Lou and Oscar will be sore about it."

"I suppose they will," Alexandra sat down on the lounge beside him. "They are very angry with me, Emil. We have had a quarrel. They will not come here again."

Emil scarcely heard what she was saying; he did not notice the sadness of her tone. He was thinking about the reckless life he meant to live in Mexico.

"What about?" he asked absently.

"About Carl Linstrum. They are afraid I am going to marry him, and that some of my property will get away from them."

Emil shrugged his shoulders. "What nonsense!" he murmured. "Just like them."

Alexandra drew back. "Why nonsense, Emil?"

"Why, you've never thought of such a thing, have you? They always have to have something to fuss about."

"Emil," said his sister slowly, "you ought not to take things for granted. Do you agree with them that I have no right to change my way of living?"

Emil looked at the outline of his sister's head in the dim light. They were sitting close together and he somehow felt that she could hear his thoughts. He was silent for a moment, and then said in an embarrassed tone, "Why, no, certainly not. You ought to do whatever you want to. I'll always back you."

"But it would seem a little bit ridiculous to you if I married Carl?"

Emil fidgeted. The issue seemed to him too far-fetched to warrant discussion. "Why, no. I should be surprised if you wanted to. I can't see exactly why. But that's none of my business. You ought to do as you please. Certainly you ought not to pay any attention to what the boys say."

Alexandra sighed. "I had hoped you might understand, a little, why I do want to. But I suppose that's too much to expect. I've had a pretty lonely life, Emil. Besides Marie, Carl is the only friend I have ever had."

Emil was awake now; a name in her last sentence roused him. He put out his hand and took his sister's awkwardly. "You ought to do just as you wish, and I think Carl's a fine fellow. He and I would always get on. I don't believe any of the things the boys say about him, honest I don't. They are suspicious of him because he's intelligent. You know their way. They've been sore at me ever since you let me go away to college. They're always trying to catch me up. If I were you, I wouldn't pay any attention to them. There's nothing to get upset about. Carl's a sensible fellow. He won't mind them."

"I don't know. If they talk to him the way they did to me, I think he'll go away."

Emil grew more and more uneasy. "Think so? Well, Marie said it would serve us all right if you walked off with him."

"Did she? Bless her little heart! *She* would." Alexandra's voice broke.

Emil began unlacing his leggings. "Why don't you talk to her about it? There's Carl, I hear his horse. I guess I'll go upstairs and get my boots off. No, I don't want any supper. We had supper at five o'clock, at the fair."

Emil was glad to escape and get to his own room. He was a little ashamed for his sister, though he had tried not to show it. He felt that there was something indecorous in her proposal, and she did seem to him somewhat ridiculous. There was trouble enough in the world, he reflected, as he threw himself upon his bed, without people who were forty years old imagining they wanted to get married. In the darkness and silence Emil was not likely to think long about Alexandra. Every image slipped away but one. He had seen Marie in the crowd that afternoon. She sold candy at the fair. *Why* had she ever run away with Frank Shabata, and how could she go on laughing and working and taking an interest in things? Why did she like so many people, and why had she seemed pleased when all the French and Bohemian boys, and the priest himself, crowded round her candy stand? Why did she care about any one but him? Why could he never, never find the thing he looked for in her playful, affectionate eyes?

Then he fell to imagining that he looked once more and found it there, and what it would be like if she loved him,—she who, as Alexandra said, could give her whole heart. In that dream he could lie for hours, as if in a trance. His spirit went out of his body and crossed the fields to Marie Shabata.

At the University dances the girls had often looked wonderingly at the tall young Swede with the fine head, leaning against the wall and frowning, his arms folded, his eyes fixed on the ceiling or the floor. All the girls were a little afraid of him. He was distinguished-looking, and not the jollying kind. They felt that he was too intense and preoccupied. There was something queer about him. Emil's fraternity rather prided itself upon its dances, and sometimes he did his duty and danced every dance. But whether he was on the floor or brooding in a corner, he was always thinking about Marie Shabata. For two years the storm had been gathering in him.

XII

Carl came into the sitting-room while Alexandra was lighting the lamp. She looked up at him as she adjusted the shade. His sharp shoulders stooped as if he were very tired, his face was pale, and there were bluish shadows under his dark eyes. His anger had burned itself out and left him sick and disgusted.

"You have seen Lou and Oscar?" Alexandra asked.

"Yes." His eyes avoided hers.

Alexandra took a deep breath. "And now you are going away. I thought so."

Carl threw himself into a chair and pushed the dark lock back from his forehead with his white, nervous hand. "What a hopeless position you are in, Alexandra!" he exclaimed feverishly. "It is your fate to be always surrounded by little men. And I am no better than the rest. I am too little to face the criticism of even such men as Lou and Oscar. Yes, I am going away; to-morrow. I cannot even ask you to give me a promise until I have something to offer you. I thought, perhaps, I could do that; but I find I can't."

"What good comes of offering people things they don't need?" Alexandra asked sadly. "I don't need money. But I have needed you for a great many years. I wonder why I have been permitted to prosper, if it is only to take my friends away from me."

"I don't deceive myself," Carl said frankly. "I know that I am going away on my own account. I must make the usual effort. I must have something to show for myself. To take what you would give me, I should have to be either a very large man or a very small one, and I am only in the middle class."

Alexandra sighed. "I have a feeling that if you go away, you will not come back. Something will happen to one of us, or to both. People have to snatch at happiness when they can, in this world. It is always easier to lose than to find. What I have is yours, if you care enough about me to take it."

Carl rose and looked up at the picture of John Bergson. "But I can't, my dear, I can't! I will go North at once. Instead of idling about in California all winter, I shall be getting my bearings up there. I won't waste another week. Be patient with me, Alexandra. Give me a year!"

"As you will," said Alexandra wearily. "All at once, in a single day, I lose everything; and I do not know why. Emil, too, is going away." Carl was still studying John Bergson's face and Alexandra's eyes followed his. "Yes," she said, "if he could have seen all that would come of the task he gave me, he would have been sorry. I hope he does not see me now. I hope that he is among the old people of his blood and country, and that tidings do not reach him from the New World."

PART III
WINTER MEMORIES

I

Winter has settled down over the Divide again; the season in which Nature recuperates, in which she sinks to sleep between the fruitfulness of autumn and the passion of spring. The birds have gone. The teeming life that goes on down in the long grass is exterminated. The prairie-dog keeps his hole. The rabbits run shivering from one frozen garden patch to another and are hard put to it to find frost-bitten cabbage-stalks. At night the coyotes roam the wintry waste, howling for food. The variegated fields are all one color now; the pastures, the stubble, the roads, the sky are the same leaden gray. The hedgerows and trees are scarcely perceptible against the bare earth, whose slaty hue they have taken on. The ground is frozen so hard that it bruises the foot to walk in the roads or in the ploughed fields. It is like an iron country, and the spirit is oppressed by its rigor and melancholy. One could easily believe that in that dead landscape the germs of life and fruitfulness were extinct forever.

Alexandra has settled back into her old routine. There are weekly letters from Emil. Lou and Oscar she has not seen since Carl went away. To avoid awkward encounters in the presence of curious spectators, she has stopped going to the Norwegian Church and drives up to the Reform Church at Hanover, or goes with Marie Shabata to the Catholic Church, locally known as "the French Church." She has not told Marie about Carl, or her differences with her brothers. She was never very communicative about her own affairs, and when she came to the point, an instinct told her that about such things she and Marie would not understand one another.

Old Mrs. Lee had been afraid that family misunderstandings

might deprive her of her yearly visit to Alexandra. But on the first day of December Alexandra telephoned Annie that to-morrow she would send Ivar over for her mother, and the next day the old lady arrived with her bundles. For twelve years Mrs. Lee had always entered Alexandra's sitting-room with the same exclamation, "Now we be yust-a like old times!" She enjoyed the liberty Alexandra gave her, and hearing her own language about her all day long. Here she could wear her nightcap and sleep with all her windows shut, listen to Ivar reading the Bible, and here she could run about among the stables in a pair of Emil's old boots. Though she was bent almost double, she was as spry as a gopher. Her face was as brown as if it had been varnished, and as full of wrinkles as a washerwoman's hands. She had three jolly old teeth left in the front of her mouth, and when she grinned she looked very knowing, as if when you found out how to take it, life wasn't half bad. While she and Alexandra patched and pieced and quilted, she talked incessantly about stories she read in a Swedish family paper, telling the plots in great detail; or about her life on a dairy farm in Gottland when she was a girl. Sometimes she forgot which were the printed stories and which were the real stories, it all seemed so far away. She loved to take a little brandy, with hot water and sugar, before she went to bed, and Alexandra always had it ready for her. "It sends good dreams," she would say with a twinkle in her eye.

When Mrs. Lee had been with Alexandra for a week, Marie Shabata telephoned one morning to say that Frank had gone to town for the day, and she would like them to come over for coffee in the afternoon. Mrs. Lee hurried to wash out and iron her new cross-stitched apron, which she had finished only the night before; a checked gingham apron worked with a design ten inches broad across the bottom; a hunting scene, with fir trees and a stag and dogs and huntsmen. Mrs. Lee was firm with herself at dinner, and refused a second helping of apple dumplings. "I ta-ank I save up," she said with a giggle.

At two o'clock in the afternoon Alexandra's cart drove up to

the Shabatas' gate, and Marie saw Mrs. Lee's red shawl come bob-
bing up the path. She ran to the door and pulled the old woman
into the house with a hug, helping her to take off her wraps while
Alexandra blanketed the horse outside. Mrs. Lee had put on her
best black satine dress—she abominated woolen stuffs, even in
winter—and a crocheted collar, fastened with a big pale gold pin,
containing faded daguerreotypes of her father and mother. She
had not worn her apron for fear of rumpling it, and now she
shook it out and tied it round her waist with a conscious air.
Marie drew back and threw up her hands, exclaiming, "Oh, what
a beauty! I've never seen this one before, have I, Mrs. Lee?"

The old woman giggled and ducked her head. "No, yust las'
night I ma-ake. See dis tread; verra strong, no wa-ash out, no fade.
My sister send from Sveden. I yust-a ta-ank you like dis."

Marie ran to the door again. "Come in, Alexandra. I have been
looking at Mrs. Lee's apron. Do stop on your way home and show
it to Mrs. Hiller. She's crazy about cross-stitch."

While Alexandra removed her hat and veil, Mrs. Lee went out
to the kitchen and settled herself in a wooden rocking-chair by
the stove, looking with great interest at the table, set for three,
with a white cloth, and a pot of pink geraniums in the middle.
"My, a-an't you gotta fine plants; such-a much flower. How you
keep from freeze?"

She pointed to the window-shelves, full of blooming fuchsias
and geraniums.

"I keep the fire all night, Mrs. Lee, and when it's very cold I
put them all on the table, in the middle of the room. Other nights
I only put newspapers behind them. Frank laughs at me for fussing, but when they don't bloom he says, 'What's the matter with
the darned things?'—What do you hear from Carl, Alexandra?"

"He got to Dawson before the river froze, and now I suppose I
won't hear any more until spring. Before he left California he sent
me a box of orange flowers, but they didn't keep very well. I have
brought a bunch of Emil's letters for you." Alexandra came out
from the sitting-room and pinched Marie's cheek playfully. "You

don't look as if the weather ever froze you up. Never have colds, do you? That's a good girl. She had dark red cheeks like this when she was a little girl, Mrs. Lee. She looked like some queer foreign kind of a doll. I've never forgot the first time I saw you in Mieklejohn's store, Marie, the time father was lying sick. Carl and I were talking about that before he went away."

"I remember, and Emil had his kitten along. When are you going to send Emil's Christmas box?"

"It ought to have gone before this. I'll have to send it by mail now, to get it there in time."

Marie pulled a dark purple silk necktie from her workbasket. "I knit this for him. It's a good color, don't you think? Will you please put it in with your things and tell him it's from me, to wear when he goes serenading."

Alexandra laughed. "I don't believe he goes serenading much. He says in one letter that the Mexican ladies are said to be very beautiful, but that don't seem to me very warm praise."

Marie tossed her head. "Emil can't fool me. If he's bought a guitar, he goes serenading. Who wouldn't, with all those Spanish girls dropping flowers down from their windows! I'd sing to them every night, wouldn't you, Mrs. Lee?"

The old lady chuckled. Her eyes lit up as Marie bent down and opened the oven door. A delicious hot fragrance blew out into the tidy kitchen. "My, somet'ing smell good!" She turned to Alexandra with a wink, her three yellow teeth making a brave show, "I ta-ank dat stop my yaw from ache no more!" she said contentedly.

Marie took out a pan of delicate little rolls, stuffed with stewed apricots, and began to dust them over with powdered sugar. "I hope you'll like these, Mrs. Lee; Alexandra does. The Bohemians always like them with their coffee. But if you don't, I have a coffee-cake with nuts and poppy seeds. Alexandra, will you get the cream jug? I put it in the window to keep cool."

"The Bohemians," said Alexandra, as they drew up to the table, "certainly know how to make more kinds of bread than any other people in the world. Old Mrs. Hiller told me once at the church supper that she could make seven kinds of fancy bread, but Marie could make a dozen."

Mrs. Lee held up one of the apricot rolls between her brown thumb and forefinger and weighed it critically. "Yust like-a fedders," she pronounced with satisfaction. "My, a-an't dis nice!" she exclaimed as she stirred her coffee. "I yust ta-ake a liddle yelly now, too, I ta-ank."

Alexandra and Marie laughed at her forehandedness, and fell to talking of their own affairs. "I was afraid you had a cold when I talked to you over the telephone the other night, Marie. What was the matter, had you been crying?"

"Maybe I had," Marie smiled guiltily. "Frank was out late that night. Don't you get lonely sometimes in the winter, when everybody has gone away?"

"I thought it was something like that. If I hadn't had company, I'd have run over to see for myself. If you get down-hearted, what will become of the rest of us?" Alexandra asked.

"I don't, very often. There's Mrs. Lee without any coffee!"

Later, when Mrs. Lee declared that her powers were spent, Marie and Alexandra went upstairs to look for some crochet patterns the old lady wanted to borrow. "Better put on your coat, Alexandra. It's cold up there, and I have no idea where those patterns are. I may have to look through my old trunks." Marie caught up a shawl and opened the stair door, running up the steps ahead of her guest. "While I go through the bureau drawers, you might look in those hat-boxes on the closet-shelf, over where Frank's clothes hang. There are a lot of odds and ends in them."

She began tossing over the contents of the drawers, and Alexandra went into the clothes-closet. Presently she came back, holding a slender elastic yellow stick in her hand.

"What in the world is this, Marie? You don't mean to tell me Frank ever carried such a thing?"

Marie blinked at it with astonishment and sat down on the floor. "Where did you find it? I didn't know he had kept it. I haven't seen it for years."

"It really is a cane, then?"

"Yes. One he brought from the old country. He used to carry it when I first knew him. Isn't it foolish? Poor Frank!"

Alexandra twirled the stick in her fingers and laughed. "He must have looked funny!"

Marie was thoughtful. "No, he didn't, really. It didn't seem out of place. He used to be awfully gay like that when he was a young man. I guess people always get what's hardest for them, Alexandra." Marie gathered the shawl closer about her and still looked hard at the cane. "Frank would be all right in the right place," she said reflectively. "He ought to have a different kind of wife, for one thing. Do you know, Alexandra, I could pick out exactly the right sort of woman for Frank—now. The trouble is you almost have to marry a man before you can find out the sort of wife he needs; and usually it's exactly the sort you are not. Then what are you going to do about it?" she asked candidly.

Alexandra confessed she didn't know. "However," she added, "it seems to me that you get along with Frank about as well as any woman I've ever seen or heard of could."

Marie shook her head, pursing her lips and blowing her warm breath softly out into the frosty air. "No; I was spoiled at home. I like my own way, and I have a quick tongue. When Frank brags, I say sharp things, and he never forgets. He goes over and over it in his mind; I can feel him. Then I'm too giddy. Frank's wife ought to be timid, and she ought not to care about another living thing in the world but just Frank! I didn't, when I married him, but I suppose I was too young to stay like that." Marie sighed.

Alexandra had never heard Marie speak so frankly about her husband before, and she felt that it was wiser not to encourage her. No good, she reasoned, ever came from talking about such things, and while Marie was thinking aloud, Alexandra had been steadily searching the hat-boxes. "Aren't these the patterns, Maria?"

Marie sprang up from the floor. "Sure enough, we were looking for patterns, weren't we? I'd forgot everything but Frank's other wife. I'll put that away."

She poked the cane behind Frank's Sunday clothes, and though she laughed, Alexandra saw there were tears in her eyes.

When they went back to the kitchen, the snow had begun to fall, and Marie's visitors thought they must be getting home. She went out to the cart with them, and tucked the robes about old Mrs. Lee while Alexandra took the blanket off her horse. As they drove away, Marie turned and went slowly back to the house. She took up the package of letters Alexandra had brought, but she did not read them. She turned them over and looked at the foreign stamps, and then sat watching the flying snow while the dusk deepened in the kitchen and the stove sent out a red glow.

Marie knew perfectly well that Emil's letters were written more for her than for Alexandra. They were not the sort of letters that a young man writes to his sister. They were both more personal and more painstaking; full of descriptions of the gay life in the old Mexican capital in the days when the strong hand of Porfirio Diaz was still strong. He told about bull-fights and cock-fights, churches and *fiestas*, the flower-markets and the fountains, the music and dancing, the people of all nations he met in the Italian restaurants on San Francisco Street. In short, they were the kind of letters a young man writes to a woman when he wishes himself and his life to seem interesting to her, when he wishes to enlist her imagination in his behalf.

Marie, when she was alone or when she sat sewing in the evening, often thought about what it must be like down there where Emil was; where there were flowers and street bands everywhere, and carriages rattling up and down, and where there was a little blind bootblack in front of the cathedral who could play any tune you asked for by dropping the lids of blacking-boxes on the stone steps. When everything is done and over for one at twenty-three, it is pleasant to let the mind wander forth and follow a young adventurer who has life before him. "And if it had not been for me," she thought, "Frank might still be free like that, and having a good time making people admire him. Poor Frank, getting married wasn't very good for him either. I'm afraid I do set people against him, as he says. I seem, somehow, to give him away all the time. Perhaps he would try to be agreeable to people again, if I were not around. It seems as if I always make him just as bad as he can be."

Later in the winter, Alexandra looked back upon that afternoon as the last satisfactory visit she had had with Marie. After that day the younger woman seemed to shrink more and more into herself. When she was with Alexandra she was not spontaneous and frank as she used to be. She seemed to be brooding over something, and holding something back. The weather had a good deal to do with their seeing less of each other than usual. There had not been such snowstorms in twenty years, and the path across the fields was drifted deep from Christmas until March. When the two neighbors went to see each other, they had to go round by the wagon-road, which was twice as far. They telephoned each other almost every night, though in January there was a stretch of three weeks when the wires were down, and when the postman did not come at all.

Marie often ran in to see her nearest neighbor, old Mrs. Hiller, who was crippled with rheumatism and had only her son, the lame shoemaker, to take care of her; and she went to the French Church, whatever the weather. She was a sincerely devout girl. She prayed for herself and for Frank, and for Emil, among the temptations of that gay, corrupt old city. She found more comfort in the Church that winter than ever before. It seemed to come closer to her, and to fill an emptiness that ached in her heart. She tried to be patient with her husband. He and his hired man usually played California Jack in the evening. Marie sat sewing or crocheting and tried to take a friendly interest in the game, but she was always thinking about the wide fields outside, where the snow was drifting over the fences; and about the orchard, where the snow was falling and packing, crust over crust. When she went out into the dark kitchen to fix her plants for the night, she used to stand by the window and look out at the white fields, or watch the currents of snow whirling over the orchard. She seemed to feel the weight of all the snow that lay down there. the branches had become so hard that they wounded your hand if you but tried to break a twig. And yet, down under the frozen crusts, at the roots of the trees, the secret of life was still safe, warm as the blood in one's heart; and the spring would come again! Oh, it would come again!

II

If Alexandra had had much imagination she might have guessed what was going on in Marie's mind, and she would have seen long before what was going on in Emil's. But that, as Emil himself had more than once reflected, was Alexandra's blind side, and her life had not been of the kind to sharpen her vision. Her training had all been toward the end of making her proficient in what she had undertaken to do. Her personal life, her own realization of herself, was almost a subconscious existence; like an underground river that came to the surface only here, and there, at intervals months apart, and then sank again to flow on under her own fields. Nevertheless, the underground stream was there, and it was because she had so much personality to put into her enterprises and succeeded in putting it into them so completely, that her affairs prospered better than those of her neighbors.

There were certain days in her life, outwardly uneventful, which Alexandra remembered as peculiarly happy; days when she was close to the flat, fallow world about her, and felt, as it were, in her own body the joyous germination in the soil. There were days, too, which she and Emil had spent together, upon which she loved to look back. There had been such a day when they were down on the river in the dry year, looking over the land. They had made an early start one morning and had driven a long way before noon. When Emil said he was hungry, they drew back from the road, gave Brigham his oats among the bushes, and climbed up to the top of a grassy bluff to eat their lunch under the shade of some little elm trees. The river was clear there, and shallow, since there had been no rain, and it ran in ripples over the sparkling sand. Under the overhanging willows of the opposite bank there was an inlet where the water was deeper and flowed so slowly that it seemed to sleep in the sun. In this little bay a single wild duck was swimming and diving and preening her feathers, disporting herself very happily in the flickering light and shade. They sat for a long time, watching the solitary bird take its pleasure. No living thing had ever seemed to Alexandra as beautiful as that wild duck. Emil must have felt about it as she did, for afterward, when they were at home, he used sometimes to say, "Sister, you know our duck down there—" Alexandra remembered that day as one of the happiest in her life. Years afterward she thought of the duck as still there, swimming and diving all by herself in the sunlight, a kind of enchanted bird that did not know age or change.

Most of Alexandra's happy memories were as impersonal as this one; yet to her they were very personal. Her mind was a white book, with clear writing about weather and beasts and growing things. Not many people would have cared to read it; only a happy few. She had never been in love, she had never indulged in sentimental reveries. Even as a girl she had looked upon men as work-fellows. She had grown up in serious times.

There was one fancy indeed, which persisted through her girlhood. It most often came to her on Sunday mornings, the one day in the week when she lay late abed listening to the familiar morning sounds; the windmill singing in the brisk breeze, Emil whistling as he blacked his boots down by the kitchen door. Sometimes, as she lay thus luxuriously idle, her eyes closed, she used to have an illusion of being lifted up bodily and carried lightly by some one very strong. It was a man, certainly, who carried her, but he was like no man she knew; he was much larger and stronger and swifter, and he carried her as easily as if she were a sheaf of wheat. She never saw him, but, with eyes closed, she could feel that he was yellow like the sunlight, and there was the smell of ripe cornfields about him. She could feel him approach, bend over her and lift her, and then she could feel herself being carried swiftly off across the fields. After such a reverie she would rise hastily, angry with herself, and go down to the bath-house that was partitioned off the kitchen shed. There she would stand in a tin tub and prosecute her bath with vigor, finishing it by pouring buckets of cold well-water over her gleaming white body which no man on the Divide could have carried very far.

As she grew older, this fancy more often came to her when she was tired than when she was fresh and strong. Sometimes, after she had been in the open all day, overseeing the branding of the cattle or the loading of the pigs, she would come in chilled, take a concoction of spices and warm home-made wine, and go to bed with her body actually aching with fatigue. Then, just before she went to sleep, she had the old sensation of being lifted and carried by a strong being who took from her all her bodily weariness.

PART IV
THE WHITE MULBERRY TREE

I

The French Church, properly the Church of Sainte-Agnes, stood upon a hill. The high, narrow, red-brick building, with its tall steeple and steep roof, could be seen for miles across the wheat-fields, though the little town of Sainte-Agnes was completely hidden away at the foot of the hill. The church looked powerful and triumphant there on its eminence, so high above the rest of the landscape, with miles of warm color lying at its feet, and by its position and setting it reminded one of some of the churches built long ago in the wheat-lands of middle France.

Late one June afternoon Alexandra Bergson was driving along one of the many roads that led through the rich French farming country to the big church. The sunlight was shining directly in her face, and there was a blaze of light all about the red church on the hill. Beside Alexandra lounged a strikingly exotic figure in a tall Mexican hat, a silk sash, and a black velvet jacket sewn with silver buttons. Emil had returned only the night before, and his sister was so proud of him that she decided at once to take him up to the church supper, and to make him wear the Mexican costume he had brought home in his trunk. "All the girls who have stands are going to wear fancy costumes," she argued, "and some of the boys. Marie is going to tell fortunes, and she sent to Omaha for a Bohemian dress her father brought back from a visit to the old country. If you wear those clothes, they will all be pleased. And you must take your guitar. Everybody ought to do what they can to help along, and we have never done much. We are not a talented family."

The supper was to be at six o'clock, in the basement of the church, and afterward there would be a fair, with charades and an auction. Alexandra had set out from home early, leaving the house to Signa and Nelse Jensen, who were to be married next week. Signa had shyly asked to have the wedding put off until Emil came home.

Alexandra was well satisfied with her brother. As they drove through the rolling French country toward the westering sun and the stalwart church, she was thinking of that time long ago when she and Emil drove back from the river valley to the still unconquered Divide. Yes, she told herself, it had been worth while; both Emil and the country had become what she had hoped. Out of her father's children there was one who was fit to cope with the world, who had not been tied to the plow, and who had a personality apart from the soil. And that, she reflected, was what she had worked for. She felt well satisfied with her life.

When they reached the church, a score of teams were hitched in front of the basement doors that opened from the hillside upon the sanded terrace, where the boys wrestled and had jumping-matches. Amédée Chevalier, a proud father of one week, rushed out and embraced Emil. Amédée was an only son,—hence he was a very rich young man,—but he meant to have twenty children himself, like his uncle Xavier. "Oh, Emil," he cried, hugging his old friend rapturously, "why ain't you been up to see my boy? You come to-morrow, sure? Emil, you wanna get a boy right off! It's the greatest thing ever! No, no, no! Angel not sick at all. Everything just fine. That boy he come into this world laughin', and he been laughin' ever since. You come an' see!" He pounded Emil's ribs to emphasize each announcement.

Emil caught his arms. "Stop, Amédée. You're knocking the wind out of me. I brought him cups and spoons and blankets and moccasins enough for an orphan asylum. I'm awful glad it's a boy, sure enough!"

The young men crowded round Emil to admire his costume and to tell him in a breath everything that had happened since he went away. Emil had more friends up here in the French country than down on Norway Creek. The French and Bohemian boys were spirited and jolly, liked variety, and were as much

predisposed to favor anything new as the Scandinavian boys were
to reject it. The Norwegian and Swedish lads were much more
self-centred, apt to be egotistical and jealous. They were cautious
and reserved with Emil because he had been away to college, and
were prepared to take him down if he should try to put on airs
with them. The French boys liked a bit of swagger, and they were
always delighted to hear about anything new: new clothes, new
games, new songs, new dances. Now they carried Emil off to show
him the club room they had just fitted up over the post-office,
down in the village. They ran down the hill in a drove, all laughing
and chattering at once, some in French, some in English.

Alexandra went into the cool, whitewashed basement where
the women were setting the tables. Marie was standing on a chair,
building a little tent of shawls where she was to tell fortunes.
She sprang down and ran toward Alexandra, stopping short and
looking at her in disappointment. Alexandra nodded to her
encouragingly.

"Oh, he will be here, Marie. The boys have taken him off to
show him something. You won't know him. He is a man now, sure
enough. I have no boy left. He smokes terrible-smelling Mexican
cigarettes and talks Spanish. How pretty you look, child. Where
did you get those beautiful earrings?"

"They belonged to father's mother. He always promised them
to me. He sent them with the dress and said I could keep them."

Marie wore a short red skirt of stoutly woven cloth, a white
bodice and kirtle, a yellow silk turban wound low over her brown
curls, and long coral pendants in her ears. Her ears had been
pierced against a piece of cork by her great-aunt when she was
seven years old. In those germless days she had worn bits of
broom-straw, plucked from the common sweeping-broom, in the
lobes until the holes were healed and ready for little gold rings.

When Emil came back from the village, he lingered outside on
the terrace with the boys. Marie could hear him talking and
strumming on his guitar while Raoul Marcel sang falsetto. She
was vexed with him for staying out there. It made her very

nervous to hear him and not to see him; for, certainly, she told herself, she was not going out to look for him. When the supper bell rang and the boys came trooping in to get seats at the first table, she forgot all about her annoyance and ran to greet the tallest of the crowd, in his conspicuous attire. She didn't mind showing her embarrassment at all. She blushed and laughed excitedly as she gave Emil her hand, and looked delightedly at the black velvet coat that brought out his fair skin and fine blond head. Marie was incapable of being lukewarm about anything that pleased her. She simply did not know how to give a half-hearted response. When she was delighted, she was as likely as not to stand on her tip-toes and clap her hands. If people laughed at her, she laughed with them.

"Do the men wear clothes like that every day, in the street?" She caught Emil by his sleeve and turned him about. "Oh, I wish I lived where people wore things like that! Are the buttons real silver? Put on the hat, please. What a heavy thing! How do you ever wear it? Why don't you tell us about the bull-fights?"

She wanted to wring all his experiences from him at once, without waiting a moment. Emil smiled tolerantly and stood looking down at her with his old, brooding gaze, while the French girls fluttered about him in their white dresses and ribbons, and Alexandra watched the scene with pride. Several of the French girls, Marie knew, were hoping that Emil would take them to supper, and she was relieved when he took only his sister. Marie caught Frank's arm and dragged him to the same table, managing to get seats opposite the Bergsons, so that she could hear what they were talking about. Alexandra made Emil tell Mrs. Xavier Chevalier, the mother of the twenty, about how he had seen a famous matador killed in the bull-ring. Marie listened to every word, only taking her eyes from Emil to watch Frank's plate and keep it filled. When Emil finished his account,—bloody enough to satisfy Mrs. Xavier and to make her feel thankful that she was not a matador,—Marie broke out with a volley of questions. How did the women dress when they went to bull-fights? Did they wear mantillas? Did they never wear hats?

After supper the young people played charades for the amusement of their elders, who sat gossiping between their guesses. All
the shops in Sainte-Agnes were closed at eight o'clock that night,
so that the merchants and their clerks could attend the fair. The
auction was the liveliest part of the entertainment, for the French
boys always lost their heads when they began to bid, satisfied that
their extravagance was in a good cause. After all the pincushions
and sofa pillows and embroidered slippers were sold, Emil precip-
itated a panic by taking out one of his turquoise shirt studs,
which every one had been admiring, and handing it to the auc-
tioneer. All the French girls clamored for it, and their sweethearts
bid against each other recklessly. Marie wanted it, too, and she
kept making signals to Frank, which he took a sour pleasure in
disregarding. He didn't see the use of making a fuss over a fellow
just because he was dressed like a clown. When the turquoise
went to Malvina Sauvage, the French banker's daughter, Marie
shrugged her shoulders and betook herself to her little tent of
shawls, where she began to shuffle her cards by the light of a tallow candle, calling out, "Fortunes, fortunes!"

The young priest, Father Duchesne, went first to have his fortune read. Marie took his long white hand, looked at it, and then
began to run off her cards. "I see a long journey across water for
you, Father. You will go to a town all cut up by water; built on
islands, it seems to be, with rivers and green fields all about. And
you will visit an old lady with a white cap and gold hoops in her
ears, and you will be very happy there."

"Mais, oui," said the priest, with a melancholy smile. "C'est
L'Isle-Adam, chez ma mère. Vous êtes très savante, ma fille." He
patted her yellow turban, calling, "Venez donc, mes garçons! Il y
a ici une véritable clairvoyante!"

Marie was clever at fortune-telling, indulging in a light irony
that amused the crowd. She told old Brunot, the miser, that he
would lose all his money, marry a girl of sixteen, and live happily
on a crust. Sholte, the fat Russian boy, who lived for his stomach,

was to be disappointed in love, grow thin, and shoot himself from despondency. Amédée was to have twenty children, and nineteen of them were to be girls. Amédée slapped Frank on the back and asked him why he didn't see what the fortune-teller would promise him. But Frank shook off his friendly hand and grunted, "She tell my fortune long ago; bad enough!" Then he withdrew to a corner and sat glowering at his wife.

Frank's case was all the more painful because he had no one in particular to fix his jealousy upon. Sometimes he could have thanked the man who would bring him evidence against his wife. He had discharged a good farm-boy, Jan Smirka, because he thought Marie was fond of him; but she had not seemed to miss Jan when he was gone, and she had been just as kind to the next boy. The farm-hands would always do anything for Marie; Frank couldn't find one so surly that he would not make an effort to please her. At the bottom of his heart Frank knew well enough that if he could once give up his grudge, his wife would come back to him. But he could never in the world do that. The grudge was fundamental. Perhaps he could not have given it up if he had tried. Perhaps he got more satisfaction out of feeling himself abused than he would have got out of being loved. If he could once have made Marie thoroughly unhappy, he might have relented and raised her from the dust. But she had never humbled herself. In the first days of their love she had been his slave; she had admired him abandonedly. But the moment he began to bully her and to be unjust, she began to draw away; at first in tearful amazement, then in quiet, unspoken disgust. The distance between them had widened and hardened. It no longer contracted and brought them suddenly together. The spark of her life went somewhere else, and he was always watching to surprise it. He knew that somewhere she must get a feeling to live upon, for she was not a woman who could live without loving. He wanted to prove to himself the wrong he felt. What did she hide in her heart? Where did it go? Even Frank had his churlish delicacies; he never reminded her of how much she had once loved him. For that Marie was grateful to him.

While Marie was chattering to the French boys, Amédée called Emil to the back of the room and whispered to him that they were going to play a joke on the girls. At eleven o'clock, Amédée was to go up to the switchboard in the vestibule and turn off the electric lights, and every boy would have a chance to kiss his sweetheart before Father Duchesne could find his way up the stairs to turn the current on again. The only difficulty was the candle in Marie's tent; perhaps, as Emil had no sweetheart, he would oblige the boys by blowing out the candle. Emil said he would undertake to do that.

At five minutes to eleven he sauntered up to Marie's booth, and the French boys dispersed to find their girls. He leaned over the card-table and gave himself up to looking at her. "Do you think you could tell my fortune?" he murmured. It was the first word he had had alone with her for almost a year. "My luck hasn't changed any. It's just the same."

Marie had often wondered whether there was anyone else who could look his thoughts to you as Emil could. To-night, when she met his steady, powerful eyes, it was impossible not to feel the sweetness of the dream he was dreaming; it reached her before she could shut it out, and hid itself in her heart. She began to shuffle her cards furiously. "I'm angry with you, Emil," she broke out with petulance. "Why did you give them that lovely blue stone to sell? You might have known Frank wouldn't buy it for me, and I wanted it awfully!"

Emil laughed shortly. "People who want such little things surely ought to have them," he said dryly. He thrust his hand into the pocket of his velvet trousers and brought out a handful of uncut turquoises, as big as marbles. Leaning over the table he dropped them into her lap. "There, will those do? Be careful, don't let any one see them. Now, I suppose you want me to go away and let you play with them?"

Marie was gazing in rapture at the soft blue color of the stones. "Oh, Emil! Is everything down there beautiful like these? How could you ever come away?"

At that instant Amédée laid hands on the switchboard. There was a shiver and a giggle, and every one looked toward the red blur that Marie's candle made in the dark. Immediately that, too, was gone. Little shrieks and currents of soft laughter ran up and down the dark hall. Marie started up,—directly into Emil's arms. In the same instant she felt his lips. The veil that had hung uncertainly between them for so long was dissolved. Before she knew what she was doing, she had committed herself to that kiss that was at once a boy's and a man's, as timid as it was tender; so like Emil and so unlike any one else in the world. Not until it was over did she realize what it meant. And Emil, who had so often imagined the shock of this first kiss, was surprised at its gentleness and naturalness. It was like a sigh which they had breathed together; almost sorrowful, as if each were afraid of wakening something in the other.

When the lights came on again, everybody was laughing and shouting, and all the French girls were rosy and shining with mirth. Only Marie, in her little tent of shawls, was pale and quiet. Under her yellow turban the red coral pendants swung against white cheeks. Frank was still staring at her, but he seemed to see nothing. Years ago, he himself had had the power to take the blood from her cheeks like that. Perhaps he did not remember— perhaps he had never noticed! Emil was already at the other end of the hall, walking about with the shoulder-motion he had acquired among the Mexicans, studying the floor with his intent, deep-set eyes. Marie began to take down and fold her shawls. She did not glance up again. The young people drifted to the other end of the hall where the guitar was sounding. In a moment she heard Emil and Raoul singing:—

> "Across the Rio Grand-e
> There lies a sunny land-e,
> My bright-eyed Mexico!"

Alexandra Bergson came up to the card booth. "Let me help you, Marie. You look tired."

She placed her hand on Marie's arm and felt her shiver. Marie stiffened under that kind, calm hand. Alexandra drew back, perplexed and hurt.

There was about Alexandra something of the impervious calm of the fatalist, always disconcerting to very young people, who cannot feel that the heart lives at all unless it is still at the mercy of storms; unless its strings can scream to the touch of pain.

II

Signa's wedding supper was over. The guests, and the tiresome little Norwegian preacher who had performed the marriage ceremony, were saying good-night. Old Ivar was hitching the horses to the wagon to take the wedding presents and the bride and groom up to their new home, on Alexandra's north quarter. When Ivar drove up to the gate, Emil and Marie Shabata began to carry out the presents, and Alexandra went into her bedroom to bid Signa good-bye and to give her a few words of good counsel. She was surprised to find that the bride had changed her slippers for heavy shoes and was pinning up her skirts. At that moment Nelse appeared at the gate with the two milk cows that Alexandra had given Signa for a wedding present.

Alexandra began to laugh. "Why, Signa, you and Nelse are to ride home. I'll send Ivar over with the cows in the morning."

Signa hesitated and looked perplexed. When her husband called her, she pinned her hat on resolutely. "I ta-ank I better do yust like he say," she murmured in confusion.

Alexandra and Marie accompanied Signa to the gate and saw the party set off, old Ivar driving ahead in the wagon and the bride and groom following on foot, each leading a cow. Emil burst into a laugh before they were out of hearing.

"Those two will get on," said Alexandra as they turned back to the house. "They are not going to take any chances. They will feel safer with those cows in their own stable. Marie, I am going to send for an old woman next. As soon as I get the girls broken in, I marry them off."

"I've no patience with Signa, marrying that grumpy fellow!" Marie declared. "I wanted her to marry that nice Smirka boy who worked for us last winter. I think she liked him, too."

"Yes, I think she did," Alexandra assented, "but I suppose she was too much afraid of Nelse to marry any one else. Now that I think of it, most of my girls have married men they were afraid of. I believe there is a good deal of the cow in most Swedish girls. You high-strung Bohemians can't understand us. We're a terribly practical people, and I guess we think a cross man makes a good manager."

Marie shrugged her shoulders and turned to pin up a lock of hair that had fallen on her neck. Somehow Alexandra had irritated her of late. Everybody irritated her. She was tired of everybody. "I'm going home alone, Emil, so you needn't get your hat," she said as she wound her scarf quickly about her head. "Good-night, Alexandra," she called back in a strained voice, running down the gravel walk.

Emil followed with long strides until he overtook her. Then she began to walk slowly. It was a night of warm wind and faint starlight, and the fireflies were glimmering over the wheat.

"Marie," said Emil after they had walked for a while, "I wonder if you know how unhappy I am?"

Marie did not answer him. Her head, in its white scarf, drooped forward a little.

Emil kicked a clod from the path and went on:—

"I wonder whether you are really shallow-hearted, like you seem? Sometimes I think one boy does just as well as another for you. It never seems to make much difference whether it is me or Raoul Marcel or Jan Smirka. Are you really like that?"

"Perhaps I am. What do you want me to do? Sit round and cry all day? When I've cried until I can't cry any more, then—then I must do something else."

"Are you sorry for me?" he persisted.

"No, I'm not. If I were big and free like you, I wouldn't let anything make me unhappy. As old Napoleon Brunot said at the fair, I wouldn't go lovering after no woman. I'd take the first train and go off and have all the fun there is."

"I tried that, but it didn't do any good. Everything reminded me. The nicer the place was, the more I wanted you." They had come to the stile and Emil pointed to it persuasively. "Sit down a moment, I want to ask you something." Marie sat down on the top step and Emil drew nearer. "Would you tell me something that's none of my business if you thought it would help me out? Well, then, tell me, *please* tell me, why you ran away with Frank Shabata!"

Marie drew back. "Because I was in love with him," she said firmly.

"Really?" he asked incredulously.

"Yes, indeed. Very much in love with him. I think I was the one who suggested our running away. From the first it was more my fault than his."

Emil turned away his face.

"And now," Marie went on, "I've got to remember that. Frank is just the same now as he was then, only then I would see him as I wanted him to be. I would have my own way. And now I pay for it."

"You don't do all the paying."

"That's it. When one makes a mistake, there's no telling where it will stop. But you can go away; you can leave all this behind you."

"Not everything. I can't leave you behind. Will you go away with me, Marie?"

Marie started up and stepped across the stile. "Emil! How wickedly you talk! I am not that kind of a girl, and you know it. But what am I going to do if you keep tormenting me like this!" she added plaintively.

"Marie, I won't bother you any more if you will tell me just one thing. Stop a minute and look at me. No, nobody can see us. Everybody's asleep. That was only a firefly. Marie, *stop* and tell me!"

Emil overtook her and catching her by the shoulders shook her gently, as if he were trying to awaken a sleepwalker.

Marie hid her face on his arm. "Don't ask me anything more. I don't know anything except how miserable I am. And I thought it would be all right when you came back. Oh, Emil," she clutched his sleeve and began to cry, "what am I to do if you don't go away? I can't go, and one of us must. Can't you see?"

Emil stood looking down at her, holding his shoulders stiff and stiffening the arm to which she clung. Her white dress looked gray in the darkness. She seemed like a troubled spirit, like some shadow out of the earth, clinging to him and entreating him to give her peace. Behind her the fireflies were weaving in and out over the wheat. He put his hand on her bent head. "On my honor, Marie, if you will say you love me, I will go away."

She lifted her face to his. "How could I help it? Didn't you know?"

Emil was the one who trembled, through all his frame. After he left Marie at her gate, he wandered about the fields all night, till morning put out the fireflies and the stars.

III

One evening, a week after Signa's wedding, Emil was kneeling before a box in the sitting room, packing his books. From time to time he rose and wandered about the house, picking up stray volumes and bringing them listlessly back to his box. He was packing without enthusiasm. He was not very sanguine about his future. Alexandra sat sewing by the table. She had helped him pack his trunk in the afternoon. As Emil came and went by her chair with his books, he thought to himself that it had not been so hard to leave his sister since he first went away to school. He was going directly to Omaha, to read law in the office of a Swedish lawyer until October, when he would enter the law school at Ann Arbor. They had planned that Alexandra was to come to

Michigan—a long journey for her—at Christmas time, and spend several weeks with him. Nevertheless, he felt that this leavetaking would be more final than his earlier ones had been; that it meant a definite break with his old home and the beginning of something new—he did not know what. His ideas about the future would not crystallize; the more he tried to think about it, the vaguer his conception of it became. But one thing was clear, he told himself; it was high time that he made good to Alexandra, and that ought to be incentive enough to begin with.

As he went about gathering up his books he felt as if he were uprooting things. At last he threw himself down on the old slat lounge where he had slept when he was little, and lay looking up at the familiar cracks in the ceiling.

"Tired, Emil?" his sister asked.

"Lazy," he murmured, turning on his side and looking at her. He studied Alexandra's face for a long time in the lamplight. It had never occurred to him that his sister was a handsome woman until Marie Shabata had told him so. Indeed, he had never thought of her as being a woman at all, only a sister. As he studied her bent head, he looked up at the picture of John Bergson above the lamp. "No," he thought to himself, "she didn't get it there. I suppose I am more like that."

"Alexandra," he said suddenly, "that old walnut secretary you use for a desk was father's wasn't it?"

Alexandra went on stitching. "Yes. It was one of the first things he bought for the old log house. It was a great extravagance in those days. But he wrote a great many letters back to the old country. He had many friends there, and they wrote to him up to the time he died. No one ever blamed him for grandfather's disgrace. I can see him now, sitting there on Sundays, in his white shirt, writing pages and pages, so carefully. He wrote a fine, regular hand, almost like engraving. Yours is something like his, when you take pains."

"Grandfather was really crooked, was he?"

"He married an unscrupulous woman, and then—then I'm afraid he was really crooked. When we first came here father used to have dreams about making a great fortune and going back to Sweden to pay back to the poor sailors the money grandfather had lost."

Emil stirred on the lounge. "I say, that would have been worth while, wouldn't it? Father wasn't a bit like Lou or Oscar, was he? I can't remember much about him before he got sick."

"Oh, not at all!" Alexandra dropped her sewing on her knee. "He had better opportunities; not to make money, but to make something of himself. He was a quiet man, but he was very intelligent. You would have been proud of him, Emil."

Alexandra felt that he would like to know there had been a man of his kin whom he could admire. She knew that Emil was ashamed of Lou and Oscar, because they were bigoted and self-satisfied. He never said much about them, but she could feel his disgust. His brothers had shown their disapproval of him ever since he first went away to school. The only thing that would have satisfied them would have been his failure at the University. As it was, they resented every change in his speech, in his dress, in his point of view; though the latter they had to conjecture, for Emil avoided talking to them about any but family matters. All his interests they treated as affectations.

Alexandra took up her sewing again. "I can remember father when he was quite a young man. He belonged to some kind of a musical society, a male chorus, in Stockholm. I can remember going with mother to hear them sing. There must have been a hundred of them, and they all wore long black coats and white neckties. I was used to seeing father in a blue coat, a sort of jacket, and when I recognized him on the platform, I was very proud. Do you remember that Swedish song he taught you, about the ship boy?"

"Yes. I used to sing it to the Mexicans. They like anything different." Emil paused. "Father had a hard fight here, didn't he?" he added thoughtfully.

"Yes, and he died in a dark time. Still, he had hope. He believed in the land."

"And in you, I guess," Emil said to himself. There was another period of silence; that warm, friendly silence, full of perfect understanding, in which Emil and Alexandra had spent many of their happiest half-hours.

At last Emil said abruptly, "Lou and Oscar would be better off if they were poor, wouldn't they?"

Alexandra smiled. "Maybe. But their children wouldn't. I have great hopes of Milly."

Emil shivered. "I don't know. Seems to me it gets worse as it goes on. The worst of the Swedes is that they're never willing to find out how much they don't know. It was like that at the University. Always so pleased with themselves! There's no getting behind that conceited Swedish grin. The Bohemians and Germans were so different."

"Come, Emil, don't go back on your own people. Father wasn't conceited, Uncle Otto wasn't. Even Lou and Oscar weren't when they were boys."

Emil looked incredulous, but he did not dispute the point. He turned on his back and lay still for a long time, his hands locked under his head, looking up at the ceiling. Alexandra knew that he was thinking of many things. She felt no anxiety about Emil. She had always believed in him, as she had believed in the land. He had been more like himself since he got back from Mexico; seemed glad to be at home, and talked to her as he used to do. She had no doubt that his wandering fit was over, and that he would soon be settled in life.

"Alexandra," said Emil suddenly, "do you remember the wild duck we saw down on the river that time?"

His sister looked up. "I often think of her. It always seems to me she's there still, just like we saw her."

"I know. It's queer what things one remembers and what things one forgets." Emil yawned and sat up. "Well, it's time to turn in." He rose, and going over to Alexandra stooped down and kissed her lightly on the cheek. "Good-night, sister. I think you did pretty well by us."

Emil took up his lamp and went upstairs. Alexandra sat finishing his new nightshirt, that must go in the top tray of his trunk.

IV

The next morning Angélique, Amédée's wife, was in the kitchen baking pies, assisted by old Mrs. Chevalier. Between the mixing-board and the stove stood the old cradle that had been Amédée's, and in it was his black-eyed son. As Angélique, flushed and excited, with flour on her hands, stopped to smile at the baby, Emil Bergson rode up to the kitchen door on his mare and dismounted.

"'Médée is out in the field, Emil," Angélique called as she ran across the kitchen to the oven. "He begins to cut his wheat today; the first wheat ready to cut anywhere about here. He bought a new header, you know, because all the wheat's so short this year. I hope he can rent it to the neighbors, it cost so much. He and his cousins bought a steam thresher on shares. You ought to go out and see that header work. I watched it an hour this morning, busy as I am with all the men to feed. He has a lot of hands, but he's the only one that knows how to drive the header or how to run the engine, so he has to be everywhere at once. He's sick, too, and ought to be in his bed."

Emil bent over Hector Baptiste, trying to make him blink his round, bead-like black eyes. "Sick? What's the matter with your daddy, kid? Been making him walk the floor with you?"

Angélique sniffed. "Not much! We don't have that kind of babies. It was his father that kept Baptiste awake. All night I had to be getting up and making mustard plasters to put on his stomach. He had an awful colic. He said he felt better this morning, but I don't think he ought to be out in the field, overheating himself."

Angélique did not speak with much anxiety, not because she was indifferent, but because she felt so secure in their good fortune. Only good things could happen to a rich, energetic, handsome young man like Amédée, with a new baby in the cradle and a new header in the field.

Emil stroked the black fuzz on Baptiste's head. "I say, Angélique, one of 'Médée's grandmothers, 'way back, must have been a squaw. This kid looks exactly like the Indian babies."

Angélique made a face at him, but old Mrs. Chevalier had been touched on a sore point, and she let out such a stream of fiery *patois* that Emil fled from the kitchen and mounted his mare.

Opening the pasture gate from the saddle, Emil rode across the field to the clearing where the thresher stood, driven by a stationary engine and fed from the header boxes. As Amédée was not on the engine, Emil rode on to the wheatfield, where he recognized, on the header, the slight, wiry figure of his friend, coatless, his white shirt puffed out by the wind, his straw hat stuck jauntily on the side of his head. The six big work-horses that drew, or rather pushed, the header, went abreast at a rapid walk, and as they were still green at the work they required a good deal of management on Amédée's part; especially when they turned the corners, where they divided, three and three, and then swung round into line again with a movement that looked as complicated as a wheel of artillery. Emil felt a new thrill of admiration for his friend, and with it the old pang of envy at the way in which Amédée could do with his might what his hand found to do, and feel that, whatever it was, it was the most important thing in the world. "I'll have to bring Alexandra up to see this thing work," Emil thought; "it's splendid!"

When he saw Emil, Amédée waved to him and called to one of his twenty cousins to take the reins. Stepping off the header without stopping it, he ran up to Emil who had dismounted. "Come along," he called. "I have to go over to the engine for a minute. I gotta green man running it, and I gotta to keep an eye on him."

Emil thought the lad was unnaturally flushed and more excited than even the cares of managing a big farm at a critical time warranted. As they passed behind a last year's stack, Amédée clutched at his right side and sank down for a moment on the straw.

"Ouch! I got an awful pain in me, Emil. Something's the matter with my insides, for sure."

Emil felt his fiery cheek. "You ought to go straight to bed, 'Médée, and telephone for the doctor; that's what you ought to do."

Amédée staggered up with a gesture of despair. "How can I? I got no time to be sick. Three thousand dollars' worth of new machinery to manage, and the wheat so ripe it will begin to shatter next week. My wheat's short, but it's gotta grand full berries. What's he slowing down for? We haven't got header boxes enough to feed the thresher, I guess."

Amédée started hot-foot across the stubble, leaning a little to the right as he ran, and waved to the engineer not to stop the engine.

Emil saw that this was no time to talk about his own affairs. He mounted his mare and rode on to Sainte-Agnes, to bid his friends there good-bye. He went first to see Raoul Marcel, and found him innocently practising the "Gloria" for the big confirmation service on Sunday while he polished the mirrors of his father's saloon.

As Emil rode homewards at three o'clock in the afternoon, he saw Amédée staggering out of the wheatfield, supported by two of his cousins. Emil stopped and helped them put the boy to bed.

V

When Frank Shabata came in from work at five o'clock that evening, old Moses Marcel, Raoul's father, telephoned him that Amédée had had a seizure in the wheatfield, and that Doctor Paradis was going to operate on him as soon as the Hanover doctor got there to help. Frank dropped a word of this at the table, bolted his supper, and rode off to Sainte-Agnes, where there would be sympathetic discussion of Amédée's case at Marcel's saloon.

As soon as Frank was gone, Marie telephoned Alexandra. It was a comfort to hear her friend's voice. Yes, Alexandra knew what there was to be known about Amédée. Emil had been there when they carried him out of the field, and had stayed with him until the doctors operated for appendicitis at five o'clock. They were afraid it was too late to do much good; it should have been done three days ago. Amédée was in a very bad way. Emil had just come home, worn out and sick himself. She had given him some brandy and put him to bed.

Marie hung up the receiver. Poor Amédée's illness had taken

on a new meaning to her, now that she knew Emil had been with him. And it might so easily have been the other way—Emil who was ill and Amédée who was sad! Marie looked about the dusky sitting-room. She had seldom felt so utterly lonely. If Emil was asleep, there was not even a chance of his coming; and she could not go to Alexandra for sympathy. She meant to tell Alexandra everything, as soon as Emil went away. Then whatever was left between them would be honest.

But she could not stay in the house this evening. Where should she go? She walked slowly down through the orchard, where the evening air was heavy with the smell of wild cotton. The fresh, salty scent of the wild roses had given way before this more powerful perfume of midsummer. Wherever those ashes-of-rose balls hung on their milky stalks, the air about them was saturated with their breath. The sky was still red in the west and the evening star hung directly over the Bergsons' windmill. Marie crossed the fence at the wheatfield corner, and walked slowly along the path that led to Alexandra's. She could not help feeling hurt that Emil had not come to tell her about Amédée. It seemed to her most unnatural that he should not have come. If she were in trouble, certainly he was the one person in the world she would want to see. Perhaps he wished her to understand that for her he was as good as gone already.

Marie stole slowly, flutteringly, along the path, like a white night-moth out of the fields. The years seemed to stretch before her like the land; spring, summer, autumn, winter, spring; always the same patient fields, the patient little trees, the patient lives; always the same yearning, the same pulling at the chain—until the instinct to live had torn itself and bled and weakened for the last time, until the chain secured a dead woman, who might cautiously be released. Marie walked on, her face lifted toward the remote, inaccessible evening star.

When she reached the stile she sat down and waited. How terrible it was to love people when you could not really share their lives!

Yes, in so far as she was concerned, Emil was already gone.

They couldn't meet anymore. There was nothing for them to say. They had spent the last penny of their small change; there was nothing left but gold. The day of love-tokens was past. They had now only their hearts to give each other. And Emil being gone, what was her life to be like? In some ways, it would be easier. She would not, at least, live in perpetual fear. If Emil were once away and settled at work, she would not have the feeling that she was spoiling his life. With the memory he left her, she could be as rash as she chose. Nobody could be the worse for it but herself; and that, surely, did not matter. Her own case was clear. When a girl had loved one man, and then loved another while that man was still alive, everybody knew what to think of her. What happened to her was of little consequence, so long as she did not drag other people down with her. Emil once away, she could let everything else go and live a new life of perfect love.

Marie left the stile reluctantly. She had, after all, thought he might come. And how glad she ought to be, she told herself, that he was asleep. She left the path and went across the pasture. The moon was almost full. An owl was hooting somewhere in the fields. She had scarcely thought about where she was going when the pond glittered before her, where Emil had shot the ducks. She stopped and looked at it. Yes, there would be a dirty way out of life, if one chose to take it. But she did not want to die. She wanted to live and dream—a hundred years, forever! As long as this sweetness welled up in her heart, as long as her breast could hold this treasure of pain! She felt as the pond must feel when it held the moon like that; when it encircled and swelled with that image of gold.

In the morning, when Emil came downstairs, Alexandra met him in the sitting-room and put her hands on his shoulders. "Emil, I went to your room as soon as it was light, but you were sleeping so sound I hated to wake you. There was nothing you could do, so I let you sleep. They telephoned from Sainte-Agnes that Amédée died at three o'clock this morning."

VI

The Church has always held that life is for the living. On Saturday, while half the village of Sainte-Agnes was mourning for Amédée and preparing the funeral black for his burial on Monday, the other half was busy with white dresses and white veils for the great confirmation service to-morrow, when the bishop was to confirm a class of one hundred boys and girls. Father Duchesne divided his time between the living and the dead. All day Saturday the church was a scene of bustling activity, a little hushed by the thought of Amédée. The choir were busy rehearsing a mass of Rossini, which they had studied and practised for this occasion. The women were trimming the altar, the boys and girls were bringing flowers.

On Sunday morning the bishop was to drive overland to Sainte-Agnes from Hanover, and Emil Bergson had been asked to take the place of one of Amédée's cousins in the cavalcade of forty French boys who were to ride across country to meet the bishop's carriage. At six o'clock on Sunday morning the boys met at the church. As they stood holding their horses by the bridle, they talked in low tones of their dead comrade. They kept repeating that Amédée had always been a good boy, glancing toward the red brick church which had played so large a part in Amédée's life, had been the scene of his most serious moments and of his happiest hours. He had played and wrestled and sung and courted under its shadow. Only three weeks ago he had proudly carried his baby there to be christened. They could not doubt that that invisible arm was still about Amédée; that through the church on earth he had passed to the church triumphant, the goal of the hopes and faith of so many hundred years.

When the word was given to mount, the young men rode at a walk out of the village; but once out among the wheatfields in the morning sun, their horses and their own youth got the better of them. A wave of zeal and fiery enthusiasm swept over them. They longed for a Jerusalem to deliver. The thud of their galloping hoofs interrupted many a country breakfast and brought many a woman and child to the door of the farmhouses as they passed. Five miles east of Sainte-Agnes they met the bishop in his open carriage, attended by two priests. Like one man the boys swung off their hats in a broad salute, and bowed their heads as the handsome old man lifted his two fingers in the Episcopal blessing. The horsemen closed about the carriage like a guard, and whenever a restless horse broke from control and shot down the road ahead of the body, the bishop laughed and rubbed his plump hands together. "What fine boys!" he said to his priests. "The Church still has her cavalry."

As the troop swept past the graveyard half a mile east of the town,—the first frame church of the parish had stood there,—old Pierre Séguin was already out with his pick and spade, digging Amédée's grave. He knelt and uncovered as the bishop passed. The boys with one accord looked away from old Pierre to the red church on the hill, with the gold cross flaming on its steeple.

Mass was at eleven. While the church was filling, Emil Bergson waited outside, watching the wagons and buggies drive up the hill. After the bell began to ring, he saw Frank Shabata ride up on horseback and tie his horse to the hitch-bar. Marie, then, was not coming. Emil turned and went into the church. Amédée's was the only empty pew, and he sat down in it. Some of Amédée's cousins were there, dressed in black and weeping. When all the pews were full, the old men and boys packed the open space at the back of the church, kneeling on the floor. There was scarcely a family in town that was not represented in the confirmation class, by a cousin, at least. The new communicants, with their clear, reverent faces, were beautiful to look upon as they entered in a body and took the front benches reserved for them. Even before the Mass began, the air was charged with feeling. The choir had never sung so well and Raoul Marcel, in the "Gloria," drew even the bishop's eyes to the organ loft. For the offertory he sang Gounod's "Ave Maria,"—always spoken of in Sainte-Agnes as "the Ave Maria."

Emil began to torture himself with questions about Marie. Was she ill? Had she quarreled with her husband? Was she too unhappy to find comfort even here? Had she, perhaps, thought that he would come to her? Was she waiting for him? Overtaxed by excitement and sorrow as he was, the rapture of the service took hold upon his body and mind. As he listened to Raoul, he seemed to emerge from the conflicting emotions which had been whirling him about and sucking him under. He felt as if a clear light broke upon his mind, and with it a conviction that good was, after all, stronger than evil, and that good was possible to men. He seemed to discover that there was a kind of rapture in which he could love forever without faltering and without sin. He looked across the head of the people at Frank Shabata with calmness. That rapture was for those who could feel it; for people who could not, it was non-existent. He coveted nothing that was Frank Shabata's. The spirit he had met in music was his own. Frank Shabata had never found it; would never find it if he lived beside it a thousand years; would have destroyed it if he had found it, as Herod slew the innocents, as Rome slew the martyrs.

> *San — cta Mari-i-i-a,*

wailed Raoul from the organ loft;

> *O — ra pro no-o-bis!*

And it did not occur to Emil that any one had ever reasoned thus before, that music had ever before given a man this equivocal revelation.

The confirmation service followed the Mass. When it was over, the congregation thronged about the newly confirmed. The girls, and even the boys, were kissed and embraced and wept over. All the aunts and grandmothers wept with joy. The housewives had much ado to tear themselves away from the general rejoicing and hurry back to their kitchens. The country parishioners were staying in town for dinner, and nearly every house in Sainte-Agnes entertained visitors that day. Father Duchesne, the bishop, and the visiting priests dined with Fabien Sauvage, the banker. Emil and Frank Shabata were both guests of old Moïse Marcel. After dinner Frank and old Moïse retired to the rear room of the saloon to play California Jack and drink their cognac, and Emil went over to the banker's with Raoul, who had been asked to sing for the bishop.

At three o'clock, Emil felt that he could stand it no longer. He slipped out under cover of "The Holy City," followed by Malvina's wistful eye, and went to the stable for his mare. He was at that height of excitement from which everything is foreshortened, from which life seems short and simple, death very near, and the soul seems to soar like an eagle. As he rode past the graveyard he looked at the brown hole in the earth where Amédée was to lie, and felt no horror. That, too, was beautiful, that simple doorway into forgetfulness. The heart, when it is too much alive, aches for that brown earth, and ecstasy has no fear of death. It is the old and the poor and the maimed who shrink from that brown hole; its wooers are found among the young, the passionate, the gallant-hearted. It was not until he had passed the graveyard that Emil realized where he was going. It was the hour for saying good-bye. It might be the last time that he would see her alone, and today he could leave her without rancor, without bitterness.

Everywhere the grain stood ripe and the hot afternoon was full of the smell of the ripe wheat, like the smell of bread baking in an oven. The breath of the wheat and the sweet clover passed him like pleasant things in a dream. He could feel nothing but the sense of diminishing distance. It seemed to him that his mare was flying, or running on wheels, like a railway train. The sunlight, flashing on the window-glass of the big red barns, drove him wild with joy. He was like an arrow shot from the bow. His life poured itself out along the road before him as he rode to the Shabata farm.

When Emil alighted at the Shabatas' gate, his horse was in a lather. He tied her in the stable and hurried to the house. It was empty. She might be at Mrs. Hiller's or with Alexandra. But anything that reminded him of her would be enough, the orchard, the mulberry tree . . . When he reached the orchard the sun was hanging low over the wheatfield. Long fingers of light reached through the apple branches as through a net; the orchard was riddled and shot with gold; light was the reality, the trees were merely interferences that reflected and refracted light. Emil went softly down between the cherry trees toward the wheatfield. When he came to the corner, he stopped short and put his hand over his mouth. Marie was lying on her side under the white mulberry tree, her face half hidden in the grass, her eyes closed, her hands lying limply where they had happened to fall. She had lived a day of her new life of perfect love, and it had left her like this. Her breast rose and fell faintly, as if she were asleep. Emil threw himself down beside her and took her in his arms. The blood came back to her cheeks, her amber eyes opened slowly, and in them Emil saw his own face and the orchard and the sun. "I was dreaming this," she whispered, hiding her face against him, "don't take my dream away!"

VII

When Frank Shabata got home that night, he found Emil's mare in his stable. Such an impertinence amazed him. Like everybody else, Frank had had an exciting day. Since noon he had been drinking too much, and he was in a bad temper. He talked bitterly to himself while he put his own horse away, and as he went up the path and saw that the house was dark he felt an added sense of injury. He approached quietly and listened on the doorstep. Hearing nothing, he opened the kitchen door and went softly from one room to another. Then he went through the house again, upstairs and down, with no better result. He sat down on the bottom step of the box stairway and tried to get his wits together. In that unnatural quiet there was no sound but his own heavy breathing. Suddenly an owl began to hoot out in the fields. Frank lifted his head. An idea flashed into his mind, and his sense of injury and outrage grew. He went into his bedroom and took his murderous 405 Winchester from the closet.

When Frank took up his gun and walked out of the house, he had not the faintest purpose of doing anything with it. He did not believe that he had any real grievance. But it gratified him to feel like a desperate man. He had got into the habit of seeing himself always in desperate straits. His unhappy temperament was like a cage; he could never get out of it; and he felt that other people, his wife in particular, must have put him there. It had never more than dimly occurred to Frank that he made his own unhappiness. Though he took up his gun with dark projects in his mind, he would have been paralyzed with fright had he known that there was the slightest probability of his ever carrying any of them out.

Frank went slowly down to the orchard gate, stopped and stood for a moment lost in thought. He retraced his steps and looked through the barn and the hayloft. Then he went out to the road, where he took the footpath along the outside of the orchard hedge. The hedge was twice as tall as Frank himself, and so dense that one could see through it only by peering closely between the leaves. He could see the empty path a long way in the moonlight. His mind traveled ahead to the stile, which he always thought of as haunted by Emil Bergson. But why had he left his horse?

At the wheatfield corner, where the orchard hedge ended and the path led across the pasture to the Bergsons', Frank stopped. In the warm, breathless night air he heard a murmuring sound, perfectly inarticulate, as low as the sound of water coming from a spring, where there is no fall, and where there are no stones to fret it. Frank strained his ears. It ceased. He held his breath and began to tremble. Resting the butt of his gun on the ground, he parted the mulberry leaves softly with his fingers and peered through the hedge at the dark figures on the grass, in the shadow of the mulberry tree. It seemed to him that they must feel his eyes, that they must hear him breathing. But they did not. Frank, who had always wanted to see things blacker than they were, for once wanted to believe less than he saw. The woman lying in the

shadow might so easily be one of the Bergsons' farm-girls. . . .
Again the murmur, like water welling out of the ground. This
time he heard it more distinctly, and his blood was quicker than
his brain. He began to act, just as a man who falls into the fire
begins to act. The gun sprang to his shoulder, he sighted mechan-
ically and fired three times without stopping, stopped without
knowing why. Either he shut his eyes or he had vertigo. He did
not see anything while he was firing. He thought he heard a cry
simultaneous with the second report, but he was not sure. He
peered again through the hedge, at the two dark figures under the
tree. They had fallen a little apart from each other, and were perfectly still—No, not quite; in a white patch of light, where the
moon shone through the branches, a man's hand was plucking
spasmodically at the grass.

Suddenly the woman stirred and uttered a cry, then another,
and another. She was living! She was dragging herself toward the
hedge! Frank dropped his gun and ran back along the path, shaking, stumbling, gasping. He had never imagined such horror. The
cries followed him. They grew fainter and thicker, as if she were
choking. He dropped on his knees beside the hedge and crouched
like a rabbit, listening; fainter, fainter; a sound like a whine; again
—a moan—another—silence. Frank scrambled to his feet and
ran on, groaning and praying. From habit he went toward the
house, where he was used to being soothed when he had worked
himself into a frenzy, but at the sight of the black, open door, he
started back. He knew that he had murdered somebody, that a
woman was bleeding and moaning in the orchard, but he had not
realized before that it was his wife. The gate stared him in the
face. He threw his hands over his head. Which way to turn? He
lifted his tormented face and looked at the sky. "Holy Mother of
God, not to suffer! She was a good girl—not to suffer!"

Frank had been wont to see himself in dramatic situations; but
now, when he stood by the windmill, in the bright space between
the barn and the house, facing his own black doorway, he did not
see himself at all. He stood like the hare when the dogs are

approaching from all sides. And he ran like a hare, back and forth
about that moonlit space, before he could make up his mind to go
into the dark stable for a horse. The thought of going into a doorway was terrible to him. He caught Emil's horse by the bit and led
it out. He could not have buckled a bridle on his own. After two
or three attempts, he lifted himself into the saddle and started for
Hanover. If he could catch the one o'clock train, he had money
enough to get as far as Omaha.

While he was thinking dully of this in some less sensitized
part of his brain, his acuter faculties were going over and over the
cries he had heard in the orchard. Terror was the only thing that
kept him from going back to her, terror that she might still be she,
that she might still be suffering. A woman, mutilated and bleeding in his orchard—it was because it was a woman that he was so
afraid. It was inconceivable that he should have hurt a woman.
He would rather be eaten by wild beasts than see her move on the
ground as she had moved in the orchard. Why had she been so
careless? She knew he was like a crazy man when he was angry.
She had more than once taken that gun away from him and held
it, when he was angry with other people. Once it had gone off
while they were struggling over it. She was never afraid. But,
when she knew him, why hadn't she been more careful? Didn't
she have all summer before her to love Emil Bergson in, without
taking such chances? Probably she had met the Smirka boy, too,
down there in the orchard. He didn't care. She could have met all
the men on the Divide there, and welcome, if only she hadn't
brought this horror on him.

There was a wrench in Frank's mind. He did not honestly
believe that of her. He knew that he was doing her wrong. He
stopped his horse to admit this to himself the more directly, to
think it out the more clearly. He knew that he was to blame. For
three years he had been trying to break her spirit. She had a way of
making the best of things that seemed to him a sentimental affecta-
tion. He wanted his wife to resent that he was wasting his best
years among these stupid and unappreciative people; but she had

seemed to find the people quite good enough. If he ever got rich he meant to buy her pretty clothes and take her to California in a Pullman car, and treat her like a lady; but in the mean time he wanted her to feel that life was as ugly and as unjust as he felt it. He had tried to make her life ugly. He had refused to share any of the little pleasures she was so plucky about making for herself. She could be gay about the least thing in the world; but she must be gay! When she first came to him, her faith in him, her adoration—Frank struck the mare with his fist. Why had Marie made him do this thing; why had she brought this upon him? He was overwhelmed by sickening misfortune. All at once he heard her cries again—he had forgotten for a moment. "Maria," he sobbed aloud, "Maria!"

When Frank was halfway to Hanover, the motion of his horse brought on a violent attack of nausea. After it had passed, he rode on again, but he could think of nothing except his physical weakness and his desire to be comforted by his wife. He wanted to get into his own bed. Had his wife been at home, he would have turned and gone back to her meekly enough.

VIII

When old Ivar climbed down from his loft at four o'clock the next morning, he came upon Emil's mare, jaded and lather-stained, her bridle broken, chewing the scattered tufts of hay outside the stable door. The old man was thrown into a fright at once. He put the mare in her stall, threw her a measure of oats, and then set out as fast as his bow-legs could carry him on the path to the nearest neighbor.

"Something is wrong with that boy. Some misfortune has come upon us. He would never have used her so, in his right senses. It is not his way to abuse his mare," the old man kept muttering, as he scuttled through the short, wet pasture grass on his bare feet.

While Ivar was hurrying across the fields, the first long rays of the sun were reaching down between the orchard boughs to those two dew-drenched figures. The story of what had happened was written plainly on the orchard grass, and on the white mulberries that had fallen in the night and were covered with dark stain. For Emil the chapter had been short. He was shot in the heart, and had rolled over on his back and died. His face was turned up to the sky and his brows were drawn in a frown, as if he had realized that something had befallen him. But for Marie Shabata it had not been so easy. One ball had torn through her right lung, another had shattered the carotid artery. She must have started up and gone toward the hedge, leaving a trail of blood. There she had fallen and bled. From that spot there was another trail, heavier than the first, where she must have dragged herself back to Emil's body. Once there, she seemed not to have struggled any more. She had lifted her head to her lover's breast, taken his hand in both her own, and bled quietly to death. She was lying on her right side in an easy and natural position, her cheek on Emil's shoulder. On her face there was a look of ineffable content. Her lips were parted a little; her eyes were lightly closed, as if in a day-dream or a light slumber. After she lay down there, she seemed not to have moved an eyelash. The hand she held was covered with dark stains, where she had kissed it.

But the stained, slippery grass, the darkened mulberries, told only half the story. Above Marie and Emil, two white butterflies from Frank's alfalfa-field were fluttering in and out among the interlacing shadows; diving and soaring, now close together, now far apart; and in the long grass by the fence the last wild roses of the year opened their pink hearts to die.

When Ivar reached the path by the hedge, he saw Shabata's rifle lying in the way. He turned and peered through the branches, falling upon his knees as if his legs had been mowed from under him. "Merciful God!" he groaned; "merciful, merciful God!"

Alexandra, too, had risen early that morning, because of her anxiety about Emil. She was in Emil's room upstairs when, from the window, she saw Ivar coming along the path that led from the Shabatas'. He was running like a spent man, tottering and lurching from side to side. Ivar never drank, and Alexandra thought at once that one of his spells had come upon him, and that he must be in a very bad way indeed. She ran downstairs and hurried out to meet him, to hide his infirmity from the eyes of her household. The old man fell in the road at her feet and caught her hand, over which he bowed his shaggy head. "Mistress, mistress," he sobbed, "it has fallen! Sin and death for the young ones! God have mercy upon us!"

PART V

ALEXANDRA

I

Ivar was sitting at a cobbler's bench in the barn, mending harness
by the light of a lantern and repeating to himself the 101st Psalm.
It was only five o'clock of a mid-October day, but a storm had
come up in the afternoon, bringing black clouds, a cold wind and
torrents of rain. The old man wore his buffalo-skin coat, and
occasionally stopped to warm his fingers at the lantern. Suddenly
a woman burst into the shed, as if she had been blown in, accompanied by a shower of rain-drops. It was Signa, wrapped in a
man's overcoat and wearing a pair of boots over her shoes. In time
of trouble Signa had come back to stay with her mistress, for she
was the only one of the maids from whom Alexandra would
accept much personal service. It was three months now since the
news of the terrible thing that had happened in Frank Shabata's
orchard had first run like a fire over the Divide. Signa and Nelse
were staying on with Alexandra until winter.

"Ivar," Signa exclaimed as she wiped the rain from her face,
"do you know where she is?"

The old man put down his cobbler's knife. "Who, the mistress?"

"Yes. She went away about three o'clock. I happened to look
out of the window and saw her going across the fields in her thin
dress and sun-hat. And now this storm has come on. I thought
she was going to Mrs. Hiller's, and I telephoned as soon as the
thunder stopped, but she had not been there. I'm afraid she is out
somewhere and will get her death of cold."

Ivar put on his cap and took up the lantern. "Ja, ja, we will
see. I will hitch the boy's mare to the cart and go."

Signa followed him across the wagon-shed to the horses'

stable. She was shivering with cold and excitement. "Where do you suppose she can be, Ivar?"

The old man lifted a set of single harness carefully from its peg. "How should I know?"

"But you think she is at the graveyard, don't you?" Signa persisted. "So do I. Oh, I wish she would be more like herself! I can't believe it's Alexandra Bergson come to this, with no head about anything. I have to tell her when to eat and when to go to bed."

"Patience, patience, sister," muttered Ivar as he settled the bit in the horse's mouth. "When the eyes of the flesh are shut, the eyes of the spirit are open. She will have a message from those who are gone, and that will bring her peace. Until then we must bear with her. You and I are the only ones who have weight with her. She trusts us."

"How awful it's been these last three months." Signa held the lantern so that he could see to buckle the straps. "It don't seem right that we must all be so miserable. Why do we all have to be punished? Seems to me like good times would never come again."

Ivar expressed himself in a deep sigh, but said nothing. He stooped and took a sandburr from his toe.

"Ivar," Signa asked suddenly, "will you tell me why you go barefoot? All the time I lived here in the house I wanted to ask you. Is it for a penance, or what?"

"No, sister. It is for the indulgence of the body. From my youth up I have had a strong, rebellious body, and have been subject to every kind of temptation. Even in age my temptations are prolonged. It was necessary to make some allowances; and the feet, as I understand it, are free members. There is no divine prohibition for them in the Ten Commandments. The hands, the tongue, the eyes, the heart, all the bodily desires we are commanded to subdue; but the feet are free members. I indulge them without harm to any one, even to trampling in filth when my desires are low. They are quickly cleaned again."

Signa did not laugh. She looked thoughtful as she followed Ivar out to the wagon-shed and held the shafts up for him, while he backed in the mare and buckled the hold-backs. "You have been a good friend to the mistress, Ivar," she murmured.

"And you, God be with you," replied Ivar as he clambered into the cart and put the lantern under the oilcloth lap-cover. "Now for a ducking, my girl," he said to the mare, gathering up the reins.

As they emerged from the shed, a stream of water, running off the thatch, struck the mare on the neck. She tossed her head indignantly, then struck out bravely on the soft ground, slipping back again and again as she climbed the hill to the main road. Between the rain and the darkness Ivar could see very little, so he let Emil's mare have the rein, keeping her head in the right direction. When the ground was level, he turned her out of the dirt road upon the sod, where she was able to trot without slipping.

Before Ivar reached the graveyard, three miles from the house, the storm had spent itself, and the downpour had died into a soft, dripping rain. The sky and the land were a dark smoke color, and seemed to be coming together, like two waves. When Ivar stopped at the gate and swung out his lantern, a white figure rose from beside John Bergson's white stone.

The old man sprang to the ground and shuffled toward the gate calling, "Mistress, mistress!"

Alexandra hurried to meet him and put her hand on his shoulder. "*Tyst!* Ivar. There's nothing to be worried about. I'm sorry if I've scared you all. I didn't notice the storm till it was on me, and I couldn't walk against it. I'm glad you've come. I am so tired I didn't know how I'd ever get home."

Ivar swung the lantern up so that it shone in her face. "*Gud!* You are enough to frighten us, mistress. You look like a drowned woman. How could you do such a thing!"

Groaning and mumbling he led her out of the gate and helped her into the cart, wrapping her in the dry blankets on which he had been sitting.

Alexandra smiled at his solicitude. "Not much use in that, Ivar. You will only shut the wet in. I don't feel so cold now; but I'm heavy and numb. I'm glad you came."

Ivar turned the mare and urged her into a sliding trot. Her feet sent back a continual spatter of mud.

Alexandra spoke to the old man as they jogged along through the sullen gray twilight of the storm. "Ivar, I think it has done me good to get cold clear through like this, once. I don't believe I shall suffer so much any more. When you get so near the dead, they seem more real than the living. Worldly thoughts leave one. Ever since Emil died, I've suffered so when it rained. Now that I've been out in it with him, I shan't dread it. After you once get cold clear through, the feeling of the rain on you is sweet. It seems to bring back feelings you had when you were a baby. It carries you back into the dark, before you were born; you can't see things, but they come to you, somehow, and you know them and aren't afraid of them. Maybe it's like that with the dead. If they feel anything at all, it's the old things, before they were born, that comfort people like the feeling of their own bed does when they are little."

"Mistress," said Ivar reproachfully, "those are bad thoughts. The dead are in Paradise."

Then he hung his head, for he did not believe that Emil was in Paradise.

When they got home, Signa had a fire burning in the sitting-room stove. She undressed Alexandra and gave her a hot footbath, while Ivar made ginger tea in the kitchen. When Alexandra was in bed, wrapped in hot blankets, Ivar came in with his tea and saw that she drank it. Signa asked permission to sleep on the slat lounge outside her door. Alexandra endured their attentions patiently, but she was glad when they put out the lamp and left her. As she lay alone in the dark, it occurred to her for the first time that perhaps she was actually tired of life. All the physical operations of life seemed difficult and painful. She longed to be free from her own body, which ached and was so heavy. And longing itself was heavy: she yearned to be free of that.

As she lay with her eyes closed, she had again, more vividly than for many years, the old illusion of her girlhood, of being lifted and carried lightly by some one very strong. He was with her a long while this time, and carried her very far, and in his arms she felt free from pain. When he laid her down on her bed again, she opened her eyes, and, for the first time in her life, she saw him, saw him clearly, though the room was dark, and his face was covered. He was standing in the doorway of her room. His white cloak was thrown over his face, and his head was bent a little forward. His shoulders seemed as strong as the foundations of the world. His right arm, bared from the elbow, was dark and gleaming, like bronze, and she knew at once that it was the arm of the mightiest of all lovers. She knew at last for whom it was she had waited, and where he would carry her. That, she told herself, was very well. Then she went to sleep.

Alexandra wakened in the morning with nothing worse than a hard cold and a stiff shoulder. She kept her bed for several days, and it was during that time that she formed a resolution to go to Lincoln to see Frank Shabata. Ever since she last saw him in the courtroom, Frank's haggard face and wild eyes had haunted her. The trial had lasted only three days. Frank had given himself up to the police in Omaha and pleaded guilty of killing without malice and without premeditation. The gun was, of course, against him, and the judge had given him the full sentence,—ten years. He had now been in the State Penitentiary for a month.

Frank was the only one, Alexandra told herself, for whom anything could be done. He had been less in the wrong than any of them, and he was paying the heaviest penalty. She often felt that she herself had been more to blame than poor Frank. From the time the Shabatas had first moved to the neighboring farm, she had omitted no opportunity of throwing Marie and Emil together. Because she knew Frank was surly about doing little things to help his wife, she was always sending Emil over to spade or plant or carpenter for Marie. She was glad to have Emil see as much as possible of an intelligent, city-bred girl like their neighbor; she noticed that it improved his manners. She knew that Emil was fond of Marie, but it had never occurred to her that Emil's feeling might be different from her own. She wondered at herself now, but she had never thought of danger in that direction. If Marie had been unmarried,—oh, yes! Then she would have kept her eyes open. But the mere fact that she was Shabata's wife, for Alexandra, settled everything. That she was beautiful, impulsive, barely two years older than Emil, these facts had had no weight with Alexandra. Emil was a good boy, and only bad boys ran after married women.

Now, Alexandra could in a measure realize that Marie was, after all, Marie; not merely a "married woman." Sometimes, when Alexandra thought of her, it was with an aching tenderness. The moment she had reached them in the orchard that morning, everything was clear to her. There was something about those two lying in the grass, something in the way Marie had settled her cheek on Emil's shoulder, that told her everything. She wondered then how they could have helped loving each other; how she could have helped knowing that they must. Emil's cold, frowning face, the girl's content—Alexandra had felt awe of them, even in the first shock of her grief.

The idleness of those days in bed, the relaxation of body which attended them, enabled Alexandra to think more calmly than she had done since Emil's death. She and Frank, she told herself, were left out of that group of friends who had been overwhelmed by disaster. She must certainly see Frank Shabata. Even in the courtroom her heart had grieved for him. He was in a strange country, he had no kinsmen or friends, and in a moment he had ruined his life. Being what he was, she felt, Frank could not have acted otherwise. She could understand his behavior more easily than she could understand Marie's. Yes, she must go to Lincoln to see Frank Shabata.

The day after Emil's funeral, Alexandra had written to Carl Linstrum; a single page of notepaper, a bare statement of what had happened. She was not a woman who could write much about such a thing, and about her own feelings she could never write very freely. She knew that Carl was away from post-offices, prospecting somewhere in the interior. Before he started he had written her where he expected to go, but her ideas about Alaska were vague. As the weeks went by and she heard nothing from him, it seemed to Alexandra that her heart grew hard against Carl. She began to wonder whether she would not do better to finish her life alone. What was left of life seemed unimportant.

II

Late in the afternoon of a brilliant October day, Alexandra Bergson, dressed in a black suit and traveling-hat, alighted at the Burlington depot in Lincoln. She drove to the Lindell Hotel, where she had stayed two years ago when she came up for Emil's Commencement. In spite of her usual air of sureness and self-possession, Alexandra felt ill at ease in hotels, and she was glad, when she went to the clerk's desk to register, that there were not many people in the lobby. She had her supper early, wearing her hat and black jacket down to the dining-room and carrying her handbag. After supper she went out for a walk.

It was growing dark when she reached the university campus. She did not go into the grounds, but walked slowly up and down the stone walk outside the long iron fence, looking through at the young men who were running from one building to another, at the lights shining from the armory and the library. A squad of cadets were going through their drill behind the armory, and the commands of their young officer rang out at regular intervals, so sharp and quick that Alexandra could not understand them. Two stalwart girls came down the library steps and out through one of the iron gates. As they passed her, Alexandra was pleased to hear them speaking Bohemian to each other. Every few moments a boy would come running down the flagged walk and dash out into the street as if he were rushing to announce some wonder to the world. Alexandra felt a great tenderness for them all. She wished one of them would stop and speak to her. She wished she could ask them whether they had known Emil.

As she lingered by the south gate she actually did encounter one of the boys. He had on his drill cap and was swinging his books at the end of a long strap. It was dark by this time; he did not see her and ran against her. He snatched off his cap and stood bareheaded and panting. "I'm awfully sorry," he said in a bright, clear voice, with a rising inflection, as if he expected her to say something.

"Oh, it was my fault!" said Alexandra eagerly. "Are you an old student here, may I ask?"

"No, ma'am. I'm a Freshie, just off the farm. Cherry County. Were you hunting somebody?"

"No, thank you. That is—" Alexandra wanted to detain him. "That is, I would like to find some of my brother's friends. He graduated two years ago."

"Then you'd have to try the Seniors, wouldn't you? Let's see; I don't know any of them yet, but there'll be sure to be some of them around the library. That red building, right there," he pointed.

"Thank you, I'll try there," said Alexandra lingeringly.

"Oh, that's all right! Good-night." The lad clapped his cap on his head and ran straight down Eleventh Street. Alexandra looked after him wistfully.

She walked back to her hotel unreasonably comforted. "What a nice voice that boy had, and how polite he was. I know Emil was always like that to women." And again, after she had undressed and was standing in her nightgown, brushing her long, heavy hair by the electric light, she remembered him and said to herself: "I don't think I ever heard a nicer voice than that boy had. I hope he will get on well here. Cherry County; that's where the hay is so fine, and the coyotes can scratch down to water."

At nine o'clock the next morning Alexandra presented herself at the warden's office in the State Penitentiary. The warden was a German, a ruddy, cheerful-looking man who had formerly been a harness-maker. Alexandra had a letter to him from the German banker in Hanover. As he glanced at the letter, Mr. Schwartz put away his pipe.

"That big Bohemian, is it? Sure, he's gettin' along fine," said Mr. Schwartz cheerfully.

"I am glad to hear that. I was afraid he might be quarrelsome and get himself into more trouble. Mr. Schwartz, if you have time, I would like to tell you a little about Frank Shabata, and why I am interested in him."

The warden listened genially while she told him briefly something of Frank's history and character, but he did not seem to find anything unusual in her account.

"Sure, I'll keep an eye on him. We'll take care of him all right," he said, rising. "You can talk to him here, while I go to see to things in the kitchen. I'll have him sent in. He ought to be done washing out his cell by this time. We have to keep 'em clean, you know."

The warden paused at the door, speaking back over his shoulder to a pale young man in convicts' clothes who was seated at a desk in the corner, writing in a big ledger.

"Bertie, when 1037 is brought in, you just step out and give this lady a chance to talk."

The young man bowed his head and bent over his ledger again.

When Mr. Schwartz disappeared, Alexandra thrust her black-edged handkerchief nervously into her handbag. Coming out on the street-car she had not had the least dread of meeting Frank. But since she had been here the sounds and smells in the corridor, the look of the men in convicts' clothes who passed the glass door of the warden's office, affected her unpleasantly.

The warden's clock ticked, the young convict's pen scratched busily in the big book, and his sharp shoulders were shaken every few seconds by a loose cough which he tried to smother. It was easy to see that he was a sick man. Alexandra looked at him timidly, but he did not raise his eyes. He wore a white shirt under his striped jacket, a high collar, and a necktie, very carefully tied. His hands were thin and white and well cared for, and he had a seal ring on his little finger. When he heard steps approaching in the corridor, he rose, blotted his book, put his pen in the rack, and left the room without raising his eyes. Through the door he opened a guard came in, bringing Frank Shabata.

"You the lady that wanted to talk to 1037? Here he is. Be on your good behavior, now. He can set down, lady," seeing that Alexandra remained standing. "Push that white button when you're through with him, and I'll come."

The guard went out and Alexandra and Frank were left alone.

Alexandra tried not to see his hideous clothes. She tried to look straight into his face, which she could scarcely believe was his. It was already bleached to a chalky gray. His lips were color-less, his fine teeth looked yellowish. He glanced at Alexandra sullenly, blinked as if he had come from a dark place, and one eyebrow twitched continually. She felt at once that this interview was a terrible ordeal to him. His shaved head, showing the con-formation of his skull, gave him a criminal look which he had not had during the trial.

Alexandra held out her hand. "Frank," she said, her eyes fill-ing suddenly, "I hope you'll let me be friendly with you. I understand how you did it. I don't feel hard toward you. They were more to blame than you."

Frank jerked a dirty blue handkerchief from his trousers pocket. He had begun to cry. He turned away from Alexandra. "I never did mean to do not'ing to dat woman," he muttered. "I never mean to do not'ing to dat boy. I ain't had not'ing ag'in' dat boy. I always like dat boy fine. An' then I find him—" He stopped. The feeling went out of his face and eyes. He dropped into a chair and sat looking stolidly at the floor, his hands hanging loosely between his knees, the handkerchief lying across his striped leg. He seemed to have stirred up in his mind a disgust that had para-lyzed his faculties.

"I haven't come up here to blame you, Frank. I think they were more to blame than you." Alexandra, too, felt benumbed.

Frank looked up suddenly and stared out of the office window. "I guess dat place all go to hell what I work so hard on," he said with a slow, bitter smile. "I not care a damn." He stopped and rubbed the palm of his hand over the light bristles on his head with annoyance. "I no can t'ink without my hair," he complained. "I forget English. We not talk here, except swear."

Alexandra was bewildered. Frank seemed to have undergone a change of personality. There was scarcely anything by which she could recognize her handsome Bohemian neighbor. He seemed, somehow, not altogether human. She did not know what to say to him.

"You do not feel hard to me, Frank?" she asked at last.

Frank clenched his fist and broke out in excitement. "I not feel hard at no woman. I tell you I not that kind-a man. I never hit my wife. No, never I hurt her when she devil me something awful!" He struck his fist down on the warden's desk so hard that he afterward stroked it absently. A pale pink crept over his neck and face. "Two, t'ree years I know dat woman don' care no more 'bout me, Alexandra Bergson. I know she after some other man. I know her, oo-oo! An' I ain't never hurt her. I never would-a done dat, if I ain't had dat gun along. I don' know what in hell make me take dat gun. She always say I ain't no man to carry gun. If she been in dat house, where she ought-a been— But das a foolish talk."

Frank rubbed his head and stopped suddenly, as he had stopped before. Alexandra felt that there was something strange in the way he chilled off, as if something came up in him that extinguished his power of feeling or thinking.

"Yes, Frank," she said kindly. "I know you never meant to hurt Marie."

Frank smiled at her queerly. His eyes filled slowly with tears. "You know, I most forgit dat woman's name. She ain't got no name for me no more. I never hate my wife, but dat woman what make me do dat— Honest to God, but I hate her! I no man to fight. I don' want to kill no boy and no woman. I not care how many men she take under dat tree. I no care for not'ing but dat fine boy I kill, Alexandra Bergson. I guess I go crazy sure 'nough."

Alexandra remembered the little yellow cane she had found in Frank's clothes-closet. She thought of how he had come to this

country a gay young fellow, so attractive that the prettiest Bohemian girl in Omaha had run away with him. It seemed
unreasonable that life should have landed him in such a place as
this. She blamed Marie bitterly. And why, with her happy, affectionate nature, should she have brought destruction and sorrow
to all who had loved her, even to poor old Joe Tovesky, the uncle
who used to carry her about so proudly when she was a little girl?
That was the strangest thing of all. Was there, then, something
wrong in being warm-hearted and impulsive like that? Alexandra
hated to think so. But there was Emil, in the Norwegian graveyard at home, and here was Frank Shabata. Alexandra rose and
took him by the hand.

"Frank Shabata, I am never going to stop trying until I get you
pardoned. I'll never give the Governor any peace. I know I can get
you out of this place."

Frank looked at her distrustfully, but he gathered confidence
from her face. "Alexandra," he said earnestly, "if I git out-a here, I
not trouble dis country no more. I go back where I come from;
see my mother."

Alexandra tried to withdraw her hand, but Frank held on to
it nervously. He put out his finger and absently touched a button
on her black jacket. "Alexandra," he said in a low tone, looking steadily at the button, "you ain' t'ink I use dat girl awful
bad before—"

"No, Frank. We won't talk about that," Alexandra said, pressing his hand. "I can't help Emil now, so I'm going to do what I can
for you. You know I don't go away from home often, and I came
up here on purpose to tell you this."

The warden at the glass door looked in inquiringly. Alexandra
nodded, and he came in and touched the white button on his
desk. The guard appeared, and with a sinking heart Alexandra
saw Frank led away down the corridor. After a few words with
Mr. Schwartz, she left the prison and made her way to the street-
car. She had refused with horror the warden's cordial invitation to
"go through the institution." As the car lurched over its uneven

roadbed, back toward Lincoln, Alexandra thought of how she and Frank had been wrecked by the same storm and of how, although she could come out into the sunlight, she had not much more left in her life than he. She remembered some lines from a poem she had liked in her schooldays:—

> Henceforth the world will only be
> A wider prison-house to me,—

and sighed. A disgust of life weighed upon her heart; some such feeling as had twice frozen Frank Shabata's features while they talked together. She wished she were back on the Divide.

When Alexandra entered her hotel, the clerk held up one finger and beckoned to her. As she approached his desk, he handed her a telegram. Alexandra took the yellow envelope and looked at it in perplexity, then stepped into the elevator without opening it. As she walked down the corridor toward her room, she reflected that she was, in a manner, immune from evil tidings. On reaching her room she locked the door, and sitting down on a chair by the dresser, opened the telegram. It was from Hanover, and it read:—

> Arrived Hanover last night. Shall wait here until you come. Please hurry.
>
> CARL LINSTRUM.

Alexandra put her head down on the dresser and burst into tears.

III

The next afternoon Carl and Alexandra were walking across the fields from Mrs. Hiller's. Alexandra had left Lincoln after midnight, and Carl had met her at the Hanover station early in the morning. After they reached home, Alexandra had gone over to Mrs. Hiller's to leave a little present she had bought for her in the city. They stayed at the old lady's door but a moment, and then came out to spend the rest of the afternoon in the sunny fields.

Alexandra had taken off her black traveling-suit and put on a white dress; partly because she saw that her black clothes made Carl uncomfortable and partly because she felt oppressed by them herself. They seemed a little like the prison where she had worn them yesterday, and to be out of place in the open fields. Carl had changed very little. His cheeks were browner and fuller. He looked less like a tired scholar than when he went away a year ago, but no one, even now, would have taken him for a man of business. His soft, lustrous black eyes, his whimsical smile, would be less against him in the Klondike than on the Divide. There are always dreamers on the frontier.

Carl and Alexandra had been talking since morning. Her letter had never reached him. He had first learned of her misfortune from a San Francisco paper, four weeks old, which he had picked up in a saloon, and which contained a brief account of Frank Shabata's trial. When he put down the paper, he had already made up his mind that he could reach Alexandra as quickly as a letter could; and ever since he had been on the way; day and night, by the fastest boats and trains he could catch. His steamer had been held back two days by rough weather.

As they came out of Mrs. Hiller's garden they took up their talk again where they had left it.

"But could you come away like that, Carl, without arranging things? Could you just walk off and leave your business?" Alexandra asked.

Carl laughed. "Prudent Alexandra! You see, my dear, I happen to have an honest partner. I trust him with everything. In fact, it's been his enterprise from the beginning, you know. I'm in it only because he took me in. I'll have to go back in the spring. Perhaps you will want to go with me then. We haven't turned up millions yet, but we've got a start that's worth following. But this winter I'd like to spend with you. You won't feel that we ought to wait longer, on Emil's account, will you, Alexandra?"

Alexandra shook her head. "No, Carl; I don't feel that way about it. And surely you needn't mind anything Lou and Oscar say now. They are much angrier with me about Emil, now, than about you. They say it was all my fault. That I ruined him by sending him to college."

"No, I don't care a button for Lou or Oscar. The moment I knew you were in trouble, the moment I thought you might need me, it all looked different. You've always been a triumphant kind of person." Carl hesitated, looking sidewise at her strong, full figure. "But you do need me now, Alexandra?"

She put her hand on his arm. "I needed you terribly when it happened, Carl. I cried for you at night. Then everything seemed to get hard inside of me, and I thought perhaps I should never care for you again. But when I got your telegram yesterday, then—then it was just as it used to be. You are all I have in the world, you know."

Carl pressed her hand in silence. They were passing the Shabatas' empty house now, but they avoided the orchard path and took one that led over by the pasture pond.

"Can you understand it, Carl?" Alexandra murmured. "I have had nobody but Ivar and Signa to talk to. Do talk to me. Can you understand it? Could you have believed that of Marie Tovesky? I would have been cut to pieces, little by little, before I would have betrayed her trust in me!"

Carl looked at the shining spot of water before them. "Maybe she was cut to pieces, too, Alexandra. I am sure she tried hard; they both did. That was why Emil went to Mexico, of course. And he was going away again, you tell me, though he had only been home three weeks. You remember that Sunday when I went with Emil up to the French Church fair? I thought that day there was some kind of feeling, something unusual, between them. I meant to talk to you about it. But on my way back I met Lou and Oscar and got so angry that I forgot everything else. You mustn't be hard on them, Alexandra. Sit down here by the pond a minute. I want to tell you something."

They sat down on the grass-tufted bank and Carl told her how he had seen Emil and Marie out by the pond that morning, more than a year ago, and how young and charming and full of grace they had seemed to him. "It happens like that in the world some-times, Alexandra," he added earnestly. "I've seen it before. There are women who spread ruin around them through no fault of theirs, just by being too beautiful, too full of life and love. They can't help it. People come to them as people go to a warm fire in winter. I used to feel that in her when she was a little girl. Do you remember how all the Bohemians crowded round her in the store that day, when she gave Emil her candy? You remember those yel-low sparks in her eyes?"

Alexandra sighed. "Yes. People couldn't help loving her. Poor Frank does, even now, I think; though he's got himself in such a tangle that for a long time his love has been bitterer than his hate. But if you saw there was anything wrong, you ought to have told me, Carl."

Carl took her hand and smiled patiently. "My dear, it was something one felt in the air, as you feel the spring coming, or a storm in summer. I didn't *see* anything. Simply, when I was with those two young things, I felt my blood go quicker, I felt—how shall I say it?—an acceleration of life. After I got away, it was all too delicate, too intangible, to write about."

Alexandra looked at him mournfully. "I try to be more liberal about such things than I used to be. I try to realize that we are not all made alike. Only, why couldn't it have been Raoul Marcel, or Jan Smirka? Why did it have to be my boy?"

"Because he was the best there was, I suppose. They were both the best you had here."

The sun was dropping low in the west when the two friends rose and took the path again. The straw-stacks were throwing long shadows, the owls were flying home to the prairie-dog town. When they came to the corner where the pastures joined, Alexan-dra's twelve young colts were galloping in a drove over the brow of the hill.

"Carl," said Alexandra, "I should like to go up there with you in the spring. I haven't been on the water since we crossed the ocean, when I was a little girl. After we first came out here I used to dream sometimes about the shipyard where father worked, and a little sort of inlet, full of masts." Alexandra paused. After a moment's thought she said, "But you would never ask me to go away for good, would you?"

"Of course not, my dearest. I think I know how you feel about this country as well as you do yourself." Carl took her hand in both his own and pressed it tenderly.

"Yes, I still feel that way, though Emil is gone. When I was on the train this morning, and we got near Hanover, I felt something like I did when I drove back with Emil from the river that time, in the dry year. I was glad to come back to it. I've lived here a long time. There is great peace here, Carl, and freedom. . . . I thought when I came out of that prison, where poor Frank is, that I should never feel free again. But I do, here." Alexandra took a deep breath and looked off into the red west.

"You belong to the land," Carl murmured, "as you have always said. Now more than ever."

"Yes, now more than ever. You remember what you once said about the graveyard, and the old story writing itself over? Only it is we who write it, with the best we have."

They paused on the last ridge of the pasture overlooking the house and the windmill and the stables that marked the site of John Bergson's homestead. On every side the brown waves of the earth rolled away to meet the sky.

"Lou and Oscar can't see those things," said Alexandra suddenly. "Suppose I do will my land to their children, what difference will that make? The land belongs to the future, Carl; that's the way it seems to me. How many of the names on the county clerk's plat will be there in fifty years? I might as well try to will the sunset over there to my brother's children. We come and go, but the land is always here. And the people who love it and understand it are the people who own it—for a little while."

Carl looked at her wonderingly. She was still gazing into the west, and in her face there was that exalted serenity that sometimes came to her at moments of deep feeling. The level rays of the sinking sun shone in her clear eyes.

"Why are you thinking of such things now, Alexandra?"

"I had a dream before I went to Lincoln—But I will tell you about that afterward, after we are married. It will never come true, now, in the way I thought it might." She took Carl's arm and they walked toward the gate. "How many times we have walked this path together, Carl. How many times we will walk it again! Does it seem to you like coming back to your own place? Do you feel at peace with the world here? I think we shall be very happy. I haven't any fears. I think when friends marry, they are safe. We don't suffer like—those young ones." Alexandra ended with a sigh.

They had reached the gate. Before Carl opened it, he drew Alexandra to him and kissed her softly, on her lips and on her eyes.

She leaned heavily on his shoulder. "I am tired," she murmured. "I have been very lonely, Carl."

They went into the house together, leaving the Divide behind them, under the evening star. Fortunate country, that is one day to receive hearts like Alexandra's into its bosom, to give them out again in the yellow wheat, in the rustling corn, in the shining eyes of youth!

THE END

. . .

My Ántonia

INTRODUCTION

Last summer I happened to be crossing the plains of Iowa in a season of intense heat, and it was my good fortune to have for a traveling companion James Quayle Burden—Jim Burden, as we still call him in the West. He and I are old friends—we grew up together in the same Nebraska town—and we had much to say to each other. While the train flashed through never-ending miles of ripe wheat, by country towns and bright-flowered pastures and oak groves wilting in the sun, we sat in the observation car, where the woodwork was hot to the touch and red dust lay deep over everything. The dust and heat, the burning wind, reminded us of many things. We were talking about what it is like to spend one's childhood in little towns like these, buried in wheat and corn, under stimulating extremes of climate: burning summers when the world lies green and billowy beneath a brilliant sky, when one is fairly stifled in vegetation, in the color and smell of strong weeds and heavy harvests; blustery winters with little snow, when the whole country is stripped bare and gray as sheet-iron. We agreed that no one who had not grown up in a little prairie town could know anything about it. It was a kind of freemasonry, we said.

Although Jim Burden and I both live in New York, and are old friends, I do not see much of him there. He is legal counsel for one of the great Western railways, and is sometimes away from his New York office for weeks together. That is one reason why we do not often meet. Another is that I do not like his wife.

When Jim was still an obscure young lawyer, struggling to make his way in New York, his career was suddenly advanced by

a brilliant marriage. Genevieve Whitney was the only daughter of
a distinguished man. Her marriage with young Burden was the
subject of sharp comment at the time. It was said she had been
brutally jilted by her cousin, Rutland Whitney, and that she married this unknown man from the West out of bravado. She was a
restless, headstrong girl, even then, who liked to astonish her
friends. Later, when I knew her, she was always doing something
unexpected. She gave one of her town houses for a Suffrage head-
quarters, produced one of her own plays at the Princess Theater,
was arrested for picketing during a garment-makers' strike, etc. I
am never able to believe that she has much feeling for the causes
to which she lends her name and her fleeting interest. She is
handsome, energetic, executive, but to me she seems unimpres-
sionable and temperamentally incapable of enthusiasm. Her
husband's quiet tastes irritate her, I think, and she finds it worth
while to play the patroness to a group of young poets and painters
of advanced ideas and mediocre ability. She has her own fortune
and lives her own life. For some reason, she wishes to remain
Mrs. James Burden.

As for Jim, no disappointments have been severe enough to
chill his naturally romantic and ardent disposition. This disposition, though it often made him seem very funny when he was a
boy, has been one of the strongest elements in his success. He
loves with a personal passion the great country through which his
railway runs and branches. His faith in it and his knowledge of it
have played an important part in its development. He is always
able to raise capital for new enterprises in Wyoming or Montana,
and has helped young men out there to do remarkable things in
mines and timber and oil. If a young man with an idea can once
get Jim Burden's attention, can manage to accompany him when
he goes off into the wilds hunting for lost parks or exploring new
canyons, then the money which means action is usually forth-
coming. Jim is still able to lose himself in those big Western
dreams. Though he is over forty now, he meets new people and
new enterprises with the impulsiveness by which his boyhood

friends remember him. He never seems to me to grow older. His fresh color and sandy hair and quick-changing blue eyes are those of a young man, and his sympathetic, solicitous interest in women is as youthful as it is Western and American.

During that burning day when we were crossing Iowa, our talk kept returning to a central figure, a Bohemian girl whom we had known long ago and whom both of us admired. More than any other person we remembered, this girl seemed to mean to us the country, the conditions, the whole adventure of our childhood. To speak her name was to call up pictures of people and places, to set a quiet drama going in one's brain. I had lost sight of her altogether, but Jim had found her again after long years, had renewed a friendship that meant a great deal to him, and out of his busy life had set apart time enough to enjoy that friendship. His mind was full of her that day. He made me see her again, feel her presence, revived all my old affection for her.

"I can't see," he said impetuously, "why you have never written anything about Ántonia."

I told him I had always felt that other people—he himself, for one—knew her much better than I. I was ready, however, to make an agreement with him; I would set down on paper all that I remembered of Ántonia if he would do the same. We might, in this way, get a picture of her.

He rumpled his hair with a quick, excited gesture, which with him often announces a new determination, and I could see that my suggestion took hold of him. "Maybe I will, maybe I will!" he declared. He stared out of the window for a few moments, and when he turned to me again his eyes had the sudden clearness that comes from something the mind itself sees. "Of course," he said, "I should have to do it in a direct way, and say a great deal about myself. It's through myself that I knew and felt her, and I've had no practice in any other form of presentation."

I told him that how he knew her and felt her was exactly what I most wanted to know about Ántonia. He had had opportunities that I, as a little girl who watched her come and go, had not.

Months afterward Jim Burden arrived at my apartment one stormy winter afternoon, with a bulging legal portfolio sheltered under his fur overcoat. He brought it into the sitting-room with him and tapped it with some pride as he stood warming his hands.

"I finished it last night—the thing about Ántonia," he said. "Now, what about yours?"

I had to confess that mine had not gone beyond a few straggling notes.

"Notes? I didn't make any." He drank his tea all at once and put down the cup. "I didn't arrange or rearrange. I simply wrote down what of herself and myself and other people Ántonia's name recalls to me. I suppose it hasn't any form. It hasn't any title, either." He went into the next room, sat down at my desk and wrote on the pinkish face of the portfolio the word, "Ántonia." He frowned at this a moment, then prefixed another word, making it "My Ántonia." That seemed to satisfy him.

"Read it as soon as you can," he said, rising, "but don't let it influence your own story."

My own story was never written, but the following narrative is Jim's manuscript, substantially as he brought it to me.

BOOK I
THE SHIMERDAS

I

I first heard of Ántonia[1] on what seemed to me an interminable journey across the great midland plain of North America. I was ten years old then; I had lost both my father and mother within a year, and my Virginia relatives were sending me out to my grandparents, who lived in Nebraska. I traveled in the care of a mountain boy, Jake Marpole, one of the "hands" on my father's old farm under the Blue Ridge, who was now going West to work for my grandfather. Jake's experience of the world was not much wider than mine. He had never been in a railway train until the morning when we set out together to try our fortunes in a new world.

We went all the way in day-coaches, becoming more sticky and grimy with each stage of the journey. Jake bought everything the newsboys offered him: candy, oranges, brass collar buttons, a watch-charm, and for me a "Life of Jesse James," which I remember as one of the most satisfactory books I have ever read. Beyond Chicago we were under the protection of a friendly passenger conductor, who knew all about the country to which we were going and gave us a great deal of advice in exchange for our confidence. He seemed to us an experienced and worldly man who had been almost everywhere; in his conversation he threw out lightly the names of distant States and cities. He wore the rings and pins and badges of different fraternal orders to which he belonged. Even his cuff-buttons were engraved with hieroglyphics, and he was more inscribed than an Egyptian obelisk. Once

---

[1] The Bohemian name *Ántonia* is strongly accented on the first syllable, like the English name *Anthony,* and the *i* is, of course, given the sound of long *e*. The name is pronounced An´-ton-ee-ah.

when he sat down to chat, he told us that in the immigrant car ahead there was a family from "across the water" whose destination was the same as ours.

"They can't any of them speak English, except one little girl, and all she can say is 'We go Black Hawk, Nebraska.' She's not much older then you, twelve or thirteen, maybe, and she's as bright as a new dollar. Don't you want to go ahead and see her, Jimmy? She's got the pretty brown eyes, too!"

This last remark made me bashful, and I shook my head and settled down to "Jesse James." Jake nodded at me approvingly and said you were likely to get diseases from foreigners.

I do not remember crossing the Missouri River, or anything about the long day's journey through Nebraska. Probably by that time I had crossed so many rivers that I was dull to them. The only thing very noticeable about Nebraska was that it was still, all day long, Nebraska.

I had been sleeping, curled up in a red plush seat, for a long while when we reached Black Hawk. Jake roused me and took me by the hand. We stumbled down from the train to a wooden siding, where men were running about with lanterns. I couldn't see any town, or even distant lights; we were surrounded by utter darkness. The engine was panting heavily after its long run. In the red glow from the fire-box, a group of people stood huddled together on the platform, encumbered by bundles and boxes. I knew this must be the immigrant family the conductor had told us about. The woman wore a fringed shawl tied over her head, and she carried a little tin trunk in her arms, hugging it as if it were a baby. There was an old man, tall and stooped. Two half-grown boys and a girl stood holding oil-cloth bundles, and a little girl clung to her mother's skirts. Presently a man with a lantern approached them and began to talk, shouting and exclaiming. I pricked up my ears, for it was positively the first time I had ever heard a foreign tongue.

Another lantern came along. A bantering voice called out: "Hello, are you Mr. Burden's folks? If you are, it's me you're looking for. I'm Otto Fuchs. I'm Mr. Burden's hired man, and I'm to drive you out. Hello, Jimmy, ain't you scared to come so far west?"

I looked up with interest at the new face in the lantern light. He might have stepped out of the pages of "Jesse James." He wore a sombrero hat, with a wide leather band and a bright buckle, and the ends of his mustache were twisted up stiffly, like little horns. He looked lively and ferocious, I thought, and as if he had a history. A long scar ran across one cheek and drew the corner of his mouth up in a sinister curl. The top of his left ear was gone, and his skin was brown as an Indian's. Surely this was the face of a desperado. As he walked about the platform in his high-heeled boots, looking for our trunks, I saw that he was a rather slight man, quick and wiry, and light on his feet. He told us we had a long night drive ahead of us, and had better be on the hike. He led us to a hitching-bar where two farm wagons were tied, and I saw the foreign family crowding into one of them. The other was for us. Jake got on the front seat with Otto Fuchs, and I rode on the straw in the bottom of the wagon-box, covered up with a buffalo hide. The immigrants rumbled off into the empty darkness, and we followed them.

I tried to go to sleep, but the jolting made me bite my tongue, and I soon began to ache all over. When the straw settled down I had a hard bed. Cautiously I slipped from under the buffalo hide, got up on my knees and peered over the side of the wagon. There seemed to be nothing to see; no fences, no creeks or trees, no hills or fields. If there was a road, I could not make it out in the faint starlight. There was nothing but land: not a country at all, but the material out of which countries are made. No, there was nothing but land—slightly undulating, I knew, because often our wheels ground against the brake as we went down into a hollow and lurched up again on the other side. I had the feeling that the world was left behind, that we had got over the edge of it, and were outside man's jurisdiction. I had never before looked up at the sky when there was not a familiar mountain ridge against it. But this was the complete dome of heaven, all there was of it. I

did not believe that my dead father and mother were watching me
from up there; they would still be looking for me at the sheep-
fold down by the creek, or along the white road that led to the
mountain pastures. I had left even their spirits behind me. The
wagon jolted on, carrying me I knew not whither. I don't think I
was homesick. If we never arrived anywhere, it did not matter.
Between that earth and that sky I felt erased, blotted out. I did not
say my prayers that night: here, I felt, what would be would be.

II

I do not remember our arrival at my grandfather's farm sometime
before daybreak, after a drive of nearly twenty miles with heavy
work-horses. When I awoke, it was afternoon. I was lying in a little
room, scarcely larger than the bed that held me, and the window-
shade at my head was flapping softly in a warm wind. A tall
woman, with wrinkled brown skin and black hair, stood looking
down at me; I knew that she must be my grandmother. She had
been crying, I could see, but when I opened my eyes she smiled,
peered at me anxiously, and sat down on the foot of my bed.

"Had a good sleep, Jimmy?" she asked briskly. Then in a very
different tone she said, as if to herself, "My, how you do look like
your father!" I remembered that my father had been her little boy;
she must often have come to wake him like this when he over-
slept. "Here are your clean clothes," she went on, stroking my
coverlid with her brown hand as she talked. "But first you come
down to the kitchen with me, and have a nice warm bath behind
the stove. Bring your things; there's nobody about."

"Down to the kitchen" struck me as curious; it was always
"out in the kitchen" at home. I picked up my shoes and stockings
and followed her through the living-room and down a flight of
stairs into a basement. This basement was divided into a dining-
room at the right of the stairs and a kitchen at the left. Both
rooms were plastered and whitewashed—the plaster laid directly

upon the earth walls, as it used to be in dugouts. The floor was of hard cement. Up under the wooden ceiling there were little half-windows with white curtains, and pots of geraniums and wandering Jew in the deep sills. As I entered the kitchen I sniffed a pleasant smell of gingerbread baking. The stove was very large, with bright nickel trimmings, and behind it there was a long wooden bench against the wall, and a tin washtub, into which grandmother poured hot and cold water. When she brought the soap and towels, I told her that I was used to taking my bath without help.

"Can you do your ears, Jimmy? Are you sure? Well, now, I call you a right smart little boy."

It was pleasant there in the kitchen. The sun shone into my bath-water through the west half-window, and a big Maltese cat came up and rubbed himself against the tub, watching me curiously. While I scrubbed, my grandmother busied herself in the dining-room until I called anxiously, "Grandmother, I'm afraid the cakes are burning!" Then she came laughing, waving her apron before her as if she were shooing chickens.

She was a spare, tall woman, a little stooped, and she was apt to carry her head thrust forward in an attitude of attention, as if she were looking at something, or listening to something, far away. As I grew older, I came to believe that it was only because she was so often thinking of things that were far away. She was quick-footed and energetic in all her movements. Her voice was high and rather shrill, and she often spoke with an anxious inflection, for she was exceedingly desirous that everything should go with due order and decorum. Her laugh, too, was high, and perhaps a little strident, but there was a lively intelligence in it. She was then fifty-five years old, a strong woman, of unusual endurance.

After I was dressed I explored the long cellar next the kitchen. It was dug out under the wing of the house, was plastered and cemented, with a stairway and an outside door by which the men came and went. Under one of the windows there was a place for them to wash when they came in from work.

While my grandmother was busy about supper I settled myself on the wooden bench behind the stove and got acquainted with the cat—he caught not only rats and mice, but gophers, I was told. The patch of yellow sunlight on the floor traveled back toward the stairway, and grandmother and I talked about my journey, and about the arrival of the new Bohemian family; she said they were to be our nearest neighbors. We did not talk about the farm in Virginia, which had been her home for so many years. But after the men came in from the fields, and we were all seated at the supper-table, then she asked Jake about the old place and about our friends and neighbors there.

My grandfather said little. When he first came in he kissed me and spoke kindly to me, but he was not demonstrative. I felt at once his deliberateness and personal dignity, and was a little in awe of him. The thing one immediately noticed about him was his beautiful, crinkly, snow-white beard. I once heard a missionary say it was like the beard of an Arabian sheik. His bald crown only made it more impressive.

Grandfather's eyes were not at all like those of an old man; they were bright blue, and had a fresh, frosty sparkle. His teeth were white and regular—so sound that he had never been to a dentist in his life. He had a delicate skin, easily roughened by sun and wind. When he was a young man his hair and beard were red; his eyebrows were still coppery.

As we sat at the table Otto Fuchs and I kept stealing covert glances at each other. Grandmother had told me while she was getting supper that he was an Austrian who came to this country a young boy and had led an adventurous life in the Far West among mining-camps and cow outfits. His iron constitution was somewhat broken by mountain pneumonia, and he had drifted back to live in a milder country for a while. He had relatives in Bismarck, a German settlement to the north of us, but for a year now he had been working for grandfather.

The minute supper was over, Otto took me into the kitchen to whisper to me about a pony down in the barn that had been bought for me at a sale; he had been riding him to find out whether he had any bad tricks, but he was a "perfect gentleman," and his name was Dude. Fuchs told me everything I wanted to know: how he had lost his ear in a Wyoming blizzard when he was a stage-driver, and how to throw a lasso. He promised to rope a steer for me before sundown next day. He got out his "chaps" and silver spurs to show them to Jake and me, and his best cowboy boots, with tops stitched in bold design—roses, and true-lover's knots, and undraped female figures. These, he solemnly explained, were angels.

Before we went to bed Jake and Otto were called up to the living-room for prayers. Grandfather put on silver-rimmed spectacles and read several Psalms. His voice was so sympathetic and he read so interestingly that I wished he had chosen one of my favorite chapters in the Book of Kings. I was awed by his intonation of the word "Selah." *"He shall choose our inheritance for us, the excellency of Jacob whom He loved. Selah."* I had no idea what the word meant; perhaps he had not. But, as he uttered it, it became oracular, the most sacred of words.

Early the next morning, I ran out of doors to look about me. I had been told that ours was the only wooden house west of Black Hawk—until you came to the Norwegian settlement, where there were several. Our neighbors lived in sod houses and dugouts—comfortable, but not very roomy. Our white frame house, with a story and half-story above the basement, stood at the east end of what I might call the farmyard, with the windmill close by the kitchen door. From the windmill the ground sloped westward, down to the barns and granaries and pig-yards. This slope was trampled hard and bare, and washed out in winding gullies by the rain. Beyond the corncribs, at the bottom of the shallow draw, was a muddy little pond, with rusty willow bushes growing about it. The road from the post-office came directly by our door, crossed the farmyard, and curved round this little pond, beyond which it began to climb the gentle swell of unbroken prairie to the west. There, along the western sky-line, it skirted a great cornfield, much larger than any field I had ever seen. This cornfield, and the sorghum patch behind the barn, were the only broken land in sight. Everywhere, as far as the eye could reach, there was nothing but rough, shaggy, red grass, most of it as tall as I.

North of the house, inside the ploughed fire-breaks, grew a thick-set strip of box-elder trees, low and bushy, their leaves already turning yellow. This hedge was nearly a quarter of a mile long, but I had to look very hard to see it at all. The little trees were insignificant against the grass. It seemed as if the grass were about to run over them, and over the plum-patch behind the sod chicken-house.

As I looked about me I felt that the grass was the country, as the water is the sea. The red of the grass made all the great prairie the color of wine-stains, or of certain seaweeds when they are first washed up. And there was so much motion in it; the whole country seemed, somehow, to be running.

I had almost forgotten that I had a grandmother, when she came out, her sunbonnet on her head, a grain-sack in her hand, and asked me if I did not want to go to the garden with her to dig potatoes for dinner. The garden, curiously enough, was a quarter of a mile from the house, and the way to it led up a shallow draw past the cattle corral. Grandmother called my attention to a stout hickory cane, tipped with copper, which hung by a leather thong from her belt. This, she said, was her rattlesnake cane. I must never go to the garden without a heavy stick or a corn-knife; she had killed a good many rattlers on her way back and forth. A little girl who lived on the Black Hawk road was bitten on the ankle and had been sick all summer.

I can remember exactly how the country looked to me as I walked beside my grandmother along the faint wagon-tracks on that early September morning. Perhaps the glide of long railway travel was still with me, for more than anything else I felt motion in the landscape; in the fresh, easy-blowing morning wind, and in the earth itself, as if the shaggy grass were a sort of loose hide, and underneath it herds of wild buffalo were galloping, galloping . . .

Alone, I should never have found the garden—except, perhaps, for the big yellow pumpkins that lay about unprotected by their withering vines—and I felt very little interest in it when I got there. I wanted to walk straight on through the red grass and over the edge of the world, which could not be very far away. The light air about me told me that the world ended here: only the ground and sun and sky were left, and if one went a little farther there would be only sun and sky, and one would float off into them, like the tawny hawks which sailed over our heads making slow shadows on the grass. While grandmother took the pitchfork we found standing in one of the rows and dug potatoes, while I picked them up out of the soft brown earth and put them into the bag, I kept looking up at the hawks that were doing what I might so easily do.

When grandmother was ready to go, I said I would like to stay up there in the garden awhile.

She peered down at me from under her sunbonnet. "Aren't you afraid of snakes?"

"A little," I admitted, "but I'd like to stay anyhow."

"Well, if you see one, don't have anything to do with him. The big yellow and brown ones won't hurt you; they're bull-snakes and help to keep the gophers down. Don't be scared if you see anything look out of that hole in the bank over there. That's a badger hole. He's about as big as a big 'possum, and his face is striped, black and white. He takes a chicken once in a while, but I won't let the men harm him. In a new country a body feels friendly to the animals. I like to have him come out and watch me when I'm at work."

Grandmother swung the bag of potatoes over her shoulder and went down the path, leaning forward a little. The road followed the windings of the draw; when she came to the first bend she waved at me and disappeared. I was left alone with this new feeling of lightness and content.

I sat down in the middle of the garden, where snakes could scarcely approach unseen, and leaned my back against a warm

yellow pumpkin. There were some ground-cherry bushes growing along the furrows, full of fruit. I turned back the papery
triangular sheaths that protected the berries and ate a few. All
about me giant grasshoppers, twice as big as any I had ever seen,
were doing acrobatic feats among the dried vines. The gophers
scurried up and down the ploughed ground. There in the sheltered draw-bottom the wind did not blow very hard, but I could
hear it singing its humming tune up on the level, and I could see
the tall grasses wave. The earth was warm under me, and warm as
I crumbled it through my fingers. Queer little red bugs came out
and moved in slow squadrons around me. Their backs were
polished vermilion, with black spots. I kept as still as I could.
Nothing happened. I did not expect anything to happen. I was
something that lay under the sun and felt it, like the pumpkins,
and I did not want to be anything more. I was entirely happy.
Perhaps we feel like that when we die and become a part of something entire, whether it is sun and air, or goodness and
knowledge. At any rate, that is happiness; to be dissolved into
something complete and great. When it comes to one, it comes as
naturally as sleep.

III

On Sunday morning Otto Fuchs was to drive us over to make the
acquaintance of our new Bohemian neighbors. We were taking
them some provisions, as they had come to live on a wild place
where there was no garden or chicken-house, and very little broken land. Fuchs brought up a sack of potatoes and a piece of
cured pork from the cellar, and grandmother packed some loaves
of Saturday's bread, a jar of butter, and several pumpkin pies in
the straw of the wagon-box. We clambered up to the front seat
and jolted off past the little pond and along the road that climbed
to the big cornfield.

I could hardly wait to see what lay beyond that cornfield; but there was only red grass like ours, and nothing else, though from the high wagon-seat one could look off a long way. The road ran about like a wild thing, avoiding the deep draws, crossing them where they were wide and shallow. And all along it, wherever it looped or ran, the sunflowers grew; some of them were as big as little trees, with great rough leaves and many branches which bore dozens of blossoms. They made a gold ribbon across the prairie. Occasionally one of the horses would tear off with his teeth a plant full of blossoms, and walk along munching it, the flowers nodding in time to his bites as he ate down toward them.

The Bohemian family, grandmother told me as we drove along, had bought the homestead of a fellow-countryman, Peter Krajiek, and had paid him more than it was worth. Their agreement with him was made before they left the old country, through a cousin of his, who was also a relative of Mrs. Shimerda. The Shimerdas were the first Bohemian family to come to this part of the county. Krajiek was their only interpreter, and could tell them anything he chose. They could not speak enough English to ask for advice, or even to make their most pressing wants known. One son, Fuchs said, was well-grown, and strong enough to work the land; but the father was old and frail and knew nothing about farming. He was a weaver by trade; had been a skilled workman on tapestries and upholstery materials. He had brought his fiddle with him, which wouldn't be of much use here, though he used to pick up money by it at home.

"If they're nice people, I hate to think of them spending the winter in that cave of Krajiek's," said grandmother. "It's no better than a badger hole; no proper dugout at all. And I hear he's made them pay twenty dollars for his old cookstove that ain't worth ten."

"Yes'm," said Otto; "and he's sold 'em his oxen and his two bony old horses for the price of good work-teams. I'd have interfered about the horses—the old man can understand some German—if I'd 'a' thought it would do any good. But Bohemians has a natural distrust of Austrians."

Grandmother looked interested. "Now, why is that, Otto?"

Fuchs wrinkled his brow and nose. "Well, ma'm, it's politics. It would take me a long while to explain."

The land was growing rougher; I was told that we were approaching Squaw Creek, which cut up the west half of the Shimerdas' place and made the land of little value for farming. Soon we could see the broken, grassy clay cliffs which indicated the windings of the stream, and the glittering tops of the cottonwoods and ash trees that grew down in the ravine. Some of the cottonwoods had already turned, and the yellow leaves and shining white bark made them look like the gold and silver trees in fairy tales.

As we approached the Shimerdas' dwelling, I could still see nothing but rough red hillocks, and draws with shelving banks and long roots hanging out where the earth had crumbled away. Presently, against one of those banks, I saw a sort of shed, thatched with the same wine-colored grass that grew everywhere. Near it tilted a shattered windmill-frame, that had no wheel. We drove up to this skeleton to tie our horses, and then I saw a door and window sunk deep in the draw-bank. The door stood open, and a woman and a girl of fourteen ran out and looked up at us hopefully. A little girl trailed along behind them. The woman had on her head the same embroidered shawl with silk fringes that she wore when she had alighted from the train at Black Hawk. She was not old, but she was certainly not young. Her face was alert and lively, with a sharp chin and shrewd little eyes. She shook grandmother's hand energetically.

"Very glad, very glad!" she ejaculated. Immediately she pointed to the bank out of which she had emerged and said, "House no good, house no good!"

Grandmother nodded consolingly. "You'll get fixed up comfortable after while, Mrs. Shimerda; make good house."

My grandmother always spoke in a very loud tone to foreigners, as if they were deaf. She made Mrs. Shimerda understand the friendly intention of our visit, and the Bohemian woman handled the loaves of bread and even smelled them, and examined the pies with lively curiosity, exclaiming, "Much good, much thank!"—and again she wrung grandmother's hand.

The oldest son, Ambrož,—they called it Ambrosch,—came out of the cave and stood beside his mother. He was nineteen years old, short and broad-backed, with a close-cropped, flat head, and a wide, flat face. His hazel eyes were little and shrewd, like his mother's, but more sly and suspicious; they fairly snapped at the food. The family had been living on corncakes and sorghum molasses for three days.

The little girl was pretty, but Án-tonia—they accented the name thus, strongly, when they spoke to her—was still prettier. I remembered what the conductor had said about her eyes. They were big and warm and full of light, like the sun shining on brown pools in the wood. Her skin was brown, too, and in her cheeks she had a glow of rich, dark color. Her brown hair was curly and wild-looking. The little sister, whom they called Yulka (Julka), was fair, and seemed mild and obedient. While I stood awkwardly confronting the two girls, Krajiek came up from the barn to see what was going on. With him was another Shimerda son. Even from a distance one could see that there was something strange about this boy. As he approached us, he began to make uncouth noises, and held up his hands to show us his fingers, which were webbed to the first knuckle, like a duck's foot. When he saw me draw back, he began to crow delightedly, "Hoo, hoo-hoo, hoo-hoo!" like a rooster. His mother scowled and said sternly, "Marek!" then spoke rapidly to Krajiek in Bohemian.

"She wants me to tell you he won't hurt nobody, Mrs. Burden. He was born like that. The others are smart. Ambrosch, he make good farmer." He struck Ambrosch on the back, and the boy smiled knowingly.

At that moment the father came out of the hole in the bank. He wore no hat, and his thick, iron-gray hair was brushed straight back from his forehead. It was so long that it bushed out behind his ears, and made him look like the old portraits I remembered in Virginia. He was tall and slender, and his thin shoulders stooped.

He looked at us understandingly, then took grandmother's hand and bent over it. I noticed how white and well-shaped his own hands were. They looked calm, somehow, and skilled. His eyes were melancholy, and were set back deep under his brow. His face was ruggedly formed, but it looked like ashes—like something from which all the warmth and light had died out. Everything about this old man was in keeping with his dignified manner. He was neatly dressed. Under his coat he wore a knitted gray vest, and, instead of a collar, a silk scarf of a dark bronze-green, carefully crossed and held together by a red coral pin. While Krajiek was translating for Mr. Shimerda, Ántonia came up to me and held out her hand coaxingly. In a moment we were running up the steep drawside together, Yulka trotting after us.

When we reached the level and could see the gold tree-tops, I pointed toward them, and Ántonia laughed and squeezed my hand as if to tell me how glad she was I had come. We raced off toward Squaw Creek and did not stop until the ground itself stopped—fell away before us so abruptly that the next step would have been out into the tree-tops. We stood panting on the edge of the ravine, looking down at the trees and bushes that grew below us. The wind was so strong that I had to hold my hat on, and the girls' skirts were blown out before them. Ántonia seemed to like it; she held her little sister by the hand and chattered away in that language which seemed to me spoken so much more rapidly than mine. She looked at me, her eyes fairly blazing with things she could not say.

"Name? What name?" she asked, touching me on the shoulder. I told her my name, and she repeated it after me and made Yulka say it. She pointed into the gold cottonwood tree behind whose top we stood and said again, "What name?"

We sat down and made a nest in the long red grass. Yulka curled up like a baby rabbit and played with a grasshopper. Ántonia pointed up to the sky and questioned me with her glance. I gave her the word, but she was not satisfied and pointed to my eyes. I told her, and she repeated the word, making it sound like "ice." She pointed up to the sky, then to my eyes, then back to the sky, with movements so quick and impulsive that she distracted me, and I had no idea what she wanted. She got up on her knees and wrung her hands. She pointed to her own eyes and shook her head, then to mine and to the sky, nodding violently.

"Oh," I exclaimed, "blue; blue sky."

She clapped her hands and murmured, "Blue sky, blue eyes," as if it amused her. While we snuggled down there out of the wind she learned a score of words. She was quick, and very eager. We were so deep in the grass that we could see nothing but the blue sky over us and the gold tree in front of us. It was wonderfully pleasant. After Ántonia had said the new words over and over, she wanted to give me a little chased silver ring she wore on her middle finger. When she coaxed and insisted, I repulsed her quite sternly. I didn't want her ring, and I felt there was something reckless and extravagant about her wishing to give it away to a boy she had never seen before. No wonder Krajiek got the better of these people, if this was how they behaved.

While we were disputing about the ring, I heard a mournful voice calling, "Án-tonia, Án-tonia!" She sprang up like a hare. "*Tatinek, Tatinek!*" she shouted, and we ran to meet the old man who was coming toward us. Ántonia reached him first, took his hand and kissed it. When I came up, he touched my shoulder and looked searchingly down into my face for several seconds. I became somewhat embarrassed, for I was used to being taken for granted by my elders.

We went with Mr. Shimerda back to the dugout, where grandmother was waiting for me. Before I got into the wagon, he took a book out of his pocket, opened it, and showed me a page with two alphabets, one English and the other Bohemian. He placed this book in my grandmother's hands, looked at her entreatingly, and said with an earnestness which I shall never forget, "Te-e-ach, te-e-ach my Án-tonia!"

IV

On the afternoon of that same Sunday I took my first long ride on my pony, under Otto's direction. After that Dude and I went twice a week to the post-office, six miles east of us, and I saved the men a good deal of time by riding on errands to our neighbors. When we had to borrow anything, or to send about word that there would be preaching at the sod schoolhouse, I was always the messenger. Formerly Fuchs attended to such things after working hours.

All the years that have passed have not dimmed my memory of that first glorious autumn. The new country lay open before me: there were no fences in those days, and I could choose my own way over the grass uplands, trusting the pony to get me home again. Sometimes I followed the sunflower-bordered roads. Fuchs told me that the sunflowers were introduced into that country by the Mormons; that at the time of the persecution, when they left Missouri and struck out into the wilderness to find a place where they could worship God in their own way, the members of the first exploring party, crossing the plains to Utah, scattered sunflower seed as they went. The next summer, when the long trains of wagons came through with all the women and children, they had the sunflower trail to follow. I believe that botanists do not confirm Jake's story, but insist that the sunflower was native to those plains. Nevertheless, that legend has stuck in my mind, and sunflower-bordered roads always seem to me the roads to freedom.

I used to love to drift along the pale yellow cornfields, looking for the damp spots one sometimes found at their edges, where the smartweed soon turned a rich copper color and the narrow brown leaves hung curled like cocoons about the swollen joints of the stem. Sometimes I went south to visit our German neighbors and to admire their catalpa grove, or to see the big elm tree that grew up out of a deep crack in the earth and had a hawk's nest in its branches. Trees were so rare in that country, and they had to make such a hard fight to grow, that we used to feel anxious about them, and visit them as if they were persons. It must have been the scarcity of detail in that tawny landscape that made detail so precious.

Sometimes I rode north to the big prairie-dog town to watch the brown, earth-owls fly home in the late afternoon and go down to their nests underground with the dogs. Ántonia Shimerda liked to go with me, and we used to wonder a great deal about these birds of subterranean habit. We had to be on our guard there, for rattlesnakes were always lurking about. They came to pick up an easy living among the dogs and owls, which were quite defenseless against them; took possession of their comfortable houses and ate the eggs and puppies. We felt sorry for the owls. It was always mournful to see them come flying home at sunset and disappear under the earth. But, after all, we felt, winged things who would live like that must be rather degraded creatures. The dogtown was a long way from any pond or creek. Otto Fuchs said he had seen populous dog-towns in the desert where there was no surface water for fifty miles; he insisted that some of the holes must go down to water—nearly two hundred feet, hereabouts. Ántonia said she didn't believe it; that the dogs probably lapped up the dew in the early morning, like the rabbits.

Ántonia had opinions about everything, and she was soon able to make them known. Almost every day she came running across the prairie to have her reading lesson with me. Mrs. Shimerda grumbled, but realized it was important that one member of the family should learn English. When the lesson was over, we used to go up to the watermelon patch behind the garden. I split the melons with an old corn-knife, and we lifted out the hearts and ate them with the juice trickling through our fingers. The white Christmas melons we did not touch, but we watched them with curiosity. They were to be picked late, when the hard frosts had set in, and put away for winter use. After weeks on the ocean, the Shimerdas were famished for fruit. The two girls would wander for miles along the edge of the cornfields, hunting for ground-cherries.

Ántonia loved to help grandmother in the kitchen and to learn about cooking and housekeeping. She would stand beside her, watching her every movement. We were willing to believe that Mrs. Shimerda was a good housewife in her own country, but she managed poorly under new conditions: the conditions were bad enough, certainly!

I remember how horrified we were at the sour, ashy-gray bread she gave her family to eat. She mixed her dough, we discovered, in an old tin peck-measure that Krajiek had used about the barn. When she took the paste out to bake it, she left smears of dough sticking to the sides of the measure, put the measure on the shelf behind the stove, and let this residue ferment. The next time she made bread, she scraped this sour stuff down into the fresh dough to serve as yeast.

During those first months the Shimerdas never went to town. Krajiek encouraged them in the belief that in Black Hawk they would somehow be mysteriously separated from their money. They hated Krajiek, but they clung to him because he was the only human being with whom they could talk or from whom they could get information. He slept with the old man and the two boys in the dugout barn, along with the oxen. They kept him in their hole and fed him for the same reason that the prairie dogs and the brown owls housed the rattlesnakes—because they did not know how to get rid of him.

V

We knew that things were hard for our Bohemian neighbors, but the two girls were light-hearted and never complained. They were always ready to forget their troubles at home, and to run away with me over the prairie, scaring rabbits or starting up flocks of quail.

I remember Ántonia's excitement when she came into our kitchen one afternoon and announced: "My papa find friends up north, with Russian mans. Last night he take me for see, and I can understand very much talk. Nice mans, Mrs. Burden. One is fat and all the time laugh. Everybody laugh. The first time I see my papa laugh in this kawn-tree. Oh, very nice!"

I asked her if she meant the two Russians who lived up by the big dog-town. I had often been tempted to go to see them when I was riding in that direction, but one of them was a wild-looking fellow and I was a little afraid of him. Russia seemed to me more remote than any other country—farther away than China, almost as far as the North Pole. Of all the strange, uprooted people among the first settlers, those two men were the strangest and the most aloof. Their last names were unpronounceable, so they were called Pavel and Peter. They went about making signs to people, and until the Shimerdas came they had no friends. Krajiek could understand them a little, but he had cheated them in a trade, so they avoided him. Pavel, the tall one, was said to be an anarchist; since he had no means of imparting his opinions, probably his wild gesticulations and his generally excited and rebellious manner gave rise to this supposition. He must once have been a very strong man, but now his great frame, with big, knotty joints, had a wasted look, and the skin was drawn tight over his high cheekbones. His breathing was hoarse, and he always had a cough.

Peter, his companion, was a very different sort of fellow; short, bow-legged, and as fat as butter. He always seemed pleased when he met people on the road, smiled and took off his cap to every one, men as well as women. At a distance, on his wagon, he looked like an old man; his hair and beard were of such a pale flaxen color that they seemed white in the sun. They were as thick and curly as carded wool. His rosy face, with its snub nose, set in this fleece, was like a melon among its leaves. He was usually called "Curly Peter," or "Rooshian Peter."

The two Russians made good farmhands, and in summer they worked out together. I had heard our neighbors laughing when they told how Peter always had to go home at night to milk his cow. Other bachelor homesteaders used canned milk, to save trouble. Sometimes Peter came to church at the sod schoolhouse. It was there I first saw him, sitting on a low bench by the door, his

plush cap in his hands, his bare feet tucked apologetically under
the seat.

After Mr. Shimerda discovered the Russians, he went to see
them almost every evening, and sometimes took Ántonia with
him. She said they came from a part of Russia where the language
was not very different from Bohemian, and if I wanted to go to
their place, she could talk to them for me. One afternoon, before
the heavy frosts began, we rode up there together on my pony.

The Russians had a neat log house built on a grassy slope,
with a windlass well beside the door. As we rode up the draw we
skirted a big melon patch, and a garden where squashes and yellow cucumbers lay about on the sod. We found Peter out behind
his kitchen, bending over a washtub. He was working so hard
that he did not hear us coming. His whole body moved up and
down as he rubbed, and he was a funny sight from the rear, with
his shaggy head and bandy legs. When he straightened himself up
to greet us, drops of perspiration were rolling from his thick nose
down on to his curly beard. Peter dried his hands and seemed
glad to leave his washing. He took us down to see his chickens,
and his cow that was grazing on the hillside. He told Ántonia that
in his country only rich people had cows, but here any man could
have one who would take care of her. The milk was good for
Pavel, who was often sick, and he could make butter by beating
sour cream with a wooden spoon. Peter was very fond of his cow.
He patted her flanks and talked to her in Russian while he pulled
up her lariat pin and set it in a new place.

After he had shown us his garden, Peter trundled a load of
watermelons up the hill in his wheelbarrow. Pavel was not at
home. He was off somewhere helping to dig a well. The house I
thought very comfortable for two men who were "batching."
Besides the kitchen, there was a living-room, with a wide double
bed built against the wall, properly made up with blue gingham
sheets and pillows. There was a little storeroom, too, with a window, where they kept guns and saddles and tools, and old coats
and boots. That day the floor was covered with garden things,

drying for winter; corn and beans and fat yellow cucumbers. There were no screens or window-blinds in the house, and all the doors and windows stood wide open, letting in flies and sunshine alike.

Peter put the melons in a row on the oil-cloth-covered table and stood over them, brandishing a butcher knife. Before the blade got fairly into them, they split of their own ripeness, with a delicious sound. He gave us knives, but no plates, and the top of the table was soon swimming with juice and seeds. I had never seen any one eat so many melons as Peter ate. He assured us that they were good for one—better than medicine; in his country people lived on them at this time of year. He was very hospitable and jolly. Once, while he was looking at Ántonia, he sighed and told us that if he had stayed at home in Russia perhaps by this time he would have had a pretty daughter of his own to cook and keep house for him. He said he had left his country because of a "great trouble."

When we got up to go, Peter looked about in perplexity for something that would entertain us. He ran into the storeroom and brought out a gaudily painted harmonica, sat down on a bench, and spreading his fat legs apart began to play like a whole band. The tunes were either very lively or very doleful, and he sang words to some of them.

Before we left, Peter put ripe cucumbers into a sack for Mrs. Shimerda and gave us a lard-pail full of milk to cook them in. I had never heard of cooking cucumbers, but Ántonia assured me they were very good. We had to walk the pony all the way home to keep from spilling the milk.

VI

One afternoon we were having our reading lesson on the warm, grassy bank where the badger lived. It was a day of amber sunlight, but there was a shiver of coming winter in the air. I had seen ice on the little horse-pond that morning, and as we went through the garden we found the tall asparagus, with its red berries, lying on the ground, a mass of slimy green.

Tony was barefooted, and she shivered in her cotton dress and was comfortable only when we were tucked down on the baked earth, in the full blaze of the sun. She could talk to me about almost anything by this time. That afternoon she was telling me how highly esteemed our friend the badger was in her part of the world, and how men kept a special kind of dog, with very short legs, to hunt him. Those dogs, she said, went down into the hole after the badger and killed him there in a terrific struggle underground; you could hear the barks and yelps outside. Then the dog dragged himself back, covered with bites and scratches, to be rewarded and petted by his master. She knew a dog who had a star on his collar for every badger he had killed.

The rabbits were unusually spry that afternoon. They kept starting up all about us, and dashing off down the draw as if they were playing a game of some kind. But the little buzzing things that lived in the grass were all dead—all but one. While we were lying there against the warm bank, a little insect of the palest, frailest green hopped painfully out of the buffalo grass and tried to leap into a bunch of bluestem. He missed it, fell back, and sat with his head sunk between his long legs, his antennae quivering, as if he were waiting for something to come and finish him. Tony make a warm nest for him in her hands; talked to him gayly and indulgently in Bohemian. Presently he began to sing for us—a thin, rusty little chirp. She held him close to her ear and laughed, but a moment afterward I saw there were tears in her eyes. She told me that in her village at home there was an old beggar woman who went about selling herbs and roots she had dug up in the forest. If you took her in and gave her a warm place by the fire, she sang old songs to the children in a cracked voice, like this. Old Hata, she was called, and the children loved to see her coming and saved their cakes and sweets for her.

When the bank on the other side of the draw began to throw a narrow shelf of shadow, we knew we ought to be starting homeward; the chill came on quickly when the sun got low, and Ántonia's dress was thin. What were we to do with the frail little creature we had lured back to life by false pretenses? I offered my pockets, but Tony shook her head and carefully put the green insect in her hair, tying her big handkerchief down loosely over her curls. I said I would go with her until we could see Squaw Creek, and then turn and run home. We drifted along lazily, very happy, through the magical light of the late afternoon.

All those fall afternoons were the same, but I never got used to them. As far as we could see, the miles of copper-red grass were drenched in sunlight that was stronger and fiercer than at any other time of the day. The blond cornfields were red gold, the haystacks turned rosy and threw long shadows. The whole prairie was like the bush that burned with fire and was not consumed. That hour always had the exultation of victory, of triumphant ending, like a hero's death—heroes who died young and gloriously. It was a sudden transfiguration, a lifting-up of day.

How many an afternoon Ántonia and I have trailed along the prairie under that magnificence! And always two long black shadows flitted before us or followed after, dark spots on the ruddy grass.

We had been silent a long time, and the edge of the sun sank nearer and nearer the prairie floor, when we saw a figure moving on the edge of the upland, a gun over his shoulder. He was walking slowly, dragging his feet along as if he had no purpose. We broke into a run to overtake him.

"My papa sick all the time," Tony panted as we flew. "He not look good, Jim."

As we neared Mr. Shimerda she shouted, and he lifted his head and peered about. Tony ran up to him, caught his hand and pressed it against her cheek. She was the only one of his family who could rouse the old man from the torpor in which he seemed to live. He took the bag from his belt and showed us three rabbits he had shot, looked at Ántonia with a wintry flicker of a smile and began to tell her something. She turned to me.

"My *tatinek* make me little hat with the skins, little hat for win-ter!" she exclaimed joyfully. "Meat for eat, skin for hat,"— she told off these benefits on her fingers.

Her father put his hand on her hair, but she caught his wrist and lifted it carefully away, talking to him rapidly. I heard the name of old Hata. He untied the handkerchief, separated her hair with his fingers, and stood looking down at the green insect. When it began to chirp faintly, he listened as if it were a beautiful sound.

I picked up the gun he had dropped; a queer piece from the old country, short and heavy, with a stag's head on the cock. When he saw me examining it, he turned to me with his faraway look that always made me feel as if I were down at the bottom of a well. He spoke kindly and gravely, and Ántonia translated:—

"My *tatinek* say when you are big boy, he give you his gun. Very fine, from Bohemie. It was belong to a great man, very rich, like what you not got here; many fields, many forests, many big house. My papa play for his wedding, and he give my papa fine gun, and my papa give you."

I was glad that this project was one of futurity. There never were such people as the Shimerdas for wanting to give away everything they had. Even the mother was always offering me things, though I knew she expected substantial presents in return. We stood there in friendly silence, while the feeble minstrel sheltered in Ántonia's hair went on with its scratchy chirp. The old man's smile, as he listened, was so full of sadness, of pity for things, that I never afterward forgot it. As the sun sank there came a sudden coolness and the strong smell of earth and drying grass. Ántonia and her father went off hand in hand, and I buttoned up my jacket and raced my shadow home.

VII

Much as I liked Ántonia, I hated a superior tone that she some-times took with me. She was four years older than I, to be sure, and had seen more of the world; but I was a boy and she was a girl, and I resented her protecting manner. Before the autumn was over she began to treat me more like an equal and to defer to me in other things than reading lessons. This change came about from an adventure we had together.

One day when I rode over to the Shimerdas' I found Ántonia starting off on foot for Russian Peter's house, to borrow a spade Ambrosch needed. I offered to take her on the pony, and she got up behind me. There had been another black frost the night before, and the air was clear and heady as wine. Within a week all the blooming roads had been despoiled—hundreds of miles of yellow sunflowers had been transformed into brown, rattling, burry stalks.

We found Russian Peter digging his potatoes. We were glad to go in and get warm by his kitchen stove and to see his squashes and Christmas melons, heaped in the storeroom for winter. As we rode away with the spade, Ántonia suggested that we stop at the prairie-dog town and dig into one of the holes. We could find out whether they ran straight down, or were horizontal, like mole-holes; whether they had underground connections; whether the owls had nests down there, lined with feathers. We might get some puppies, or owl eggs, or snake-skins.

The dog-town was spread out over perhaps ten acres. The grass had been nibbled short and even, so this stretch was not shaggy and red like the surrounding country, but gray and velvety. The holes were several yards apart, and were disposed with a good deal of regularity, almost as if the town had been laid out in streets and avenues. One always felt that an orderly and very sociable kind of life was going on there. I picketed Dude down in a draw, and we went wandering about, looking for a hole that would be easy to dig. The dogs were out, as usual, dozens of them, sitting up on their hind legs over the doors of their houses. As we approached, they barked, shook their tails at us, and scurried underground. Before the mouths of the holes were little patches of sand and gravel, scratched up, we supposed, from a long way below the surface. Here and there, in the town, we came on larger gravel patches, several yards away from any hole. If the dogs had scratched the sand up in excavating, how had they carried it so far? It was on one of these gravel beds that I met my adventure.

We were examining a big hole with two entrances. The burrow sloped into the ground at a gentle angle, so that we could see where the two corridors united, and the floor was dusty from use, like a little highway over which much travel went. I was walking backward, in a crouching position, when I heard Ántonia scream. She was standing opposite me, pointing behind me and shouting something in Bohemian. I whirled round, and there, on one of those dry gravel beds, was the biggest snake I had ever seen. He was sunning himself, after the cold night, and he must have been asleep when Ántonia screamed. When I turned he was lying in long loose waves, like a letter "W." He twitched and began to coil slowly. He was not merely a big snake, I thought—he was a circus monstrosity. His abominable muscularity, his loathsome, fluid motion, somehow made me sick. He was as thick as my leg, and looked as if millstones couldn't crush the disgusting vitality out of him. He lifted his hideous little head, and rattled. I didn't run because I didn't think of it—if my back had been against a stone wall I couldn't have felt more cornered. I saw his coils tighten—now he would spring, spring his length, I remembered. I ran up and drove at his head with my spade, struck him fairly across the neck, and in a minute he was all about my feet in wavy loops. I struck now from hate. Ántonia, barefooted as she was, ran up behind me. Even after I had pounded his ugly head flat, his body kept on coiling and winding, doubling and falling back on itself. I walked away and turned my back. I felt seasick. Ántonia came after me, crying, "O Jimmy, he not bite you? You sure? Why you not run when I say?"

"What did you jabber Bohunk for? You might have told me there was a snake behind me!" I said petulantly.

"I know I am just awful, Jim, I was so scared." She took my handkerchief from my pocket and tried to wipe my face with it, but I snatched it away from her. I suppose I looked as sick as I felt.

"I never know you was so brave, Jim," she went on comfortingly. "You is just like big mans; you wait for him lift his head and then you go for him. Ain't you feel scared a bit? Now we take that snake home and show everybody. Nobody ain't seen in this kawn-tree so big snake like you kill."

She went on in this strain until I began to think that I had longed for this opportunity, and had hailed it with joy. Cautiously we went back to the snake; he was still groping with his tail, turning up his ugly belly in the light. A faint, fetid smell came from him, and a thread of green liquid oozed from his crushed head.

"Look, Tony, that's his poison," I said.

I took a long piece of string from my pocket, and she lifted his head with the spade while I tied a noose around it. We pulled him out straight and measured him by my riding-quirt; he was about five and a half feet long. He had twelve rattles, but they were broken off before they began to taper, so I insisted that he must once have had twenty-four. I explained to Ántonia how this meant that he was twenty-four years old, that he must have been there when white men first came, left on from buffalo and Indian times. As I turned him over I began to feel proud of him, to have a kind of respect for his age and size. He seemed like the ancient, eldest Evil. Certainly his kind have left horrible unconscious memories in all warm-blooded life. When we dragged him down into the draw, Dude sprang off to the end of his tether and shivered all over—wouldn't let us come near him.

We decided that Ántonia should ride Dude home, and I would walk. As she rode along slowly, her bare legs swinging against the pony's sides, she kept shouting back to me about how astonished everybody would be. I followed with the spade over my shoulder, dragging my snake. Her exultation was contagious. The great land had never looked to me so big and free. If the red grass were full of rattlers, I was equal to them all. Nevertheless, I stole furtive glances behind me now and then to see that no avenging mate, older and bigger than my quarry, was racing up from the rear.

The sun had set when we reached our garden and went down the draw toward the house. Otto Fuchs was the first one we met.

He was sitting on the edge of the cattle-pond, having a quiet pipe before supper. Ántonia called him to come quick and look. He did not say anything for a minute, but scratched his head and turned the snake over with his boot.

"Where did you run onto that beauty, Jim?"

"Up at the dog-town," I answered laconically.

"Kill him yourself? How come you to have a weepon?"

"We'd been up to Russian Peter's, to borrow a spade for Ambrosch."

Otto shook the ashes out of his pipe and squatted down to count the rattles. "It was just luck you had a tool," he said cautiously. "Gosh! I wouldn't want to do any business with that fellow myself, unless I had a fence-post along. Your grandmother's snake-cane wouldn't more than tickle him. He could stand right up and talk to you, he could. Did he fight hard?"

Ántonia broke in: "He fight something awful! He is all over Jimmy's boots. I scream for him to run, but he just hit and hit that snake like he was crazy."

Otto winked at me. After Ántonia rode on he said: "Got him in the head first crack, didn't you? That was just as well."

We hung him up to the windmill, and when I went down to the kitchen I found Ántonia standing in the middle of the floor, telling the story with a great deal of color.

Subsequent experiences with rattlesnakes taught me that my first encounter was fortunate in circumstance. My big rattler was old, and had led too easy a life; there was not much fight in him. He had probably lived there for years, with a fat prairie dog for breakfast whenever he felt like it, a sheltered home, even an owl-feather bed, perhaps, and he had forgot that the world doesn't owe rattlers a living. A snake of his size, in fighting trim, would be more than any boy could handle. So in reality it was a mock adventure; the game was fixed for me by chance, as it probably was for many a dragon-slayer. I had been adequately armed by Russian Peter; the snake was old and lazy; and I had Ántonia beside me, to appreciate and admire.

That snake hung on our corral fence for several days; some of the neighbors came to see it and agreed that it was the biggest rattler ever killed in those parts. This was enough for Ántonia. She liked me better from that time on, and she never took a supercilious air with me again. I had killed a big snake—I was now a big fellow.

VIII

While the autumn color was growing pale on the grass and cornfields, things went badly with our friends the Russians. Peter told his troubles to Mr. Shimerda: he was unable to meet a note which fell due on the first of November; had to pay an exorbitant bonus on renewing it, and to give a mortgage on his pigs and horses and even his milk cow. His creditor was Wick Cutter, the merciless Black Hawk money-lender, a man of evil name throughout the county, of whom I shall have more to say later. Peter could give no very clear account of his transactions with Cutter. He only knew that he had first borrowed two hundred dollars, then another hundred, then fifty—that each time a bonus was added to the principal, and the debt grew faster than any crop he planted. Now everything was plastered with mortgages.

Soon after Peter renewed his note, Pavel strained himself lifting timbers for a new barn, and fell over among the shavings with such a gush of blood from the lungs that his fellow-workmen thought he would die on the spot. They hauled him home and put him into his bed, and there he lay, very ill indeed. Misfortune seemed to settle like an evil bird on the roof of the log house, and to flap its wings there, warning human beings away. The Russians had such bad luck that people were afraid of them and liked to put them out of mind.

One afternoon Ántonia and her father came over to our house to get buttermilk, and lingered, as they usually did, until the sun was low. Just as they were leaving, Russian Peter drove up. Pavel was very bad, he said, and wanted to talk to Mr. Shimerda and his daughter; he had come to fetch them. When Ántonia and her father got into the wagon, I entreated grandmother to let me go with them: I would gladly go without my supper, I would sleep in the Shimerdas' barn and run home in the morning. My plan must have seemed very foolish to her, but she was often large-minded about humoring the desires of other people. She asked Peter to wait a moment, and when she came back from the kitchen she brought a bag of sandwiches and doughnuts for us.

Mr. Shimerda and Peter were on the front seat; Ántonia and I sat in the straw behind and ate our lunch as we bumped along. After the sun sank, a cold wind sprang up and moaned over the prairie. If this turn in the weather had come sooner, I should not have got away. We burrowed down in the straw and curled up close together, watching the angry red die out of the west and the stars begin to shine in the clear, windy sky. Peter kept sighing and groaning. Tony whispered to me that he was afraid Pavel would never get well. We lay still and did not talk. Up there the stars grew magnificently bright. Though we had come from such different parts of the world, in both of us there was some dusky superstition that those shining groups have their influence upon what is and what is not to be. Perhaps Russian Peter, come from farther away than any of us, had brought from his land, too, some such belief.

The little house on the hillside was so much the color of the night that we could not see it as we came up the draw. The ruddy windows guided us—the light from the kitchen stove, for there was no lamp burning.

We entered softly. The man in the wide bed seemed to be asleep. Tony and I sat down on the bench by the wall and leaned our arms on the table in front of us. The firelight flickered on the hewn logs that supported the thatch overhead. Pavel made a rasping sound when he breathed, and he kept moaning. We waited. The wind shook the doors and windows impatiently, then swept on again, singing through the big spaces. Each gust, as it bore down, rattled the panes, and swelled off like the others. They made me think of defeated armies, retreating; or of ghosts who were trying desperately to get in for shelter, and then went moaning on. Presently, in one of those sobbing intervals between the blasts, the coyotes tuned up with their whining howl; one, two, three, then all together—to tell us that winter was coming. This sound brought an answer from the bed,—a long complaining cry,—as if Pavel were having bad dreams or were waking to some old misery. Peter listened, but did not stir. He was sitting on the floor by the kitchen stove. The coyotes broke out again; yap, yap, yap—then the high whine. Pavel called for something and struggled up on his elbow.

"He is scared of the wolves," Ántonia whispered to me. "In his country there are very many, and they eat men and women." We slid closer together along the bench.

I could not take my eyes off the man in the bed. His shirt was hanging open, and his emaciated chest, covered with yellow bristle, rose and fell horribly. He began to cough. Peter shuffled to his feet, caught up the tea-kettle and mixed him some hot water and whiskey. The sharp smell of spirits went through the room.

Pavel snatched the cup and drank, then made Peter give him the bottle and slipped it under his pillow, grinning disagreeably, as if he had outwitted some one. His eyes followed Peter about the room with a contemptuous, unfriendly expression. It seemed to me that he despised him for being so simple and docile.

Presently Pavel began to talk to Mr. Shimerda, scarcely above a whisper. He was telling a long story, and as he went on, Ántonia took my hand under the table and held it tight. She leaned forward and strained her ears to hear him. He grew more and more excited, and kept pointing all around his bed, as if there were things there and he wanted Mr. Shimerda to see them.

"It's wolves, Jimmy," Ántonia whispered. "It's awful, what he ways!"

The sick man raged and shook his fist. He seemed to be cursing people who had wronged him. Mr. Shimerda caught him by

the shoulders, but could hardly hold him in bed. At last he was
shut off by a coughing fit which fairly choked him. He pulled a
cloth from under his pillow and held it to his mouth. Quickly it
was covered with bright red spots—I thought I had never seen
any blood so bright. When he lay down and turned his face to the
wall, all the rage had gone out of him. He lay patiently fighting for
breath, like a child with croup. Ántonia's father uncovered one of
his long bony legs and rubbed it rhythmically. From our bench
we could see what a hollow case his body was. His spine and
shoulder-blades stood out like bones under the hide of a dead
steer left in the fields. That sharp backbone must have hurt him
when he lay on it.

Gradually, relief came to all of us. Whatever it was, the worst
was over. Mr. Shimerda signed to us that Pavel was asleep. Without a word Peter got up and lit his lantern. He was going out to
get his team to drive us home. Mr. Shimerda went with him. We
sat and watched the long bowed back under the blue sheet,
scarcely daring to breathe.

On the way home, when we were lying in the straw, under the
jolting and rattling Ántonia told me as much of the story as she
could. What she did not tell me then, she told later; we talked of
nothing else for days afterward.

When Pavel and Peter were young men, living at home in
Russia, they were asked to be groomsmen for a friend who was to
marry the belle of another village. It was in the dead of winter and
the groom's party went over to the wedding in sledges. Peter and
Pavel drove in the groom's sledge, and six sledges followed with
all his relatives and friends.

After the ceremony at the church, the party went to a dinner
given by the parents of the bride. The dinner lasted all afternoon;
then it became a supper and continued far into the night. There
was much dancing and drinking. At midnight the parents of the
bride said good-bye to her and blessed her. The groom took her
up in his arms and carried her out to his sledge and tucked her

under the blankets. He sprang in beside her, and Pavel and Peter (our Pavel and Peter!) took the front seat. Pavel drove. The party set out with singing and the jingle of sleigh-bells, the groom's sledge going first. All the drivers were more or less the worse for merry-making, and the groom was absorbed in his bride.

The wolves were bad that winter, and every one knew it, yet when they heard the first wolf-cry, the drivers were not much alarmed. They had too much good food and drink inside them. The first howls were taken up and echoed and with quickening repetitions. The wolves were coming together. There was no moon, but the starlight was clear on the snow. A black drove came up over the hill behind the wedding party. The wolves ran like streaks of shadow; they looked no bigger than dogs, but there were hundreds of them.

Something happened to the hindmost sledge: the driver lost control,—he was probably very drunk,—the horses left the road, the sledge was caught in a clump of trees, and overturned. The occupants rolled out over the snow, and the fleetest of the wolves sprang upon them. The shrieks that followed made everybody sober. The drivers stood up and lashed their horses. The groom had the best team and his sledge was lightest—all the others carried from six to a dozen people.

Another driver lost control. The screams of the horses were more terrible to hear than the cries of the men and women. Nothing seemed to check the wolves. It was hard to tell what was happening in the rear; the people who were falling behind shrieked as piteously as those who were already lost. The little bride hid her face on the groom's shoulder and sobbed. Pavel sat still and watched his horses. The road was clear and white, and the groom's three blacks went like the wind. It was only necessary to be calm and to guide them carefully.

At length, as they breasted a long hill, Peter rose cautiously and looked back. "There are only three sledges left," he whispered.

"And the wolves?" Pavel asked.

"Enough! Enough for all of us."

Pavel reached the brow of the hill, but only two sledges followed him down the other side. In that moment on the hilltop, they saw behind them a whirling black group on the snow. Presently the groom screamed. He saw his father's sledge overturned, with his mother and sisters. He sprang up as if he meant to jump, but the girl shrieked and held him back. It was even then too late. The black ground-shadows were already crowding over the heap in the road, and one horse ran out across the fields, his harness hanging to him, wolves at his heels. But the groom's movement had given Pavel an idea.

They were within a few miles of their village now. The only sledge left out of six was not very far behind them, and Pavel's middle horse was failing. Beside a frozen pond something happened to the other sledge; Peter saw it plainly. Three big wolves got abreast of the horses, and the horses went crazy. They tried to jump over each other, got tangled up in the harness, and overturned the sledge.

When the shrieking behind them died away, Pavel realized that he was alone upon the familiar road. "They still come?" he asked Peter.

"Yes."

"How many?"

"Twenty, thirty—enough."

Now his middle horse was being almost dragged by the other two. Pavel gave Peter the reins and stepped carefully into the back of the sledge. He called to the groom that they must lighten—and pointed to the bride. The young man cursed him and held her tighter. Pavel tried to drag her away. In the struggle, the groom rose. Pavel knocked him over the side of the sledge and threw the girl after him. He said he never remembered exactly how he did it, or what happened afterward. Peter, crouching in the front seat, saw nothing. The first thing either of them noticed was a new sound that broke into the clear air, louder than they had ever heard it before—the bell of the monastery of their own village, ringing for early prayers.

Pavel and Peter drove into the village alone, and they had been alone ever since. They were run out of their village. Pavel's own mother would not look at him. They went away to strange towns, but when people learned where they came from, they were always asked if they knew the two men who had fed the bride to the wolves. Wherever they went, the story followed them. It took them five years to save money enough to come to America. They worked in Chicago, Des Moines, Fort Wayne, but they were always unfortunate. When Pavel's health grew so bad, they decided to try farming.

Pavel died a few days after he unburdened his mind to Mr. Shimerda, and was buried in the Norwegian graveyard. Peter sold off everything, and left the country—went to be cook in a railway construction camp where gangs of Russians were employed.

At his sale we bought Peter's wheelbarrow and some of his harness. During the auction he went about with his head down, and never lifted his eyes. He seemed not to care about anything. The Black Hawk money-lender who held mortgages on Peter's livestock was there, and he bought in the sale notes at about fifty cents on the dollar. Every one said Peter kissed the cow before she was led away by her new owner. I did not see him do it, but this I know: after all his furniture and his cook-stove and pots and pans had been hauled off by the purchasers, when his house was stripped and bare, he sat down on the floor with his clasp-knife and ate all the melons that he had put away for winter. When Mr. Shimerda and Krajiek drove up in their wagon to take Peter to the train, they found him with a dripping beard, surrounded by heaps of melon rinds.

The loss of his two friends had a depressing effect upon old Mr. Shimerda. When he was out hunting, he used to go into the empty log house and sit there, brooding. This cabin was his hermitage until the winter snows penned him in his cave. For Ántonia and me, the story of the wedding party was never at an end. We did not tell Pavel's secret to any one, but guarded it jealously—as if the wolves of the Ukraine had gathered that night long ago, and the wedding party been sacrificed, to give us a painful and peculiar pleasure. At night, before I went to sleep, I often found myself in a sledge drawn by three horses, dashing through a country that looked something like Nebraska and something like Virginia.

IX

The first snowfall came early in December. I remember how the world looked from our sitting-room window as I dressed behind the stove that morning: the low sky was like a sheet of metal; the blond cornfields had faded out into ghostliness at last; the little pond was frozen under its stiff willow bushes. Big white flakes were whirling over everything and disappearing in the red grass.

Beyond the pond, on the slope that climbed to the cornfield, there was, faintly marked in the grass, a great circle where the Indians used to ride. Jake and Otto were sure that when they galloped round that ring the Indians tortured prisoners, bound to a stake in the center; but grandfather thought they merely ran races or trained horses there. Whenever one looked at this slope against the setting sun, the circle showed like a pattern in the grass; and this morning, when the first light spray of snow lay over it, it came out with wonderful distinctness, like strokes of Chinese white on canvas. The old figure stirred me as it had never done before and seemed a good omen for the winter.

As soon as the snow had packed hard I began to drive about the country in a clumsy sleigh that Otto Fuchs made for me by fastening a wooden goods-box on bobs. Fuchs had been apprenticed to a cabinet-maker in the old country and was very handy with tools. He would have done a better job if I hadn't hurried him. My first trip was to the post-office, and the next day I went over to take Yulka and Ántonia for a sleigh-ride.

It was a bright, cold day. I piled straw and buffalo robes into the box, and took two hot bricks wrapped in old blankets. When

I got to the Shimerdas' I did not go up to the house, but sat in my sleigh at the bottom of the draw and called. Ántonia and Yulka came running out, wearing little rabbit-skin hats their father had made for them. They had heard about my sledge from Ambrosch and knew why I had come. They tumbled in beside me and we set off toward the north, along a road that happened to be broken.

The sky was brilliantly blue, and the sunlight on the glittering white stretches of prairie was almost blinding. As Ántonia said, the whole world was changed by the snow; we kept looking in vain for familiar landmarks. The deep arroyo through which Squaw Creek wound was now only a cleft between snowdrifts— very blue when one looked down into it. The tree-tops that had been gold all the autumn were dwarfed and twisted, as if they would never have any life in them again. The few little cedars, which were so dull and dingy before, now stood out a strong, dusky green. The wind had the burning taste of fresh snow; my throat and nostrils smarted as if some one had opened a harts-horn bottle. The cold stung, and at the same time delighted one. My horse's breath rose like steam, and whenever we stopped he smoked all over. The cornfields got back a little of their color under the dazzling light, and stood the palest possible gold in the sun and snow. All about us the snow was crusted in shallow ter-races, with tracings like ripple-marks at the edges, curly waves that were the actual impression of the stinging lash in the wind.

The girls had on cotton dresses under their shawls; they kept shivering beneath the buffalo robes and hugging each other for warmth. But they were so glad to get away from their ugly cave and their mother's scolding that they begged me to go on and on, as far as Russian Peter's house. The great fresh open, after the stu-pefying warmth indoors, made them behave like wild things. They laughed and shouted, and said they never wanted to go home again. Couldn't we settle down and live in Russian Peter's house, Yulka asked, and couldn't I go to town and buy things for us to keep house with?

All the way to Russian Peter's we were extravagantly happy, but when we turned back,—it must have been about four o'clock,—the east wind grew stronger and began to howl; the sun lost its heartening power and the sky became gray and somber. I took off my long woolen comforter and wound it around Yulka's throat. She got so cold that we made her hide her head under the buffalo robe. Ántonia and I sat erect, but I held the reins clumsily, and my eyes were blinded by the wind a good deal of the time. It was growing dark when we got to their house, but I refused to go in with them and get warm. I knew my hands would ache terribly if I went near a fire. Yulka forgot to give me back my comforter, and I had to drive home directly against the wind. The next day I came down with an attack of quinsy, which kept me in the house for nearly two weeks.

The basement kitchen seemed heavenly safe and warm in those days—like a tight little boat in a winter sea. The men were out in the fields all day, husking corn, and when they came in at noon, with long caps pulled down over their ears and their feet in red-lined overshoes, I used to think they were like Arctic explorers.

In the afternoons, when grandmother sat upstairs darning, or making husking-gloves, I read "The Swiss Family Robinson" aloud to her, and I felt that the Swiss family had no advantages over us in the way of an adventurous life. I was convinced that man's strongest antagonist is the cold. I admired the cheerful zest with which grandmother went about keeping us warm and comfortable and well-fed. She often reminded me, when she was preparing for the return of the hungry men, that this country was not like Virginia, and that here a cook had, as she said, "very little to do with." On Sundays she gave us as much chicken as we could eat, and on other days we had ham or bacon or sausage meat. She baked either pies or cake for us every day, unless, for a change, she made my favorite pudding, striped with currants and boiled in a bag.

Next to getting warm and keeping warm, dinner and supper were the most interesting things we had to think about. Our lives centered around warmth and food and the return of the men at nightfall. I used to wonder, when they came in tired from the fields, their feet numb and their hands cracked and sore, how they could do all the chores so conscientiously: feed and water and bed the horses, milk the cows, and look after the pigs. When supper was over, it took them a long while to get the cold out of their bones. While grandmother and I washed the dishes and grandfather read his paper upstairs, Jake and Otto sat on the long bench behind the stove, "easing" their inside boots, or rubbing mutton tallow into their cracked hands.

Every Saturday night we popped corn or made taffy, and Otto Fuchs used to sing, "For I Am a Cowboy and Know I've Done Wrong," or, "Bury Me Not on the Lone Prairee." He had a good baritone voice and always led the singing when we went to church services at the sod schoolhouse.

I can still see those two men sitting on the bench; Otto's close-clipped head and Jake's shaggy hair slicked flat in front by a wet comb. I can see the sag of their tired shoulders against the white-washed wall. What good fellows they were, how much they knew, and how many things they had kept faith with!

Fuchs had been a cowboy, a stage-driver, a bar-tender, a miner; had wandered all over that great Western country and done hard work everywhere, though, as grandmother said, he had nothing to show for it. Jake was duller than Otto. He could scarcely read, wrote even his name with difficulty, and he had a violent temper which sometimes made him behave like a crazy man—tore him all to pieces and actually made him ill. But he was so soft-hearted that any one could impose upon him. If he, as he said, "forgot himself" and swore before grandmother, he went about depressed and shamefaced all day. They were both of them jovial about the cold in winter and the heat in summer, always ready to work overtime and to meet emergencies. It was a matter of pride with them not to spare themselves. Yet they were the sort of men who never get on, somehow, or do anything but work hard for a dollar or two a day.

On those bitter, starlit nights, as we sat around the old stove that fed us and warmed us and kept us cheerful, we could hear the coyotes howling down by the corrals, and their hungry, wintry cry used to remind the boys of wonderful animal stories; about gray wolves and bears in the Rockies, wildcats and panthers in the Virginia mountains. Sometimes Fuchs could be persuaded to talk about the outlaws and desperate characters he had known. I remember one funny story about himself that made grandmother, who was working her bread on the bread-board, laugh until she wiped her eyes with her bare arm, her hands being floury. It was like this:—

When Otto left Austria to come to America, he was asked by one of his relatives to look after a woman who was crossing on the same boat, to join her husband in Chicago. The woman started off with two children, but it was clear that her family might grow larger on the journey. Fuchs said he "got on fine with the kids," and liked the mother, though she played a sorry trick on him. In mid-ocean she proceeded to have not one baby, but three! This event made Fuchs the object of undeserved notoriety, since he was traveling with her. The steerage stewardess was indignant with him, the doctor regarded him with suspicion. The first-cabin passengers, who made up a purse for the woman, took an embarrassing interest in Otto, and often inquired of him about his charge. When the triplets were taken ashore at New York, he had, as he said, "to carry some of them." The trip to Chicago was even worse than the ocean voyage. On the train it was very difficult to get milk for the babies and to keep their bottles clean. The mother did her best, but no woman, out of her natural resources, could feed three babies. The husband, in Chicago, was working in a furniture factory for modest wages, and when he met his family at the station he was rather crushed by the size of it. He, too, seemed to consider Fuchs in some fashion to blame. "I was sure glad," Otto concluded, "that he didn't take his hard feeling out on that poor woman; but he had a sullen eye for me, all right! Now, did you ever hear of a young feller's having such hard luck, Mrs. Burden?"

Grandmother told him she was sure the Lord had remembered these things to his credit, and had helped him out of many a scrape when he didn't realize that he was being protected by Providence.

X

For several weeks after my sleigh-ride, we heard nothing from the Shimerdas. My sore throat kept me indoors, and grandmother had a cold which made the housework heavy for her. When Sunday came she was glad to have a day of rest. One night at supper Fuchs told us he had seen Mr. Shimerda out hunting.

"He's made himself a rabbit-skin cap, Jim, and a rabbit-skin collar that he buttons on outside his coat. They ain't got but one overcoat among 'em over there, and they take turns wearing it. They seem awful scared of cold, and stick in that hole in the bank like badgers."

"All but the crazy boy," Jake put in. "He never wears the coat. Krajiek says he's terrible strong and can stand anything. I guess rabbits must be getting scarce in this locality. Ambrosch come along by the cornfield yesterday where I was at work and showed me three prairie dogs he'd shot. He asked me if they was good to eat. I spit and made a face and took on, to scare him, but he just looked like he was smarter'n me and put 'em back in his sack and walked off."

Grandmother looked up in alarm and spoke to grandfather. "Josiah, you don't suppose Krajiek would let them poor creatures eat prairie dogs, do you?"

"You had better go over and see our neighbors to-morrow, Emmaline," he replied gravely.

Fuchs put in a cheerful word and said prairie dogs were clean beasts and ought to be good for food, but their family connections were against them. I asked what he meant, and he grinned and said they belonged to the rat family.

When I went downstairs in the morning, I found grandmother and Jake packing a hamper basket in the kitchen.

"Now, Jake," grandmother was saying, "if you can find that old rooster that got his comb froze, just give his neck a twist, and we'll take him along. There's no good reason why Mrs. Shimerda couldn't have got hens from her neighbors last fall and had a hen-house going by now. I reckon she was confused and didn't know where to begin. I've come strange to a new country myself, but I never forgot hens are a good thing to have, no matter what you don't have."

"Just as you say, mam," said Jake, "but I hate to think of Krajiek getting a leg of that old rooster." He tramped out through the long cellar and dropped the heavy door behind him.

After breakfast grandmother and Jake and I bundled ourselves up and climbed into the cold front wagon-seat. As we approached the Shimerdas' we heard the frosty whine of the pump and saw Ántonia, her head tied up and her cotton dress blown about her, throwing all her weight on the pump-handle as it went up and down. She heard our wagon, looked back over her shoulder, and catching up her pail of water, started at a run for the hole in the bank.

Jake helped grandmother to the ground, saying he would bring the provisions after he had blanketed his horses. We went slowly up the icy path toward the door sunk in the drawside. Blue puffs of smoke came from the stovepipe that stuck out through the grass and snow, but the wind whisked them roughly away.

Mrs. Shimerda opened the door before we knocked and seized grandmother's hand. She did not say "How do!" as usual, but at once began to cry, talking very fast in her own language, pointing to her feet which were tied up in rags, and looking about accusingly at every one.

The old man was sitting on a stump behind the stove, crouching over as if he were trying to hide from us. Yulka was on the floor at his feet, her kitten in her lap. She peeped out at me and smiled, but, glancing up at her mother, hid again. Ántonia was washing pans and dishes in a dark corner. The crazy boy lay under the only window, stretched on a gunnysack stuffed with straw. As soon as we entered he threw a grainsack over the crack at the bottom of the door. The air in the cave was stifling, and it was very dark, too. A lighted lantern, hung over the stove, threw out a feeble yellow glimmer.

Mrs. Shimerda snatched off the covers of two barrels behind the door, and made us look into them. In one there were some potatoes that had been frozen and were rotting, in the other was a little pile of flour. Grandmother murmured something in embarrassment, but the Bohemian woman laughed scornfully, a kind of whinny-laugh, and catching up an empty coffee-pot from the shelf, shook it at us with a look positively vindictive.

Grandmother went on talking in her polite Virginia way, not admitting their stark need or her own remissness, until Jake arrived with the hamper, as if in direct answer to Mrs. Shimerda's reproaches. Then the poor woman broke down. She dropped on the floor beside her crazy son, hid her face on her knees, and sat crying bitterly. Grandmother paid no heed to her, but called Ántonia to come and help empty the basket. Tony left her corner reluctantly. I had never seen her crushed like this before.

"You not mind my poor *mamenka*, Mrs. Burden. She is so sad," she whispered, as she wiped her wet hands on her skirt and took the things grandmother handed her.

The crazy boy, seeing the food, began to make soft, gurgling noises and stroked his stomach. Jake came in again, this time with a sack of potatoes. Grandmother looked about in perplexity.

"Haven't you got any sort of cave or cellar outside, Ántonia? This is no place to keep vegetables. How did your potatoes get frozen?"

"We get from Mr. Bushy, at the post-office,—what he throw out. We got no potatoes, Mrs. Burden," Tony admitted mournfully.

When Jake went out, Marek crawled along the floor and stuffed up the door-crack again. Then, quietly as a shadow, Mr. Shimerda came out from behind the stove. He stood brushing his hand over his smooth gray hair, as if he were trying to clear away a fog about his head. He was clean and neat as usual, with his green neckcloth and his coral pin. He took grandmother's arm and led her behind the stove, to the back of the room. In the rear wall was another little cave; a round hole, not much bigger than an oil barrel, scooped out in the black earth. When I got up on one of the stools and peered into it, I saw some quilts and a pile of straw. The old man held the lantern. "Yulka," he said in a low, despairing voice, "Yulka; my Ántonia!"

Grandmother drew back. "You mean they sleep in there,— your girls?" He bowed his head.

Tony slipped under his arm. "It is very cold on the floor, and this is warm like the badger hole. I like for sleep there," she insisted eagerly. "My *mamenka* have nice bed, with pillows from our own geese in Bohemie. See, Jim?" She pointed to the narrow bunk which Krajiek had built against the wall for himself before the Shimerdas came.

Grandmother sighed. "Sure enough, where *would* you sleep, dear! I don't doubt you're warm there. You'll have a better house after while, Ántonia, and then you'll forget these hard times."

Mr. Shimerda made grandmother sit down on the only chair and pointed his wife to a stool beside her. Standing before them with his hand on Ántonia's shoulder, he talked in a low tone, and his daughter translated. He wanted us to know that they were not beggars in the old country; he made good wages, and his family were respected there. He left Bohemia with more than a thousand dollars in savings, after their passage money was paid. He had in some way lost on exchange in New York, and the railway fare to Nebraska was more than they had expected. By the time they paid Krajiek for the land, and bought his horses and oxen and some old farm machinery, they had very little money left. He wished grandmother to know, however, that he still had some money. If they could get through until spring came, they would buy a cow and chickens and plant a garden, and would then do very well. Ambrosch and Ántonia were both old enough to work in the fields, and they were willing to work. But the snow and the bitter weather had disheartened them all.

Ántonia explained that her father meant to build a new house for them in the spring; he and Ambrosch had already split the logs for it, but the logs were all buried in the snow, along the creek where they had been felled.

While grandmother encouraged and gave them advice, I sat down on the floor with Yulka and let her show me her kitten. Marek slid cautiously toward us and began to exhibit his webbed fingers. I knew he wanted to make his queer noises for me—to bark like a dog or whinny like a horse,—but he did not dare in the presence of his elders. Marek was always trying to be agreeable, poor fellow, as if he had it on his mind that he must make up for his deficiencies.

Mrs. Shimerda grew more calm and reasonable before our visit was over, and, while Ántonia translated, put in a word now and then on her own account. The woman had a quick ear, and caught up phrases whenever she heard English spoken. As we rose to go, she opened her wooden chest and brought out a bag made of bed-ticking, about as long as a flour sack and half as wide, stuffed full of something. At sight of it, the crazy boy began to smack his lips. When Mrs. Shimerda opened the bag and stirred the contents with her hand, it gave out a salty, earthy smell, very pungent, even among the other odors of that cave. She measured a teacup full, tied it up in a bit of sacking, and presented it ceremoniously to grandmother.

"For cook," she announced. "Little now; be very much when cook," spreading out her hands as if to indicate that the pint would swell to a gallon. "Very good. You no have in this country. All things for eat better in my country."

"Maybe so, Mrs. Shimerda," grandmother said drily. "I can't say but I prefer our bread to yours, myself."

Ántonia undertook to explain. "This very good, Mrs. Burden,"—she clasped her hands as if she could not express how good,—"it make very much when you cook, like what my

mama say. Cook with rabbit, cook with chicken, in the gravy,—
oh, so good!"

All the way home grandmother and Jake talked about how
easily good Christian people could forget they were their brothers'
keepers.

"I will say, Jake, some of our brothers and sisters are hard to
keep. Where's a body to begin, with these people? They're wanting in everything, and most of all in horse-sense. Nobody can give
'em that, I guess. Jimmy, here, is about as able to take over a
homestead as they are. Do you reckon that boy Ambrosch has any
real push in him?"

"He's a worker, all right, mam, and he's got some ketch-on
about him; but he's a mean one. Folks can be mean enough to get
on in this world; and then, ag'in, they can be too mean."

That night, while grandmother was getting supper, we opened
the package Mrs. Shimerda had given her. It was full of little
brown chips that looked like the shavings of some root. They
were as light as feathers, and the most noticeable thing about
them was their penetrating, earthy odor. We could not determine
whether they were animal or vegetable.

"They might be dried meat from some queer beast, Jim. They
ain't dried fish, and they never grew on stalk or vine. I'm afraid of
'em. Anyhow, I shouldn't want to eat anything that had been shut
up for months with old clothes and goose pillows."

She threw the package into the stove, but I bit off a corner of
one of the chips I held in my hand, and chewed it tentatively.
I never forgot the strange taste; though it was many years before I
knew that those little brown shavings, which the Shimerdas
had brought so far and treasured so jealously, were dried mush-
rooms. They had been gathered, probably, in some deep
Bohemian forest . . . .

XI

During the week before Christmas, Jake was the most important person of our household, for he was to go to town and do all our Christmas shopping. But on the 21st of December, the snow began to fall. The flakes came down so thickly that from the sitting-room windows I could not see beyond the windmill—its frame looked dim and gray, unsubstantial like a shadow. The snow did not stop falling all day, or during the night that followed. The cold was not severe, but the storm was quiet and resistless. The men could not go farther than the barns and corral. They sat about the house most of the day as if it were Sunday; greasing their boots, mending their suspenders, plaiting whiplashes.

On the morning of the 22nd, grandfather announced at breakfast that it would be impossible to go to Black Hawk for Christmas purchases. Jake was sure he could get through on horseback, and bring home our things in saddle-bags; but grandfather told him the roads would be obliterated, and a newcomer in the country would be lost ten times over. Anyway, he would never allow one of his horses to be put to such a strain.

We decided to have a country Christmas, without any help from town. I had wanted to get some picture-books for Yulka and Ántonia; even Yulka was able to read a little now. Grandmother took me into the ice-cold storeroom, where she had some bolts of gingham and sheeting. She cut squares of cotton cloth and we sewed them together into a book. We bound it between pasteboards, which I covered with brilliant calico, representing scenes from a circus. For two days I sat at the dining-room table, pasting this book full of pictures for Yulka. We had files of those good old family magazines which used to publish colored lithographs of popular paintings, and I was allowed to use some of these. I took "Napoleon Announcing the Divorce to Josephine" for my frontispiece. On the white pages I grouped Sunday-School cards and advertising cards which I had brought from my "old country." Fuchs got out the old candle-moulds and made tallow candles. Grandmother hunted up her fancy cake-cutters and baked gingerbread men and roosters, which we decorated with burnt sugar and red cinnamon drops.

On the day before Christmas, Jake packed the things we were sending to the Shimerdas in his saddle-bags and set off on grandfather's gray gelding. When he mounted his horse at the door, I saw that he had a hatchet slung to his belt, and he gave grandmother a meaning look which told me he was planning a surprise for me. That afternoon I watched long and eagerly from the sitting-room window. At last I saw a dark spot moving on the west hill, beside the half-buried cornfield, where the sky was taking on a coppery flush from the sun that did not quite break through. I put on my cap and ran out to meet Jake. When I got to the pond I could see that he was bringing in a little cedar tree across his pommel. He used to help my father cut Christmas trees for me in Virginia, and he had not forgotten how much I liked them.

By the time we had placed the cold, fresh-smelling little tree in a corner of the sitting-room, it was already Christmas Eve. After supper we all gathered there, and even grandfather, reading his paper by the table, looked up with friendly interest now and then. The cedar was about five feet high and very shapely. We hung it with the gingerbread animals, strings of popcorn, and bits of candle which Fuchs had fitted into pasteboard sockets. Its real splendors, however, came from the most unlikely place in the world—from Otto's cowboy trunk. I had never seen anything in that trunk but old boots and spurs and pistols, and a fascinating mixture of yellow leather thongs, cartridges, and shoemaker's wax. From under the lining he now produced a collection of brilliantly colored paper figures, several inches high and stiff enough to stand alone. They had been sent to him year after year, by his old mother in Austria. There was a bleeding heart, in tufts of paper lace; there were the three kings, gorgeously appareled, and the ox and the ass and the shepherds; there was the Baby in the manger, and a group of angels, singing; there were camels and leopards, held by the black slaves of the three kings. Our tree became the talking tree of the fairy tale; legends and stories

nestled like birds in its branches. Grandmother said it reminded
her of the Tree of Knowledge. We put sheets of cotton wool under
it for a snow-field, and Jake's pocket-mirror for a frozen lake.

I can see them now, exactly as they looked, working about the
table in the lamplight: Jake with his heavy features, so rudely
moulded that his face seemed, somehow, unfinished; Otto with his
half-ear and the savage scar that made his upper lip curl so fero-
ciously under his twisted mustache. As I remember them, what
unprotected faces they were; their very roughness and violence
made them defenseless. These boys had no practiced manner
behind which they could retreat and hold people at a distance.
They had only their hard fists to batter at the world with. Otto was
already one of those drifting, case-hardened laborers who never
marry or have children of their own. Yet he was so fond of children!

XII

On Christmas morning, when I got down to the kitchen, the men
were just coming in from their morning chores—the horses and
pigs always had their breakfast before we did. Jake and Otto
shouted "Merry Christmas"! to me, and winked at each other
when they saw the waffle-irons on the stove. Grandfather came
down, wearing a white shirt and his Sunday coat. Morning
prayers were longer than usual. He read the chapters from
St. Matthew about the birth of Christ, and as we listened it all
seemed like something that had happened lately, and near at
hand. In his prayer he thanked the Lord for the first Christmas,
and for all that it had meant to the world ever since. He gave
thanks for our food and comfort, and prayed for the poor and
destitute in great cities, where the struggle for life was harder than
it was here with us. Grandfather's prayers were often very interesting. He had the gift of simple and moving expression. Because
he talked so little, his words had a peculiar force; they were not
worn dull from constant use. His prayers reflected what he was

thinking about at the time, and it was chiefly through them that we got to know his feelings and his views about things.

After we sat down to our waffles and sausage, Jake told us how pleased the Shimerdas had been with their presents; even Ambrosch was friendly and went to the creek with him to cut the Christmas tree. It was a soft gray day outside, with heavy clouds working across the sky, and occasional squalls of snow. There were always odd jobs to be done about the barn on holidays, and the men were busy until afternoon. Then Jake and I played dominoes, while Otto wrote a long letter home to his mother. He always wrote to her on Christmas Day, he said, no matter where he was, and no matter how long it had been since his last letter. All afternoon he sat in the dining-room. He would write for a while, then sit idle, his clenched fist lying on the table, his eyes following the pattern of the oilcloth. He spoke and wrote his own language so seldom that it came to him awkwardly. His effort to remember entirely absorbed him.

At about four o'clock a visitor appeared: Mr. Shimerda, wearing his rabbit-skin cap and collar, and new mittens his wife had knitted. He had come to thank us for the presents, and for all grandmother's kindness to his family. Jake and Otto joined us from the basement and we sat about the stove, enjoying the deepening gray of the winter afternoon and the atmosphere of comfort and security in my grandfather's house. This feeling seemed completely to take possession of Mr. Shimerda. I suppose, in the crowded clutter of their cave, the old man had come to believe that peace and order had vanished from the earth, or existed only in the old world he had left so far behind. He sat still and passive, his head resting against the back of the wooden rocking-chair, his hands relaxed upon the arms. His face had a look of weariness and pleasure, like that of sick people when they feel relief from pain. Grandmother insisted on his drinking a glass of Virginia apple-brandy after his long walk in the cold, and when a faint flush came up in his cheeks, his features might have been cut out of a shell, they were so transparent. He said almost nothing, and smiled rarely; but as he rested there we all had a sense of his utter content.

As it grew dark, I asked whether I might light the Christmas tree before the lamp was brought. When the candle ends sent up their conical yellow flames, all the colored figures from Austria stood out clear and full of meaning against the green boughs. Mr. Shimerda rose, crossed himself, and quietly knelt down before the tree, his head sunk forward. His long body formed a letter "S." I saw grandmother look apprehensively at grandfather. He was rather narrow in religious matters, and sometimes spoke out and hurt people's feelings. There had been nothing strange about the tree before, but now, with some one kneeling before it,—images, candles, . . . Grandfather merely put his fingertips to his brow and bowed his venerable head, thus Protestantizing the atmosphere.

We persuaded our guest to stay for supper with us. He needed little urging. As we sat down to the table, it occurred to me that he liked to look at us, and that our faces were open books to him. When his deep-seeing eyes rested on me, I felt as if he were looking far ahead into the future for me, down the road I would have to travel.

At nine o'clock Mr. Shimerda lighted one of our lanterns and put on his overcoat and fur collar. He stood in the little entry hall, the lantern and his fur cap under his arm, shaking hands with us. When he took grandmother's hand, he bent over it as he always did, and said slowly, "Good wo-man!" He made the sign of the cross over me, put on his cap and went off in the dark. As we turned back to the sitting-room, grandfather looked at me searchingly. "The prayers of all good people are good," he said quietly.

XIII

The week following Christmas brought in a thaw, and by New Year's Day all the world about us was a broth of gray slush, and the guttered slope between the windmill and the barn was running black water. The soft black earth stood out in patches along the roadsides. I resumed all my chores, carried in the cobs and wood and water, and spent the afternoons at the barn, watching Jake shell corn with a hand-sheller.

One morning, during this interval of fine weather, Ántonia and her mother rode over on one of their shaggy old horses to pay us a visit. It was the first time Mrs. Shimerda had been to our house, and she ran about examining our carpets and curtains and furniture, all the while commenting upon them to her daughter in an envious, complaining tone. In the kitchen she caught up an iron pot that stood on the back of the stove and said: "You got many, Shimerdas no got." I thought it weak-minded of grandmother to give the pot to her.

After dinner, when she was helping to wash the dishes, she said, tossing her head: "You got many things for cook. If I got all things like you, I make much better."

She was a conceited, boastful old thing, and even misfortune could not humble her. I was so annoyed that I felt coldly even toward Ántonia and listened unsympathetically when she told me her father was not well.

"My papa sad for the old country. He not look good. He never make music any more. At home he play violin all the time; for weddings and for dance. Here never. When I beg him for play, he shake his head no. Some days he take his violin out of his box and make with his fingers on the strings, like this, but never he make the music. He don't like this kawn-tree."

"People who don't like this country ought to stay at home," I said severely. "We don't make them come here."

"He not want to come, nev-er!" she burst out. "My *mamenka* make him come. All the time she say: 'America big country; much money, much land for my boys, much husband for my girls.' My papa, he cry for leave his old friends what make music with him. He love very much the man what play the long horn like this"— she indicated a slide trombone. "They go to school together and are friends from boys. But my mama, she want Ambrosch for be rich, with many cattle."

"Your mama," I said angrily, "wants other people's things."

"Your grandfather is rich," she retorted fiercely. "Why he not help my papa? Ambrosch be rich, too, after while, and he pay back. He is very smart boy. For Ambrosch my mama come here."

Ambrosch was considered the important person in the family. Mrs. Shimerda and Ántonia always deferred to him, though he was often surly with them and contemptuous toward his father. Ambrosch and his mother had everything their own way. Though Ántonia loved her father more than she did any one else, she stood in awe of her elder brother.

After I watched Ántonia and her mother go over the hill on their miserable horse, carrying our iron pot with them, I turned to grandmother, who had taken up her darning, and said I hoped that snooping old woman wouldn't come to see us any more.

Grandmother chuckled and drove her bright needle across a hole in Otto's sock. "She's not old, Jim, though I expect she seems old to you. No, I wouldn't mourn if she never came again. But, you see, a body never knows what traits poverty might bring out in 'em. It makes a woman grasping to see her children want for things. Now read me a chapter in 'The Prince of the House of David.' Let's forget the Bohemians."

We had three weeks of this mild, open weather. The cattle in the corral ate corn almost as fast as the men could shell it for them, and we hoped they would be ready for an early market. One morning the two big bulls, Gladstone and Brigham Young, thought spring had come, and they began to tease and butt at each other across the barbed wire that separated them. Soon they got angry. They bellowed and pawed up the soft earth with their hoofs, rolling their eyes and tossing their heads. Each withdrew to a far corner of his own corral, and then they made for each other at a gallop. Thud, thud, we could hear the impact of their great heads, and their bellowing shook the pans on the kitchen shelves. Had they not been dehorned, they would have torn each other to pieces. Pretty soon the fat steers took it up and began butting and horning each other. Clearly, the affair had to be stopped. We all

stood by and watched admiringly while Fuchs rode into the corral with a pitchfork and prodded the bulls again and again, finally
driving them apart.

The big storm of the winter began on my eleventh birthday,
the 20th of January. When I went down to breakfast that morning, Jake and Otto came in white as snow-men, beating their
hands and stamping their feet. They began to laugh boisterously
when they saw me, calling:—

"You've got a birthday present this time, Jim, and no mistake.
They was a full-grown blizzard ordered for you."

All day the storm went on. The snow did not fall this time, it
simply spilled out of heaven, like thousands of feather-beds being
emptied. That afternoon the kitchen was a carpenter-shop; the
men brought in their tools and made two great wooden shovels
with long handles. Neither grandmother nor I could go out in the
storm, so Jake fed the chickens and brought in a pitiful contribu-
tion of eggs.

Next day our men had to shovel until noon to reach the
barn—and the snow was still falling! There had not been such a
storm in the ten years my grandfather had lived in Nebraska. He
said at dinner that we would not try to reach the cattle—they
were fat enough to go without their corn for a day or two; but to-
morrow we must feed them and thaw out their water-tap so that
they could drink. We could not so much as see the corrals, but we
knew the steers were over there, huddled together under the
north bank. Our ferocious bulls, subdued enough by this time,
were probably warming each other's backs. "This'll take the bile
out of 'em!" Fuchs remarked gleefully.

At noon that day the hens had not been heard from. After dinner Jake and Otto, their damp clothes now dried on them,
stretched their stiff arms and plunged again into the drifts. They
made a tunnel under the snow to the henhouse, with walls so
solid that grandmother and I could walk back and forth in it. We
found the chickens asleep; perhaps they thought night had come
to stay. One old rooster was stirring about, pecking at the solid

lump of ice in their water-tin. When we flashed the lantern in their eyes, the hens set up a great cackling and flew about clumsily, scattering down-feathers. The mottled, pin-headed guinea-hens, always resentful of captivity, ran screeching out into the tunnel and tried to poke their ugly, painted faces through the snow walls. By five o'clock the chores were done—just when it was time to begin them all over again! That was a strange, unnatural sort of day.

XIV

On the morning of the 22nd I wakened with a start. Before I opened my eyes, I seemed to know that something had happened. I heard excited voices in the kitchen—grandmother's was so shrill that I knew she must be almost beside herself. I looked forward to any new crisis with delight. What could it be, I wondered, as I hurried into my clothes. Perhaps the barn had burned; perhaps the cattle had frozen to death; perhaps a neighbor was lost in the storm.

Down in the kitchen grandfather was standing before the stove with his hands behind him. Jake and Otto had taken off their boots and were rubbing their woolen socks. Their clothes and boots were steaming, and they both looked exhausted. On the bench behind the stove lay a man, covered up with a blanket. Grandmother motioned me to the dining-room. I obeyed reluctantly. I watched her as she came and went, carrying dishes. Her lips were tightly compressed and she kept whispering to herself: "Oh, dear Saviour!" "Lord, Thou knowest!"

Presently grandfather came in and spoke to me: "Jimmy, we will not have prayers this morning, because we have a great deal to do. Old Mr. Shimerda is dead, and his family are in great distress. Ambrosch came over here in the middle of the night, and Jake and Otto went back with him. The boys have had a hard night, and you must not bother them with questions. That is Ambrosch, asleep on the bench. Come in to breakfast, boys."

After Jake and Otto had swallowed their first cup of coffee, they began to talk excitedly, disregarding grandmother's warning glances. I held my tongue, but I listened with all my ears.

"No, sir," Fuchs said in answer to a question from grandfather, "nobody heard the gun go off. Ambrosch was out with the ox team, trying to break a road, and the women folks was shut up tight in their cave. When Ambrosch come in it was dark and he didn't see nothing, but the oxen acted kind of queer. One of 'em ripped around and got away from him—bolted clean out of the stable. His hands is blistered where the rope run through. He got a lantern and went back and found the old man, just as we seen him."

"Poor soul, poor soul!" grandmother groaned. "I'd like to think he never done it. He was always considerate and un-wishful to give trouble. How could he forget himself and bring this on us!"

"I don't think he was out of his head for a minute, Mrs. Burden," Fuchs declared. "He done everything natural. You know he was always sort of fixy, and fixy he was to the last. He shaved after dinner, and washed hisself all over after the girls was done the dishes. Ántonia heated the water for him. Then he put on a clean shirt and clean socks, and after he was dressed he kissed her and the little one and took his gun and said he was going out to hunt rabbits. He must have gone right down to the barn and done it then. He layed down on that bunk-bed, close to the ox stalls, where he always slept. When we found him, everything was decent except,"—Fuchs wrinkled his brow and hesitated,—"except what he couldn't nowise foresee. His coat was hung on a peg, and his boots was under the bed. He'd took off that silk neckcloth he always wore, and folded it smooth and stuck his pin through it. He turned back his shirt at the neck and rolled up his sleeves."

"I don't see how he could do it!" grandmother kept saying.

Otto misunderstood her. "Why, mam, it was simple enough; he pulled the trigger with his big toe. He layed over on his side and put the end of the barrel in his mouth, then he drew up one foot and felt for the trigger. He found it all right!"

"Maybe he did," said Jake grimly. "There's something mighty queer about it."

"Now what do you mean, Jake?" grandmother asked sharply.

"Well, mam, I found Krajiek's axe under the manger, and I picks it up and carries it over to the corpse, and I take my oath it just fit the gash in the front of the old man's face. That there Krajiek had been sneakin' round, pale and quiet, and when he seen me examinin' the axe, he begun whimperin', 'My God, man, don't do that!' 'I reckon I'm a-goin' to look into this,' says I. Then he begun to squeal like a rat and run about wringin' his hands. 'They'll hang me!' says he. 'My God, they'll hang me sure!'"

Fuchs spoke up impatiently. Krajiek's gone silly, Jake, and so have you. The old man wouldn't have made all them preparations for Krajiek to murder him, would he? It don't hang together. The gun was right beside him when Ambrosch found him."

"Krajiek could 'a' put it there, couldn't he?" Jake demanded.

Grandmother broke in excitedly: "See here, Jake Marpole, don't you go trying to add murder to suicide. We're deep enough in trouble. Otto reads you too many of them detective stories."

"It will be easy to decide all that, Emmaline," said grandfather quietly. "If he shot himself in the way they think, the gash will be torn from inside outward."

"Just so it is, Mr. Burden," Otto affirmed. "I seen bunches of hair and stuff sticking to the poles and straw along the roof. They was blown up there by gunshot, no question."

Grandmother told grandfather she meant to go over to the Shimerdas with him.

"There is nothing you can do," he said doubtfully. "The body can't be touched until we get the coroner here from Black Hawk, and that will be a matter of several days, this weather."

"Well, I can take them some victuals, anyway, and say a word of comfort to them poor little girls. The oldest one was his darling, and was like a right hand to him. He might have thought of her. He's left her alone in a hard world." She glanced distrustfully at Ambrosch, who was now eating his breakfast at the kitchen table.

Fuchs, although he had been up in the cold nearly all night, was going to make the long ride to Black Hawk to fetch the priest and the coroner. On the gray gelding, our best horse, he would try to pick his way across the country with no roads to guide him.

"Don't you worry about me, Mrs. Burden," he said cheerfully, as he put on a second pair of socks. "I've got a good nose for directions, and I never did need much sleep. It's the gray I'm worried about. I'll save him what I can, but it'll strain him, as sure as I'm telling you!"

"This is no time to be over-considerate of animals, Otto; do the best you can for yourself. Stop at the Widow Steavens's for dinner. She's a good woman, and she'll do well by you."

After Fuchs rode away, I was left with Ambrosch. I saw a side of him I had not seen before. He was deeply, even slavishly, devout. He did not say a word all morning, but sat with his rosary in his hands, praying, now silently, now aloud. He never looked away from his beads, nor lifted his hands except to cross himself. Several times the poor boy fell asleep where he sat, wakened with a start, and began to pray again.

No wagon could be got to the Shimerdas' until a road was broken, and that would be a day's job. Grandfather came from the barn on one of our big black horses, and Jake lifted grandmother up behind him. She wore her black hood and was bundled up in shawls. Grandfather tucked his bushy white beard inside his overcoat. They looked very Biblical as they set off, I thought. Jake and Ambrosch followed them, riding the other black and my pony, carrying bundles of clothes that we had got together for Mrs. Shimerda. I watched them go past the pond and over the hill by the drifted cornfield. Then, for the first time, I realized that I was alone in the house.

I felt a considerable extension of power and authority, and was anxious to acquit myself creditably. I carried in cobs and wood from the long cellar, and filled both the stoves. I remembered that in the hurry and excitement of the morning nobody had thought of the chickens, and the eggs had not been gathered. Going out through the tunnel, I gave the hens their corn, emptied the ice from their drinking-pan, and filled it with water. After the cat had had his milk, I could think of nothing else to do, and I sat down to get warm. The quiet was delightful, and the ticking clock was the most pleasant of companions. I got "Robinson Crusoe" and tried to read, but his life on the island seemed dull compared with ours. Presently, as I looked with satisfaction about our comfortable sitting-room, it flashed upon me that if Mr. Shimerda's soul were lingering about in this world at all, it would be here, in our house, which had been more to his liking than any other in the neighborhood. I remembered his contented face when he was with us on Christmas Day. If he could have lived with us, this terrible thing would never have happened.

I knew it was homesickness that had killed Mr. Shimerda, and I wondered whether his released spirit would not eventually find its way back to his own country. I thought of how far it was to Chicago, and then to Virginia, to Baltimore,—and then the great wintry ocean. No, he would not at once set out upon that long journey. Surely, his exhausted spirit, so tired of cold and crowding and the struggle with the ever-falling snow, was resting now in this quiet house.

I was not frightened, but I made no noise. I did not wish to disturb him. I went softly down to the kitchen which, tucked away so snugly underground, always seemed to me the heart and center of the house. There, on the bench behind the stove, I thought and thought about Mr. Shimerda. Outside I could hear the wind singing over hundreds of miles of snow. It was as if I had let the old man in out of the tormenting winter, and were sitting there with him. I went over all that Ántonia had ever told me about his life before he came to this country; how he used to play the fiddle at weddings and dances. I thought about the friends he had mourned to leave, the trombone-player, the great forest full of game,—belonging, as Ántonia said, to the "nobles,"—from which she and her mother used to steal wood on moonlight nights. There was a white hart that lived in that forest, and if any one killed it, he would be hanged, she said. Such vivid pictures came to me that they might have been Mr. Shimerda's memories, not yet faded out from the air in which they had haunted him.

It had begun to grow dark when my household returned, and grandmother was so tired that she went at once to bed. Jake and I got supper, and while we were washing the dishes he told me in loud whispers about the state of things over at the Shimerdas'. Nobody could touch the body until the coroner came. If any one did, something terrible would happen, apparently. The dead man was frozen through, "just as stiff as a dressed turkey you hang out to freeze," Jake said. The horses and oxen would not go into the barn until he was frozen so hard that there was no longer any smell of blood. They were stabled there now, with the dead man, because there was no other place to keep them. A lighted lantern was kept hanging over Mr. Shimerda's head. Ántonia and Ambrosch and the mother took turns going down to pray beside him. The crazy boy went with them, because he did not feel the cold. I believed he felt cold as much as any one else, but he liked to be thought insensible to it. He was always coveting distinction, poor Marek!

Ambrosch, Jake said, showed more human feeling than he would have supposed him capable of; but he was chiefly concerned about getting a priest, and about his father's soul, which he believed was in a place of torment and would remain there until his family and the priest had prayed a great deal for him. "As I understand it," Jake concluded, "it will be a matter of years to pray his soul out of Purgatory, and right now he's in torment."

"I don't believe it," I said stoutly. "I almost know it isn't true." I did not, of course, say that I believed he had been in that very kitchen all afternoon, on his way back to his own country. Nevertheless, after I went to bed, this idea of punishment and Purgatory came back on me crushingly. I remembered the account of Dives in torment, and shuddered. But Mr. Shimerda had not been rich and selfish; he had only been so unhappy that he could not live any longer.

XV

Otto Fuchs got back from Black Hawk at noon the next day. He reported that the coroner would reach the Shimerdas' sometime that afternoon, but the missionary priest was at the other end of his parish, a hundred miles away, and the trains were not running. Fuchs had got a few hours' sleep at the livery barn in town, but he was afraid the gray gelding had strained himself. Indeed, he was never the same horse afterward. That long trip through the deep snow had taken all the endurance out of him.

Fuchs brought home with him a stranger, a young Bohemian who had taken a homestead near Black Hawk, and who came on his only horse to help his fellow-countrymen in their trouble. That was the first time I ever saw Anton Jelinek. He was a strapping young fellow in the early twenties then, handsome, warm-hearted, and full of life, and he came to us like a miracle in the midst of that grim business. I remember exactly how he strode into our kitchen in his felt boots and long wolfskin coat, his eyes and cheeks bright with the cold. At sight of grandmother, he snatched off his fur cap, greeting her in a deep, rolling voice which seemed older than he.

"I want to thank you very much, Mrs. Burden, for that you are so kind to poor strangers from my kawn-tree."

He did not hesitate like a farmer boy, but looked one eagerly in the eye when he spoke. Everything about him was warm and spontaneous. He said he would have come to see the Shimerdas before, but he had hired out to husk corn all the fall, and since winter began he had been going to the school by the mill, to learn English, along with the little children. He told me he had a nice "lady-teacher" and that he liked to go to school.

At dinner grandfather talked to Jelinek more than he usually did to strangers.

"Will they be much disappointed because we cannot get a priest?" he asked.

Jelinek looked serious. "Yes, sir, that is very bad for them.

Their father has done a great sin," he looked straight at grand-father. "Our Lord has said that."

Grandfather seemed to like his frankness. "We believe that, too, Jelinek. But we believe that Mr. Shimerda's soul will come to its Creator as well off without a priest. We believe that Christ is our only intercessor."

The young man shook his head. "I know how you think. My teacher at the school has explain. But I have seen too much. I believe in prayer for the dead. I have seen too much."

We asked him what he meant.

He glanced around the table. "You want I shall tell you? When I was a little boy like this one, I begin to help the priest at the altar. I make my first communion very young; what the Church teach seem plain to me. By 'n' by war-times come, when the Austrians fight us. We have very many soldiers in camp near my village, and the cholera break out in that camp, and the men die like flies. All day long our priest go about there to give the Sacrament to dying men, and I go with him to carry the vessels with the Holy Sacra-ment. Everybody that go near that camp catch the sickness but me and the priest. But we have no sickness, we have no fear, because we carry that blood and that body of Christ, and it preserve us." He paused, looking at grandfather. "That I know, Mr. Burden, for it happened to myself. All the soldiers know, too. When we walk along the road, the old priest and me, we meet all the time soldiers marching and officers on horse. All those officers, when they see what I carry under the cloth, pull up their horses and kneel down on the ground in the road until we pass. So I feel very bad for my kawntree-man to die without the Sacrament, and to die in a bad way for his soul, and I feel sad for his family."

We had listened attentively. It was impossible not to admire his frank, manly faith.

"I am always glad to meet a young man who thinks seriously about these things," said grandfather, "and I would never be the one to say you were not in God's care when you were among the soldiers."

After dinner it was decided that young Jelinek should hook our two strong black farmhorses to the scraper and break a road through to the Shimerdas', so that a wagon could go when it was necessary. Fuchs, who was the only cabinet-maker in the neighborhood, was set to work on a coffin.

Jelinek put on his long wolfskin coat, and when we admired it, he told us that he had shot and skinned the coyotes, and the young man who "batched" with him, Jan Bouska, who had been a fur-worker in Vienna, made the coat. From the windmill I watched Jelinek come out of the barn with the blacks, and work his way up the hillside toward the cornfield. Sometimes he was completely hidden by the clouds of snow that rose about him; then he and the horses would emerge black and shining.

Our heavy carpenter's bench had to be brought from the barn and carried down into the kitchen. Fuchs selected boards from a pile of planks grandfather had hauled out from town in the fall to make a new floor for the oats bin. When at last the lumber and tools were assembled, and the doors were closed again and the cold drafts shut out, grandfather rode away to meet the coroner at the Shimerdas', and Fuchs took off his coat and settled down to work. I sat on his work-table and watched him. He did not touch his tools at first, but figured for a long while on a piece of paper, and measured the planks and made marks on them. While he was thus engaged, he whistled softly to himself, or teasingly pulled at his half-ear. Grandmother moved about quietly, so as not to disturb him. At last he folded his ruler and turned a cheerful face to us.

"The hardest part of my job's done," he announced. "It's the head end of it that comes hard with me, especially when I'm out of practice. The last time I made one of these, Mrs. Burden," he continued, as he sorted and tried his chisels, "was for a fellow in the Black Tiger mine, up above Silverton, Colorado. The mouth of that mine goes right into the face of the cliff, and they used to put us in a bucket and run us over on a trolley and shoot us into the shaft. The bucket traveled across a box cañon three hundred feet deep, and about a third full of water. Two Swedes had fell out of that bucket once, and hit the water, feet down. If you'll believe it, they went to work the next day. You can't kill a Swede. But in my time a little Eye-talian tried the high dive, and it turned out different with him. We was snowed in then, like we are now, and I happened to be the only man in camp that could make a coffin for him. It's a handy thing to know, when you knock about like I've done."

"We'd be hard put to it now, if you didn't know, Otto," grandmother said.

"Yes, 'm," Fuchs admitted with modest pride. "So few folks does know how to make a good tight box that'll turn water. I sometimes wonder if there'll be anybody about to do it for me. However, I'm not at all particular that way."

All afternoon, wherever one went in the house, one could hear the panting wheeze of the saw or the pleasant purring of the plane. They were such cheerful noises, seeming to promise new things for living people: it was a pity that those freshly planed pine boards were to be put underground so soon. The lumber was hard to work because it was full of frost, and the boards gave off a sweet smell of pine woods, as the heap of yellow shavings grew higher and higher. I wondered why Fuchs had not stuck to cabinet-work, he settled down to it with such ease and content. He handled the tools as if he liked the feel of them; and when he planed, his hands went back and forth over the boards in an eager, beneficent way as if he were blessing them. He broke out now and then into German hymns, as if this occupation brought back old times to him.

At four o'clock Mr. Bushy, the postmaster, with another neighbor who lived east of us, stopped in to get warm. They were on their way to the Shimerdas'. The news of what had happened over there had somehow got abroad through the snow-blocked country. Grandmother gave the visitors sugar-cakes and hot coffee. Before these callers were gone, the brother of the Widow Steavens, who lived on the Black Hawk road, drew up at our door, and after him came the father of the German family, our nearest neighbors on the south. They dismounted and joined us in the dining-room.

They were all eager for any details about the suicide, and they were greatly concerned as to where Mr. Shimerda would be buried. The nearest Catholic cemetery was at Black Hawk, and it might be weeks before a wagon could get so far. Besides, Mr. Bushy and grandmother were sure that a man who had killed himself could not be buried in a Catholic graveyard. There was a burying-ground over by the Norwegian church, west of Squaw Creek; perhaps the Norwegians would take Mr. Shimerda in.

After our visitors rode away in single file over the hill, we returned to the kitchen. Grandmother began to make the icing for a chocolate cake, and Otto again filled the house with the exciting, expectant song of the plane. One pleasant thing about this time was that everybody talked more than usual. I had never heard the postmaster say anything but "Only papers, to-day," or, "I've got a sackful of mail for ye," until this afternoon. Grandmother always talked, dear woman; to herself or to the Lord, if there was no one else to listen; but grandfather was naturally taciturn, and Jake and Otto were often so tired after supper that I used to feel as if I were surrounded by a wall of silence. Now every one seemed eager to talk. That afternoon Fuchs told me story after story; about the Black Tiger mine, and about violent deaths and casual buryings, and the queer fancies of dying men. You never really knew a man, he said, until you saw him die. Most men were game, and went without a grudge.

The postmaster, going home, stopped to say that grandfather would bring the coroner back with him to spend the night. The officers of the Norwegian church, he told us, had held a meeting and decided that the Norwegian graveyard could not extend its hospitality to Mr. Shimerda.

Grandmother was indignant. "If these foreigners are so clannish, Mr. Bushy, we'll have to have an American graveyard that will be more liberal-minded. I'll get right after Josiah to start one in the spring. If anything was to happen to me, I don't want the Norwegians holding inquisitions over me to see whether I'm good enough to be laid amongst 'em."

Soon grandfather returned, bringing with him Anton Jelinek, and that important person, the coroner. He was a mild, flurried old man, a Civil War veteran, with one sleeve hanging empty. He seemed to find this case very perplexing, and said if it had not been for grandfather he would have sworn out a warrant against Krajiek. "The way he acted, and the way his axe fit the wound, was enough to convict any man."

Although it was perfectly clear that Mr. Shimerda had killed himself, Jake and the coroner thought something ought to be done to Krajiek because he behaved like a guilty man. He was badly frightened, certainly, and perhaps he even felt some stirrings of remorse for his indifference to the old man's misery and loneliness.

At supper the men ate like vikings, and the chocolate cake, which I had hoped would linger on until to-morrow in a muti-lated condition, disappeared on the second round. They talked excitedly about where they should bury Mr. Shimerda; I gathered that the neighbors were all disturbed and shocked about some-thing. It developed that Mrs. Shimerda and Ambrosch wanted the old man buried on the southwest corner of their own land; indeed, under the very stake that marked the corner. Grandfather had explained to Ambrosch that some day, when the country was put under fence and the roads were confined to section lines, two roads would cross exactly on that corner. But Ambrosch only said, "It makes no matter."

Grandfather asked Jelinek whether in the old country there was some superstition to the effect that a suicide must be buried at the cross-roads.

Jelinek said he didn't know; he seemed to remember hearing there had once been such a custom in Bohemia. "Mrs. Shimerda is made up her mind," he added. "I try to persuade her, and say it looks bad for her to all the neighbors; but she say so it must be. 'There I will bury him, if I dig the grave myself,' she say. I have to promise her I help Ambrosch make the grave to-morrow."

Grandfather smoothed his beard and looked judicial. "I don't know whose wish should decide the matter, if not hers. But if she thinks she will live to see the people of this country ride over that old man's head, she is mistaken."

XVI

Mr. Shimerda lay dead in the barn four days, and on the fifth they buried him. All day Friday Jelinek was off with Ambrosch digging the grave, chopping out the frozen earth with old axes. On Saturday we breakfasted before daylight and got into the wagon with the coffin. Jake and Jelinek went ahead on horseback to cut the body loose from the pool of blood in which it was frozen fast to the ground.

When grandmother and I went into the Shimerdas' house, we found the women-folk alone; Ambrosch and Marek were at the barn. Mrs. Shimerda sat crouching by the stove, Ántonia was washing dishes. When she saw me she ran out of her dark corner and threw her arms around me. "Oh, Jimmy," she sobbed, "what you tink for my lovely papa!" It seemed to me that I could feel her heart breaking as she clung to me.

Mrs. Shimerda, sitting on the stump by the stove, kept looking over her shoulder toward the door while the neighbors were arriving. They came on horseback, all except the postmaster, who brought his family in a wagon over the only broken wagon-trail. The Widow Steavens rode up from her farm eight miles down the Black Hawk road. The cold drove the women into the cave-house, and it was soon crowded. A fine, sleety snow was beginning to fall, and every one was afraid of another storm and anxious to have the burial over with.

Grandfather and Jelinek came to tell Mrs. Shimerda that it was time to start. After bundling her mother up in clothes the neighbors had brought, Ántonia put on an old cape from our house and the rabbit-skin hat her father had made for her. Four men carried Mr. Shimerda's box up the hill; Krajiek slunk along behind

them. The coffin was too wide for the door, so it was put down on
the slope outside. I slipped out from the cave and looked at Mr.
Shimerda. He was lying on his side, with his knees drawn up. His
body was draped in a black shawl, and his head was bandaged in
white muslin, like a mummy's; one of his long, shapely hands lay
out on the black cloth; that was all one could see of him.

Mrs. Shimerda came out and placed an open prayer-book
against the body, making the sign of the cross on the bandaged
head with her fingers. Ambrosch knelt down and made the same
gesture, and after him Ántonia and Marek. Yulka hung back. Her
mother pushed her forward, and kept saying something to her
over and over. Yulka knelt down, shut her eyes, and put out her
hand a little way, but she drew it back and began to cry wildly.
She was afraid to touch the bandage. Mrs. Shimerda caught her
by the shoulders and pushed her toward the coffin, but grandmother interfered.

"No, Mrs. Shimerda," she said firmly, "I won't stand by and see
that child frightened into spasms. She is too little to understand
what you want of her. Let her alone."

At a look from grandfather, Fuchs and Jelinek placed the lid
on the box, and began to nail it down over Mr. Shimerda. I was
afraid to look at Ántonia. She put her arms round Yulka and held
the little girl close to her.

The coffin was put into the wagon. We drove slowly away,
against the fine, icy snow which cut our faces like a sand-blast.
When we reached the grave, it looked a very little spot in that
snow-covered waste. The men took the coffin to the edge of the
hole and lowered it with ropes. We stood about watching them,
and the powdery snow lay without melting on the caps and shoulders of the men and the shawls of the women. Jelinek spoke in a
persuasive tone to Mrs. Shimerda, and then turned to grandfather.

"She says, Mr. Burden, she is very glad if you can make some
prayer for him here in English, for the neighbors to understand."

Grandmother looked anxiously at grandfather. He took off
his hat, and the other men did likewise. I thought his prayer

remarkable. I still remember it. He began, "Oh, great and just God, no man among us knows what the sleeper knows, nor is it for us to judge what lies between him and Thee." He prayed that if any man there had been remiss toward the stranger come to a far country, God would forgive him and soften his heart. He recalled the promises to the widow and the fatherless, and asked God to smooth the way before this widow and her children, and to "incline the hearts of men to deal justly with her." In closing, he said we were leaving Mr. Shimerda at "Thy judgment seat, which is also Thy mercy seat."

All the time he was praying, grandmother watched him through the black fingers of her glove, and when he said "Amen," I thought she looked satisfied with him. She turned to Otto and whispered, "Can't you start a hymn, Fuchs? It would seem less heathenish."

Fuchs glanced about to see if there was general approval of her suggestion, then began, "Jesus, Lover of my Soul," and all the men and women took it up after him. Whenever I have heard the hymn since, it has made me remember that white waste and the little group of people; and the bluish air, full of fine, eddying snow, like long veils flying:—

> "While the nearer waters roll,
> While the tempest still is high."

. . .

Years afterward, when the open-grazing days were over, and the red grass had been ploughed under and under until it had almost disappeared from the prairie; when all the fields were under fence, and the roads no longer ran about like wild things, but followed the surveyed section-lines, Mr. Shimerda's grave was still there, with a sagging wire fence around it, and an unpainted wooden cross. As grandfather had predicted, Mrs. Shimerda never saw the roads going over his head. The road from the north curved a little to the east just there, and the road from the west swung out a little to the south; so that the grave, with its tall red grass that was never mowed, was like a little island; and at twilight, under a new moon or the clear evening star, the dusty roads used to look like soft gray rivers flowing past it. I never came upon the place without emotion, and in all that country it was the spot most dear to me. I loved the dim superstition, the propitiatory intent, that had put the grave there; and still more I loved the spirit that could not carry out the sentence—the error from the surveyed lines, the clemency of the soft earth roads along which the home-coming wagons rattled after sunset. Never a tired driver passed the wooden cross, I am sure, without wishing well to the sleeper.

XVII

When spring came, after that hard winter, one could not get enough of the nimble air. Every morning I wakened with a fresh consciousness that winter was over. There were none of the signs of spring for which I used to watch in Virginia, no budding woods or blooming gardens. There was only—spring itself; the throb of it, the light restlessness, the vital essence of it everywhere; in the sky, in the swift clouds, in the pale sunshine, and in the warm, high wind—rising suddenly, sinking suddenly, impulsive and playful like a big puppy that pawed you and then lay down to be petted. If I had been tossed down blindfold on that red prairie, I should have known that it was spring.

Everywhere now there was the smell of burning grass. Our neighbors burned off their pasture before the new grass made a start, so that the fresh growth would not be mixed with the dead stand of last year. Those light, swift fires, running about the country, seemed a part of the same kindling that was in the air.

The Shimerdas were in their new log house by then. The neighbors had helped them to build it in March. It stood directly in front of their old cave, which they used as a cellar. The family were now fairly equipped to begin their struggle with the soil.

They had four comfortable rooms to live in, a new windmill,—bought on credit,—a chicken-house and poultry. Mrs. Shimerda had paid grandfather ten dollars for a milk cow, and was to give him fifteen more as soon as they harvested their first crop.

When I rode up to the Shimerdas' one bright windy afternoon in April, Yulka ran out to meet me. It was to her, now, that I gave reading lessons; Ántonia was busy with other things. I tied my pony and went into the kitchen where Mrs. Shimerda was baking bread, chewing poppy seeds as she worked. By this time she could speak enough English to ask me a great many questions about what our men were doing in the fields. She seemed to think that my elders withheld helpful information, and that from me she might get valuable secrets. On this occasion she asked me very craftily when grandfather expected to begin planting corn. I told her, adding that he thought we should have a dry spring and that the corn would not be held back by too much rain, as it had been last year.

She gave me a shrewd glance. "He not Jesus," she blustered; "he not know about the wet and the dry."

I did not answer her; what was the use? As I sat waiting for the hour when Ambrosch and Ántonia would return from the fields, I watched Mrs. Shimerda at her work. She took from the oven a coffee-cake which she wanted to keep warm for supper, and wrapped it in a quilt stuffed with feathers. I have seen her put even a roast goose in this quilt to keep it hot. When the neighbors were there building the new house they saw her do this, and the story got abroad that the Shimerdas kept their food in their feather beds.

When the sun was dropping low, Ántonia came up the big south draw with her team. How much older she had grown in eight months! She had come to us a child, and now she was a tall, strong young girl, although her fifteenth birthday had just slipped by. I ran out and met her as she brought her horses up to the windmill to water them. She wore the boots her father had so thoughtfully taken off before he shot himself, and his old fur cap. Her outgrown cotton dress switched about her calves, over the boot-tops. She kept her sleeves rolled up all day, and her arms and throat were burned as brown as a sailor's. Her neck came up strongly out of her shoulders, like the bole of a tree out of the turf. One sees that draft-horse neck among the peasant women in all old countries.

She greeted me gayly, and began at once to tell me how much ploughing she had done that day. Ambrosch, she said, was on the north quarter, breaking sod with the oxen.

"Jim, you ask Jake how much he ploughed to-day. I don't want that Jake get more done in one day than me. I want we have very much corn this fall."

While the horses drew in the water, and nosed each other, and then drank again, Ántonia sat down on the windmill step and rested her head on her hand. "You see the big prairie fire from your place last night? I hope your grandpa ain't lose no stacks?"

"No, we didn't. I came to ask you something, Tony. Grandmother wants to know if you can't go to the term of school that begins next week over at the sod schoolhouse. She says there's a good teacher, and you'd learn a lot."

Ántonia stood up, lifting and dropping her shoulders as if they were stiff. "I ain't got time to learn. I can work like mans now. My mother can't say no more how Ambrosch do all and nobody to help him. I can work as much as him. School is all right for little boys. I help make this land one good farm."

She clucked to her team and started for the barn. I walked beside her, feeling vexed. Was she going to grow up boastful like her mother, I wondered? Before we reached the stable, I felt something tense in her silence, and glancing up I saw that she was crying. She turned her face from me and looked off at the red streak of dying light, over the dark prairie.

I climbed up into the loft and threw down the hay for her, while she unharnessed her team. We walked slowly back toward the house. Ambrosch had come in from the north quarter, and was watering his oxen at the tank.

Ántonia took my hand. "Sometime you will tell me all those

nice things you learn at the school, won't you, Jimmy?" she asked with a sudden rush of feeling in her voice. "My father, he went much to school. He know a great deal; how to make the fine cloth like what you not got here. He play horn and violin, and he read so many books that the priests in Bohemie come to talk to him. You won't forget my father, Jim?"

"No," I said, "I will never forget him."

Mrs. Shimerda asked me to stay for supper. After Ambrosch and Ántonia had washed the field dust from their hands and faces at the wash-basin by the kitchen door, we sat down at the oil-cloth-covered table. Mrs. Shimerda ladled meal mush out of an iron pot and poured milk on it. After the mush we had fresh bread and sorghum molasses, and coffee with the cake that had been kept warm in the feathers. Ántonia and Ambrosch were talking in Bohemian; disputing about which of them had done more ploughing that day. Mrs. Shimerda egged them on, chuckling while she gobbled her food.

Presently Ambrosch said sullenly in English: "You take them ox to-morrow and try the sod plough. Then you not be so smart."

His sister laughed. "Don't be mad. I know it's awful hard work for break sod. I milk the cow for you to-morrow, if you want."

Mrs. Shimerda turned quickly to me. "That cow not give so much milk like what your grandpa say. If he make talk about fifteen dollars, I send him back the cow."

"He doesn't talk about the fifteen dollars," I exclaimed indignantly. "He doesn't find fault with people."

"He say I break his saw when we build, and I never," grumbled Ambrosch.

I knew he had broken the saw, and then hid it and lied about it. I began to wish I had not stayed for supper. Everything was disagreeable to me. Ántonia ate so noisily now, like a man, and she yawned often at the table and kept stretching her arms over her head, as if they ached. Grandmother had said, "Heavy field work'll spoil that girl. She'll lose all her nice ways and get rough ones." She had lost them already.

After supper I rode home through the sad, soft spring twilight. Since winter I had seen very little of Ántonia. She was out in the fields from sun-up until sun-down. If I rode over to see her where she was ploughing, she stopped at the end of a row to chat for a moment, then gripped her plough-handles, clucked to her team, and waded on down the furrow, making me feel that she was now grown up and had no time for me. On Sundays she helped her mother make garden or sewed all day. Grandfather was pleased with Ántonia. When we complained of her, he only smiled and said, "She will help some fellow get ahead in the world."

Nowadays Tony could talk of nothing but the prices of things, or how much she could lift and endure. She was too proud of her strength. I knew, too, that Ambrosch put upon her some chores a girl ought not to do, and that the farmhands around the country joked in a nasty way about it. Whenever I saw her come up the furrow, shouting to her beasts, sunburned, sweaty, her dress open at the neck, and her throat and chest dust-plastered, I used to think of the tone in which poor Mr. Shimerda, who could say so little, yet managed to say so much when he exclaimed, "My Án-tonia!"

XVIII

After I began to go to the country school, I saw less of the Bohemians. We were sixteen pupils at the sod schoolhouse, and we all came on horseback and brought our dinner. My schoolmates were none of them very interesting, but I somehow felt that by making comrades of them I was getting even with Ántonia for her indifference. Since the father's death, Ambrosch was more than ever the head of the house and he seemed to direct the feelings as well as the fortunes of his women-folk. Ántonia often quoted his opinions to me, and she let me see that she admired him, while she thought of me only as a little boy. Before the spring was over, there was a distinct coldness between us and the Shimerdas. It came about in this way.

One Sunday I rode over there with Jake to get a horse-collar which Ambrosch had borrowed from him and had not returned. It was a beautiful blue morning. The buffalo-peas were blooming in pink and purple masses along the roadside, and the larks, perched on last year's dried sunflower stalks, were singing straight at the sun, their heads thrown back and their yellow breasts a-quiver. The wind blew about us in warm, sweet gusts. We rode slowly, with a pleasant sense of Sunday indolence.

We found the Shimerdas working just as if it were a week-day. Marek was cleaning out the stable, and Ántonia and her mother were making garden, off across the pond in the draw-head. Ambrosch was up on the windmill tower, oiling the wheel. He came down, not very cordially. When Jake asked for the collar, he grunted and scratched his head. The collar belonged to grand-father, of course, and Jake, feeling responsible for it, flared up.

"Now, don't you say you haven't got it, Ambrosch, because I know you have, and if you ain't a-going to look for it, I will."

Ambrosch shrugged his shoulders and sauntered down the hill toward the stable. I could see that it was one of his mean days. Presently he returned, carrying a collar that had been badly used—trampled in the dirt and gnawed by rats until the hair was sticking out of it.

"This what you want?" he asked surlily.

Jake jumped off his horse. I saw a wave of red come up under the rough stubble on his face. "That ain't the piece of harness I loaned you, Ambrosch; or if it is, you've used it shameful. I ain't a-going to carry such a looking thing back to Mr. Burden."

Ambrosch dropped the collar on the ground. "All right," he said coolly, took up his oil-can, and began to climb the mill. Jake caught him by the belt of his trousers and yanked him back. Ambrosch's feet had scarcely touched the ground when he lunged out with a vicious kick at Jake's stomach. Fortunately Jake was in such a posi-tion that he could dodge it. This was not the sort of thing country boys did when they played at fisticuffs, and Jake was furious. He landed Ambrosch a blow on the head—it sounded like the crack of an axe on a cow-pumpkin. Ambrosch dropped over, stunned.

We heard squeals, and looking up saw Ántonia and her mother coming on the run. They did not take the path around the pond, but plunged through the muddy water, without even lifting their skirts. They came on, screaming and clawing the air. By this time Ambrosch had come to his senses and was sputtering with nose-bleed. Jake sprang into his saddle. "Let's get out of this, Jim," he called.

Mrs. Shimerda threw her hands over her head and clutched as if she were going to pull down lightning. "Law, law!" she shrieked after us. "Law for knock my Ambrosch down!"

"I never like you no more, Jake and Jim Burden," Ántonia panted. "No friends any more!"

Jake stopped and turned his horse for a second. "Well, you're a damned ungrateful lot, the whole pack of you," he shouted back. "I guess the Burdens can get along without you. You've been a sight of trouble to them, anyhow!"

We rode away, feeling so outraged that the fine morning was spoiled for us. I hadn't a word to say, and poor Jake was white as paper and trembling all over. It made him sick to get so angry. "They ain't the same, Jimmy," he kept saying in a hurt tone. "These foreigners ain't the same. You can't trust 'em to be fair. It's dirty to kick a feller. You heard how the women turned on you—and after all we went through on account of 'em last winter! They ain't to be trusted. I don't want to see you get too thick with any of 'em."

"I'll never be friends with them again, Jake," I declared hotly. "I believe they are all like Krajiek and Ambrosch underneath."

Grandfather heard our story with a twinkle in his eye. He advised Jake to ride to town to-morrow, go to a justice of the peace, tell him he had knocked young Shimerda down, and pay his fine. Then if Mrs. Shimerda still inclined to make trouble— her son was still under age—she would be forestalled. Jake said he might as well take the wagon and haul to market the pig he had been fattening. On Monday, about an hour after Jake had started, we saw Mrs. Shimerda and her Ambrosch proudly driving by, looking neither to the right nor left. As they rattled out of sight down the Black Hawk road, grandfather chuckled, saying he had rather expected she would follow the matter up.

Jake paid his fine with a ten-dollar bill grandfather had given him for that purpose. But when the Shimerdas found that Jake sold his pig in town that day, Ambrosch worked it out in his shrewd head that Jake had to sell his pig to pay his fine. This theory afforded the Shimerdas great satisfaction, apparently. For weeks afterward, whenever Jake and I met Ántonia on her way to the post-office, or going along the road with her work-team, she would clap her hands and call to us in a spiteful, crowing voice:—

"Jake-y, Jake-y, sell the pig and pay the slap!"

Otto pretended not to be surprised at Ántonia's behavior. He only lifted his brows and said, "You can't tell me anything new about a Czech; I'm an Austrian."

Grandfather was never a party to what Jake called our feud with the Shimerdas. Ambrosch and Ántonia always greeted him respectfully, and he asked them about their affairs and gave them advice as usual. He thought the future looked hopeful for them. Ambrosch was a far-seeing fellow; he soon realized that his oxen were too heavy for any work except breaking sod, and he succeeded in selling them to a newly arrived German. With the money he bought another team of horses, which grandfather selected for him. Marek was strong, and Ambrosch worked him hard; but he could never teach him to cultivate corn, I remember. The one idea that had ever got through poor Marek's thick head was that all exertion was meritorious. He always bore down on the handles of the cultivator and drove the blades so deep into the earth that the horses were soon exhausted.

In June Ambrosch went to work at Mr. Bushy's for a week, and took Marek with him at full wages. Mrs. Shimerda then drove the second cultivator; she and Ántonia worked in the fields all day and did the chores at night. While the two women were running the place alone, one of the new horses got colic and gave them a terrible fright.

Ántonia had gone down to the barn one night to see that all was well before she went to bed, and she noticed that one of the roans had swollen about the middle and stood with its head hanging. She mounted another horse, without waiting to saddle him, and hammered on our door just as we were going to bed. Grandfather answered her knock. He did not send one of his men, but rode back with her himself, taking a syringe and an old piece of carpet he kept for hot applications when our horses were sick. He found Mrs. Shimerda sitting by the horse with her lantern, groaning and wringing her hands. It took but a few moments to release the gases pent up in the poor beast, and the two women heard the rush of wind and saw the roan visibly diminish in girth.

"If I lose that horse, Mr. Burden," Ántonia exclaimed, "I never stay here till Ambrosch come home! I go drown myself in the pond before morning."

When Ambrosch came back from Mr. Bushy's, we learned that he had given Marek's wages to the priest at Black Hawk, for masses for their father's soul. Grandmother thought Ántonia needed shoes more than Mr. Shimerda needed prayers, but grandfather said tolerantly, "If he can spare six dollars, pinched as he is, it shows he believes what he professes."

It was grandfather who brought about a reconciliation with the Shimerdas. One morning he told us that the small grain was coming on so well, he thought he would begin to cut his wheat on the first of July. He would need more men, and if it were agreeable to every one he would engage Ambrosch for the reaping and thrashing, as the Shimerdas had no small grain of their own.

"I think, Emmaline," he concluded, "I will ask Ántonia to come over and help you in the kitchen. She will be glad to earn something, and it will be a good time to end misunderstandings. I may as well ride over this morning and make arrangements. Do you want to go with me, Jim?" His tone told me that he had already decided for me.

After breakfast we set off together. When Mrs. Shimerda saw

us coming, she ran from her door down into the draw behind the stable, as if she did not want to meet us. Grandfather smiled to himself while he tied his horse, and we followed her.

Behind the barn we came upon a funny sight. The cow had evidently been grazing somewhere in the draw. Mrs. Shimerda had run to the animal, pulled up the lariat pin, and, when we came upon her, she was trying to hide the cow in an old cave in the bank. As the hole was narrow and dark, the cow held back, and the old woman was slapping and pushing at her hind quarters, trying to spank her into the draw-side.

Grandfather ignored her singular occupation and greeted her politely. "Good-morning, Mrs. Shimerda. Can you tell me where I will find Ambrosch? Which field?"

"He with the sod corn." She pointed toward the north, still standing in front of the cow as if she hoped to conceal it.

"His sod corn will be good for fodder this winter," said grandfather encouragingly. "And where is Ántonia?"

"She go with." Mrs. Shimerda kept wiggling her bare feet about nervously in the dust.

"Very well. I will ride up there. I want them to come over and help me cut my oats and wheat next month. I will pay them wages. Good-morning. By the way, Mrs. Shimerda," he said as he turned up the path, "I think we may as well call it square about the cow."

She started and clutched the rope tighter. Seeing that she did not understand, grandfather turned back. "You need not pay me anything more; no more money. The cow is yours."

"Pay no more, keep cow?" she asked in a bewildered tone, her narrow eyes snapping at us in the sunlight.

"Exactly. Pay no more, keep cow." He nodded.

Mrs. Shimerda dropped the rope, ran after us, and crouching down beside grandfather, she took his hand and kissed it. I doubt if he had ever been so much embarrassed before. I was a little startled, too. Somehow, that seemed to bring the Old World very close.

We rode away laughing, and grandfather said: "I expect she

thought we had come to take the cow away for certain, Jim. I wonder if she wouldn't have scratched a little if we'd laid hold of that lariat rope!"

Our neighbors seemed glad to make peace with us. The next Sunday Mrs. Shimerda came over and brought Jake a pair of socks she had knitted. She presented them with an air of great magnanimity, saying, "Now you not come any more for knock my Ambrosch down?"

Jake laughed sheepishly. "I don't want to have no trouble with Ambrosch. If he'll let me alone, I'll let him alone."

"If he slap you, we ain't got no pig for pay the fine," she said insinuatingly.

Jake was not at all disconcerted. "Have the last word, mam," he said cheerfully. "It's a lady's privilege."

XIX

July came on with that breathless, brilliant heat which makes the plains of Kansas and Nebraska the best corn country in the world. It seemed as if we could hear the corn growing in the night; under the stars one caught a faint crackling in the dewy, heavy-odored cornfields where the feathered stalks stood so juicy and green. If all the great plain from the Missouri to the Rocky Mountains had been under glass, and the heat regulated by a thermometer, it could not have been better for the yellow tassels that were ripening and fertilizing each other day by day. The cornfields were far apart in those times, with miles of wild grazing land between. It took a clear, meditative eye like my grandfather's to foresee that they would enlarge and multiply until they would be, not the Shimerdas' cornfields, or Mr. Bushy's, but the world's cornfields; that their yield would be one of the great economic facts, like the wheat crop of Russia, which underlie all the activities of men, in peace or war.

The burning sun of those few weeks, with occasional rains at night, secured the corn. After the milky ears were once formed, we had little to fear from dry weather. The men were working so hard in the wheatfields that they did not notice the heat,—though I was kept busy carrying water for them,—and grandmother and Ántonia had so much to do in the kitchen that they could not have told whether one day was hotter than another. Each morning, while the dew was still on the grass, Ántonia went with me up to the garden to get early vegetables for dinner. Grandmother made her wear a sunbonnet, but as soon as we reached the garden she threw it on the grass and let her hair fly in the breeze. I remember how, as we bent over the pea-vines, beads of perspiration used to gather on her upper lip like a little mustache.

"Oh, better I like to work out of doors than in a house!" she used to sing joyfully. "I not care that your grandmother say it makes me like a man. I like to be like a man." She would toss her head and ask me to feel the muscles swell in her brown arm.

We were glad to have her in the house. She was so gay and responsive that one did not mind her heavy, running step, or her clattery way with pans. Grandmother was in high spirits during the weeks that Ántonia worked for us.

All the nights were close and hot during that harvest season. The harvesters slept in the hayloft because it was cooler there than in the house. I used to lie in my bed by the open window, watching the heat lightning play softly along the horizon, or looking up at the gaunt frame of the windmill against the blue night sky. One night there was a beautiful electric storm, though not enough rain fell to damage the cut grain. The men went down to the barn immediately after supper, and when the dishes were washed Ántonia and I climbed up on the slanting roof of the chicken-house to watch the clouds. The thunder was loud and metallic, like the rattle of sheet iron, and the lightning broke in great zigzags across the heavens, making everything stand out and come close to us for a moment. Half the sky was checkered with black thunderheads, but all the west was luminous and clear: in the lightning-flashes it looked like deep blue water, with the sheen of moonlight on it; and the mottled part of the sky was like marble pavement, like the quay of some splendid sea-coast city, doomed to destruction. Great warm splashes of rain fell on our upturned faces. One black cloud, no bigger than a little boat, drifted out into the clear space unattended, and kept moving westward. All about us we could hear the felty beat of the rain-drops on the soft dust of the farmyard. Grandmother came to the door and said it was late, and we would get wet out there.

"In a minute we come," Ántonia called back to her. "I like your grandmother, and all things here," she sighed. "I wish my papa live to see this summer. I wish no winter ever come again."

"It will be summer a long while yet," I reassured her. "Why aren't you always nice like this, Tony?"

"How nice?"

"Why, just like this; like yourself. Why do you all the time try to be like Ambrosch?"

She put her arms under her head and lay back, looking up at the sky. "If I live here, like you, that is different. Things will be easy for you. But they will be hard for us."

BOOK II
THE HIRED GIRLS

I

I had been living with my grandfather for nearly three years when he decided to move to Black Hawk. He and grandmother were getting old for the heavy work of a farm, and as I was now thirteen they thought I ought to be going to school. Accordingly our homestead was rented to "that good woman, the Widow Steavens," and her bachelor brother, and we bought Preacher White's house, at the north end of Black Hawk. This was the first town house one passed driving in from the farm, a landmark which told country people their long ride was over.

We were to move to Black Hawk in March, and as soon as grandfather had fixed the date he let Jake and Otto know of his intention. Otto said he would not be likely to find another place that suited him so well; that he was tired of farming and thought he would go back to what he called the "wild West." Jake Marpole, lured by Otto's stories of adventure, decided to go with him. We did our best to dissuade Jake. He was so handicapped by illiteracy and by his trusting disposition that he would be an easy prey to sharpers. Grandmother begged him to stay among kindly, Christian people, where he was known; but there was no reasoning with him. He wanted to be a prospector. He thought a silver mine was waiting for him in Colorado.

Jake and Otto served us to the last. They moved us into town, put down the carpets in our new house, made shelves and cupboards for grandmother's kitchen, and seemed loath to leave us. But at last they went, without warning. Those two fellows had been faithful to us through sun and storm, had given us things that cannot be bought in any market in the world. With me they had been like older brothers; had restrained their speech and

manners out of care for me, and given me so much good com-
radeship. Now they got on the west-bound train one morning, in
their Sunday clothes, with their oilcloth valises—and I never saw
them again. Months afterward we got a card from Otto, saying
that Jake had been down with mountain fever, but now they were
both working in the Yankee Girl mine, and were doing well. I
wrote to them at that address, but my letter was returned to me,
"unclaimed." After that we never heard from them.

Black Hawk, the new world in which we had come to live, was
a clean, well-planted little prairie town, with white fences and
good green yards about the dwellings, wide, dusty streets, and
shapely little trees growing along the wooden sidewalks. In the
center of the town there were two rows of new brick "store"
buildings, a brick schoolhouse, the courthouse, and four white
churches. Our own house looked down over the town, and from
our upstairs windows we could see the winding line of the river
bluffs, two miles south of us. That river was to be my compensa-
tion for the lost freedom of the farming country.

We came to Black Hawk in March, and by the end of April we
felt like town people. Grandfather was a deacon in the new Baptist Church, grandmother was busy with church suppers and
missionary societies, and I was quite another boy, or thought I
was. Suddenly put down among boys of my own age, I found I
had a great deal to learn. Before the spring term of school was
over I could fight, play "keeps," tease the little girls, and use for-
bidden words as well as any boy in my class. I was restrained
from utter savagery only by the fact that Mrs. Harling, our nearest
neighbor, kept an eye on me, and if my behavior went beyond
certain bounds I was not permitted to come into her yard or to
play with her jolly children.

We saw more of our country neighbors now than when we
lived on the farm. Our house was a convenient stopping-place for
them. We had a big barn where the farmers could put up their
teams, and their women-folk more often accompanied them, now
that they could stay with us for dinner, and rest and set their

bonnets right before they went shopping. The more our house was like a country hotel, the better I liked it. I was glad, when I came home from school at noon, to see a farm wagon standing in the back yard, and I was always ready to run downtown to get beefsteak or baker's bread for unexpected company. All through that first spring and summer I kept hoping that Ambrosch would being Ántonia and Yulka to see our new house. I wanted to show them our red plush furniture, and the trumpet-blowing cherubs the German paper-hanger had put on our parlor ceiling.

When Ambrosch came to town, however, he came alone, and though he put his horses in our barn, he would never stay for dinner, or tell us anything about his mother and sisters. If we ran out and questioned him as he was slipping through the yard, he would merely work his shoulders about in his coat and say, "They all right, I guess."

Mrs. Steavens, who now lived on our farm, grew as fond of Ántonia as we had been, and always brought us news of her. All through the wheat season, she told us, Ambrosch hired his sister out like a man, and she went from farm to farm, binding sheaves or working with the thrashers. The farmers liked her and were kind to her; said they would rather have her for a hand than Ambrosch. When fall came she was to husk corn for the neighbors until Christmas, as she had done the year before; but grandmother saved her from this by getting her a place to work with our neighbors, the Harlings.

II

Grandmother often said that if she had to live in town, she thanked God she lived next the Harlings. They had been farming people, like ourselves, and their place was like a little farm, with a big barn and a garden, and an orchard and grazing lots,—even a windmill. The Harlings were Norwegians, and Mrs. Harling had lived in Christiania until she was ten years old. Her husband was born in

Minnesota. He was a grain merchant and cattle buyer, and was generally considered the most enterprising business man in our county. He controlled a line of grain elevators in the little towns along the railroad to the west of us, and was away from home a great deal. In his absence his wife was the head of the household.

Mrs. Harling was short and square and sturdy-looking, like her house. Every inch of her was charged with an energy that made itself felt the moment she entered a room. Her face was rosy and solid, with bright, twinkling eyes and a stubborn little chin. She was quick to anger, quick to laughter, and jolly from the depths of her soul. How well I remember her laugh; it had in it the same sudden recognition that flashed into her eyes, was a burst of humor, short and intelligent. Her rapid footsteps shook her own floors, and she routed lassitude and indifference wherever she came. She could not be negative or perfunctory about anything. Her enthusiasm, and her violent likes and dislikes, asserted themselves in all the every-day occupations of life. Washday was interesting, never dreary, at the Harlings'. Preserving-time was a prolonged festival, and house-cleaning was like a revolution. When Mrs. Harling made garden that spring, we could feel the stir of her undertaking through the willow hedge that separated our place from hers.

Three of the Harling children were near me in age. Charley, the only son,—they had lost an older boy,—was sixteen; Julia, who was known as the musical one, was fourteen when I was; and Sally, the tomboy with short hair, was a year younger. She was nearly as strong as I, and uncannily clever at all boys' sports. Sally was a wild thing, with sunburned yellow hair, bobbed about her ears, and a brown skin, for she never wore a hat. She raced all over town on one roller skate, often cheated at "keeps," but was such a quick shot one couldn't catch her at it.

The grown-up daughter, Frances, was a very important person in our world. She was her father's chief clerk, and virtually managed his Black Hawk office during his frequent absences. Because of her unusual business ability, he was stern and exacting with her. He paid her a good salary, but she had few holidays and never got away from her responsibilities. Even on Sundays she went to the office to open the mail and read the markets. With Charley, who was not interested in business, but was already preparing for Annapolis, Mr. Harling was very indulgent; bought him guns and tools and electric batteries, and never asked what he did with them.

Frances was dark, like her father, and quite as tall. In winter she wore a sealskin coat and cap, and she and Mr. Harling used to walk home together in the evening, talking about grain-cars and cattle, like two men. Sometimes she came over to see grandfather after supper, and her visits flattered him. More than once they put their wits together to rescue some unfortunate farmer from the clutches of Wick Cutter, the Black Hawk money-lender. Grandfather said Frances Harling was as good a judge of credits as any banker in the county. The two or three men who had tried to take advantage of her in a deal acquired celebrity by their defeat. She knew every farmer for miles about; how much land he had under cultivation, how many cattle he was feeding, what his liabilities were. Her interest in these people was more than a business interest. She carried them all in her mind as if they were characters in a book or a play.

When Frances drove out into the country on business, she would go miles out of her way to call on some of the old people, or to see the women who seldom got to town. She was quick at understanding the grandmothers who spoke no English, and the most reticent and distrustful of them would tell her their story without realizing they were doing so. She went to country funerals and weddings in all weathers. A farmer's daughter who was to be married could count on a wedding present from Frances Harling.

In August the Harlings' Danish cook had to leave them. Grandmother entreated them to try Ántonia. She cornered Ambrosch the next time he came to town, and pointed out to him that any connection with Christian Harling would strengthen his credit and be of advantage to him. One Sunday Mrs. Harling took the long ride out to the Shimerdas' with Frances. She said she wanted

to see "what the girl came from" and to have a clear understanding with her mother. I was in our yard when they came
driving home, just before sunset. They laughed and waved to me
as they passed, and I could see they were in great good humor.
After supper, when grandfather set off to church, grandmother
and I took my short cut through the willow hedge and went over
to hear about the visit to the Shimerdas.

We found Mrs. Harling with Charley and Sally on the front
porch, resting after her hard drive. Julia was in the hammock—she
was fond of repose—and Frances was at the piano, playing without a light and talking to her mother through the open window.

Mrs. Harling laughed when she saw us coming. "I expect you
left your dishes on the table to-night, Mrs. Burden," she called.
Frances shut the piano and came out to join us.

They had liked Ántonia from their first glimpse of her; felt
they knew exactly what kind of girl she was. As for Mrs. Shimerda, they found her very amusing. Mrs. Harling chuckled
whenever she spoke of her. "I expect I am more at home with that
sort of bird than you are, Mrs. Burden. They're a pair, Ambrosch
and that old woman!"

They had had a long argument with Ambrosch about Ántonia's
allowance for clothes and pocket-money. It was his plan that
every cent of his sister's wages should be paid over to him each
month, and he would provide her with such clothing as he
thought necessary. When Mrs. Harling told him firmly that she
would keep fifty dollars a year for Ántonia's own use, he declared
they wanted to take his sister to town and dress her up and make
a fool of her. Mrs. Harling gave us a lively account of Ambrosch's
behavior throughout the interview; how he kept jumping up and
putting on his cap as if he were through with the whole business,
and how his mother tweaked his coat-tail and prompted him in
Bohemian. Mrs. Harling finally agreed to pay three dollars a week
for Ántonia's services—good wages in those days—and keep her
in shoes. There had been hot dispute about the shoes, Mrs.
Shimerda finally saying persuasively that she would send Mrs.

Harling three fat geese every year to "make even." Ambrosch was to bring his sister to town next Saturday.

"She'll be awkward and rough at first, like enough," grandmother said anxiously, "but unless she's been spoiled by the hard life she's led, she has it in her to be a real helpful girl."

Mrs. Harling laughed her quick, decided laugh. "Oh, I'm not worrying, Mrs. Burden! I can bring something out of that girl. She's barely seventeen, not too old to learn new ways. She's good-looking, too!" she added warmly.

Frances turned to grandmother. "Oh, yes, Mrs. Burden, you didn't tell us that! She was working in the garden when we got there, barefoot and ragged. But she has such fine brown legs and arms, and splendid color in her cheeks—like those big dark red plums."

We were pleased at this praise. Grandmother spoke feelingly. "When she first came to this country, Frances, and had that genteel old man to watch over her, she was as pretty a girl as ever I saw. But, dear me, what a life she's led, out in the fields with those rough thrashers! Things would have been very different with poor Ántonia if her father had lived."

The Harlings begged us to tell them about Mr. Shimerda's death and the big snowstorm. By the time we saw grandfather coming home from church we had told them pretty much all we knew of the Shimerdas.

"The girl will be happy here, and she'll forget those things," said Mrs. Harling confidently, as we rose to take our leave.

III

On Saturday Ambrosch drove up to the back gate, and Ántonia jumped down from the wagon and ran into our kitchen just as she used to do. She was wearing shoes and stockings, and was breathless and excited. She gave me a playful shake by the shoulders. "You ain't forget about me, Jim?"

Grandmother kissed her. "God bless you, child! Now you've come, you must try to do right and be a credit to us."

Ántonia looked eagerly about the house and admired everything. "Maybe I be the kind of girl you like better, now I come to town," she suggested hopefully.

How good it was to have Ántonia near us again; to see her every day and almost every night! Her greatest fault, Mrs. Harling found, was that she so often stopped her work and fell to playing with the children. She would race about the orchard with us, or take sides in our hay-fights in the barn, or be the old bear that came down from the mountain and carried off Nina. Tony learned English so quickly that by the time school began she could speak as well as any of us.

I was jealous of Tony's admiration for Charley Harling. Because he was always first in his classes at school, and could mend the water-pipes or the door-bell and take the clock to pieces, she seemed to think him a sort of prince. Nothing that Charley wanted was too much trouble for her. She loved to put up lunches for him when he went hunting, to mend his ball-gloves and sew buttons on his shooting-coat, baked the kind of nut-cake he liked, and fed his setter dog when he was away on trips with his father. Ántonia had made herself cloth working-slippers out of Mr. Harling's old coats, and in these she went padding about after Charley, fairly panting with eagerness to please him.

Next to Charley, I think she loved Nina best. Nina was only six, and she was rather more complex than the other children. She was fanciful, had all sorts of unspoken preferences, and was easily offended. At the slightest disappointment or displeasure her velvety brown eyes filled with tears, and she would lift her chin and walk silently away. If we ran after her and tried to appease her, it did no good. She walked on unmollified. I used to think that no eyes in the world could grow so large or hold so many tears as Nina's. Mrs. Harling and Ántonia invariably took her part. We were never given a chance to explain. The charge was simply: "You have made Nina cry. Now, Jimmy can go home, and Sally must get her arithmetic." I liked Nina, too; she was so quaint and unexpected, and her eyes were lovely; but I often wanted to shake her.

We had jolly evenings at the Harlings when the father was away. If he was at home, the children had to go to bed early, or they came over to my house to play. Mr. Harling not only demanded a quiet house, he demanded all his wife's attention. He used to take her away to their room in the west ell, and talk over his business with her all evening. Though we did not realize it then, Mrs. Harling was our audience when we played, and we always looked to her for suggestions. Nothing flattered one like her quick laugh.

Mr. Harling had a desk in his bedroom, and his own easy-chair by the window, in which no one else ever sat. On the nights when he was at home, I could see his shadow on the blind, and it seemed to me an arrogant shadow. Mrs. Harling paid no heed to any one else if he was there. Before he went to bed she always got him a lunch of smoked salmon or anchovies and beer. He kept an alcohol lamp in his room, and a French coffee-pot, and his wife made coffee for him at any hour of the night he happened to want it.

Most Black Hawk fathers had no personal habits outside their domestic ones; they paid the bills, pushed the baby carriage after office hours, moved the sprinkler about over the lawn, and took the family driving on Sunday. Mr. Harling, therefore, seemed to me autocratic and imperial in his ways. He walked, talked, put on his gloves, shook hands, like a man who felt that he had power. He was not tall, but he carried his head so haughtily that he looked a commanding figure, and there was something daring and challenging in his eyes. I used to imagine that the "nobles" of whom Ántonia was always talking probably looked very much like Christian Harling, wore caped overcoats like his, and just such a glittering diamond upon the little finger.

Except when the father was at home, the Harling house was never quiet. Mrs. Harling and Nina and Ántonia made as much noise as a houseful of children, and there was usually somebody at the piano. Julia was the only one who was held down to regular hours of practicing, but they all played. When Frances came home at noon, she played until dinner was ready. When Sally got back from school, she sat down in her hat and coat and drummed the plantation melodies that negro minstrel troupes brought to town. Even Nina played the Swedish Wedding March.

Mrs. Harling had studied the piano under a good teacher, and somehow she managed to practice every day. I soon learned that if I were sent over on an errand and found Mrs. Harling at the piano, I must sit down and wait quietly until she turned to me. I can see her at this moment; her short, square person planted firmly on the stool, her little fat hands moving quickly and neatly over the keys, her eyes fixed on the music with intelligent concentration.

IV

"I won't have none of your weevily wheat,
and I won't have none of your barley,
But I'll take a measure of fine white flour,
to make a cake for Charley."

We were singing rhymes to tease Ántonia while she was beating up one of Charley's favorite cakes in her big mixing-bowl. It was a crisp autumn evening, just cold enough to make one glad to quit playing tag in the yard, and retreat into the kitchen. We had begun to roll popcorn balls with syrup when we heard a knock at the back door, and Tony dropped her spoon and went to open it. A plump, fair-skinned girl was standing in the doorway. She looked demure and pretty, and made a graceful picture in her blue cashmere dress and little blue hat, with a plaid shawl drawn neatly about her shoulders and a clumsy pocketbook in her hand.

"Hello, Tony. Don't you know me?" she asked in a smooth, low voice, looking in at us archly.

Ántonia gasped and stepped back. "Why, it's Lena! Of course I didn't know you, so dressed up!"

Lena Lingard laughed, as if this pleased her. I had not recognized her for a moment, either. I had never seen her before with a hat on her head—or with shoes and stockings on her feet, for that matter. And here she was, brushed and smoothed and dressed like a town girl, smiling at us with perfect composure.

"Hello, Jim," she said carelessly as she walked into the kitchen and looked about her. "I've come to town to work, too, Tony."

"Have you, now? Well, ain't that funny!" Ántonia stood ill at ease, and didn't seem to know just what to do with her visitor.

The door was open into the dining-room, where Mrs. Harling sat crocheting and Frances was reading. Frances asked Lena to come in and join them.

"You are Lena Lingard, aren't you? I've been to see your mother, but you were off herding cattle that day. Mama, this is Chris Lingard's oldest girl."

Mrs. Harling dropped her worsted and examined the visitor with quick, keen eyes. Lena was not at all disconcerted. She sat down in the chair Frances pointed out, carefully arranging her pocketbook and gray cotton gloves on her lap. We followed with our popcorn, but Ántonia hung back—said she had to get her cake into the oven.

"So you have come to town," said Mrs. Harling, her eyes still fixed on Lena. "Where are you working?"

"For Mrs. Thomas, the dressmaker. She is going to teach me to sew. She says I have quite a knack. I'm through with the farm. There ain't any end to the work on a farm, and always so much trouble happens. I'm going to be a dressmaker."

"Well, there have to be dressmakers. It's a good trade. But I wouldn't run down the farm, if I were you," said Mrs. Harling rather severely. "How is your mother?"

"Oh, mother's never very well; she has too much to do. She'd get away from the farm, too, if she could. She was willing for me to come. After I learn to do sewing, I can make money and help her."

"See that you don't forget to," said Mrs. Harling skeptically, as she took up her crocheting again and sent the hook in and out with nimble fingers.

"No, 'm, I won't," said Lena blandly. She took a few grains of the popcorn we pressed upon her, eating them discreetly and taking care not to get her fingers sticky.

Frances drew her chair up nearer to the visitor. "I thought you were going to be married, Lena," she said teasingly. "Didn't I hear that Nick Svendsen was rushing you pretty hard?"

Lena looked up with her curiously innocent smile. "He did go with me quite a while. But his father made a fuss about it and said he wouldn't give Nick any land if he married me, so he's going to marry Annie Iverson. I wouldn't like to be her; Nick's awful sullen, and he'll take it out on her. He ain't spoke to his father since he promised."

Frances laughed. "And how do you feel about it?"

"I don't want to marry Nick, or any other man," Lena murmured. "I've seen a good deal of married life, and I don't care for it. I want to be so I can help my mother and the children at home, and not have to ask lief of anybody."

"That's right," said Frances. "And Mrs. Thomas thinks you can learn dressmaking?"

"Yes, 'm. I've always liked to sew, but I never had much to do with. Mrs. Thomas makes lovely things for all the town ladies. Did you know Mrs. Gardener is having a purple velvet made? The velvet came from Omaha. My, but it's lovely!" Lena sighed softly and stroked her cashmere folds. "Tony knows I never did like out-of-door work," she added.

Mrs. Harling glanced at her. "I expect you'll learn to sew all right, Lena, if you'll only keep your head and not go gadding about to dances all the time and neglect your work, the way some country girls do."

"Yes, 'm. Tiny Soderball is coming to town, too. She's going to work at the Boys' Home Hotel. She'll see lots of strangers," Lena added wistfully.

"Too many, like enough," said Mrs. Harling. "I don't think a hotel is a good place for a girl; though I guess Mrs. Gardener keeps an eye on her waitresses."

Lena's candid eyes, that always looked a little sleepy under their long lashes, kept straying about the cheerful rooms with naïve admiration. Presently she drew on her cotton gloves. "I guess I must be leaving," she said irresolutely.

Frances told her to come again, whenever she was lonesome or wanted advice about anything. Lena replied that she didn't believe she would ever get lonesome in Black Hawk.

She lingered at the kitchen door and begged Ántonia to come and see her often. "I've got a room of my own at Mrs. Thomas's, with a carpet."

Tony shuffled uneasily in her cloth slippers. "I'll come sometime, but Mrs. Harling don't like to have me run much," she said evasively.

"You can do what you please when you go out, can't you?" Lena asked in a guarded whisper. "Ain't you crazy about town, Tony? I don't care what anybody says, I'm done with the farm!" She glanced back over her shoulder toward the dining-room, where Mrs. Harling sat.

When Lena was gone, Frances asked Ántonia why she hadn't been a little more cordial to her.

"I didn't know if your mother would like her coming here," said Ántonia, looking troubled. "She was kind of talked about, out there."

"Yes, I know. But mother won't hold it against her if she behaves well here. You needn't say anything about that to the children. I guess Jim has heard all that gossip?"

When I nodded, she pulled my hair and told me I knew too much, anyhow. We were good friends, Frances and I.

I ran home to tell grandmother that Lena Lingard had come to town. We were glad of it, for she had a hard life on the farm.

Lena lived in the Norwegian settlement west of Squaw Creek, and she used to herd her father's cattle in the open country between his place and the Shimerdas'. Whenever we rode over in that direction we saw her out among her cattle, bareheaded and barefooted, scantily dressed in tattered clothing, always knitting as she watched her herd. Before I knew Lena, I thought of her as something wild, that always lived on the prairie, because I had never seen her under a roof. Her yellow hair was burned to a ruddy thatch on her head; but her legs and arms, curiously enough, in spite of constant exposure to the sun, kept a miraculous whiteness which somehow made her seem more undressed than other girls who went scantily clad. The first time I stopped to talk to her, I was astonished at her soft voice and easy, gentle ways. The girls out there usually got rough and mannish after they went to herding. But Lena asked Jake and me to get off our horses and stay awhile, and behaved exactly as if she were in a house and were accustomed to having visitors. She was not embarrassed by her ragged clothes, and treated us as if we were old acquaintances. Even then I noticed the unusual color of her eyes—a shade of deep violet—and their soft, confiding expression.

Chris Lingard was not a very successful farmer, and he had a large family. Lena was always knitting stockings for little brothers and sisters, and even the Norwegian women, who disapproved of her, admitted that she was a good daughter to her mother. As Tony said, she had been talked about. She was accused of making Ole Benson lose the little sense he had—and that at an age when she should still have been in pinafores.

Ole lived in a leaky dugout somewhere at the edge of the settlement. He was fat and lazy and discouraged, and bad luck had become a habit with him. After he had had every other kind of misfortune, his wife, "Crazy Mary," tried to set a neighbor's barn on fire, and was sent to the asylum at Lincoln. She was kept there for a few months, then escaped and walked all the way home, nearly two hundred miles, traveling by night and hiding in barns and haystacks by day. When she got back to the Norwegian settlement, her poor feet were as hard as hoofs. She promised to be good, and was allowed to stay at home—though every one realized she was as crazy as ever, and she still ran about barefooted through the snow, telling her domestic troubles to her neighbors.

Not long after Mary came back from the asylum, I heard a young Dane, who was helping us to thrash, tell Jake and Otto that Chris Lingard's oldest girl had put Ole Benson out of his head, until he had no more sense than his crazy wife. When Ole was cultivating his corn that summer, he used to get discouraged in the field, tie up his team, and wander off to wherever Lena Lingard was herding. There he would sit down on the draw-side and help her watch her cattle. All the settlement was talking about it. The Norwegian preacher's wife went to Lena and told her she ought not to allow this; she begged Lena to come to church on Sundays. Lena said she hadn't a dress in the world any less ragged than the one on her back. Then the minister's wife went through her old trunks and found some things she had worn before her marriage.

The next Sunday Lena appeared at church, a little late, with her hair done up neatly on her head, like a young woman, wearing shoes and stockings, and the new dress, which she had made over for herself very becomingly. The congregation stared at her. Until that morning no one—unless it were Ole—had realized how pretty she was, or that she was growing up. The swelling lines of her figure had been hidden under the shapeless rags she wore in the fields. After the last hymn had been sung, and the congregation was dismissed, Ole slipped out to the hitch-bar and lifted Lena on her horse. That, in itself, was shocking; a married man was not expected to do such things. But it was nothing to the scene that followed. Crazy Mary darted out from the group of women at the church door, and ran down the road after Lena, shouting horrible threats.

"Look out, you Lena Lingard, look out! I'll come over with a corn-knife one day and trim some of that shape off you. Then you won't sail round so fine, making eyes at the men! . . ."

The Norwegian women didn't know where to look. They were formal housewives, most of them, with a severe sense of decorum. But Lena Lingard only laughed her lazy, good-natured laugh and rode on, gazing back over her shoulder at Ole's infuriated wife.

The time came, however, when Lena didn't laugh. More than once Crazy Mary chased her across the prairie and round and round the Shimerdas' cornfield. Lena never told her father; perhaps she was ashamed; perhaps she was more afraid of his anger than of the corn-knife. I was at the Shimerdas' one afternoon when Lena came bounding through the red grass as fast as her white legs could carry her. She ran straight into the house and hid in Ántonia's feather-bed. Mary was not far behind; she came right up to the door and made us feel how sharp her blade was, showing us very graphically just what she meant to do to Lena. Mrs. Shimerda, leaning out of the window, enjoyed the situation keenly, and was sorry when Ántonia sent Mary away, mollified by an apronful of bottle-tomatoes. Lena came out from Tony's room behind the kitchen, very pink from the heat of the feathers, but otherwise calm. She begged Ántonia and me to go with her, and help get her cattle together; they were scattered and might be gorging themselves in somebody's cornfield.

"Maybe you lose a steer and learn not to make somethings with your eyes at married men," Mrs. Shimerda told her hectoringly.

Lena only smiled her sleepy smile. "I never made anything to him with my eyes. I can't help it if he hangs around, and I can't order him off. It ain't my prairie."

V

After Lena came to Black Hawk I often met her downtown, where she would be matching sewing silk or buying "findings" for Mrs. Thomas. If I happened to walk home with her, she told me all about the dresses she was helping to make, or about what she saw and heard when she was with Tiny Soderball at the hotel on Saturday nights.

The Boys' Home was the best hotel on our branch of the Burlington, and all the commercial travelers in that territory tried to get into Black Hawk for Sunday. They used to assemble in the parlor after supper on Saturday nights. Marshall Field's man, Anson Kirkpatrick, played the piano and sang all the latest sentimental songs. After Tiny had helped the cook wash the dishes, she and Lena sat on the other side of the double doors between the parlor and the dining-room, listening to the music and giggling at the jokes and stories. Lena often said she hoped I would be a traveling man when I grew up. They had a gay life of it; nothing to do but ride about on trains all day and go to theaters when they were in big cities. Behind the hotel there was an old store building, where the salesmen opened their big trunks and spread out their samples on the counters. The Black Hawk merchants went to look at these things and order goods, and Mrs. Thomas, though she was "retail trade," was permitted to see them and to "get ideas." They were all generous, these traveling men; they gave Tiny Soderball handkerchiefs and gloves and ribbons and striped stockings, and so many bottles of perfume and cakes of scented soap that she bestowed some of them on Lena.

One afternoon in the week before Christmas I came upon Lena and her funny, square-headed little brother Chris, standing before the drug-store, gazing in at the wax dolls and blocks and Noah's arks arranged in the frosty show window. The boy had come to town with a neighbor to do his Christmas shopping, for he had money of his own this year. He was only twelve, but that winter he had got the job of sweeping out the Norwegian church and making the fire in it every Sunday morning. A cold job it must have been, too!

We went into Duckford's dry-goods store, and Chris unwrapped all his presents and showed them to me—something for each of the six younger than himself, even a rubber pig for the baby. Lena had given him one of Tiny Soderball's bottles of perfume for his mother, and he thought he would get some handkerchiefs to go with it. They were cheap, and he hadn't much money left. We found a tableful of handkerchiefs spread out for view at Duckford's. Chris wanted those with initial letters in the corner, because he had never seen any before. He studied them seriously, while Lena looked over his shoulder, telling him she thought the red letters would hold their color best. He seemed so perplexed that I thought perhaps he hadn't enough money, after all. Presently he said gravely,—

"Sister, you know mother's name is Berthe. I don't know if I ought to get B for Berthe or M for Mother."

Lena patted his bristly head. "I'd get the B, Christy. It will please her for you to think about her name. Nobody ever calls her by it now."

That satisfied him. His face cleared at once, and he took three reds and three blues. When the neighbor came in to say that it was time to start, Lena wound Chris's comforter about his neck and turned up his jacket collar—he had no overcoat—and we watched him climb into the wagon and start on his long, cold drive. As we walked together up the windy street, Lena wiped her eyes with the back of her woolen glove. "I get awful homesick for them, all the same," she murmured, as if she were answering some remembered reproach.

VI

Winter comes down savagely over a little town on the prairie. The wind that sweeps in from the open country strips away all the leafy screens that hide one yard from another in summer, and the houses seem to draw closer together. The roofs, that looked so far away across the green tree-tops, now stare you in the face, and they are so much uglier than when their angles were softened by vines and shrubs.

In the morning, when I was fighting my way to school against the wind, I couldn't see anything but the road in front of me; but in the late afternoon, when I was coming home, the town looked bleak and desolate to me. The pale, cold light of the winter sunset did not beautify—it was like the light of truth itself. When the smoky clouds hung low in the west and the red sun went down behind them, leaving a pink flush on the snowy roofs and the blue drifts, then the wind sprang up afresh, with a kind of bitter song, as if it said: "This is reality, whether you like it or not. All those frivolities of summer, the light and shadow, the living mask of green that trembled over everything, they were lies, and this is what was underneath. This is the truth." It was as if we were being punished for loving the loveliness of summer.

If I loitered on the playground after school, or went to the post-office for the mail and lingered to hear the gossip about the cigar-stand, it would be growing dark by the time I came home. The sun was gone; the frozen streets stretched long and blue before me; the lights were shining pale in kitchen windows, and I could smell the suppers cooking as I passed. Few people were abroad, and each one of them was hurrying toward a fire. The glowing stoves in the houses were like magnets. When one passed an old man, one could see nothing of his face but a red nose sticking out between a frosted beard and a long plush cap. The young men capered along with their hands in their pockets, and sometimes tried a slide on the icy sidewalk. The children, in their bright hoods and comforters, never walked, but always ran from the moment they left their door, beating their mittens against their sides. When I got as far as the Methodist Church, I was about halfway home. I can remember how glad I was when there happened to be a light in the church, and the painted glass window shone out at us as we came along the frozen street. In the winter bleakness a hunger for color came over people, like the Laplander's craving for fats and sugar. Without knowing why, we used to linger on the sidewalk outside the church when the lamps were lighted early for choir practice or prayer-meeting, shivering and talking until our feet were like lumps of ice. The crude reds and greens and blues of that colored glass held us there.

On winter nights, the lights in the Harlings' windows drew me like the painted glass. Inside that warm, roomy house there was color, too. After supper I used to catch up my cap, stick my hands in my pockets, and dive through the willow hedge as if witches were after me. Of course, if Mr. Harling was at home, if his shadow stood out on the blind of the west room, I did not go in, but turned and walked home by the long way, through the street, wondering what book I should read as I sat down with the two old people.

Such disappointments only gave greater zest to the nights when we acted charades, or had a costume ball in the back parlor, with Sally always dressed like a boy. Frances taught us to dance that winter, and she said, from the first lesson, that Ántonia would make the best dancer among us. On Saturday nights, Mrs. Harling used to play the old operas for us,—"Martha," "Norma," "Rigoletto,"—telling us the story while she played. Every Saturday night was like a party. The parlor, the back parlor, and the dining-room were warm and brightly lighted, with comfortable chairs and sofas, and gay pictures on the walls. One always felt at ease there. Ántonia brought her sewing and sat with us—she was already beginning to make pretty clothes for herself. After the long winter evenings on the prairie, with Ambrosch's sullen silences and her mother's complaints, the Harlings' house seemed, as she said, "like Heaven" to her. She was never too tired to make taffy or chocolate cookies for us. If Sally whispered in her ear, or Charley gave her three winks, Tony would rush into the kitchen and build a fire in the range on which she had already cooked three meals that day.

While we sat in the kitchen waiting for the cookies to bake or the taffy to cool, Nina used to coax Ántonia to tell her stories—about the calf that broke its leg, or how Yulka saved her little turkeys from drowning in the freshet, or about old Christmases and weddings in Bohemia. Nina interpreted the stories about the crèche fancifully, and in spite of our derision she cherished a belief that Christ was born in Bohemia a short time before the Shimerdas left that country. We all liked Tony's stories. Her voice had a peculiarly engaging quality; it was deep, a little husky, and one always heard the breath vibrating behind it. Everything she said seemed to come right out of her heart.

One evening when we were picking out kernels for walnut taffy, Tony told us a new story.

"Mrs. Harling, did you ever hear about what happened up in the Norwegian settlement last summer, when I was thrashing there? We were at Iversons', and I was driving one of the grain wagons."

Mrs. Harling came out and sat down among us. "Could you throw the wheat into the bin yourself, Tony?" She knew what heavy work it was.

"Yes, mam, I did. I could shovel just as fast as that fat Andern boy that drove the other wagon. One day it was just awful hot. When we got back to the field from dinner, we took things kind of easy. The men put in the horses and got the machine going, and Ole Iverson was up on the deck, cutting bands. I was sitting against a straw stack, trying to get some shade. My wagon wasn't going out first, and somehow I felt the heat awful that day. The sun was so hot like it was going to burn the world up. After a while I see a man coming across the stubble, and when he got close I see it was a tramp. His toes stuck out of his shoes, and he hadn't shaved for a long while, and his eyes was awful red and wild, like he had some sickness. He comes right up and begins to talk like he knows me already. He says: 'The ponds in this country is done got so low a man couldn't drownd himself in one of 'em.'

"I told him nobody wanted to drownd themselves, but if we didn't have rain soon we'd have to pump water for the cattle.

"'Oh, cattle,' he says, 'you'll all take care of your cattle! Ain't you got no beer here?' I told him he'd have to go to the Bohemians for beer; the Norwegians didn't have none when they thrashed. 'My God!' he says, 'so it's Norwegians now, is it? I thought this was Americy.'

"Then he goes up to the machine and yells out to Ole Iverson, 'Hello, partner, let me up there. I can cut bands, and I'm tired of trampin'. I won't go no farther.'

"I tried to make signs to Ole, 'cause I thought that man was crazy and might get the machine stopped up. But Ole, he was glad to get down out of the sun and chaff—it gets down your neck and sticks to you something awful when it's hot like that. So Ole jumped down and crawled under one of the wagons for shade, and the tramp got on the machine. He cut bands all right for a few minutes, and then, Mrs. Harling, he waved his hand to me and jumped head-first right into the thrashing machine after the wheat.

"I begun to scream, and the men run to stop the horses, but the belt had sucked him down, and by the time they got her stopped he was all beat and cut to pieces. He was wedged in so tight it was a hard job to get him out, and the machine ain't never worked right since."

"Was he clear dead, Tony?" we cried.

"Was he dead? Well, I guess so! There, now Nina's all upset. We won't talk about it. Don't you cry, Nina. No old tramp won't get you while Tony's here."

Mrs. Harling spoke up sternly. "Stop crying, Nina, or I'll always send you upstairs when Ántonia tells us about the country. Did they never find out where he came from, Ántonia?"

"Never, mam. He hadn't been seen nowhere except in a little town they call Conway. He tried to get beer there, but there wasn't any saloon. Maybe he came in on a freight, but the brakeman hadn't seen him. They couldn't find no letters nor nothing on him; nothing but an old penknife in his pocket and the wishbone of a chicken wrapped up in a piece of paper, and some poetry."

"Some poetry?" we exclaimed.

"I remember," said Frances. "It was 'The Old Oaken Bucket,' cut out of a newspaper and nearly worn out. Ole Iverson brought it into the office and showed it to me."

"Now, wasn't that strange, Miss Frances?" Tony asked thought-fully. "What would anybody want to kill themselves in summer for? In thrashing time, too! It's nice everywhere then."

"So it is, Ántonia," said Mrs. Harling heartily. "Maybe I'll go home and help you thrash next summer. Isn't that taffy nearly ready to eat? I've been smelling it a long while."

There was a basic harmony between Ántonia and her mistress. They had strong, independent natures, both of them. They knew what they liked, and were not always trying to imitate other people. They loved children and animals and music, and rough play and digging in the earth. They liked to prepare rich, hearty food and to see people eat it; to make up soft white beds and to see youngsters asleep in them. They ridiculed conceited people and were quick to help unfortunate ones. Deep down in each of them there was a kind of hearty joviality, a relish of life, not overdelicate, but very invigorating. I never tried to define it, but I was distinctly conscious of it. I could not imagine Ántonia's living for a week in any other house in Black Hawk than the Harlings'.

VII

Winter lies too long in country towns; hangs on until it is stale and shabby, old and sullen. On the farm the weather was the great fact, and men's affairs went on underneath it, as the streams creep under the ice. But in Black Hawk the scene of human life was spread out shrunken and pinched, frozen down to the bare stalk.

Through January and February I went to the river with the Harlings on clear nights, and we skated up to the big island and made bonfires on the frozen sand. But by March the ice was rough and choppy, and the snow on the river bluffs was gray and mournful-looking. I was tired of school, tired of winter clothes, of the rutted streets, of the dirty drifts and the piles of cinders that had lain in the yards so long. There was only one break in the dreary monotony of that month; when Blind d'Arnault, the negro pianist, came to town. He gave a concert at the Opera House on Monday night, and he and his manager spent Saturday and Sunday at our comfortable hotel. Mrs. Harling had known d'Arnault for years. She told Ántonia she had better go to see Tiny that Saturday evening, as there would certainly be music at the Boys' Home.

Saturday night after supper I ran downtown to the hotel and

slipped quietly into the parlor. The chairs and sofas were already occupied, and the air smelled pleasantly of cigar smoke. The parlor had once been two rooms, and the floor was sway-backed where the partition had been cut away. The wind from without made waves in the long carpet. A coal stove glowed at either end of the room, and the grand piano in the middle stood open.

There was an atmosphere of unusual freedom about the house that night, for Mrs. Gardener had gone to Omaha for a week. Johnnie had been having drinks with the guests until he was rather absent-minded. It was Mrs. Gardener who ran the business and looked after everything. Her husband stood at the desk and welcomed incoming travelers. He was a popular fellow, but no manager.

Mrs. Gardener was admittedly the best-dressed woman in Black Hawk, drove the best horse, and had a smart trap and a little white-and-gold sleigh. She seemed indifferent to her possessions, was not half so solicitous about them as her friends were. She was tall, dark, severe, with something Indian-like in the rigid immobility of her face. Her manner was cold, and she talked little. Guests felt that they were receiving, not conferring, a favor when they stayed at her house. Even the smartest traveling men were flattered when Mrs. Gardener stopped to chat with them for a moment. The patrons of the hotel were divided into two classes; those who had seen Mrs. Gardener's diamonds, and those who had not.

When I stole into the parlor Anson Kirkpatrick, Marshall Field's man, was at the piano, playing airs from a musical comedy then running in Chicago. He was a dapper little Irishman, very vain, homely as a monkey, with friends everywhere, and a sweetheart in every port, like a sailor. I did not know all the men who were sitting about, but I recognized a furniture salesman from Kansas City, a drug man, and Willy O'Reilly, who traveled for a jewelry house and sold musical instruments. The talk was all about good and bad hotels, actors and actresses and musical prodigies. I learned that Mrs. Gardener had gone to Omaha to hear Booth and Barrett, who were to play there next week, and that Mary Anderson was having a great success in "A Winter's Tale," in London.

The door from the office opened, and Johnnie Gardener came in, directing Blind d'Arnault,—he would never consent to be led. He was a heavy, bulky mulatto, on short legs, and he came tapping the floor in front of him with his gold-headed cane. His yellow face was lifted in the light, with a show of white teeth, all grinning, and his shrunken, papery eyelids lay motionless over his blind eyes.

"Good-evening, gentlemen. No ladies here? Good-evening, gentlemen. We going to have a little music? Some of you gentlemen going to play for me this evening?" It was the soft amiable negro voice, like those I remembered from early childhood, with the note of docile subservience in it. He had the negro head, too; almost no head at all; nothing behind the ears but folds of neck under close-clipped wool. He would have been repulsive if his face had not been so kindly and happy. It was the happiest face I had seen since I left Virginia.

He felt his way directly to the piano. The moment he sat down, I noticed the nervous infirmity of which Mrs. Harling had told me. When he was sitting, or standing still, he swayed back and forth incessantly, like a rocking toy. At the piano, he swayed in time to the music, and when he was not playing, his body kept up this motion, like an empty mill grinding on. He found the pedals and tried them, ran his yellow hands up and down the keys a few times, tinkling off scales, then turned to the company.

"She seems all right, gentlemen. Nothing happened to her since the last time I was here. Mrs. Gardener, she always has this piano tuned up before I come. Now, gentlemen, I expect you've all got grand voices. Seems like we might have some good old plantation songs to-night."

The men gathered round him, as he began to play "My Old Kentucky Home." They sang one negro melody after another, while the mulatto sat rocking himself, his head thrown back, his yellow face lifted, its shriveled eyelids never fluttering.

He was born in the Far South, on the d'Arnault plantation, where the spirit if not the fact of slavery persisted. When he was three weeks old he had an illness which left him totally blind. As soon as he was old enough to sit up alone and toddle about, another affliction, the nervous motion of his body, became apparent. His mother, a buxom young negro wench who was laundress for the d'Arnaults, concluded that her blind baby was "not right" in his head, and she was ashamed of him. She loved him devotedly, but he was so ugly, with his sunken eyes and his "fidgets," that she hid him away from people. All the dainties she brought down from the "Big House" were for the blind child, and she beat and cuffed her other children whenever she found them teasing him or trying to get his chicken-bone away from him. He began to talk early, remembered everything he heard, and his mammy said he "wasn't all wrong." She named him Samson, because he was blind, but on the plantation he was known as "yellow Martha's simple child." He was docile and obedient, but when he was six years old he began to run away from home, always taking the same direction. He felt his way through the lilacs, along the boxwood hedge, up to the south wing of the "Big House," where Miss Nellie d'Arnault practiced the piano every morning. This angered his mother more than anything else he could have done; she was so ashamed of his ugliness that she couldn't bear to have white folks see him. Whenever she caught him slipping away from the cabin, she whipped him unmercifully, and told him what dreadful things old Mr. d'Arnault would do to him if he ever found him near the "Big House." But the next time Samson had a chance, he ran away again. If Miss d'Arnault stopped practicing for a moment and went toward the window, she saw this hideous little pickaninny, dressed in an old piece of sacking, standing in the open space between the hollyhock rows, his body rocking automatically, his blind face lifted to the sun and wearing an expression of idiotic rapture. Often she was tempted to tell Martha that the child must be kept at home, but somehow the memory of his foolish, happy face deterred her. She remembered that his sense of hearing was nearly all he had,—though it did not occur to her that he might have more of it than other children.

One day Samson was standing thus while Miss Nellie was playing her lesson to her music-master. The windows were open. He heard them get up from the piano, talk a little while, and then leave the room. He heard the door close after them. He crept up to the front windows and stuck his head in: there was no one there. He could always detect the presence of any one in a room. He put one foot over the window sill and straddled it. His mother had told him over and over how his master would give him to the big mastiff if he ever found him "meddling." Samson had got too near the mastiff's kennel once, and had felt his terrible breath in his face. He thought about that, but he pulled in his other foot.

Through the dark he found his way to the Thing, to its mouth. He touched it softly, and it answered softly, kindly. He shivered and stood still. Then he began to feel it all over, ran his finger tips along the slippery sides, embraced the carved legs, tried to get some conception of its shape and size, of the space it occupied in primeval night. It was cold and hard, and like nothing else in his black universe. He went back to its mouth, began at one end of the keyboard and felt his way down into the mellow thunder, as far as he could go. He seemed to know that it must be done with the fingers, not with the fists or the feet. He approached this highly artificial instrument through a mere instinct, and coupled himself to it, as if he knew it was to piece him out and make a whole creature of him. After he had tried over all the sounds, he began to finger out passages from things Miss Nellie had been practicing, passages that were already his, that lay under the bones of his pinched, conical little skull, definite as animal desires. The door opened; Miss Nellie and her music-master stood behind it, but blind Samson, who was so sensitive to presences, did not know they were there. He was feeling out the pattern that lay all ready-made on the big and little keys. When he paused for a moment, because the sound was wrong and he wanted another, Miss Nellie spoke softly. He whirled about in a spasm of terror, leaped forward in the dark, struck his head on the open window, and fell screaming and bleeding to the floor. He had what his mother called a fit. The doctor came and gave him opium.

When Samson was well again, his young mistress led him back to the piano. Several teachers experimented with him. They found he had absolute pitch, and a remarkable memory. As a very young child he could repeat, after a fashion, any composition that was played for him. No matter how many wrong notes he struck, he never lost the intention of a passage, he brought the substance of it across by irregular and astonishing means. He wore his teachers out. He could never learn like other people, never acquired any finish. He was always a negro prodigy who played barbarously and wonderfully. As piano playing, it was perhaps abominable, but as music it was something real, vitalized by a sense of rhythm that was stronger than his other physical senses,—that not only filled his dark mind, but worried his body incessantly. To hear him, to watch him, was to see a negro enjoying himself as only a negro can. It was as if all the agreeable sensations possible to creatures of flesh and blood were heaped upon those black and white keys, and he were gloating over them and trickling them through his yellow fingers.

In the middle of a crashing waltz d'Arnault suddenly began to play softly, and, turning to one of the men who stood behind him, whispered, "Somebody dancing in there." He jerked his bullet head toward the dining-room. "I hear little feet,—girls, I 'spect."

Anson Kirkpatrick mounted a chair and peeped over the transom. Springing down, he wrenched open the doors and ran out into the dining-room. Tiny and Lena, Ántonia and Mary Dusak, were waltzing in the middle of the floor. They separated and fled toward the kitchen, giggling.

Kirkpatrick caught Tiny by the elbows. "What's the matter with you girls? Dancing out here by yourselves, when there's a roomful of lonesome men on the other side of the partition! Introduce me to your friends, Tiny."

The girls, still laughing, were trying to escape. Tiny looked alarmed. "Mrs. Gardener wouldn't like it," she protested. "She'd be awful mad if you was to come out here and dance with us."

"Mrs. Gardener's in Omaha, girl. Now, you're Lena, are you?— and you're Tony and you're Mary. Have I got you all straight?"

O'Reilly and the others began to pile the chairs on the tables. Johnnie Gardener ran in from the office.

"Easy, boys, easy!" he entreated them. "You'll wake the cook, and there'll be the devil to pay for me. She won't hear the music, but she'll be down the minute anything's moved in the dining-room."

"Oh, what do you care, Johnnie? Fire the cook and wire Molly to bring another. Come along, nobody'll tell tales."

Johnnie shook his head. "'S a fact, boys," he said confidentially. "If I take a drink in Black Hawk, Molly knows it in Omaha!"

His guests laughed and slapped him on the shoulder. "Oh, we'll make it all right with Molly. Get your back up, Johnnie."

Molly was Mrs. Gardener's name, of course. "Molly Bawn" was painted in large blue letters on the glossy white side of the hotel bus, and "Molly" was engraved inside Johnnie's ring and on his watch-case—doubtless on his heart, too. He was an affectionate little man, and he thought his wife a wonderful woman; he knew that without her he would hardly be more than a clerk in some other man's hotel.

At a word from Kirkpatrick, d'Arnault spread himself out over the piano, and began to draw the dance music out of it, while the perspiration shone on his short wool and on his uplifted face. He looked like some glistening African god of pleasure, full of strong, savage blood. Whenever the dancers paused to change partners or to catch breath, he would boom out softly, "Who's that goin' back on me? One of these city gentlemen, I bet! Now, you girls, you ain't goin' to let that floor get cold?"

Ántonia seemed frightened at first, and kept looking questioningly at Lena and Tiny over Willy O'Reilly's shoulder. Tiny Soderball was trim and slender, with lively little feet and pretty ankles—she wore her dresses very short. She was quicker in speech, lighter in movement and manner than the other girls. Mary Dusak was broad and brown of countenance, slightly marked by smallpox, but handsome for all that. She had beautiful chestnut hair, coils of it; her forehead was low and smooth, and her commanding dark eyes regarded the world indifferently and fearlessly. She looked bold and resourceful and unscrupulous, and she was all of these. They were handsome girls, had the fresh color of their country up-bringing, and in their eyes that brilliancy which is called,—by no metaphor, alas!—"the light of youth."

D'Arnault played until his manager came and shut the piano. Before he left us, he showed us his gold watch which struck the hours, and a topaz ring, given him by some Russian nobleman who delighted in negro melodies, and had heard d'Arnault play in New Orleans. At last he tapped his way upstairs, after bowing to everybody, docile and happy. I walked home with Ántonia. We were so excited that we dreaded to go to bed. We lingered a long while at the Harlings' gate, whispering in the cold until the restlessness was slowly chilled out of us.

VIII

The Harling children and I were never happier, never felt more contented and secure, than in the weeks of spring which broke that long winter. We were out all day in the thin sunshine, helping Mrs. Harling and Tony break the ground and plant the garden, dig around the orchard trees, tie up vines and clip the hedges. Every morning, before I was up, I could hear Tony singing in the garden rows. After the apple and cherry trees broke into bloom, we ran about under them, hunting for the new nests the birds were building, throwing clods at each other, and playing hide-and-seek with Nina. Yet the summer which was to change everything was coming nearer every day. When boys and girls are growing up, life can't stand still, not even in the quietest of country towns; and they have to grow up, whether they will or no. That is what their elders are always forgetting.

It must have been in June, for Mrs. Harling and Ántonia were preserving cherries, when I stopped one morning to tell them that a dancing pavilion had come to town. I had seen two drays hauling the canvas and painted poles up from the depot.

That afternoon three cheerful-looking Italians strolled about Black Hawk, looking at everything, and with them was a dark, stout woman who wore a long gold watch chain about her neck and carried a black lace parasol. They seemed especially interested in children and vacant lots. When I overtook them and stopped to say a word, I found them affable and confiding. They told me they worked in Kansas City in the winter, and in summer they went out among the farming towns with their tent and taught dancing. When business fell off in one place, they moved on to another.

The dancing pavilion was put up near the Danish laundry, on a vacant lot surrounded by tall, arched cottonwood trees. It was very much like a merry-go-round tent, with open sides and gay flags flying from the poles. Before the week was over, all the ambitious mothers were sending their children to the afternoon dancing class. At three o'clock one met little girls in white dresses and little boys in the round-collared shirts of the time, hurrying along the sidewalk on their way to the tent. Mrs. Vanni received them at the entrance, always dressed in lavender with a great deal of black lace, her important watch chain lying on her bosom. She wore her hair on the top of her head, built up in a black tower, with red coral combs. When she smiled, she showed two rows of strong, crooked yellow teeth. She taught the little children herself, and her husband, the harpist, taught the older ones.

Often the mothers brought their fancy-work and sat on the shady side of the tent during the lesson. The popcorn man wheeled his glass wagon under the big cottonwood by the door, and lounged in the sun, sure of a good trade when the dancing was over. Mr. Jensen, the Danish laundryman, used to bring a

chair from his porch and sit out in the grass plot. Some ragged little boys from the depot sold pop and iced lemonade under a
white umbrella at the corner, and made faces at the spruce youngsters who came to dance. That vacant lot soon became the most
cheerful place in town. Even on the hottest afternoons the cottonwoods made a rustling shade, and the air smelled of popcorn and
melted butter, and Bouncing Bets wilting in the sun. Those hardy
flowers had run away from the laundryman's garden, and the
grass in the middle of the lot was pink with them.

The Vannis kept exemplary order, and closed every evening at
the hour suggested by the City Council. When Mrs. Vanni gave
the signal, and the harp struck up "Home, Sweet Home," all Black
Hawk knew it was ten o'clock. You could set your watch by that
tune as confidently as by the Round House whistle.

At last there was something to do in those long, empty summer
evenings, when the married people sat like images on their front
porches, and the boys and girls tramped and tramped the board
sidewalks—northward to the edge of the open prairie, south to the
depot, then back again to the post-office, the ice-cream parlor, the
butcher shop. Now there was a place where the girls could wear
their new dresses, and where one could laugh aloud without being
reproved by the ensuing silence. That silence seemed to ooze out
of the ground, to hang under the foliage of the black maple trees
with the bats and shadows. Now it was broken by light-hearted
sounds. First the deep purring of Mr. Vanni's harp came in silvery
ripples through the blackness of the dusty-smelling night; then the
violins fell in—one of them was almost like a flute. They called so
archly, so seductively, that our feet hurried toward the tent of
themselves. Why hadn't we had a tent before?

Dancing became popular now, just as roller skating had
been the summer before. The Progressive Euchre Club arranged
with the Vannis for the exclusive use of the floor on Tuesday
and Friday nights. At other times any one could dance who
paid his money and was orderly; the railroad men, the Round
House mechanics, the delivery boys, the iceman, the farmhands

who lived near enough to ride into town after their day's work was over.

I never missed a Saturday night dance. The tent was open until midnight then. The country boys came in from farms eight and ten miles away, and all the country girls were on the floor,—Ántonia and Lena and Tiny, and the Danish laundry girls and their friends. I was not the only boy who found these dances gayer than the others. The young men who belonged to the Progressive Euchre Club used to drop in late and risk a tiff with their sweethearts and general condemnation for a waltz with "the hired girls."

IX

There was a curious social situation in Black Hawk. All the young men felt the attraction of the fine, well-set-up country girls who had come to town to earn a living, and, in nearly every case, to help the father struggle out of debt, or to make it possible for the younger children of the family to go to school.

Those girls had grown up in the first bitter-hard times, and had got little schooling themselves. But the younger brothers and sisters, for whom they made such sacrifices and who have had "advantages," never seem to me, when I meet them now, half as interesting or as well educated. The older girls, who helped to break up the wild sod, learned so much from life, from poverty, from their mothers and grandmothers, they had all, like Ántonia, been early awakened and made observant by coming at a tender age from an old country to a new. I can remember a score of these country girls who were in service in Black Hawk during the few years I lived there, and I can remember something unusual and engaging about each of them. Physically they were almost a race apart, and out-of-door work had given them a vigor which, when they got over their first shyness on coming to town, developed into a positive carriage and freedom of movement, and made them conspicuous among Black Hawk women.

That was before the day of High-School athletics. Girls who had to walk more than half a mile to school were pitied. There was not a tennis court in the town; physical exercise was thought rather inelegant for the daughters of well-to-do families. Some of the High-School girls were jolly and pretty, but they stayed indoors in winter because of the cold, and in summer because of the heat. When one danced with them their bodies never moved inside their clothes; their muscles seemed to ask but one thing—not to be disturbed. I remember those girls merely as faces in the schoolroom, gay and rosy, or listless and dull, cut off below the shoulders, like cherubs, by the ink-smeared tops of the high desks that were surely put there to make us round-shouldered and hollow-chested.

The daughters of Black Hawk merchants had a confident, unin-quiring belief that they were "refined," and that the country girls, who "worked out," were not. The American farmers in our county were quite as hard-pressed as their neighbors from other countries. All alike had come to Nebraska with little capital and no knowl-edge of the soil they must subdue. All had borrowed money on their land. But no matter in what straits the Pennsylvanian or Vir-ginian found himself, he would not let his daughters go out into service. Unless his girls could teach a country school, they sat at home in poverty. The Bohemian and Scandinavian girls could not get positions as teachers, because they had no opportunity to learn the language. Determined to help in the struggle to clear the homestead from debt, they had no alternative but to go into ser-vice. Some of them, after they came to town, remained as serious and discreet in behavior as they had been when they ploughed and herded on their father's farm. Others, like the three Bohemian Marys, tried to make up for the years of youth they had lost. But every one of them did what she had set out to do, and sent home those hard-earned dollars. The girls I knew were always helping to pay for ploughs and reapers, brood-sows, or steers to fatten.

One result of this family solidarity was that the foreign farmers in our county were the first to become prosperous. After the fathers were out of debt, the daughters married the sons of neigh-bors,—usually of like nationality,—and the girls who once worked in Black Hawk kitchens are to-day managing big farms and fine families of their own; their children are better off than the children of the town women they used to serve.

I thought the attitude of the town people toward these girls very stupid. If I told my schoolmates that Lena Lingard's grand-father was a clergyman, and much respected in Norway, they looked at me blankly. What did it matter? All foreigners were ignorant people who couldn't speak English. There was not a man in Black Hawk who had the intelligence or cultivation, much less the personal distinction, of Ántonia's father. Yet people saw no difference between her and the three Marys; they were all Bohe-mians, all "hired girls."

I always knew I should live long enough to see my country girls come into their own, and I have. To-day the best that a harassed Black Hawk merchant can hope for is to sell provisions and farm machinery and automobiles to the rich farms where that first crop of stalwart Bohemian and Scandinavian girls are now the mistresses.

The Black Hawk boys looked forward to marrying Black Hawk girls, and living in a brand-new little house with best chairs that must not be sat upon, and hand-painted china that must not be used. But sometimes a young fellow would look up from his ledger, or out through the grating of his father's bank, and let his eyes follow Lena Lingard, as she passed the window with her slow, undulating walk, or Tiny Soderball, tripping by in her short skirt and striped stockings.

The country girls were considered a menace to the social order. Their beauty shone out too boldly against a conventional background. But anxious mothers need have felt no alarm. They mistook the mettle of their sons. The respect for respectability was stronger than any desire in Black Hawk youth.

Our young man of position was like the son of a royal house; the boy who swept out his office or drove his delivery wagon might frolic with the jolly country girls, but he himself must sit all evening in a plush parlor where conversation dragged so perceptibly that the father often came in and made blundering efforts to warm up the atmosphere. On his way home from his dull call, he would perhaps meet Tony and Lena, coming along the sidewalk whispering to each other, or the three Bohemian Marys in their long plush coats and caps, comporting themselves with a dignity that only made their eventful histories the more piquant. If he went to the hotel to see a traveling man on business, there was Tiny, arching her shoulders at him like a kitten. If he went into the laundry to get his collars, there were four Danish girls, smiling up from their ironing-boards, with their white throats and their pink cheeks.

The three Marys were the heroines of a cycle of scandalous stories, which the old men were fond of relating as they sat about the cigar-stand in the drug-store. Mary Dusak had been housekeeper for a bachelor rancher from Boston, and after several years in his service she was forced to retire from the world for a short time. Later she came back to town to take the place of her friend, Mary Svoboda, who was similarly embarrassed. The three Marys were considered as dangerous as high explosives to have about the kitchen, yet they were such good cooks and such admirable housekeepers that they never had to look for a place.

The Vannis' tent brought the town boys and the country girls together on neutral ground. Sylvester Lovett, who was cashier in his father's bank, always found his way to the tent on Saturday night. He took all the dances Lena Lingard would give him, and even grew bold enough to walk home with her. If his sisters or their friends happened to be among the onlookers on "popular nights," Sylvester stood back in the shadow under the cottonwood trees, smoking and watching Lena with a harassed expression. Several times I stumbled upon him there in the dark, and I felt rather sorry for him. He reminded me of Ole Benson, who used to sit on the draw-side and watch Lena herd her cattle. Later in the summer, when Lena went home for a week to visit her mother, I heard from Ántonia that young Lovett drove all the way out there to see her, and took her buggy-riding. In my ingenuousness I hoped that Sylvester would marry Lena, and thus give all the country girls a better position in the town.

Sylvester dallied about Lena until he began to make mistakes in his work; had to stay at the bank until after dark to make his books balance. He was daft about her, and everyone knew it. To escape from his predicament he ran away with a widow six years older then himself, who owned a half-section. This remedy worked, apparently. He never looked at Lena again, nor lifted his eyes as he ceremoniously tipped his hat when he happened to meet her on the sidewalk.

So that was what they were like, I thought, these white-handed, high-collared clerks and bookkeepers! I used to glare at young Lovett from a distance and only wished I had some way of showing my contempt for him.

X

It was at the Vannis' tent that Ántonia was discovered. Hitherto she had been looked upon more as a ward of the Harlings than as one of the "hired girls." She had lived in their house and yard and garden; her thoughts never seemed to stray outside that little kingdom. But after the tent came to town she began to go about with Tiny and Lena and their friends. The Vannis often said that Ántonia was the best dancer of them all. I sometimes heard murmurs in the crowd outside the pavilion that Mrs. Harling would soon have her hands full with that girl. The young men began to joke with each other about "the Harlings' Tony" as they did about "the Marshalls' Anna" or "the Gardeners' Tiny."

Ántonia talked and thought of nothing but the tent. She hummed the dance tunes all day. When supper was late, she hurried with her dishes, dropped and smashed them in her excitement. At the first call of the music, she became irresponsible. If she hadn't time to dress, she merely flung off her apron and shot out of the kitchen door. Sometimes I went with her; the moment the lighted tent came into view she would break into a run, like a boy. There were always partners waiting for her; she began to dance before she got her breath.

Ántonia's success at the tent had its consequences. The iceman lingered too long now, when he came into the covered porch to fill the refrigerator. The delivery boys hung about the kitchen when they brought the groceries. Young farmers who were in town for Saturday came tramping through the yard to the back door to engage dances, or to invite Tony to parties and picnics. Lena and Norwegian Anna dropped in to help her with her work, so that she could get away early. The boys who brought her home after the dances sometimes laughed at the back gate and wakened Mr. Harling from his sleep. A crisis was inevitable.

One Saturday night Mr. Harling had gone down to the cellar for beer. As he came up the stairs in the dark, he heard scuffling on the back porch, and then the sound of a vigorous slap. He looked out through the side door in time to see a pair of long legs vaulting over the picket fence. Ántonia was standing there, angry and excited. Young Harry Paine, who was to marry his employer's daughter on Monday, had come to the tent with a crowd of friends and danced all evening. Afterward, he begged Ántonia to let him walk home with her. She said she supposed he was a nice young man, as he was one of Miss Frances's friends, and she didn't mind. On the back porch he tried to kiss her, and when she protested,— because he was going to be married on Monday,—he caught her and kissed her until she got one hand free and slapped him.

Mr. Harling put his beer bottles down on the table. "This is what I've been expecting, Ántonia. You've been going with girls who have a reputation for being free and easy, and now you've got the same reputation. I won't have this and that fellow tramping about my back yard all the time. This is the end of it, to-night. It stops, short. You can quit going to these dances, or you can hunt another place. Think it over."

The next morning when Mrs. Harling and Frances tried to

reason with Ántonia, they found her agitated but determined. "Stop going to the tent?" she panted. "I wouldn't think of it for a minute! My own father couldn't make me stop! Mr. Harling ain't my boss outside my work. I won't give up my friends, either. The boys I go with are nice fellows. I thought Mr. Paine was all right, too, because he used to come here. I guess I gave him a red face for his wedding, all right!" she blazed out indignantly.

"You'll have to do one thing or the other, Ántonia," Mrs. Harling told her decidedly. "I can't go back on what Mr. Harling has said. This is his house."

"Then I'll just leave, Mrs. Harling. Lena's been wanting me to get a place closer to her for a long while. Mary Svoboda's going away from the Cutters' to work at the hotel, and I can have her place."

Mrs. Harling rose from her chair. "Ántonia, if you go to the Cutters to work, you cannot come back to this house again. You know what that man is. It will be the ruin of you."

Tony snatched up the tea-kettle and began to pour boiling water over the glasses, laughing excitedly. "Oh, I can take care of myself! I'm a lot stronger than Cutter is. They pay four dollars there, and there's no children. The work's nothing; I can have every evening, and be out a lot in the afternoons."

"I thought you liked children. Tony, what's come over you?"

"I don't know, something has." Ántonia tossed her head and set her jaw. "A girl like me has got to take her good times when she can. Maybe there won't be any tent next year. I guess I want to have my fling, like the other girls."

Mrs. Harling gave a short, harsh laugh. "If you go to work for the Cutters, you're likely to have a fling that you won't get up from in a hurry."

Frances said, when she told grandmother and me about this scene, that every pan and plate and cup on the shelves trembled when her mother walked out of the kitchen. Mrs. Harling declared bitterly that she wished she had never let herself get fond of Ántonia.

XI

Wick Cutter was the money-lender who had fleeced poor Russian Peter. When a farmer once got into the habit of going to Cutter, it was like gambling or the lottery; in an hour of discouragement he went back.

Cutter's first name was Wycliffe, and he liked to talk about his pious bringing-up. He contributed regularly to the Protestant churches, "for sentiment's sake," as he said with a flourish of the hand. He came from a town in Iowa where there were a great many Swedes, and could speak a little Swedish, which gave him a great advantage with the early Scandinavian settlers.

In every frontier settlement there are men who have come there to escape restraint. Cutter was one of the "fast set" of Black Hawk business men. He was an inveterate gambler, though a poor loser. When we saw a light burning in his office late at night, we knew that a game of poker was going on. Cutter boasted that he never drank anything stronger than sherry, and said he got his start in life by saving the money that other young men spent for cigars. He was full of moral maxims for boys. When he came to our house on business, he quoted "Poor Richard's Almanack" to me, and told me he was delighted to find a town boy who could milk a cow. He was particularly affable to grandmother, and whenever they met he would begin at once to talk about "the good old times" and simple living. I detested his pink, bald head, and his yellow whiskers, always soft and glistening. It was said he brushed them every night, as a woman does her hair. His white teeth looked factory-made. His skin was red and rough, as if from perpetual sunburn; he often went away to hot springs to take mud baths. He was notoriously dissolute with women. Two Swedish girls who had lived in his house were the worse for the experience. One of them he had taken to Omaha and established in the business for which he had fitted her. He still visited her.

Cutter lived in a state of perpetual warfare with his wife, and yet, apparently, they never thought of separating. They dwelt in a fussy, scroll-work house, painted white and buried in thick evergreens, with a fussy white fence and barn. Cutter thought he knew a great deal about horses, and usually had a colt which he was training for the track. On Sunday mornings one could see him out at the fair grounds, speeding around the race-course in his trotting-buggy, wearing yellow gloves and a black-and-white-check traveling cap, his whiskers blowing back in the breeze. If there were any boys about, Cutter would offer one of them a quarter to hold the stop-watch, and then drive off, saying he had no change and would "fix it up next time." No one could cut his lawn or wash his buggy to suit him. He was so fastidious and prim about his place that a boy would go to a good deal of trouble to throw a dead cat into his back yard, or to dump a sackful of tin cans in his alley. It was a peculiar combination of old-maidishness and licentiousness that made Cutter seem so despicable.

He had certainly met his match when he married Mrs. Cutter. She was a terrifying-looking person; almost a giantess in height, raw-boned, with iron-gray hair, a face always flushed, and prominent, hysterical eyes. When she meant to be entertaining and agreeable, she nodded her head incessantly and snapped her eyes at one. Her teeth were long and curved, like a horse's; people said babies always cried if she smiled at them. Her face had a kind of fascination for me; it was the very color and shape of anger. There was a gleam of something akin to insanity in her full, intense eyes. She was formal in manner, and made calls in rustling, steel-gray brocades and a tall bonnet with bristling aigrettes.

Mrs. Cutter painted china so assiduously that even her wash-bowls and pitchers, and her husband's shaving-mug, were covered with violets and lilies. Once when Cutter was exhibiting some of his wife's china to a caller, he dropped a piece. Mrs. Cutter put her handkerchief to her lips as if she were going to faint and said grandly: "Mr. Cutter, you have broken all the Commandments—spare the finger-bowls!"

They quarreled from the moment Cutter came into the house

until they went to bed at night, and their hired girls reported these scenes to the town at large. Mrs. Cutter had several times cut paragraphs about unfaithful husbands out of the newspapers and mailed them to Cutter in a disguised handwriting. Cutter would come home at noon, find the mutilated journal in the paper-rack, and triumphantly fit the clipping into the space from which it had been cut. Those two could quarrel all morning about whether he ought to put on his heavy or his light underwear, and all evening about whether he had taken cold or not.

The Cutters had major as well as minor subjects for dispute. The chief of these was the question of inheritance: Mrs. Cutter told her husband it was plainly his fault they had no children. He insisted that Mrs. Cutter had purposely remained childless, with the determination to outlive him and to share his property with her "people," whom he detested. To this she would reply that unless he changed his mode of life, she would certainly outlive him. After listening to her insinuations about his physical sound-ness, Cutter would resume his dumb-bell practice for a month, or rise daily at the hour when his wife most liked to sleep, dress noisily, and drive out to the track with his trotting-horse.

Once when they had quarreled about household expenses, Mrs. Cutter put on her brocade and went among their friends soliciting orders for painted china, saying that Mr. Cutter had compelled her "to live by her brush." Cutter wasn't shamed as she had expected; he was delighted!

Cutter often threatened to chop down the cedar trees which half-buried the house. His wife declared she would leave him if she were stripped of the "privacy" which she felt these trees afforded her. That was his opportunity, surely; but he never cut down the trees. The Cutters seemed to find their relations to each other interesting and stimulating, and certainly the rest of us found them so. Wick Cutter was different from any other rascal I have ever known, but I have found Mrs. Cutters all over the world; sometimes founding new religions, sometimes being forcibly fed—easily recognizable, even when superficially tamed.

XII

After Ántonia went to live with the Cutters, she seemed to care about nothing but picnics and parties and having a good time. When she was not going to a dance, she sewed until midnight. Her new clothes were the subject of caustic comment. Under Lena's direction she copied Mrs. Gardener's new party dress and Mrs. Smith's street costume so ingeniously in cheap materials that those ladies were greatly annoyed, and Mrs. Cutter, who was jealous of them, was secretly pleased.

Tony wore gloves now, and high-heeled shoes and feathered bonnets, and she went downtown nearly every afternoon with Tiny and Lena and the Marshalls' Norwegian Anna. We High-School boys used to linger on the playground at the afternoon recess to watch them as they came tripping down the hill along the board sidewalk, two and two. They were growing prettier every day, but as they passed us, I used to think with pride that Ántonia, like Snow-White in the fairy tale, was still "fairest of them all."

Being a Senior now, I got away from school early. Sometimes I overtook the girls downtown and coaxed them into the ice-cream parlor, where they would sit chattering and laughing, telling me all the news from the country. I remember how angry Tiny Soderball made me one afternoon. She declared she had heard grandmother was going to make a Baptist preacher of me. "I guess you'll have to stop dancing and wear a white necktie then. Won't he look funny, girls?"

Lena laughed. "You'll have to hurry up, Jim. If you're going to be a preacher, I want you to marry me. You must promise to marry us all, and then baptize the babies."

Norwegian Anna, always dignified, looked at her reprovingly.

"Baptists don't believe in christening babies, do they, Jim?"

I told her I didn't know what they believed, and didn't care, and that I certainly wasn't going to be a preacher.

"That's too bad," Tiny simpered. She was in a teasing mood.

"You'd make such a good one. You're so studious. Maybe you'd like to be a professor. You used to teach Tony, didn't you?"

Ántonia broke in. "I've set my heart on Jim being a doctor. You'd be good with sick people, Jim. Your grandmother's trained you up so nice. My papa always said you were an awful smart boy."

I said I was going to be whatever I pleased. "Won't you be surprised, Miss Tiny, if I turn out to be a regular devil of a fellow?"

They laughed until a glance from Norwegian Anna checked them; the High-School Principal had just come into the front part of the shop to buy bread for supper. Anna knew the whisper was going about that I was a sly one. People said there must be something queer about a boy who showed no interest in girls of his own age, but who could be lively enough when he was with Tony and Lena or the three Marys.

The enthusiasm for the dance, which the Vannis had kindled, did not at once die out. After the tent left town, the Euchre Club became the Owl Club, and gave dances in the Masonic Hall once a week. I was invited to join, but declined. I was moody and restless that winter, and tired of the people I saw every day. Charley Harling was already at Annapolis, while I was still sitting in Black Hawk, answering to my name at roll-call every morning, rising from my desk at the sound of a bell and marching out like the grammar-school children. Mrs. Harling was a little cool toward me, because I continued to champion Ántonia. What was there for me to do after supper? Usually I had learned next day's lessons by the time I left the school building, and I couldn't sit still and read forever.

In the evening I used to prowl about, hunting for diversion. There lay the familiar streets, frozen with snow or liquid with mud. They led to the houses of good people who were putting the babies to bed, or simply sitting still before the parlor stove, digesting their supper. Black Hawk had two saloons. One of them was admitted, even by the church people, to be as respectable as a saloon could be. Handsome Anton Jelinek, who had rented his homestead and come to town, was the proprietor. In his saloon there were long tables where the Bohemian and German farmers could eat the lunches they brought from home while they drank their beer. Jelinek kept rye bread on hand, and smoked fish and strong imported cheeses to please the foreign palate. I liked to drop into his bar-room and listen to the talk. But one day he overtook me on the street and clapped me on the shoulder.

"Jim," he said, "I am good friends with you and I always like to see you. But you know how the church people think about saloons. Your grandpa has always treated me fine, and I don't like to have you come into my place, because I know he don't like it, and it puts me in bad with him."

So I was shut out of that.

One could hang about the drug-store, and listen to the old men who sat there every evening, talking politics and telling raw stories. One could go to the cigar factory and chat with the old German who raised canaries for sale, and look at his stuffed birds. But whatever you began with him, the talk went back to taxidermy. There was the depot, of course; I often went down to see the night train come in, and afterward sat awhile with the disconsolate telegrapher who was always hoping to be transferred to Omaha or Denver, "where there was some life." He was sure to bring out his pictures of actresses and dancers. He got them with cigarette coupons, and nearly smoked himself to death to possess those desired forms and faces. For a change, one could talk to the station agent; but he was another malcontent; spent all his spare time writing letters to officials requesting a transfer. He wanted to get back to Wyoming where he could go trout-fishing on Sundays. He used to say "there was nothing in life for him but trout streams, ever since he'd lost his twins."

These were the distractions I had to choose from. There were no other lights burning downtown after nine o'clock. On starlight nights I used to pace up and down those long, cold streets, scowling at the little, sleeping houses on either side, with their storm-windows and covered back porches. They were flimsy shelters, most of them poorly built of light wood, with spindle porch-posts horribly mutilated by the turning lathe. Yet for all their frailness, how much jealousy and envy and unhappiness some of them managed to contain! The life that went on in them seemed to me made up of evasions and negations; shifts to save cooking, to save washing and cleaning, devices to propitiate the tongue of gossip. This guarded mode of existence was like living under a tyranny. People's speech, their voices, their very glances, became furtive and repressed. Every individual taste, every natural appetite, was bridled by caution. The people asleep in those houses, I thought, tried to live like the mice in their own kitchens; to make no noise, to leave no trace, to slip over the surface of things in the dark. The growing piles of ashes and cinders in the back yards were the only evidence that the wasteful, consuming process of life went on at all. On Tuesday nights the Owl Club danced; then there was a little stir in the streets, and here and there one could see a lighted window until midnight. But the next night all was dark again.

After I refused to join "the Owls," as they were called, I made a bold resolve to go to the Saturday night dances at Firemen's Hall. I knew it would be useless to acquaint my elders with any such plan. Grandfather didn't approve of dancing anyway; he would only say that if I wanted to dance I could go to the Masonic Hall, among "the people we knew." It was just my point that I saw altogether too much of the people we knew.

My bedroom was on the ground floor, and as I studied there, I had a stove in it. I used to retire to my room early on Saturday night, change my shirt and collar and put on my Sunday coat. I waited until all was quiet and the old people were asleep, then raised my window, climbed out, and went softly through the yard. The first time I deceived my grandparents I felt rather shabby, perhaps even the second time, but I soon ceased to think about it.

The dance at the Firemen's Hall was the one thing I looked forward to all the week. There I met the same people I used to see at the Vannis' tent. Sometimes there were Bohemians from Wilber, or German boys who came down on the afternoon freight from Bismarck. Tony and Lena and Tiny were always there, and the three Bohemian Marys, and the Danish laundry girls.

The four Danish girls lived with the laundryman and his wife in their house behind the laundry, with a big garden where the clothes were hung out to dry. The laundryman was a kind, wise old fellow, who paid his girls well, looked out for them, and gave them a good home. He told me once that his own daughter died just as she was getting old enough to help her mother, and that he had been "trying to make up for it ever since." On summer afternoons he used to sit for hours on the sidewalk in front of his laundry, his newspaper lying on his knee, watching his girls through the big open window while they ironed and talked in Danish. The clouds of white dust that blew up the street, the gusts of hot wind that withered his vegetable garden, never disturbed his calm. His droll expression seemed to say that he had found the secret of contentment. Morning and evening he drove about in his spring wagon, distributing freshly ironed clothes, and collecting bags of linen that cried out for his suds and sunny drying-lines. His girls never looked so pretty at the dances as they did standing by the ironing-board, or over the tubs, washing the fine pieces, their white arms and throats bare, their cheeks bright as the brightest wild roses, their gold hair moist with the steam or the heat and curling in little damp spirals about their ears. They had not learned much English, and were not so ambitious as Tony or Lena; but they were kind, simple girls and they were always happy. When one danced with them, one smelled their clean, freshly ironed clothes that had been put away with rose-mary leaves from Mr. Jensen's garden.

There were never girls enough to go round at those dances, but every one wanted a turn with Tony and Lena. Lena moved without exertion, rather indolently, and her hand often accented the rhythm softly on her partner's shoulder. She smiled if one spoke to her, but seldom answered. The music seemed to put her into a soft, waking dream, and her violet-colored eyes looked sleepily and confidingly at one from under her long lashes. When she sighed she exhaled a heavy perfume of sachet powder. To dance "Home, Sweet Home," with Lena was like coming in with the tide. She danced every dance like a waltz, and it was always the same waltz—the waltz of coming home to something, of inevitable, fated return. After a while one got restless under it, as one does under the heat of a soft, sultry summer day.

When you spun out into the floor with Tony, you didn't return to anything. You set out every time upon a new adventure. I liked to schottische with her; she had so much spring and variety, and was always putting in new steps and slides. She taught me to dance against and around the hard-and-fast beat of the music. If, instead of going to the end of the railroad, old Mr. Shimerda had stayed in New York and picked up a living with his fiddle, how different Ántonia's life might have been!

Ántonia often went to the dances with Larry Donovan, a passenger conductor who was a kind of professional ladies' man, as we said. I remember how admiringly all the boys looked at her the night she first wore her velveteen dress, made like Mrs. Gardener's black velvet. She was lovely to see, with her eyes shining, and her lips always a little parted when she danced. That constant, dark color in her cheeks never changed.

One evening when Donovan was out on his run, Ántonia came to the hall with Norwegian Anna and her young man, and that night I took her home. When we were in Cutter's yard, sheltered by the evergreens, I told her she must kiss me good-night.

"Why, sure, Jim." A moment later she drew her face away and whispered indignantly, "Why, Jim! You know you ain't right to kiss me like that. I'll tell your grandmother on you!"

"Lena Lingard lets me kiss her," I retorted, "and I'm not half as fond of her as I am of you."

"Lena does?" Tony gasped. "If she's up to any of her nonsense with you, I'll scratch her eyes out!" She took my arm again and we walked out of the gate and up and down the sidewalk. "Now, don't you go and be a fool like some of these town boys. You're not going to sit around here and whittle store-boxes and tell stories all your life. You are going away to school and make something of yourself. I'm just awful proud of you. You won't go and get mixed up with the Swedes, will you?"

"I don't care anything about any of them but you," I said. "And you'll always treat me like a kid, I suppose."

She laughed and threw her arms around me. "I expect I will, but you're a kid I'm awful fond of, anyhow! You can like me all you want to, but if I see you hanging round with Lena much, I'll go to your grandmother, as sure as your name's Jim Burden! Lena's all right, only—well, you know yourself she's soft that way. She can't help it. It's natural to her."

If she was proud of me, I was so proud of her that I carried my head high as I emerged from the dark cedars and shut the Cutters' gate softly behind me. Her warm, sweet face, her kind arms, and the true heart in her; she was, oh, she was still my Ántonia! I looked with contempt at the dark, silent little houses about me as I walked home, and thought of the stupid young men who were asleep in some of them. I knew where the real women were, though I was only a boy; and I would not be afraid of them, either!

I hated to enter the still house when I went home from the dances, and it was long before I could get to sleep. Toward morning I used to have pleasant dreams: sometimes Tony and I were out in the country, sliding down straw-stacks as we used to do; climbing up the yellow mountains over and over, and slipping down the smooth sides into soft piles of chaff.

One dream I dreamed a great many times, and it was always the same. I was in a harvest-field full of shocks, and I was lying against one of them. Lena Lingard came across the stubble barefoot, in a short skirt, with a curved reaping-hook in her hand, and she was flushed like the dawn, with a kind of luminous rosiness all about her. She sat down beside me, turned to me with a soft sigh and said, "Now they are all gone, and I can kiss you as much as I like."

I used to wish I could have this flattering dream about Ántonia, but I never did.

XIII

I noticed one afternoon that grandmother had been crying. Her feet seemed to drag as she moved about the house, and I got up from the table where I was studying and went to her, asking if she didn't feel well, and if I couldn't help her with her work.

"No, thank you, Jim. I'm troubled, but I guess I'm well enough. Getting a little rusty in the bones, maybe," she added bitterly.

I stood hesitating. "What are you fretting about, grandmother? Has grandfather lost any money?"

"No, it ain't money. I wish it was. But I've heard things. You must 'a' known it would come back to me sometime." She dropped into a chair, and covering her face with her apron, began to cry. "Jim," she said, "I was never one that claimed old folks could bring up their grandchildren. But it came about so; there wasn't any other way for you, it seemed like."

I put my arms around her. I couldn't bear to see her cry.

"What is it, grandmother? Is it the Firemen's dances?"

She nodded.

"I'm sorry I sneaked off like that. But there's nothing wrong about the dances, and I haven't done anything wrong. I like all those country girls, and I like to dance with them. That's all there is to it."

"But it ain't right to deceive us, son, and it brings blame on us. People say you are growing up to be a bad boy, and that ain't just to us."

"I don't care what they say about me, but if it hurts you, that settles it. I won't go to the Firemen's Hall again."

I kept my promise, of course, but I found the spring months dull enough. I sat at home with the old people in the evenings now, reading Latin that was not in our High-School course. I had made up my mind to do a lot of college requirement work in the summer, and to enter the freshman class at the University without conditions in the fall. I wanted to get away as soon as possible.

Disapprobation hurt me, I found,—even that of people whom

I did not admire. As the spring came on, I grew more and more lonely, and fell back on the telegrapher and the cigarmaker and his canaries for companionship. I remember I took a melancholy pleasure in hanging a May-basket for Nina Harling that spring. I bought the flowers from an old German woman who always had more window plants than any one else, and spent an afternoon trimming a little work-basket. When dusk came on, and the new moon hung in the sky, I went quietly to the Harlings' front door with my offering, rang the bell, and then ran away as was the custom. Through the willow hedge I could hear Nina's cries of delight, and I felt comforted.

On those warm, soft spring evenings I often lingered down-town to walk home with Frances, and talked to her about my plans and about the reading I was doing. One evening she said she thought Mrs. Harling was not seriously offended with me.

"Mama is as broad-minded as mothers ever are, I guess. But you know she was hurt about Ántonia, and she can't understand why you like to be with Tiny and Lena better than with the girls of your own set."

"Can you?" I asked bluntly.

Frances laughed. "Yes, I think I can. You knew them in the country, and you like to take sides. In some ways you're older than boys of your age. It will be all right with mama after you pass your college examinations and she sees you're in earnest."

"If you were a boy," I persisted, "you wouldn't belong to the Owl Club, either. You'd be just like me."

She shook her head. "I would and I wouldn't. I expect I know the country girls better than you do. You always put a kind of glamour over them. The trouble with you, Jim, is that you're romantic. Mama's going to your Commencement. She asked me the other day if I knew what your oration is to be about. She wants you to do well."

I thought my oration very good. It stated with fervor a great many things I had lately discovered. Mrs. Harling came to the Opera House to hear the Commencement exercises, and I looked at her most of the time while I made my speech. Her keen, intelligent eyes never left my face. Afterward she came back to the dressing-room where we stood, with our diplomas in our hands, walked up to me, and said heartily: "You surprised me, Jim. I didn't believe you could do as well as that. You didn't get that speech out of books." Among my graduation presents there was a silk umbrella from Mrs. Harling, with my name on the handle.

I walked home from the Opera House alone. As I passed the Methodist Church, I saw three white figures ahead of me, pacing up and down under the arching maple trees, where the moonlight filtered through the lush June foliage. They hurried toward me; they were waiting for me—Lena and Tony and Anna Hansen.

"Oh, Jim, it was splendid!" Tony was breathing hard, as she always did when her feelings outran her language. "There ain't a lawyer in Black Hawk could make a speech like that. I just stopped your grandpa and said so to him. He won't tell you, but he told us he was awful surprised himself, didn't he, girls?"

Lena sidled up to me and said teasingly: "What made you so solemn? I thought you were scared. I was sure you'd forget."

Anna spoke wistfully. "It must make you happy, Jim, to have fine thoughts like that in your mind all the time, and to have words to put them in. I always wanted to go to school, you know."

"Oh, I just sat there and wished my papa could hear you! Jim,"—Ántonia took hold of my coat lapels,—"there was something in your speech that made me think so about my papa!"

"I thought about your papa when I wrote my speech, Tony," I said. "I dedicated it to him."

She threw her arms around me, and her dear face was all wet with tears.

I stood watching their white dresses glimmer smaller and smaller down the sidewalk as they went away. I have had no other success that pulled at my heartstrings like that one.

XIV

The day after Commencement I moved my books and desk upstairs, to an empty room where I should be undisturbed, and I fell to studying in earnest. I worked off a year's trigonometry that summer, and began Virgil alone. Morning after morning I used to pace up and down my sunny little room, looking off at the distant river bluffs and the roll of the blond pastures between, scanning the Æneid aloud and committing long passages to memory. Sometimes in the evening Mrs. Harling called to me as I passed her gate, and asked me to come in and let her play for me. She was lonely for Charley, she said, and liked to have a boy about. Whenever my grandparents had misgivings, and began to wonder whether I was not too young to go off to college alone, Mrs. Harling took up my cause vigorously. Grandfather had such respect for her judgment that I knew he would not go against her.

I had only one holiday that summer. It was in July. I met Ántonia downtown on Saturday afternoon, and learned that she and Tiny and Lena were going to the river next day with Anna Hansen—the elder was all in bloom now, and Anna wanted to make elderblow wine.

"Anna's to drive us down in the Marshalls' delivery wagon, and we'll take a nice lunch and have a picnic. Just us; nobody else. Couldn't you happen along, Jim? It would be like old times."

I considered a moment. "Maybe I can, if I won't be in the way."

On Sunday morning I rose early and got out of Black Hawk while the dew was still heavy on the long meadow grasses. It was the high season for summer flowers. The pink bee-bush stood tall along the sandy roadsides, and the cone-flowers and rose mallow grew everywhere. Across the wire fence, in the long grass, I saw a clump of flaming orange-colored milkweed, rare in that part of the State. I left the road and went around through a stretch of pasture that was always cropped short in summer, where the gaillardia came up year after year and matted over the ground with the deep, velvety red that is in Bokhara carpets.

The country was empty and solitary except for the larks that Sunday morning, and it seemed to lift itself up to me and to come very close.

The river was running strong for midsummer; heavy rains to the west of us had kept it full. I crossed the bridge and went upstream along the wooded shore to a pleasant dressing-room I knew among the dogwood bushes, all overgrown with wild grapevines. I began to undress for a swim. The girls would not be along yet. For the first time it occurred to me that I would be homesick for that river after I left it. The sandbars, with their clean white beaches and their little groves of willows and cottonwood seedlings, were a sort of No Man's Land, little newly-created worlds that belonged to the Black Hawk boys. Charley Harling and I had hunted through these woods, fished from the fallen logs, until I knew every inch of the river shores and had a friendly feeling for every bar and shallow.

After my swim, while I was playing about indolently in the water, I heard the sound of hoofs and wheels on the bridge. I struck downstream and shouted, as the open spring wagon came into view on the middle span. They stopped the horse, and the two girls in the bottom of the cart stood up, steadying themselves by the shoulders of the two in front, so that they could see me better. They were charming up there, huddled together in the cart and peering down at me like curious deer when they come out of the thicket to drink. I found bottom near the bridge and stood up, waving to them.

"How pretty you look!" I called.

"So do you!" they shouted altogether, and broke into peals of laughter. Anna Hansen shook the reins and they drove on, while I zigzagged back to my inlet and clambered up behind an overhanging elm. I dried myself in the sun, and dressed slowly, reluctant to leave that green enclosure where the sunlight flickered so bright through the grapevine leaves and the woodpecker hammered away in the crooked elm that trailed out over the water. As I went along the road back to the bridge I kept picking off little pieces of scaly chalk from the dried water gullies, and breaking them up in my hands.

When I came upon the Marshalls' delivery horse, tied in the shade, the girls had already taken their baskets and gone down the east road which wound through the sand and scrub. I could hear them calling to each other. The elder bushes did not grow back in the shady ravines between the bluffs, but in the hot, sandy bottoms along the stream, where their roots were always in moisture and their tops in the sun. The blossoms were unusually luxuriant and beautiful that summer.

I followed a cattle path through the thick underbrush until I came to a slope that fell away abruptly to the water's edge. A great chunk of the shore had been bitten out by some spring freshet, and the scar was masked by elder bushes, growing down to the water in flowery terraces. I did not touch them. I was overcome by content and drowsiness and by the warm silence about me. There was no sound but the high, sing-song buzz of wild bees and the sunny gurgle of the water underneath. I peeped over the edge of the bank to see the little stream that made the noise; it flowed along perfectly clear over the sand and gravel, cut off from the muddy main current by a long sandbar. Down there, on the lower shelf of the bank, I saw Ántonia, seated alone under the pagoda-like elders. She looked up when she heard me, and smiled, but I saw that she had been crying. I slid down into the soft sand beside her and asked her what was the matter.

"It makes me homesick, Jimmy, this flower, this smell," she said softly. "We have this flower very much at home, in the old country. It always grew in our yard and my papa had a green bench and a table under the bushes. In summer, when they were in bloom, he used to sit there with his friend that played the trombone. When I was little I used to go down there to hear them talk—beautiful talk, like what I never hear in this country."

"What did they talk about?" I asked her.

She sighed and shook her head. "Oh, I don't know! About music, and the woods, and about God, and when they were young." She turned to me suddenly and looked into my eyes. "You think, Jimmy, that maybe my father's spirit can go back to those old places?"

I told her about the feeling of her father's presence I had on that winter day when my grandparents had gone over to see his dead body and I was left alone in the house. I said I felt sure then that he was on his way back to his own country, and that even now, when I passed his grave, I always thought of him as being among the woods and fields that were so dear to him.

Ántonia had the most trusting, responsive eyes in the world; love and credulousness seemed to look out of them with open faces. "Why didn't you ever tell me that before? It makes me feel more sure for him." After a while she said: "You know, Jim, my father was different from my mother. He did not have to marry my mother, and all his brothers quarreled with him because he did. I used to hear the old people at home whisper about it. They said he could have paid my mother money, and not married her. But he was older than she was, and he was too kind to treat her like that. He lived in his mother's house, and she was a poor girl come in to do the work. After my father married her, my grand-mother never let my mother come into her house again. When I went to my grandmother's funeral was the only time I was ever in my grandmother's house. Don't that seem strange?"

While she talked, I lay back in the hot sand and looked up at the blue sky between the flat bouquets of elder. I could hear the bees humming and singing, but they stayed up in the sun above the flowers and did not come down into the shadow of the leaves. Ántonia seemed to me that day exactly like the little girl who used to come to our house with Mr. Shimerda.

"Some day, Tony, I am going over to your country, and I am going to the little town where you lived. Do you remember all about it?"

"Jim," she said earnestly, "if I was put down there in the mid-dle of the night, I could find my way all over that little town; and along the river to the next town, where my grandmother lived.

My feet remember all the little paths through the woods, and where the big roots stick out to trip you. I ain't never forgot my own country."

There was a crackling in the branches above us, and Lena Lingard peered down over the edge of the bank.

"You lazy things!" she cried. "All this elder, and you two lying there! Didn't you hear us calling you?" Almost as flushed as she had been in my dream, she leaned over the edge of the bank and began to demolish our flowery pagoda. I had never seen her so energetic; she was panting with zeal, and the perspiration stood in drops on her short, yielding upper lip. I sprang to my feet and ran up the bank.

It was noon now, and so hot that the dogwoods and scrub-oaks began to turn up the silvery under-side of their leaves, and all the foliage looked soft and wilted. I carried the lunch-basket to the top of one of the chalk bluffs, where even on the calmest days there was always a breeze. The flat-topped, twisted little oaks threw light shadows on the grass. Below us we could see the windings of the river, and Black Hawk, grouped among its trees, and, beyond, the rolling country, swelling gently until it met the sky. We could recognize familiar farmhouses and windmills. Each of the girls pointed out to me the direction in which her father's farm lay, and told me how many acres were in wheat that year and how many in corn.

"My old folks," said Tiny Soderball, "have put in twenty acres of rye. They get it ground at the mill, and it makes nice bread. It seems like my mother ain't been so homesick, ever since father's raised rye flour for her."

"It must have been a trial for our mothers," said Lena, "coming out here and having to do everything different. My mother had always lived in town. She says she started behind in farm-work, and never has caught up."

"Yes, a new country's hard on the old ones, sometimes," said Anna thoughtfully. "My grandmother's getting feeble now, and her mind wanders. She's forgot about this country, and thinks she's at home in Norway. She keeps asking mother to take her down to the waterside and the fish market. She craves fish all the time. Whenever I go home I take her canned salmon and mackerel."

"Mercy, it's hot!" Lena yawned. She was supine under a little oak, resting after the fury of her elder-hunting, and had taken off the high-heeled slippers she had been silly enough to wear. "Come here, Jim. You never got the sand out of your hair." She began to draw her fingers slowly through my hair.

Ántonia pushed her away. "You'll never get it out like that," she said sharply. She gave my head a rough touzling and finished me off with something like a box on the ear. "Lena, you oughtn't to try to wear those slippers any more. They're too small for your feet. You'd better give them to me for Yulka."

"All right," said Lena good-naturedly, tucking her white stockings under her skirt. "You get all Yulka's things, don't you? I wish father didn't have such bad luck with his farm machinery; then I could buy more things for my sisters. I'm going to get Mary a new coat this fall, if the sulky plough's never paid for!"

Tiny asked her why she didn't wait until after Christmas, when coats would be cheaper. "What do you think of poor me?" she added; "with six at home, younger than I am? And they all think I'm rich, because when I go back to the country I'm dressed so fine!" She shrugged her shoulders. "But, you know, my weakness is playthings. I like to buy them playthings better than what they need."

"I know how that is," said Anna. "When we first came here, and I was little, we were too poor to buy toys. I never got over the loss of a doll somebody gave me before we left Norway. A boy on the boat broke her, and I still hate him for it."

"I guess after you got here you had plenty of live dolls to nurse, like me!" Lena remarked cynically.

"Yes, the babies came along pretty fast, to be sure. But I never minded. I was fond of them all. The youngest one, that we didn't any of us want, is the one we love best now."

Lena sighed. "Oh, the babies are all right; if only they don't come in winter. Ours nearly always did. I don't see how mother stood it. I tell you what girls," she sat up with sudden energy; "I'm going to get my mother out of that old sod house where she's lived so many years. The men will never do it. Johnnie, that's my oldest brother, he's wanting to get married now, and build a house for his girl instead of his mother. Mrs. Thomas says she thinks I can move to some other town pretty soon, and go into business for myself. If I don't get into business, I'll maybe marry a rich gambler."

"That would be a poor way to get on," said Anna sarcastically. "I wish I could teach school, like Selma Kronn. Just think! She'll be the first Scandinavian girl to get a position in the High School. We ought to be proud of her."

Selma was a studious girl, who had not much tolerance for giddy things like Tiny and Lena; but they always spoke of her with admiration.

Tiny moved about restlessly, fanning herself with her straw hat. "If I was smart like her, I'd be at my books day and night. But she was born smart—and look how her father's trained her! He was something high up in the old country."

"So was my mother's father," murmured Lena, "but that's all the good it does us! My father's father was smart, too, but he was wild. He married a Lapp. I guess that's what's the matter with me; they say Lapp blood will out."

"A real Lapp, Lena?" I exclaimed. "The kind that wear skins?"

"I don't know if she wore skins, but she was a Lapp all right, and his folks felt dreadful about it. He was sent up north on some Government job he had, and fell in with her. He would marry her."

"But I thought Lapland women were fat and ugly, and had squint eyes, like Chinese?" I objected.

"I don't know, maybe. There must be something mighty taking about the Lapp girls, though; mother says the Norwegians up north are always afraid their boys will run after them."

In the afternoon, when the heat was less oppressive, we had a lively game of "Pussy Wants a Corner," on the flat bluff-top, with the little trees for bases. Lena was Pussy so often that she finally said she wouldn't play any more. We threw ourselves down on the grass, out of breath.

"Jim," Ántonia said dreamily, "I want you to tell the girls about how the Spanish first came here, like you and Charley Harling used to talk about. I've tried to tell them, but I leave out so much."

They sat under a little oak, Tony resting against the trunk and the other girls leaning against her and each other, and listened to the little I was able to tell them about Coronado and his search for the Seven Golden Cities. At school we were taught that he had not got so far north as Nebraska, but had given up his quest and turned back somewhere in Kansas. But Charley Harling and I had a strong belief that he had been along this very river. A farmer in the county north of ours, when he was breaking sod, had turned up a metal stirrup of fine workmanship, and a sword with a Spanish inscription on the blade. He lent these relics to Mr. Harling, who brought them home with him. Charley and I scoured them, and they were on exhibition in the Harling office all summer. Father Kelly, the priest, had found the name of the Spanish maker on the sword, and an abbreviation that stood for the city of Cordova.

"And that I saw with my own eyes," Ántonia put in triumphantly. "So Jim and Charley were right, and the teachers were wrong!"

The girls began to wonder among themselves. Why had the Spaniards come so far? What must this country have been like, then? Why had Coronado never gone back to Spain, to his riches and his castles and his king? I couldn't tell them. I only knew the school books said he "died in the wilderness, of a broken heart."

"More than him has done that," said Ántonia sadly, and the girls murmured assent.

We sat looking off across the country, watching the sun go down. The curly grass about us was on fire now. The bark of the oaks turned red as copper. There was a shimmer of gold on the brown river. Out in the stream the sandbars glittered like glass, and the light trembled in the willow thickets as if little flames were leaping among them. The breeze sank to stillness. In the ravine a ringdove mourned plaintively, and somewhere off in the bushes an owl hooted. The girls sat listless, leaning against each other. The long fingers of the sun touched their foreheads.

Presently we saw a curious thing: There were no clouds, the sun was going down in a limpid, gold-washed sky. Just as the lower edge of the red disc rested on the high fields against the horizon, a great black figure suddenly appeared on the face of the sun. We sprang to our feet, straining our eyes toward it. In a moment we realized what it was. On some upland farm, a plough had been left standing in the field. The sun was sinking just behind it. Magnified across the distance by the horizontal light, it stood out against the sun, was exactly contained within the circle of the disc; the handles, the tongue, the share—black against the molten red. There it was, heroic in size, a picture writing on the sun.

Even while we whispered about it, our vision disappeared; the ball dropped and dropped until the red tip went beneath the earth. The fields below us were dark, the sky was growing pale, and that forgotten plough had sunk back to its own littleness somewhere on the prairie.

XV

Late in August the Cutters went to Omaha for a few days, leaving Ántonia in charge of the house. Since the scandal about the Swedish girl, Wick Cutter could never get his wife to stir out of Black Hawk without him.

The day after the Cutters left, Ántonia came over to see us. Grandmother noticed that she seemed troubled and distracted. "You've got something on your mind, Ántonia," she said anxiously.

"Yes, Mrs. Burden. I couldn't sleep much last night." She hesitated, and then told us how strangely Mr. Cutter had behaved before he went away. He put all the silver in a basket and placed it under her bed, and with it a box of papers which he told her were valuable. He made her promise that she would not sleep away from the house, or be out late in the evening, while he was gone.

He strictly forbade her to ask any of the girls she knew to stay with her at night. She would be perfectly safe, he said, as he had just put a new Yale lock on the front door.

Cutter had been so insistent in regard to these details that now she felt uncomfortable about staying there alone. She hadn't liked the way he kept coming into the kitchen to instruct her, or the way he looked at her. "I feel as if he is up to some of his tricks again, and is going to try to scare me, somehow."

Grandmother was apprehensive at once. "I don't think it's right for you to stay there, feeling that way. I suppose it wouldn't be right for you to leave the place alone, either, after giving your word. Maybe Jim would be willing to go over there and sleep, and you could come here nights. I'd feel safer, knowing you were under my own roof. I guess Jim could take care of their silver and old usury notes as well as you could."

Ántonia turned to me eagerly. "Oh, would you, Jim? I'd make up my bed nice and fresh for you. It's a real cool room, and the bed's right next the window. I was afraid to leave the window open last night."

I liked my own room, and I didn't like the Cutters' house under any circumstances; but Tony looked so troubled that I consented to try this arrangement. I found that I slept there as well as anywhere, and when I got home in the morning, Tony had a good breakfast waiting for me. After prayers she sat down at the table with us, and it was like old times in the country.

The third night I spent at the Cutters', I awoke suddenly with the impression that I had heard a door open and shut. Everything was still, however, and I must have gone to sleep again immediately.

The next thing I knew, I felt some one sit down on the edge of the bed. I was only half awake, but I decided that he might take the Cutters' silver, whoever he was. Perhaps if I did not move, he would find it and get out without troubling me. I held my breath and lay absolutely still. A hand closed softly on my shoulder, and at the same moment I felt something hairy and cologne-scented brushing my face. If the room had suddenly been flooded with electric light, I couldn't have seen more clearly the detestable bearded countenance that I knew was bending over me. I caught a handful of whiskers and pulled, shouting something. The hand that held my shoulder was instantly at my throat. The man became insane; he stood over me, choking me with one fist and beating me in the face with the other, hissing and chuckling and letting out a flood of abuse.

"So this is what she's up to when I'm away, is it? Where is she, you nasty whelp, where is she? Under the bed, are you, hussy? I know your tricks! Wait till I get at you! I'll fix this rat you've got in here. He's caught, all right!"

So long as Cutter had me by the throat, there was no chance for me at all. I got hold of his thumb and bent it back, until he let go with a yell. In a bound, I was on my feet, and easily sent him sprawling to the floor. Then I made a dive for the open window, struck the wire screen, knocked it out, and tumbled after it into the yard.

Suddenly I found myself running across the north end of Black Hawk in my nightshirt, just as one sometimes finds one's self behaving in bad dreams. When I got home I climbed in the kitchen window. I was covered with blood from my nose and lip, but I was too sick to do anything about it. I found a shawl and an overcoat on the hatrack, lay down on the parlor sofa, and in spite of my hurts, went to sleep.

Grandmother found me there in the morning. Her cry of fright awakened me. Truly, I was a battered object. As she helped me to my room, I caught a glimpse of myself in the mirror. My lip was cut and stood out like a snout. My nose looked like a big blue plum, and one eye was swollen shut and hideously discolored. Grandmother said we must have the doctor at once, but I implored her, as I had never begged for anything before, not to send for him. I could stand anything, I told her, so long as nobody saw me or knew what had happened to me. I entreated her not to let grandfather, even, come into my room. She seemed to understand, though I was too faint and miserable to go into explanations.

When she took off my nightshirt, she found such bruises on my chest and shoulders that she began to cry. She spent the whole morning bathing and poulticing me, and rubbing me with arnica. I heard Ántonia sobbing outside my door, but I asked grandmother to send her away. I felt that I never wanted to see her again. I hated her almost as much as I hated Cutter. She had let me in for all this disgustingness. Grandmother kept saying how thankful we ought to be that I had been there instead of Ántonia. But I lay with my disfigured face to the wall and felt no particular gratitude. My one concern was that grandmother should keep every one away from me. If the story once got abroad, I would never hear the last of it. I could well imagine what the old men down at the drugstore would do with such a theme.

While grandmother was trying to make me comfortable, grandfather went to the depot and learned that Wick Cutter had come home on the night express from the east, and had left again on the six o'clock train for Denver that morning. The agent said his face was striped with court-plaster, and he carried his left hand in a sling. He looked so used up, that the agent asked him what had happened to him since ten o'clock the night before; whereat Cutter began to swear at him and said he would have him discharged for incivility.

That afternoon, while I was asleep, Ántonia took grandmother with her, and went over to the Cutters' to pack her trunk. They found the place locked up, and they had to break the window to get into Ántonia's bedroom. There everything was in shocking disorder. Her clothes had been taken out of her closet, thrown into the middle of the room, and trampled and torn. My own garments had been treated so badly that I never saw them again; grandmother burned them in the Cutters' kitchen range.

While Ántonia was packing her trunk and putting her room in order, to leave it, the front-door bell rang violently. There stood Mrs. Cutter,—locked out, for she had no key to the new lock— her head trembling with rage. "I advised her to control herself, or she would have a stroke," grandmother said afterwards.

Grandmother would not let her see Ántonia at all, but made her sit down in the parlor while she related to her just what had occurred the night before. Ántonia was frightened, and was going home to stay for a while, she told Mrs. Cutter; it would be useless to interrogate the girl, for she knew nothing of what had happened.

Then Mrs. Cutter told her story. She and her husband had started home from Omaha together the morning before. They had to stop over several hours at Waymore Junction to catch the Black Hawk train. During the wait, Cutter left her at the depot and went to the Waymore bank to attend to some business. When he returned, he told her that he would have to stay overnight there, but she could go on home. He bought her ticket and put her on the train. She saw him slip a twenty-dollar bill into her handbag with her ticket. That bill, she said, should have aroused her suspicions at once—but did not.

The trains are never called at little junction towns; everybody knows when they come in. Mr. Cutter showed his wife's ticket to the conductor, and settled her in her seat before the train moved off. It was not until nearly nightfall that she discovered she was on the express bound for Kansas City, that her ticket was made out to that point, and that Cutter must have planned it so. The conductor told her the Black Hawk train was due at Waymore twelve minutes after the Kansas City train left. She saw at once that her husband had played this trick in order to get back to Black Hawk without her. She had no choice but to go on to Kansas City and take the first fast train for home.

Cutter could have got home a day earlier than his wife by any one of a dozen simpler devices; he could have left her in the Omaha hotel, and said he was going on to Chicago for a few days. But apparently it was part of his fun to outrage her feelings as much as possible.

"Mr. Cutter will pay for this, Mrs. Burden. He will pay!" Mrs. Cutter avouched, nodding her horselike head and rolling her eyes.

Grandmother said she hadn't a doubt of it.

Certainly Cutter liked to have his wife think him a devil. In some way he depended upon the excitement he could arouse in her hysterical nature. Perhaps he got the feeling of being a rake more from his wife's rage and amazement than from any experiences of his own. His zest in debauchery might wane, but never Mrs. Cutter's belief in it. The reckoning with his wife at the end of an escapade was something he counted on—like the last powerful liqueur after a long dinner. The one excitement he really couldn't do without was quarreling with Mrs. Cutter!

BOOK III
LENA LINGARD

I

At the University I had the good fortune to come immediately under the influence of a brilliant and inspiring young scholar. Gaston Cleric had arrived in Lincoln only a few weeks earlier than I, to begin his work as head of the Latin Department. He came West at the suggestion of his physicians, his health having been enfeebled by a long illness in Italy. When I took my entrance examinations he was my examiner, and my course was arranged under his supervision.

I did not go home for my first summer vacation, but stayed in Lincoln, working off a year's Greek, which had been my only condition on entering the Freshman class. Cleric's doctor advised against his going back to New England, and except for a few weeks in Colorado, he, too, was in Lincoln all that summer. We played tennis, read, and took long walks together. I shall always look back on that time of mental awakening as one of the happiest in my life. Gaston Cleric introduced me to the world of ideas; when one first enters that world everything else fades for a time, and all that went before is as if it had not been. Yet I found curious survivals; some of the figures of my old life seemed to be waiting for me in the new.

In those days there were many serious young men among the students who had come up to the University from the farms and the little towns scattered over the thinly settled State. Some of those boys came straight from the cornfields with only a summer's wages in their pockets, hung on through the four years, shabby and underfed, and completed the course by really heroic self-sacrifice. Our instructors were oddly assorted; wandering pioneer school-teachers, stranded ministers of the Gospel, a few enthusiastic young men just out of graduate schools. There was an atmosphere of endeavor, of expectancy and bright hopefulness about the young college that had lifted its head from the prairie only a few years before.

Our personal life was as free as that of our instructors. There were no college dormitories; we lived where we could and as we could. I took rooms with an old couple, early settlers in Lincoln, who had married off their children and now lived quietly in their house at the edge of town, near the open country. The house was inconveniently situated for students, and on that account I got two rooms for the price of one. My bedroom, originally a linen closet, was unheated and was barely large enough to contain my cot bed, but it enabled me to call the other room my study. The dresser, and the great walnut wardrobe which held all my clothes, even my hats and shoes, I had pushed out of the way, and I considered them non-existent, as children eliminate incongruous objects when they are playing house. I worked at a commodious green-topped table placed directly in front of the west window which looked out over the prairie. In the corner at my right were all my books, in shelves I had made and painted myself. On the blank wall at my left the dark, old-fashioned wall-paper was covered by a large map of ancient Rome, the work of some German scholar. Cleric had ordered it for me when he was sending for books from abroad. Over the bookcase hung a photograph of the Tragic Theater at Pompeii, which he had given me from his collection.

When I sat at work I half faced a deep, upholstered chair which stood at the end of my table, its high back against the wall. I had bought it with great care. My instructor sometimes looked in upon me when he was out for an evening tramp, and I noticed that he was more likely to linger and become talkative if I had a comfortable chair for him to sit in, and if he found a bottle of Bénédictine and plenty of the kind of cigarettes he liked, at his elbow. He was, I had discovered, parsimonious about small expenditures—a trait absolutely inconsistent with his general character. Sometimes when he came he was silent and moody, and after a few sarcastic remarks went away again, to tramp the streets of Lincoln, which were almost as quiet and oppressively domestic as those of Black Hawk. Again, he would sit until nearly midnight, talking about Latin and English poetry, or telling me about his long stay in Italy.

I can give no idea of the peculiar charm and vividness of his talk. In a crowd he was nearly always silent. Even for his class-room he had no platitudes, no stock of professorial anecdotes. When he was tired his lectures were clouded, obscure, elliptical; but when he was interested they were wonderful. I believe that Gaston Cleric narrowly missed being a great poet, and I have sometimes thought that his bursts of imaginative talk were fatal to his poetic gift. He squandered too much in the heat of personal communication. How often I have seen him draw his dark brows together, fix his eyes upon some object on the wall or a figure in the carpet, and then flash into the lamplight the very image that was in his brain. He could bring the drama of antique life before one out of the shadows—white figures against blue backgrounds. I shall never forget his face as it looked one night when he told me about the solitary day he spent among the sea temples at Paestum: the soft wind blowing through the roofless columns, the birds flying low over the flowering marsh grasses, the changing lights on the silver, cloud-hung mountains. He had willfully stayed the short summer night there, wrapped in his coat and rug, watching the constellations on their path down the sky until "the bride of old Tithonus" rose out of the sea, and the mountains stood sharp in the dawn. It was there he caught the fever which held him back on the eve of his departure for Greece and of which he lay ill so long in Naples. He was still, indeed, doing penance for it.

I remember vividly another evening, when something led us to talk of Dante's veneration for Virgil. Cleric went through canto after canto of the "Commedia," repeating the discourse between Dante and his "sweet teacher," while his cigarette burned itself out unheeded between his long fingers. I can hear him now, speaking the lines of the poet Statius, who spoke for Dante: "*I was famous on earth with the name which endures longest and honors most. The seeds of my ardor were the sparks from that divine flame whereby more than a thousand have kindled; I speak of the Æneid, mother to me and nurse to me in poetry.*"

Although I admired scholarship so much in Cleric, I was not deceived about myself; I knew that I should never be a scholar. I could never lose myself for long among impersonal things. Mental excitement was apt to send me with a rush back to my own naked land and the figures scattered upon it. While I was in the very act of yearning toward the new forms that Cleric brought up before me, my mind plunged away from me, and I suddenly found myself thinking of the places and people of my own infinitesimal past. They stood out strengthened and simplified now, like the image of the plough against the sun. They were all I had for an answer to the new appeal. I begrudged the room that Jake and Otto and Russian Peter took up in my memory, which I wanted to crowd with other things. But whenever my consciousness was quickened, all those early friends were quickened within it, and in some strange way they accompanied me through all my new experiences. They were so much alive in me that I scarcely stopped to wonder whether they were alive anywhere else, or how.

II

One March evening in my Sophomore year I was sitting alone in my room after supper. There had been a warm thaw all day, with mushy yards and little streams of dark water gurgling cheerfully into the streets out of old snow-banks. My window was open, and the earthy wind blowing through made me indolent. On the edge of the prairie, where the sun had gone down, the sky was turquoise blue, like a lake, with gold light throbbing in it. Higher up, in the utter clarity of the western slope, the evening star hung like a lamp suspended by silver chains—like the lamp engraved upon the title-page of old Latin texts, which is always appearing in new heavens, and waking new desires in men. It reminded me, at any rate, to shut my window and light my wick in answer. I did so regretfully, and the dim objects in the room emerged from the shadows and took their place about me with the helpfulness which custom breeds.

I propped my book open and stared listlessly at the page of the Georgics where tomorrow's lesson began. It opened with the melancholy reflection that, in the lives of mortals, the best days are the first to flee. "*Optima dies . . . prima fugit.*" I turned back to the beginning of the third book, which we had read in class that morning. "*Primus ego in patriam mecum . . . deducam Musas*"; "for I shall be the first, if I live, to bring the Muse into my country." Cleric had explained to us that "patria" here meant, not a nation or even a province, but the little rural neighborhood on the Min-cio where the poet was born. This was not a boast, but a hope, at once bold and devoutly humble, that he might bring the Muse (but lately come to Italy from her cloudy Grecian mountains), not to the capital, the *palatia Romana*, but to his own little "country"; to his father's fields, "sloping down to the river and to the old beech trees with broken tops."

Cleric said he thought Virgil, when he was dying at Brindisi, must have remembered that passage. After he had faced the bitter fact that he was to leave the Æneid unfinished, and had decreed that the great canvas, crowded with figures of gods and men, should be burned rather than survive him unperfected, then his mind must have gone back to the perfect utterance of the Georg-ics, where the pen was fitted to the matter as the plough is to the furrow; and he must have said to himself with the thankfulness of a good man, "I was the first to bring the Muse into my country."

We left the classroom quietly, conscious that we had been brushed by the wing of a great feeling, though perhaps I alone knew Cleric intimately enough to guess what that feeling was. In the evening, as I sat staring at my book, the fervor of his voice stirred through the quantities on the page before me. I was wondering whether that particular rocky strip of New England coast about which he had so often told me was Cleric's *patria*. Before I had got far with my reading I was disturbed by a knock. I hurried to the door and when I opened it saw a woman standing in the dark hall.

"I expect you hardly know me, Jim."

The voice seemed familiar, but I did not recognize her until she stepped into the light of my doorway and I beheld—Lena Lingard! She was so quietly conventionalized by city clothes that I might have passed her on the street without seeing her. Her black suit fitted her figure smoothly, and a black lace hat, with pale-blue forget-me-nots, sat demurely on her yellow hair.

I led her toward Cleric's chair, the only comfortable one I had, questioning her confusedly.

She was not disconcerted by my embarrassment. She looked about her with the naïve curiosity I remembered so well. "You are quite comfortable here, aren't you? I live in Lincoln now, too, Jim. I'm in business for myself. I have a dressmaking shop in the Raleigh Block, out on O Street. I've made a real good start."

"But, Lena, when did you come?"

"Oh, I've been here all winter. Didn't your grandmother ever write you? I've thought about looking you up lots of times. But we've all heard what a studious young man you've got to be, and I felt bashful. I didn't know whether you'd be glad to see me." She laughed her mellow, easy laugh, that was either very artless or very comprehending, one never quite knew which. "You seem the same, though,—except you're a young man, now, of course. Do you think I've changed?"

"Maybe you're prettier—though you were always pretty enough. Perhaps it's your clothes that make a difference."

"You like my new suit? I have to dress pretty well in my business." She took off her jacket and sat more at ease in her blouse, of some soft, flimsy silk. She was already at home in my place, had slipped quietly into it, as she did into everything. She told me her business was going well, and she had saved a little money.

"This summer I'm going to build the house for mother I've talked about so long. I won't be able to pay up on it at first, but I want her to have it before she is too old to enjoy it. Next summer I'll take her down new furniture and carpets, so she'll have something to look forward to all winter."

I watched Lena sitting there so smooth and sunny and well cared-for, and thought of how she used to run barefoot over the prairie until after the snow began to fly, and how Crazy Mary chased her round and round the cornfields. It seemed to me wonderful that she should have got on so well in the world. Certainly she had no one but herself to thank for it.

"You must feel proud of yourself, Lena," I said heartily. "Look at me; I've never earned a dollar, and I don't know that I'll ever be able to."

"Tony says you're going to be richer than Mr. Harling some day. She's always bragging about you, you know."

"Tell me, how *is* Tony?"

"She's fine. She works for Mrs. Gardener at the hotel now. She's housekeeper. Mrs. Gardener's health isn't what it was, and she can't see after everything like she used to. She has great confidence in Tony. Tony's made it up with the Harlings, too. Little Nina is so fond of her that Mrs. Harling kind of overlooked things."

"Is she still going with Larry Donovan?"

"Oh, that's on, worse than ever! I guess they're engaged. Tony talks about him like he was president of the railroad. Everybody laughs about it, because she was never a girl to be soft. She won't hear a word against him. She's so sort of innocent."

I said I didn't like Larry, and never would.

Lena's face dimpled. "Some of us could tell her things, but it wouldn't do any good. She'd always believe him. That's Ántonia's failing, you know; if she once likes people, she won't hear anything against them."

"I think I'd better go home and look after Ántonia," I said.

"I think you had." Lena looked up at me in frank amusement. "It's a good thing the Harlings are friendly with her again. Larry's

afraid of them. They ship so much grain, they have influence with
the railroad people. What are you studying?" She leaned her
elbows on the table and drew my book toward her. I caught a
faint odor of violet sachet. "So that's Latin, is it? It looks hard. You
do go to the theater sometimes, though, for I've seen you there.
Don't you just love a good play, Jim? I can't stay at home in the
evening if there's one in town. I'd be willing to work like a slave, it
seems to me, to live in a place where there are theaters."

"Let's go to a show together sometime. You are going to let me
come to see you, aren't you?"

"Would you like to? I'd be ever so pleased. I'm never busy after
six o'clock, and I let my sewing girls go at half-past five. I board,
to save time, but sometimes I cook a chop for myself, and I'd be
glad to cook one for you. "Well,"—she began to put on her white
gloves,—"it's been awful good to see you, Jim."

"You needn't hurry, need you? You've hardly told me anything
yet."

"We can talk when you come to see me. I expect you don't
often have lady visitors. The old woman downstairs didn't want to
let me come up very much. I told her I was from your home
town, and had promised your grandmother to come and see you.
How surprised Mrs. Burden would be!" Lena laughed softly as
she rose.

When I caught up my hat she shook her head. "No, I don't
want you to go with me. I'm to meet some Swedes at the drug-
store. You wouldn't care for them. I wanted to see your room so I
could write Tony all about it, but I must tell her how I left you
right here with your books. She's always so afraid someone will
run off with you!" Lena slipped her silk sleeves into the jacket I
held for her, smoothed it over her person, and buttoned it slowly.
I walked with her to the door. "Come and see me sometimes
when you're lonesome. But maybe you have all the friends you
want. Have you?" She turned her soft cheek to me. "Have you?"
she whispered teasingly in my ear. In a moment I watched her
fade down the dusky stairway.

When I turned back to my room the place seemed much pleasanter than before. Lena had left something warm and friendly in the lamplight. How I loved to hear her laugh again! It was so soft and unexcited and appreciative—gave a favorable interpretation to everything. When I closed my eyes I could hear them all laughing—the Danish laundry girls and the three Bohemian Marys. Lena had brought them all back to me. It came over me, as it had never done before, the relation between girls like those and the poetry of Virgil. If there were no girls like them in the world, there would be no poetry. I understood that clearly, for the first time. This revelation seemed to me inestimably precious. I clung to it as if it might suddenly vanish.

As I sat down to my book at last, my old dream about Lena coming across the harvest field in her short skirt seemed to me like the memory of an actual experience. It floated before me on the page like a picture, and underneath it stood the mournful line: *Optima dies . . . prima fugit.*

III

In Lincoln the best part of the theatrical season came late, when the good companies stopped off there for one-night stands, after their long runs in New York and Chicago. That spring Lena went with me to see Joseph Jefferson in "Rip Van Winkle," and to a war play called "Shenandoah." She was inflexible about paying for her own seat; said she was in business now, and she wouldn't have a schoolboy spending his money on her. I liked to watch a play with Lena; everything was wonderful to her, and everything was true. It was like going to revival meetings with some one who was always being converted. She handed her feelings over to the actors with a kind of fatalistic resignation. Accessories of costume and scene meant much more to her than to me. She sat entranced through "Robin Hood" and hung upon the lips of the contralto who sang, "Oh, Promise Me!"

Toward the end of April, the billboards, which I watched anxiously in those days, bloomed out one morning with gleaming white posters on which two names were impressively printed in blue Gothic letters: the name of an actress of whom I had often heard, and the name "Camille."

I called at the Raleigh Block for Lena on Saturday evening, and we walked down to the theater. The weather was warm and sultry and put us both in a holiday humor. We arrived early, because Lena liked to watch the people come in. There was a note on the programme, saying that the "incidental music" would be from the opera "Traviata," which was made from the same story as the play. We had neither of us read the play, and we did not know what it was about—though I seemed to remember having heard it was a piece in which great actresses shone. "The Count of Monte Cristo," which I had seen James O'Neill play that winter, was by the only Alexandre Dumas I knew. This play, I saw, was by his son, and I expected a family resemblance. A couple of jack-rabbits, run in off the prairie, could not have been more innocent of what awaited them than were Lena and I.

Our excitement began with the rise of the curtain, when the moody Varville, seated before the fire, interrogated Nanine. Decidedly, there was a new tang about this dialogue. I had never heard in the theater lines that were alive, that presupposed and took for granted, like those which passed between Varville and Marguerite in the brief encounter before her friends entered. This introduced the most brilliant, worldly, the most enchantingly gay scene I had ever looked upon. I had never seen champagne bottles opened on the stage before—indeed, I had never seen them opened anywhere. The memory of that supper makes me hungry now; the sight of it then, when I had only a students' boarding-house dinner behind me, was delicate torment. I seem to remember gilded chairs and tables (arranged hurriedly by foot-men in white gloves and stockings), linen of dazzling whiteness, glittering glass, silver dishes, a great bowl of fruit, and the reddest of roses. The room was invaded by beautiful women and dashing young men, laughing and talking together. The men were dressed more or less after the period in which the play was written; the women were not. I saw no inconsistency. Their talk seemed to open to one the brilliant world in which they lived; every sentence made one older and wiser, every pleasantry enlarged one's horizon. One could experience excess and satiety without the inconvenience of learning what to do with one's hands in a drawing-room! When the characters all spoke at once and I missed some of the phrases they flashed at each other, I was in misery. I strained my ears and eyes to catch every exclamation.

The actress who played Marguerite was even then old-fashioned, though historic. She had been a member of Daly's famous New York company, and afterward a "star" under his direction. She was a woman who could not be taught, it is said, though she had a crude natural force which carried with people whose feelings were accessible and whose taste was not squeamish. She was already old, with a ravaged countenance and a physique curiously hard and stiff. She moved with difficulty—I think she was lame—I seem to remember some story about a malady of the spine. Her Armand was disproportionately young and slight, a handsome youth, perplexed in the extreme. But what did it matter? I believed devoutly in her power to fascinate him, in her dazzling loveliness. I believed her young, ardent, reckless, disillusioned, under sentence, feverish, avid of pleasure. I wanted to cross the footlights and help the slim-waisted Armand in the frilled shirt to convince her that there was still loyalty and devotion in the world. Her sudden illness, when the gayety was at its height, her pallor, the handkerchief she crushed against her lips, the cough she smothered under the laughter while Gaston kept playing the piano lightly—it all wrung my heart. But not so much as her cynicism in the long dialogue with her lover which followed. How far was I from questioning her unbelief! While the charmingly sincere young man pleaded with her—accompanied by the orchestra in the old "Traviata" duet, "*misterioso, misterioso!*"—she maintained her bitter skepticism, and the curtain fell on her dancing recklessly with the others, after Armand had been sent away with his flower.

Between the acts we had no time to forget. The orchestra kept sawing away at the "Traviata" music, so joyous and sad, so thin and far-away, so clap-trap and yet so heart-breaking. After the second act I left Lena in tearful contemplation of the ceiling, and went out into the lobby to smoke. As I walked about there I congratulated myself that I had not brought some Lincoln girl who would talk during the waits about the Junior dances, or whether the cadets would camp at Plattsmouth. Lena was at least a woman, and I was a man.

Through the scene between Marguerite an the elder Duval, Lena wept unceasingly, and I sat helpless to prevent the closing of that chapter of idyllic love, dreading the return of the young man whose ineffable happiness was only to be the measure of his fall.

I suppose no woman could have been further in person, voice, and temperament from Dumas' appealing heroine than the veteran actress who first acquainted me with her. Her conception of the character was as heavy and uncompromising as her diction; she bore hard on the idea and on the consonants. At all times she was highly tragic, devoured by remorse. Lightness of stress or behavior was far from her. Her voice was heavy and deep: "Ar-r-r-mond!" she would begin, as if she were summoning him to the bar of Judgment. But the lines were enough. She had only to utter them. They created the character in spite of her.

The heartless world which Marguerite re-entered with Varville had never been so glittering and reckless as on the night when it gathered in Olympe's salon for the fourth act. There were chandeliers hung from the ceiling, I remember, many servants in livery, gaming-tables where the men played with piles of gold, and a staircase down which the guests made their entrance. After all the other had gathered round the card tables, and young Duval had been warned by Prudence, Marguerite descended the staircase with Varville; such a cloak, such a fan, such jewels—and her face! One knew at a glance how it was with her. When Armand, with the terrible words, "Look, all of you, I owe this woman nothing!" flung the gold and banknotes at the half-swooning Marguerite, Lena cowered beside me and covered her face with her hands.

The curtain rose on the bedroom scene. By this time there wasn't a nerve in me that hadn't been twisted. Nanine alone could have made me cry. I loved Nanine tenderly; and Gaston, how one clung to that good fellow! The New Year's presents were not too much; nothing could be too much now. I wept unrestrainedly. Even the handkerchief in my breast-pocket, worn for elegance and not at all for use, was wet through by the time that moribund woman sank for the last time into the arms of her lover.

When we reached the door of the theater, the streets were shining with rain. I had prudently brought along Mrs. Harling's useful Commencement present, and I took Lena home under its shelter. After leaving her, I walked slowly out into the country part of the town where I lived. The lilacs were all blooming in the yards, and the smell of them after the rain, of the new leaves and the blossoms together, blew into my face with a sort of bitter sweetness. I tramped through the puddles and under the showery trees, mourning for Marguerite Gauthier as if she had died only yesterday, sighing with the spirit of 1840, which had sighed so much, and which had reached me only that night, across long years and several languages, through the person of an infirm old actress. The idea is one that no circumstances can frustrate. Wherever and whenever that piece is put on, it is April.

IV

How well I remember the stiff little parlor where I used to wait for Lena: the hard horsehair furniture, bought at some auction sale, the long mirror, the fashion-plates on the wall. If I sat down even for a moment I was sure to find threads and bits of colored silk clinging to my clothes after I went away. Lena's success puzzled me. She was so easygoing; had none of the push and self-assertiveness that get people ahead in business. She had come to Lincoln, a country girl, with no introductions except to some cousins of Mrs. Thomas who lived there, and she was already making clothes for the women of "the young married set." She evidently had great natural aptitude for her work. She knew, as she said, "what people looked well in." She never tired of poring over fashion books. Sometimes in the evening I would find her alone in her work-room, draping folds of satin on a wire figure, with a quite blissful expression of countenance. I couldn't help thinking that the years when Lena literally hadn't enough clothes to cover herself might have something to do with her untiring interest in dressing the human figure. Her clients said that Lena "had style," and overlooked her habitual inaccuracies. She never, I discovered, finished anything by the time she had promised, and she frequently spent more money on materials than her customer had authorized. Once, when I arrived at six o'clock, Lena was ushering out a fidgety mother and her awkward, overgrown daughter. The woman detained Lena at the door to say apologetically:—

"You'll try to keep it under fifty for me, won't you, Miss Lingard? You see, she's really too young to come to an expensive dressmaker, but I knew you could do more with her than anybody else."

"Oh, that will be all right, Mrs. Herron. I think we'll manage to get a good effect," Lena replied blandly.

I thought her manner with her customers very good, and wondered where she had learned such self-possession.

Sometimes after my morning classes were over, I used to encounter Lena downtown, in her velvet suit and a little black hat, with a veil tied smoothly over her face, looking as fresh as the spring morning. Maybe she would be carrying home a bunch of jonquils or a hyacinth plant. When we passed a candy store her footsteps would hesitate and linger. "Don't let me go in," she would murmur. "Get me by if you can." She was very fond of sweets, and was afraid of growing too plump.

We had delightful Sunday breakfasts together at Lena's. At the back of her long work-room was a bay-window, large enough to hold a box-couch and a reading-table. We breakfasted in this recess, after drawing the curtains that shut out the long room, with cutting-tables and wire women and sheet-draped garments on the walls. The sunlight poured in, making everything on the table shine and glitter and the flame of the alcohol lamp disappear altogether. Lena's curly black water-spaniel, Prince, breakfasted with us. He sat beside her on the couch and behaved very well until the Polish violin-teacher across the hall began to practice, when Prince would growl and sniff the air with disgust. Lena's landlord, old Colonel Raleigh, had given her the dog, and at first she was not at all pleased. She had spent too much of her life taking care of animals to have much sentiment about them. But Prince was a knowing little beast, and she grew fond of him. After breakfast I made him do his lessons; play dead dog, shake hands, stand up like a soldier. We used to put my cadet cap on his head—I had to take military drill at the University—and give him a yard-measure to hold with his front leg. His gravity made us laugh immoderately.

Lena's talk always amused me. Ántonia had never talked like the people about her. Even after she learned to speak English readily there was always something impulsive and foreign in her speech. But Lena had picked up all the conventional expressions she heard at Mrs. Thomas's dressmaking shop. Those formal phrases, the very flower of small-town proprieties, and the flat commonplaces, nearly all hypocritical in their origin, became very funny, very engaging, when they were uttered in Lena's soft voice, with her caressing intonation and arch naïveté. Nothing could be more diverting than to hear Lena, who was almost as candid as Nature, call a leg a "limb" or a house a "home."

We used to linger a long while over our coffee in that sunny corner. Lena was never so pretty as in the morning; she wakened fresh with the world every day, and her eyes had a deeper color then, like the blue flowers that are never so blue as when they first open. I could sit idle all through a Sunday morning and look at her. Ole Benson's behavior was now no mystery to me.

"There was never any harm in Ole," she said once. "People need n't have troubled themselves. He just liked to come over and sit on the draw-side and forget about his bad luck. I liked to have him. Any company's welcome when you're off with cattle all the time."

"But wasn't he always glum?" I asked. "People said he never talked at all."

"Sure he talked, in Norwegian. He'd been a sailor on an English boat and had seen lots of queer places. He had wonderful tattoos. We used to sit and look at them for hours; there wasn't much to look at out there. He was like a picture book. He had a ship and a strawberry girl on one arm, and on the other a girl standing before a little house, with a fence and gate and all, waiting for her sweetheart. Farther up his arm, her sailor had come back and was kissing her. 'The Sailor's Return,' he called it."

I admitted it was no wonder Ole liked to look at a pretty girl once in a while, with such a fright at home.

"You know," Lena said confidentially, "he married Mary because he thought she was strong-minded and would keep him straight. He never could keep straight on shore. The last time he landed in Liverpool he'd been out on a two years' voyage. He was paid off one morning, and by the next he hadn't a cent left, and his watch and compass were gone. He'd got with some women, and they'd taken everything. He worked his way to this country on a little passenger boat. Mary was a stewardess, and she tried to convert him on the way over. He thought she was just the one to keep him steady. Poor Ole! He used to bring me candy from town, hidden in his feed-bag. He couldn't refuse anything to a girl. He'd have given away his tattoos long ago, if he could. He's one of the people I'm sorriest for."

If I happened to spend an evening with Lena and stayed late, the Polish violin-teacher across the hall used to come out and watch me descend the stairs, muttering so threateningly that it would have been easy to fall into a quarrel with him. Lena had told him once that she liked to hear him practice, so he always left his door open, and watched who came and went.

There was a coolness between the Pole and Lena's landlord on her account. Old Colonel Raleigh had come to Lincoln from Kentucky and invested an inherited fortune in real estate, at the time of inflated prices. Now he sat day after day in his office in the Raleigh Block, trying to discover where his money had gone and how he could get some of it back. He was a widower, and found very little congenial companionship in this casual Western city. Lena's good looks and gentle manners appealed to him. He said her voice reminded him of Southern voices, and he found as many opportunities of hearing it as possible. He painted and papered her rooms for her that spring, and put in a porcelain bathtub in place of the tin one that had satisfied the former tenant. While these repairs were being made, the old gentleman often dropped in to consult Lena's preferences. She told me with amusement how Ordinsky, the Pole, had presented himself at her door one evening, and said that if the landlord was annoying her by his attentions, he would promptly put a stop to it.

"I don't exactly know what to do about him," she said, shaking her head, "he's so sort of wild all the time. I wouldn't like to have him say anything rough to that nice old man. The Colonel is long-winded, but then I expect he's lonesome. I don't think he cares much for Ordinsky, either. He said once that if I had any complaints to make of my neighbors, I mustn't hesitate."

One Saturday evening when I was having supper with Lena we heard a knock at her parlor door, and there stood the Pole, coatless, in a dress shirt and collar. Prince dropped on his paws and began to growl like a mastiff, while the visitor apologized, saying that he could not possibly come in thus attired, but he begged Lena to lend him some safety pins.

"Oh, you'll have to come in, Mr. Ordinsky, and let me see what's the matter." She closed the door behind him. "Jim, won't you make Prince behave?"

I rapped Prince on the nose, while Ordinsky explained that he had not had his dress clothes on for a long time, and to-night, when he was going to play for a concert, his waistcoat had split down the back. He thought he could pin it together until he got it to a tailor.

Lena took him by the elbow and turned him round. She laughed when she saw the long gap in the satin. "You could never pin that, Mr. Ordinsky. You've kept it folded too long, and the goods is all gone along the crease. Take it off. I can put a new piece of lining-silk in there for you in ten minutes." She disappeared into her work-room with the vest, leaving me to confront the Pole, who stood against the door like a wooden figure. He folded his arms and glared at me with his excitable, slanting brown eyes. His head was the shape of a chocolate drop, and was covered with dry, straw-colored hair that fuzzed up about his pointed crown. He had never done more than mutter at me as I passed him, and I was surprised when he now addressed me.

"Miss Lingard," he said haughtily, "is a young woman for whom I have the utmost, the utmost respect."

"So have I," I said coldly.

He paid no heed to my remark, but began to do rapid finger-exercises on his shirt-sleeves, as he stood with tightly folded arms.

"Kindness of heart," he went on, staring at the ceiling, "sentiment, are not understood in a place like this. The noblest qualities are ridiculed. Grinning college boys, ignorant and conceited, what do they know of delicacy!"

I controlled my features and tried to speak seriously.

"If you mean me, Mr. Ordinsky, I have known Miss Lingard a long time, and I think I appreciate her kindness. We come from the same town, and we grew up together."

His gaze traveled slowly down from the ceiling and rested on me. "Am I to understand that you have this young woman's interests at heart? That you do not wish to compromise her?"

"That's a word we don't use much here, Mr. Ordinsky. A girl who makes her own living can ask a college boy to supper without being talked about. We take some things for granted."

"Then I have misjudged you, and I ask your pardon,"—he bowed gravely. "Miss Lingard," he went on, "is an absolutely trustful heart. She has not learned the hard lessons of life. As for you and me, *noblesse oblige*,"—he watched me narrowly.

Lena returned with the vest. "Come in and let us look at you as you go out, Mr. Ordinsky. I've never seen you in your dress suit," she said as she opened the door for him.

A few moments later he reappeared with his violin case—a heavy muffler about his neck and thick woolen gloves on his bony hands. Lena spoke encouragingly to him, and he went off with such an important, professional air, that we fell to laughing as soon as we had shut the door. "Poor fellow," Lena said indulgently, "he takes everything so hard."

After that Ordinsky was friendly to me, and behaved as if there were some deep understanding between us. He wrote a furious article, attacking the musical taste of the town, and asked me to do him a great service by taking it to the editor of the morning paper. If the editor refused to print it, I was to tell him that he would be answerable to Ordinsky "in person." He declared that he would never retract one word, and that he was quite prepared to lose all his pupils. In spite of the fact that nobody ever mentioned his article to him after it appeared—full of typographical errors which he thought intentional—he got a certain satisfaction from believing that the citizens of Lincoln had meekly accepted the epithet "coarse barbarians." "You see how it is," he said to me, "where there is no chivalry, there is no *amour propre*." When I met him on his rounds now, I thought he carried his head more disdainfully than ever, and strode up the steps of front porches and rang doorbells with more assurance. He told Lena he would never forget how I had stood by him when he was "under fire."

All this time, of course, I was drifting. Lena had broken up my serious mood. I wasn't interested in my classes. I played with Lena and Prince, I played with the Pole, I went buggy-riding with the old Colonel, who had taken a fancy to me and used to talk to me about Lena and the "great beauties" he had known in his youth. We were all three in love with Lena.

Before the first of June, Gaston Cleric was offered an instruc-

torship at Harvard College, and accepted it. He suggested that I
should follow him in the fall, and complete my course at Harvard.
He had found out about Lena—not from me—and he talked to
me seriously.

"You won't do anything here now. You should either quit school
and go to work, or change your college and begin again in earnest.
You won't recover yourself while you are playing about with this
handsome Norwegian. Yes, I've seen her with you at the theater.
She's very pretty, and perfectly irresponsible, I should judge."

Cleric wrote my grandfather that he would like to take me
East with him. To my astonishment, grandfather replied that I
might go if I wished. I was both glad and sorry on the day when
the letter came. I stayed in my room all evening and thought
things over; I even tried to persuade myself that I was standing in
Lena's way—it is so necessary to be a little noble!—and that if she
had not me to play with, she would probably marry and secure
her future.

The next evening I went to call on Lena. I found her propped
up on the couch in her bay window, with her foot in a big slipper.
An awkward little Russian girl whom she had taken into her
work-room had dropped a flat-iron on Lena's toe. On the table
beside her there was a basket of early summer flowers which the
Pole had left after he heard of the accident. He always managed to
know what went on in Lena's apartment.

Lena was telling me some amusing piece of gossip about
one of her clients, when I interrupted her and picked up the
flower basket.

"This old chap will be proposing to you some day, Lena."

"Oh, he has—often!" she murmured.

"What! After you've refused him?"

"He doesn't mind that. It seems to cheer him to mention the
subject. Old men are like that, you know. It makes them feel
important to think they're in love with somebody."

"The Colonel would marry you in a minute. I hope you won't
marry some old fellow; not even a rich one."

Lena shifted her pillows and looked up at me in surprise. "Why, I'm not going to marry anybody. Didn't you know that?"

"Nonsense, Lena. That's what girls say, but you know better. Every handsome girl like you marries, of course."

She shook her head. "Not me."

"But why not? What makes you say that?" I persisted.

Lena laughed. "Well, it's mainly because I don't want a husband. Men are all right for friends, but as soon as you marry them they turn into cranky old fathers, even the wild ones. They begin to tell you what's sensible and what's foolish, and want you to stick at home all the time. I prefer to be foolish when I feel like it, and be accountable to nobody."

"But you'll be lonesome. You'll get tired of this sort of life, and you'll want a family."

"Not me. I like to be lonesome. When I went to work for Mrs. Thomas I was nineteen years old, and I had never slept a night in my life when there weren't three in the bed. I never had a minute to myself except when I was off with the cattle."

Usually, when Lena referred to her life in the country at all, she dismissed it with a single remark, humorous or mildly cynical. But to-night her mind seemed to dwell on those early years. She told me she couldn't remember a time when she was so little that she wasn't lugging a heavy baby about, helping to wash for babies, trying to keep their little chapped hands and faces clean. She remembered home as a place where there were always too many children, a cross man, and work piling up around a sick woman.

"It wasn't mother's fault. She would have made us comfortable if she could. But that was no life for a girl! After I began to herd and milk I could never get the smell of the cattle off me. The few underclothes I had I kept in a cracker box. On Saturday nights, after everybody was in bed, then I could take a bath if I wasn't too tired. I could make two trips to the windmill to carry water, and heat it in the wash-boiler on the stove. While the water was heating, I could bring in a washtub out of the cave, and take my bath in the kitchen. Then I could put on a clean nightgown and get into bed with two others, who likely hadn't had a bath unless I'd given it to them. You can't tell me anything about family life. I've had plenty to last me."

"But it's not all like that," I objected.

"Near enough. It's all being under somebody's thumb. What's on your mind, Jim? Are you afraid I'll want you to marry me some day?"

Then I told her I was going away.

"What makes you want to go away, Jim? Haven't I been nice to you?"

"You've been just awfully good to me, Lena," I blurted. "I don't think about much else. I never shall think about much else while I'm with you. I'll never settle down and grind if I stay here. You know that." I dropped down beside her and sat looking at the floor. I seemed to have forgotten all my reasonable explanations.

Lena drew close to me, and the little hesitation in her voice that had hurt me was not there when she spoke again.

"I oughtn't to have begun it, ought I?" she murmured. "I oughtn't to have gone to see you that first time. But I did want to. I guess I've always been a little foolish about you. I don't know what first put it into my head, unless it was Ántonia, always telling me I mustn't be up to any of my nonsense with you. I let you alone for a long while, though, didn't I?"

She was a sweet creature to those she loved, that Lena Lingard!

At last she sent me away with her soft, slow, renunciatory kiss. "You aren't sorry I came to see you that time?" she whispered. "It seemed so natural. I used to think I'd like to be your first sweetheart. You were such a funny kid!" She always kissed one as if she were sadly and wisely sending one away forever.

We said many good-byes before I left Lincoln, but she never tried to hinder me or hold me back. "You are going, but you haven't gone yet, have you?" she used to say.

My Lincoln chapter closed abruptly. I went home to my grandparents for a few weeks, and afterward visited my relatives in Virginia until I joined Cleric in Boston. I was then nineteen years old.

BOOK IV
THE PIONEER WOMAN'S STORY

I

Two years after I left Lincoln I completed my academic course at Harvard. Before I entered the Law School I went home for the summer vacation. On the night of my arrival Mrs. Harling and Frances and Sally came over to greet me. Everything seemed just as it used to be. My grandparents looked very little older. Frances Harling was married now, and she and her husband managed the Harling interests in Black Hawk. When we gathered in grandmother's parlor, I could hardly believe that I had been away at all. One subject, however, we avoided all evening.

When I was walking home with Frances, after we had left Mrs. Harling at her gate, she said simply, "You know, of course, about poor Ántonia."

Poor Ántonia! Every one would be saying that now, I thought bitterly. I replied that grandmother had written me how Ántonia went away to marry Larry Donovan at some place where he was working; that he had deserted her, and that there was now a baby. This was all I knew.

"He never married her," Frances said. "I haven't seen her since she came back. She lives at home, on the farm, and almost never comes to town. She brought the baby in to show it to mama once. I'm afraid she's settled down to be Ambrosch's drudge for good."

I tried to shut Ántonia out of my mind. I was bitterly disappointed in her. I could not forgive her for becoming an object of pity, while Lena Lingard, for whom people had always foretold trouble, was now the leading dressmaker of Lincoln, much respected in Black Hawk. Lena gave her heart away when she felt like it, but she kept her head for her business and had got on in the world.

Just then it was the fashion to speak indulgently of Lena and severely of Tiny Soderball, who had quietly gone West to try her fortune the year before. A Black Hawk boy, just back from Seattle, brought the news that Tiny had not gone to the coast on a venture, as she had allowed people to think, but with very definite plans. One of the roving promoters that used to stop at Mrs. Gardener's hotel owned idle property along the waterfront in Seattle, and he had offered to set Tiny up in business in one of his empty buildings. She was now conducting a sailors' lodging-house. This, every one said, would be the end of Tiny. Even if she had begun by running a decent place, she couldn't keep it up; all sailors' boarding-houses were alike.

When I thought about it, I discovered that I had never known Tiny as well as I knew the other girls. I remembered her tripping briskly about the dining-room on her high heels, carrying a big tray full of dishes, glancing rather pertly at the spruce traveling men, and contemptuously at the scrubby ones—who were so afraid of her that they didn't dare to ask for two kinds of pie. Now it occurred to me that perhaps the sailors, too, might be afraid of Tiny. How astonished we would have been, as we sat talking about her on Frances Harling's front porch, if we could have known what her future was really to be! Of all the girls and boys who grew up together in Black Hawk, Tiny Soderball was to lead the most adventurous life and to achieve the most solid worldly success.

This is what actually happened to Tiny: While she was running her lodging-house in Seattle, gold was discovered in Alaska. Miners and sailors came back from the North with wonderful stories and pouches of gold. Tiny saw it and weighed it in her hands. That daring which nobody had ever suspected in her, awoke. She sold her business and set out for Circle City, in company with a carpenter and his wife whom she had persuaded to go along with her. They reached Skaguay in a snowstorm, went in dog sledges over the Chilkoot Pass, and shot the Yukon in flatboats. They reached Circle City on the very day when some Siwash Indians came into the settlement with the report that there had been a rich gold strike farther up the river, on a certain Klondike Creek. Two days later Tiny and her friends, and nearly every one else in Circle City, started for the Klondike fields on the last steamer that went up the Yukon before it froze for the winter. That boatload of people founded Dawson City. Within a few weeks there were fifteen hundred homeless men in camp. Tiny and the carpenter's wife began to cook for them, in a tent. The miners gave her a lot, and the carpenter put up a log hotel for her. There she sometimes fed a hundred and fifty men a day. Miners came in on snowshoes from their placer claims twenty miles away to buy fresh bread from her, and paid for it in gold.

That winter Tiny kept in her hotel a Swede whose legs had been frozen one night in a storm when he was trying to find his way back to his cabin. The poor fellow thought it great good fortune to be cared for by a woman, and a woman who spoke his own tongue. When he was told that his feet must be amputated, he said he hoped he would not get well; what could a working-man do in this hard world without feet? He did, in fact, die from the operation, but not before he had deeded Tiny Soderball his claim on Hunker Creek. Tiny sold her hotel, invested half her money in Dawson building lots, and with the rest she developed her claim. She went off into the wilds and lived on it. She bought other claims from discouraged miners, traded or sold them on percentages.

After nearly ten years in the Klondike, Tiny returned, with a considerable fortune, to live in San Francisco. I met her in Salt Lake City in 1908. She was a thin, hard-faced woman, very well-dressed, very reserved in manner. Curiously enough, she reminded me of Mrs. Gardener, for whom she had worked in Black Hawk so long ago. She told me about some of the desperate chances she had taken in the gold country, but the thrill of them was quite gone. She said frankly that nothing interested her much now but making money. The only two human beings of whom she spoke with any feeling were the Swede, Johnson, who had given her his claim, and Lena Lingard. She had persuaded Lena to come to San Francisco and go into business there.

"Lincoln was never any place for her," Tiny remarked. "In a town of that size Lena would always be gossiped about. Frisco's the right field for her. She has a fine class of trade. Oh, she's just the same as she always was! She's careless, but she's level-headed. She's the only person I know who never gets any older. It's fine for me to have her there; somebody who enjoys things like that. She keeps an eye on me and won't let me be shabby. When she thinks I need a new dress, she makes it and sends it home—with a bill that's long enough, I can tell you!"

Tiny limped slightly when she walked. The claim on Hunker Creek took toll from its possessors. Tiny had been caught in a sudden turn of weather, like poor Johnson. She lost three toes from one of those pretty little feet that used to trip about Black Hawk in pointed slippers and striped stockings. Tiny mentioned this mutilation quite casually—didn't seem sensitive about it. She was satisfied with her success, but not elated. She was like some one in whom the faculty of becoming interested is worn out.

II

Soon after I got home that summer I persuaded my grandparents to have their photographs taken, and one morning I went into the photographer's shop to arrange for sittings. While I was waiting for him to come out of his developing-room, I walked about trying to recognize the likenesses on his walls: girls in Commencement dresses, country brides and grooms holding hands, family groups of three generations. I noticed, in a heavy frame, one of those depressing "crayon enlargements" often seen in farmhouse parlors, the subject being a round-eyed baby in short dresses. The photographer came out and gave a constrained, apologetic laugh.

"That's Tony Shimerda's baby. You remember her; she used to

be the Harling's Tony. Too bad! She seems proud of the baby, though; wouldn't hear to a cheap frame for the picture. I expect her brother will be in for it Saturday."

I went away feeling that I must see Ántonia again. Another girl would have kept her baby out of sight, but Tony, of course, must have its picture on exhibition at the town photographer's, in a great gilt frame. How like her! I could forgive her, I told myself, if she hadn't thrown herself away on such a cheap sort of fellow.

Larry Donovan was a passenger conductor, one of those train-crew aristocrats who are always afraid that some one may ask them to put up a car-window, and who, if requested to perform such a menial service, silently point to the button that calls the porter. Larry wore this air of official aloofness even on the street, where there were no car-windows to compromise his dignity. At the end of his run he stepped indifferently from the train along with the passengers, his street hat on his head and his conductor's cap in an alligator-skin bag, went directly into the station and changed his clothes. It was a matter of the utmost importance to him never to be seen in his blue trousers away from his train. He was usually cold and distant with men, but with all women he had a silent, grave familiarity, a special handshake, accompanied by a significant, deliberate look. He took women, married or single, into his confidence; walked them up and down in the moonlight, telling them what a mistake he had made by not entering the office branch of the service, and how much better fitted he was to fill the post of General Passenger Agent in Denver than the roughshod man who then bore that title. His un-appre..ciated worth was the tender secret Larry shared with his sweethearts, and he was always able to make some foolish heart ache over it.

As I drew near home that morning, I saw Mrs. Harling out in her yard, digging round her mountain-ash tree. It was a dry summer, and she had now no boy to help her. Charley was off in his battleship, cruising somewhere on the Caribbean sea. I turned in at the gate—it was with a feeling of pleasure that I opened and shut that gate in those days; I liked the feel of it under my hand. I took the spade away from Mrs. Harling, and while I loosened the earth around the tree, she sat down on the steps and talked about the oriole family that had a nest in its branches.

"Mrs. Harling," I said presently, "I wish I could find out exactly how Ántonia's marriage fell through."

"Why don't you go out and see your grandfather's tenant, the Widow Steavens? She knows more about it than anybody else. She helped Ántonia get ready to be married, and she was there when Ántonia came back. She took care of her when the baby was born. She could tell you everything. Besides, the Widow Steavens is a good talker, and she has a remarkable memory."

III

On the first or second day of August I got a horse and cart and set out for the high country, to visit the Widow Steavens. The wheat harvest was over, and here and there along the horizon I could see black puffs of smoke from the steam thrashing-machines. The old pasture land was now being broken up into wheatfields and corn-fields, the red grass was disappearing, and the whole face of the country was changing. There were wooden houses where the old sod dwellings used to be, and little orchards, and big red barns; all this meant happy children, contented women, and men who saw their lives coming to a fortunate issue. The windy springs and the blazing summers, one after another, had enriched and mellowed that flat tableland; all the human effort that had gone into it was coming back in long, sweeping lines of fertility. The changes seemed beautiful and harmonious to me; it was like watching the growth of a great man or of a great idea. I recognized every tree and sandbank and rugged draw. I found that I remembered the confor-mation of the land as one remembers the modeling of human faces.

When I drew up to our old windmill, the Widow Steavens came out to meet me. She was brown as an Indian woman, tall, and very strong. When I was little, her massive head had always seemed to me like a Roman senator's. I told her at once why I had come.

"You'll stay the night with us, Jimmy? I'll talk to you after supper. I can take more interest when my work is off my mind. You've no prejudice against hot biscuit for supper? Some have, these days."

While I was putting my horse away I heard a rooster squawking. I looked at my watch and sighed; it was three o'clock, and I knew that I must eat him at six.

After supper Mrs. Steavens and I went upstairs to the old sitting-room, while her grave, silent brother remained in the basement to read his farm papers. All the windows were open. The white summer moon was shining outside, the windmill was pumping hazily in the light breeze. My hostess put the lamp on a stand in the corner, and turned it low because of the heat. She sat down in her favorite rocking-chair and settled a little stool comfortably under her tired feet. "I'm troubled with callouses, Jim; getting old," she sighed cheerfully. She crossed her hands in her lap and sat as if she were at a meeting of some kind.

"Now, it's about that dear Ántonia you want to know? Well, you've come to the right person. I've watched her like she'd been my own daughter.

"When she came home to do her sewing that summer before she was to be married, she was over here about every day. They've never had a sewing machine at the Shimerdas', and she made all her things here. I taught her hemstitching, and I helped her to cut and fit. She used to sit there at that machine by the window, pedaling the life out of it—she was so strong—and always singing them queer Bohemian songs, like she was the happiest thing in the world.

"'Ántonia,' I used to say, 'don't run that machine so fast. You won't hasten the day none that way.'

"Then she'd laugh and slow down for a little, but she'd soon forget and begin to pedal and sing again. I never saw a girl work harder to go to housekeeping right and well-prepared. Lovely table linen the Harlings had given her, and Lena Lingard had sent her nice things from Lincoln. We hemstitched all the tablecloths and pillow-cases, and some of the sheets. Old Mrs. Shimerda knit yards and yards of lace for her underclothes. Tony told me just how she meant to have everything in her house. She'd even bought silver spoons and forks, and kept them in her trunk. She was always coaxing brother to go to the post-office. Her young man did write her real often, from the different towns along his run.

"The first thing that troubled her was when he wrote that his run had been changed, and they would likely have to live in Denver. 'I'm a country girl,' she said, 'and I doubt if I'll be able to manage so well for him in a city. I was counting on keeping chickens, and maybe a cow.' She soon cheered up, though.

"At last she got the letter telling her when to come. She was shaken by it; she broke the seal and read it in this room. I suspected then that she'd begun to get faint-hearted, waiting; though she'd never let me see it.

"Then there was a great time of packing. It was in March, if I remember rightly, and a terrible muddy, raw spell, with the roads bad for hauling her things to town. And here let me say, Ambrosch did the right thing. He went to Black Hawk and bought her a set of plated silver in a purple velvet box, good enough for her station. He gave her three hundred dollars in money; I saw the check. He'd collected her wages all those first years she worked out, and it was but right. I shook him by the hand in this room. 'You're behaving like a man, Ambrosch,' I said, 'and I'm glad to see it, son.'

"'Twas a cold, raw day he drove her and her three trunks into Black Hawk to take the night train for Denver—the boxes had been shipped before. He stopped the wagon here, and she ran in to tell me good-bye. She threw her arms around me and kissed me, and thanked me for all I'd done for her. She was so happy she was crying and laughing at the same time; and her red cheeks was all wet with rain.

"You're surely handsome enough for any man,' I said, looking her over.

"She laughed kind of flighty like, and whispered, 'Good-bye, dear house!' and then ran out to the wagon. I expect she meant that for you and your grandmother, as much as for me, so I'm particular to tell you. This house had always been a refuge to her.

"Well, in a few days we had a letter saying she got to Denver safe, and he was there to meet her. They were to be married in a few days. He was trying to get his promotion before he married, she said. I didn't like that, but I said nothing. The next week Yulka got a postal card, saying she was 'well and happy.' After that we heard nothing. A month went by, and old Mrs. Shimerda began to get fretful. Ambrosch was as sulky with me as if I'd picked out the man and arranged the match.

"One night brother William came in and said that on his way back from the fields he had passed a livery team from town, driving fast out the west road. There was a trunk on the front seat with the driver, and another behind. In the back seat there was a woman all bundled up; but for all her veils, he thought 't was Ántonia Shimerda, or Ántonia Donovan, as her name ought now to be.

"The next morning I got brother to drive me over. I can walk still, but my feet ain't what they used to be, and I try to save myself. The lines outside the Shimerdas' house was full of washing, though it was the middle of the week. As we got nearer I saw a sight that made my heart sink—all those underclothes we'd put so much work on, out there swinging in the wind. Yulka came bringing a dishpanful of wrung clothes, but she darted back into the house like she was loath to see us. When I went in, Ántonia was standing over the tubs, just finishing up a big washing. Mrs. Shimerda was going about her work, talking and scolding to herself. She didn't so much as raise her eyes. Tony wiped her hand on her apron and held it out to me, looking at me steady but mournful. When I took her in my arms she drew away. 'Don't, Mrs. Steavens,' she says, 'you'll make me cry, and I don't want to.'

"I whispered and asked her to come out of doors with me. I

knew she couldn't talk free before her mother. She went out with me, bareheaded, and we walked up toward the garden.

"'I'm not married, Mrs. Steavens,' she says to me very quiet and natural-like, 'and I ought to be.'

"'Oh, my child,' says I, 'what's happened to you? Don't be afraid to tell me!'

"She sat down on the draw-side, out of sight of the house. 'He's run away from me,' she said. 'I don't know if he ever meant to marry me.'

"'You mean he's thrown up his job and quit the country?' says I.

"'He didn't have any job. He'd been fired; blacklisted for knocking down fares. I didn't know. I thought he hadn't been treated right. He was sick when I got there. He'd just come out of the hospital. He lived with me till my money gave out, and afterwards I found he hadn't really been hunting work at all. Then he just didn't come back. One nice fellow at the station told me, when I kept going to look for him, to give it up. He said he was afraid Larry'd gone bad and wouldn't come back any more. I guess he's gone to Old Mexico. The conductors get rich down there, collecting half-fares off the natives and robbing the company. He was always talking about fellows who had got ahead that way.'

"I asked her, of course, why she didn't insist on a civil marriage at once—that would have given her some hold on him. She leaned her head on her hands, poor child, and said, 'I just don't know, Mrs. Steavens. I guess my patience was wore out, waiting so long. I thought if he saw how well I could do for him, he'd want to stay with me.'

"Jimmy, I sat right down on that bank beside her and made lament. I cried like a young thing. I couldn't help it. I was just about heart-broke. It was one of them lovely warm May days, and the wind was blowing and the colts jumping around in the pastures; but I felt bowed with despair. My Ántonia, that had so much good in her, had come home disgraced. And that Lena Lingard, that was always a bad one, say what you will, had turned out so well, and was coming home here every summer in her silks and her satins, and doing so much for her mother. I give credit where credit is due, but you know well enough, Jim Burden, there is a great difference in the principles of those two girls. And here it was the good one that had come to grief! I was poor comfort to her. I marveled at her calm. As we went back to the house, she stopped to feel of her clothes to see if they was drying well, and seemed to take pride in their whiteness—she said she'd been living in a brick block, where she didn't have proper conveniences to wash them.

"The next time I saw Ántonia, she was out in the fields ploughing corn. All that spring and summer she did the work of a man on the farm; it seemed to be an understood thing. Ambrosch didn't get any other hand to help him. Poor Marek had got violent and been sent away to an institution a good while back. We never even saw any of Tony's pretty dresses. She didn't take them out of her trunks. She was quiet and steady. Folks respected her industry and tried to treat her as if nothing had happened. They talked, to be sure; but not like they would if she'd put on airs. She was so crushed and quiet that nobody seemed to want to humble her. She never went anywhere. All that summer she never once came to see me. At first I was hurt, but I got to feel that it was because this house reminded her of too much. I went over there when I could, but the times when she was in from the fields were the times when I was busiest here. She talked about the grain and the weather as if she'd never had another interest, and if I went over at night she always looked dead weary. She was afflicted with toothache; one tooth after another ulcerated, and she went about with her face swollen half the time. She wouldn't go to Black Hawk to a dentist for fear of meeting people she knew. Ambrosch had got over his good spell long ago, and was always surly. Once I told him he ought not to let Ántonia work so hard and pull herself down. He said, 'If you put that in her head, you better stay home.' And after that I did.

"Ántonia worked on through harvest and thrashing, though

she was too modest to go out thrashing for the neighbors, like when she was young and free. I didn't see much of her until late that fall when she begun to herd Ambrosch's cattle in the open ground north of here, up toward the big dog town. Sometimes she used to bring them over the west hill, there, and I would run to meet her and walk north a piece with her. She had thirty cattle in her bunch; it had been dry, and the pasture was short, or she wouldn't have brought them so far.

"It was a fine open fall, and she liked to be alone. While the steers grazed, she used to sit on them grassy banks along the draws and sun herself for hours. Sometimes I slipped up to visit with her, when she hadn't gone too far.

"'It does seem like I ought to make lace or knit like Lena used to,' she said one day, 'but if I start to work, I look around and forget to go on. It seems such a little while ago when Jim Burden and I was playing all over this country. Up here I can pick out the very places where my father used to stand. Sometimes I feel like I'm not going to live very long, so I'm just enjoying every day of this fall.'

"After the winter begun she wore a man's long overcoat and boots, and a man's felt hat with a wide brim. I used to watch her coming and going, and I could see that her steps were getting heavier. One day in December, the snow began to fall. Late in the afternoon I saw Ántonia driving her cattle homeward across the hill. The snow was flying round her and she bent to face it, looking more lonesome-like to me than usual. 'Deary me,' I says to myself, 'the girl's stayed out too late. It'll be dark before she gets them cattle put into the corral.' I seemed to sense she'd been feeling too miserable to get up and drive them.

"That very night, it happened. She got her cattle home, turned them into the corral, and went into the house, into her room behind the kitchen, and shut the door. There, without calling to anybody, without a groan, she lay down on the bed and bore her child.

"I was lifting supper when old Mrs. Shimerda came running down the basement stairs, out of breath and screeching:—

" 'Baby come, baby come!' she says. 'Ambrosch much like devil!'

"Brother William is surely a patient man. He was just ready to sit down to a hot supper after a long day in the fields. Without a word he rose and went down to the barn and hooked up his team. He got us over there as quick as it was humanly possible. I went right in, and began to do for Ántonia; but she laid there with her eyes shut and took no account of me. The old woman got a tubful of warm water to wash the baby. I overlooked what she was doing and I said out loud:—

" 'Mrs. Shimerda, don't you put that strong yellow soap near that baby. You'll blister its little skin.' I was indignant.

" 'Mrs. Steavens,' Ántonia said from the bed, 'if you'll look in the top tray of my trunk, you'll see some fine soap.' That was the first word she spoke.

"After I'd dressed the baby, I took it out to show it to Ambrosch. He was muttering behind the stove and wouldn't look at it.

" 'You'd better put it out in the rain barrel,' he says.

" 'Now, see here, Ambrosch,' says I, 'there's a law in this land, don't forget that. I stand here a witness that this baby has come into the world sound and strong, and I intend to keep an eye on what befalls it.' I pride myself I cowed him.

"Well, I expect you're not much interested in babies, but Ántonia's got on fine. She loved it from the first as dearly as if she'd had a ring on her finger, and was never ashamed of it. It's a year and eight months old now, and no baby was ever better cared-for. Ántonia is a natural-born mother. I wish she could marry and raise a family, but I don't know as there's much chance now."

I slept that night in the room I used to have when I was a little boy, with the summer wind blowing in at the windows, bringing the smell of the ripe fields. I lay awake and watched the moonlight shining over the barn and the stacks and the pond, and the windmill making its old dark shadow against the blue sky.

IV

The next afternoon I walked over to the Shimerdas'. Yulka showed me the baby and told me that Ántonia was shocking wheat on the southwest quarter. I went down across the fields, and Tony saw me from a long way off. She stood still by her shocks, leaning on her pitchfork, watching me as I came. We met like the people in the old song, in silence, if not in tears. Her warm hand clasped mine.

"I thought you'd come, Jim. I heard you were at Mrs. Steavens's last night. I've been looking for you all day.'

She was thinner than I had ever seen her, and looked, as Mrs. Steavens said, "worked down,' but there was a new kind of strength in the gravity of her face, and her color still gave her that look of deep-seated health and ardor. Still? Why, it flashed across me that though so much had happened in her life and in mine, she was barely twenty-four years old.

Ántonia stuck her fork in the ground, and instinctively we walked toward that unploughed patch at the crossing of the roads as the fittest place to talk to each other. We sat down outside the sagging wire fence that shut Mr. Shimerda's plot off from the rest of the world. The tall red grass had never been cut there. It had died down in winter and come up again in the spring until it was as thick and shrubby as some tropical garden-grass. I found myself telling her everything: why I had decided to study law and to go into the law office of one of my mother's relatives in New York City; about Gaston Cleric's death from pneumonia last winter, and the difference it had made in my life. She wanted to know about my friends and my way of living, and my dearest hopes.

"Of course it means you are going away from us for good," she said with a sigh. "But that don't mean I'll lose you. Look at my papa here; he's been dead all these years, and yet he is more real to me than almost anybody else. He never goes out of my life. I talk to him and consult him all the time. The older I grow, the better I know him and the more I understand him."

She asked me whether I had learned to like big cities. "I'd always be miserable in a city. I'd die of lonesomeness. I like to be where I know every stack and tree, and where all the ground is friendly. I want to live and die here. Father Kelly says everybody's put into this world for something, and I know what I've got to do. I'm going to see that my little girl has a better chance than ever I had. I'm going to take care of that girl, Jim."

I told her I knew she would. "Do you know, Ántonia, since I've been away, I think of you more often than of any one else in this part of the world. I'd have liked to have you for a sweetheart, or a wife, or my mother or my sister—anything that a woman can be to a man. The idea of you is a part of my mind; you influence my likes and dislikes, all my tastes, hundreds of times when I don't realize it. You really are a part of me."

She turned her bright, believing eyes to me, and the tears came up in them slowly. "How can it be like that, when you know so many people, and when I've disappointed you so? Ain't it wonderful, Jim, how much people can mean to each other? I'm so glad we had each other when we were little. I can't wait till my little girl's old enough to tell her about all the things we used to do. You'll always remember me when you think about old times, won't you? And I guess everybody thinks about old times, even the happiest people."

As we walked homeward across the fields, the sun dropped and lay like a great golden globe in the low west. While it hung there, the moon rose in the east, as big as a cartwheel, pale silver and streaked with rose color, thin as a bubble or a ghost-moon. For five, perhaps ten minutes, the two luminaries confronted each other across the level land, resting on opposite edges of the world. In that singular light every little tree and shock of wheat, every sunflower stalk and clump of snow-on-the-mountain, drew itself up high and pointed; the very clods and furrows in the fields seemed to stand up sharply. I felt the old pull of the earth, the solemn magic that comes out of those fields at nightfall. I wished I could be a little boy again, and that my way could end there.

We reached the edge of the field, where our ways parted. I took her hands and held them against my breast, feeling once more how strong and warm and good they were, those brown hands, and remembering how many kind things they had done for me. I held them now a long while, over my heart. About us it was growing darker and darker, and I had to look hard to see her face, which I meant always to carry with me; the closest, realest face, under all the shadows of women's faces, at the very bottom of my memory.

"I'll come back," I said earnestly, through the soft, intrusive darkness.

"Perhaps you will"—I felt rather than saw her smile. "But even if you don't, you're here, like my father. So I won't be lonesome."

As I went back alone over that familiar road, I could almost believe that a boy and girl ran along beside me, as our shadows used to do, laughing and whispering to each other in the grass.

BOOK V
CUZAK'S BOYS

I

I told Ántonia I would come back, but life intervened, and it was twenty years before I kept my promise. I heard of her from time to time; that she married, very soon after I last saw her, a young Bohemian, a cousin of Anton Jelinek; that they were poor, and had a large family. Once when I was abroad I went into Bohemia, and from Prague I sent Ántonia some photographs of her native village. Months afterward came a letter from her, telling me the names and ages of her many children, but little else; signed, "Your old friend, Ántonia Cuzak." When I met Tiny Soderball in Salt Lake, she told me that Ántonia had not "done very well"; that her husband was not a man of much force, and she had had a hard life. Perhaps it was cowardice that kept me away so long. My business took me West several times every year, and it was always in the back of my mind that I would stop in Nebraska some day and go to see Ántonia. But I kept putting it off until the next trip. I did not want to find her aged and broken; I really dreaded it. In the course of twenty crowded years one parts with many illusions. I did not wish to lose the early ones. Some memories are realities, and are better than anything that can ever happen to one again.

I owe it to Lena Lingard that I went to see Ántonia at last. I was in San Francisco two summers ago when both Lena and Tiny Soderball were in town. Tiny lives in a house of her own, and Lena's shop is in an apartment house just around the corner. It interested me, after so many years, to see the two women together. Tiny audits Lena's accounts occasionally, and invests her money for her; and Lena, apparently, takes care that Tiny doesn't grow too miserly. "If there's anything I can't stand," she said to me in Tiny's presence, "it's a shabby rich woman." Tiny smiled grimly and assured me that Lena would never be either shabby or rich. "And I don't want to be," the other agreed complacently.

Lena gave me a cheerful account of Ántonia and urged me to make her a visit.

"You really ought to go, Jim. It would be such a satisfaction to her. Never mind what Tiny says. There's nothing the matter with Cuzak. You'd like him. He isn't a hustler, but a rough man would never have suited Tony. Tony has nice children—ten or eleven of them by this time, I guess. I shouldn't care for a family of that size myself, but somehow it's just right for Tony. She'd love to show them to you."

On my way East I broke my journey at Hastings, in Nebraska, and set off with an open buggy and a fairly good livery team to find the Cuzak farm. At a little past midday, I knew I must be nearing my destination. Set back on a swell of land at my right, I saw a wide farmhouse, with a red barn and an ash grove, and cattle yards in front that sloped down to the high road. I drew up my horses and was wondering whether I should drive in here, when I heard low voices. Ahead of me, in a plum thicket beside the road, I saw two boys bending over a dead dog. The little one, not more than four or five, was on his knees, his hands folded, and his close-clipped, bare head drooping forward in deep dejection. The other stood beside him, a hand on his shoulder, and was comforting him in a language I had not heard for a long while. When I stopped my horses opposite them, the older boy took his brother by the hand and came toward me. He, too, looked grave. This was evidently a sad afternoon for them.

"Are you Mrs. Cuzak's boys?" I asked.

The younger one did not look up; he was submerged in his own feelings, but his brother met me with intelligent gray eyes. "Yes, sir."

"Does she live up there on the hill? I am going to see her. Get in and ride up with me."

He glanced at his reluctant little brother. "I guess we'd better walk. But we'll open the gate for you."

I drove along the side-road and they followed slowly behind. When I pulled up at the windmill, another boy, barefooted and curly-headed, ran out of the barn to tie my team for me. He was a handsome one, this chap, fair-skinned and freckled, with red cheeks and a ruddy pelt as thick as a lamb's wool, growing down on his neck in little tufts. He tied my team with two flourishes of his hands, and nodded when I asked him if his mother was at home. As he glanced at me, his face dimpled with a seizure of irrelevant merriment, and he shot up the windmill tower with a lightness that struck me as disdainful. I knew he was peering down at me as I walked toward the house.

Ducks and geese ran quacking across my path. White cats were sunning themselves among yellow pumpkins on the porch steps. I looked through the wire screen into a big, light kitchen with a white floor. I saw a long table, rows of wooden chairs against the wall, and a shining range in one corner. Two girls were washing dishes at the sink, laughing and chattering, and a little one, in a short pinafore, sat on a stool playing with a rag baby. When I asked for their mother, one of the girls dropped her towel, ran across the floor with noiseless bare feet, and disappeared. The older one, who wore shoes and stockings, came to the door to admit me. She was a buxom girl with dark hair and eyes, calm and self-possessed.

"Won't you come in? Mother will be here in a minute."

Before I could sit down in the chair she offered me, the miracle happened; one of those quiet moments that clutch the heart, and take more courage than the noisy, excited passages in life. Ántonia came in and stood before me; a stalwart, brown woman, flat-chested, her curly brown hair a little grizzled. It was a shock, of course. It always is, to meet people after long years, especially if they have lived as much and as hard as this woman had. We stood looking at each other. The eyes that peered anxiously at me were—simply Ántonia's eyes. I had seen no others like them since I looked into them last, though I had looked at so many thousands of human faces. As I confronted her, the changes grew less

apparent to me, her identity stronger. She was there, in the full
vigor of her personality, battered but not diminished, looking at
me, speaking to me in the husky, breathy voice I remembered
so well.

"My husband's not at home, sir. Can I do anything?"

"Don't you remember me, Ántonia? Have I changed so much?"

She frowned into the slanting sunlight that made her brown
hair look redder than it was. Suddenly her eyes widened, her
whole face seemed to grow broader. She caught her breath and
put out two hard-worked hands.

"Why, it's Jim! Anna, Yulka, it's Jim Burden!" She had no
sooner caught my hands than she looked alarmed. "What's happened? Is anybody dead?"

I patted her arm. "No. I didn't come to a funeral this time. I
got off the train at Hastings and drove down to see you and
your family."

She dropped my hand and began rushing about. "Anton,
Yulka, Nina, where are you all? Run, Anna, and hunt for the boys.
They're off looking for that dog, somewhere. And call Leo. Where
is that Leo!" She pulled them out of corners and came bringing
them like a mother cat bringing in her kittens. "You don't have to
go right off, Jim? My oldest boy's not here. He's gone with papa to
the street fair at Wilber. I won't let you go! You've got to stay and
see Rudolph and our papa." She looked at me imploringly, panting with excitement.

While I reassured her and told her there would be plenty of
time, the barefooted boys from outside were slipping into the
kitchen and gathering about her.

"Now, tell me their names, and how old they are."

As she told them off in turn, she made several mistakes about
ages, and they roared with laughter. When she came to my light-
footed friend of the windmill, she said, "This is Leo, and he's old
enough to be better than he is."

He ran up to her and butted her playfully with his curly head,
like a little ram, but his voice was quite desperate. "You've forgot!

You always forget mine. It's mean! Please tell him, mother!" He clenched his fists in vexation and looked up at her impetuously.

She wound her forefinger in his yellow fleece and pulled it, catching him. "Well, how old are you?"

"I'm twelve," he panted, looking not at me but at her; "I'm twelve years old, and I was born on Easter day!"

She nodded to me. "It's true. He was an Easter baby."

The children all looked at me, as if they expected me to exhibit astonishment or delight at this information. Clearly, they were proud of each other, and of being so many. When they had all been introduced, Anna, the eldest daughter, who had met me at the door, scattered them gently, and came bringing a white apron which she tied round her mother's waist.

"Now, mother, sit down and talk to Mr. Burden. We'll finish the dishes quietly and not disturb you."

Ántonia looked about, quite distracted. "Yes, child, but why don't we take him into the parlor, now that we've got a nice parlor for company?"

The daughter laughed indulgently, and took my hat from me. "Well, you're here, now, mother, and if you talk here, Yulka and I can listen, too. You can show him the parlor after while." She smiled at me, and went back to the dishes, with her sister. The little girl with the rag doll found a place on the bottom step of an enclosed back stairway, and sat with her toes curled up, looking out at us expectantly.

"She's Nina, after Nina Harling," Ántonia explained. "Ain't her eyes like Nina's? I declare, Jim, I loved you children almost as much as I love my own. These children know all about you and Charley and Sally, like as if they'd grown up with you. I can't think of what I want to say, you've got me so stirred up. And then, I've forgot my English so. I don't often talk it any more. I tell the children I used to speak real well." She said they always spoke Bohemian at home. The little ones could not speak English at all—didn't learn it until they went to school.

"I can't believe it's you, sitting here, in my own kitchen. You wouldn't have known me, would you, Jim? You've kept so young, yourself. But it's easier for a man. I can't see how my Anton looks any older than the day I married him. His teeth have kept so nice. I haven't got many left. But I feel just as young as I used to, and I can do as much work. Oh, we don't have to work so hard now! We've got plenty to help us, papa and me. And how many have you got, Jim?"

When I told her I had no children she seemed embarrassed. "Oh, ain't that too bad! Maybe you could take one of my bad ones, now? That Leo; he's the worst of all." She leaned toward me with a smile. "And I love him the best," she whispered.

"Mother!" the two girls murmured reproachfully from the dishes.

Ántonia threw up her head and laughed. "I can't help it. You know I do. Maybe it's because he came on Easter day, I don't know. And he's never out of mischief one minute!"

I was thinking, as I watched her, how little it mattered—about her teeth, for instance. I know so many women who have kept all the things that she has lost, but whose inner glow has faded. Whatever else was gone, Ántonia had not lost the fire of life. Her skin, so brown and hardened, had not that look of flabbiness, as if the sap beneath it had been secretly drawn away.

While we were talking, the little boy whom they called Jan came in and sat down on the step beside Nina, under the hood of the stairway. He wore a funny long gingham apron, like a smock, over his trousers, and his hair was clipped so short that his head looked white and naked. He watched us out of his big, sorrowful gray eyes.

"He wants to tell you about the dog, mother. They found it dead," Anna said, as she passed us on her way to the cupboard.

Ántonia beckoned the boy to her. He stood by her chair, leaning his elbows on her knees and twisting her apron strings in his slender fingers, while he told her his story softly in Bohemian, and the tears brimmed over and hung on his long lashes. His mother listened, spoke soothingly to him, and in a whisper promised him something that made him give her a quick, teary smile. He slipped away and whispered his secret to Nina, sitting close to her and talking behind his hand.

When Anna finished her work and had washed her hands, she came and stood behind her mother's chair. "Why don't we show Mr. Burden our new fruit cave?" she asked.

We started off across the yard with the children at our heels. The boys were standing by the windmill, talking about the dog; some of them ran ahead to open the cellar door. When we descended, they all came down after us, and seemed quite as proud of the cave as the girls were. Ambrosch, the thoughtful-looking one who had directed me down by the plum bushes, called my attention to the stout brick walls and the cement floor. "Yes, it is a good way from the house," he admitted. "But, you see, in winter there are nearly always some of us around to come out and get things."

Anna and Yulka showed me three small barrels; one full of dill pickles, one full of chopped pickles, and one full of pickled water-melon rinds.

"You wouldn't believe, Jim, what it takes to feed them all!" their mother exclaimed. "You ought to see the bread we bake on Wednesdays and Saturdays! It's no wonder their poor papa can't get rich, he has to buy so much sugar for us to preserve with. We have our own wheat ground for flour,—but then there's that much less to sell."

Nina and Jan, and a little girl named Lucie, kept shyly pointing out to me the shelves of glass jars. They said nothing, but glancing at me, traced on the glass with their finger-tips the outline of the cherries and strawberries and crab-apples within, trying by a blissful expression of countenance to give me some idea of their deliciousness.

"Show him the spiced plums, mother. Americans don't have those," said one of the older boys. "Mother uses them to make *kolaches*," he added.

Leo, in a low voice, tossed off some scornful remark in Bohemian.

I turned to him. "You think I don't know what *kolaches* are, eh? You're mistaken, young man. I have eaten your mother's *kolaches* long before that Easter day when you were born."

"Always too fresh, Leo," Ambrosch remarked with a shrug.

Leo dived behind his mother and grinned out at me.

We turned to leave the cave; Ántonia and I went up the stairs first, and the children waited. We were standing outside talking, when they all came running up the steps together, big and little, tow heads and gold heads and brown, and flashing little naked legs; a veritable explosion of life out of the dark cave into the sunlight. It made me dizzy for a moment.

The boys escorted us to the front of the house, which I hadn't yet seen; in farmhouses, somehow, life comes and goes by the back door. The roof was so steep that the eaves were not much above the forest of tall hollyhocks, now brown and in seed. Through July, Ántonia said, the house was buried in them; the Bohemians, I remembered, always planted hollyhocks. The front yard was enclosed by a thorny locust hedge, and at the gate grew two silvery, moth-like trees of the mimosa family. From here one looked down over the cattle yards, with their two long ponds, and over a wide stretch of stubble which they told me was a rye-field in summer.

At some distance behind the house were an ash grove and two orchards; a cherry orchard, with gooseberry and currant bushes between the rows, and an apple orchard, sheltered by a high hedge from the hot winds. The older children turned back when we reached the hedge, but Jan and Nina and Lucie crept through it by a hole known only to themselves and hid under the low-branching mulberry bushes.

As we walked through the apple orchard, grown up in tall bluegrass, Ántonia kept stopping to tell me about one tree and another. "I love them as if they were people," she said, rubbing her hand over the bark. "There wasn't a tree here when we first came. We planted every one, and used to carry water for them, too—after we'd been working in the fields all day. Anton, he was a city man, and he used to get discouraged. But I couldn't feel so tired that I wouldn't fret about these trees when there was a dry time. They were on my mind like children. Many a night after he was asleep I've got up and come out and carried water to the poor things. And now, you see, we have the good of them. My man worked in the orange groves in Florida, and he knows all about grafting. There ain't one of our neighbors has an orchard that bears like ours."

In the middle of the orchard we came upon a grape-arbor, with seats built along the sides and a warped plank table. The three children were waiting for us there. They looked up at me bashfully and made some request of their mother.

"They want me to tell you how the teacher has the school picnic here every year. These don't go to school yet, so they think it's all like the picnic."

After I had admired the arbor sufficiently, the youngsters ran away to an open place where there was a rough jungle of French pinks, and squatted down among them, crawling about and measuring with a string. "Jan wants to bury his dog there," Ántonia explained. "I had to tell him he could. He's kind of like Nina Harling; you remember how hard she used to take little things? He has funny notions, like her."

We sat down and watched them. Ántonia leaned her elbows on the table. There was the deepest peace in that orchard. It was surrounded by a triple enclosure; the wire fence, then the hedge of thorny locusts, then the mulberry hedge which kept out the hot winds of summer and held fast to the protecting snows of winter. The hedges were so tall that we could see nothing but the blue sky above them, neither the barn roof nor the windmill. The afternoon sun poured down on us through the drying grape leaves. The orchard seemed full of sun, like a cup, and we could smell the ripe apples on the trees. The crabs hung on the branches as thick as beads on a string, purple-red, with a thin silvery glaze over them. Some hens and ducks had crept through the hedge and were pecking at the fallen apples. The drakes were handsome fellows, with pinkish gray bodies, their heads and necks covered with iridescent green feathers which grew close and full, changing to blue like a peacock's neck. Ántonia said they always reminded her of soldiers—some uniform she had seen in the old country, when she was a child.

"Are there any quail left now?" I asked. I reminded her how she used to go hunting with me the last summer before we moved to town. "You weren't a bad shot, Tony. Do you remember how you used to want to run away and go for ducks with Charley Harling and me?"

"I know, but I'm afraid to look at a gun now." She picked up one of the drakes and ruffled his green capote with her fingers. "Ever since I've had children, I don't like to kill anything. It makes me kind of faint to wring an old goose's neck. Ain't that strange, Jim?"

"I don't know. The young Queen of Italy said the same thing once, to a friend of mine. She used to be a great huntswoman, but now she feels as you do, and only shoots clay pigeons."

"Then I'm sure she's a good mother," Ántonia said warmly.

She told me how she and her husband had come out to this new country when the farm land was cheap and could be had on easy payments. The first ten years were a hard struggle. Her husband knew very little about farming and often grew discouraged. "We'd never have got through if I hadn't been so strong. I've always had good health, thank God, and I was able to help him in the fields until right up to the time before my babies came. Our children were good about taking care of each other. Martha, the one you saw when she was a baby, was such a help to me, and she trained Anna to be just like her. My Martha's married now, and has a baby of her own. Think of that, Jim!

"No, I never got down-hearted. Anton's a good man, and I loved my children and always believed they would turn out well. I belong on a farm. I'm never lonesome here like I used to be in town. You remember what sad spells I used to have, when I didn't know what was the matter with me? I've never had them out here. And I don't mind work a bit, if I don't have to put up with sadness." She leaned her chin on her hand and looked down through the orchard, where the sunlight was growing more and more golden.

"You ought never to have gone to town, Tony," I said, wondering at her.

She turned to me eagerly. "Oh, I'm glad I went! I'd never have known anything about cooking or housekeeping if I hadn't. I learned nice ways at the Harlings', and I've been able to bring my children up so much better. Don't you think they are pretty well-behaved for country children? If it hadn't been for what Mrs. Harling taught me, I expect I'd have brought them up like wild rabbits. No, I'm glad I had a chance to learn; but I'm thankful none of my daughters will ever have to work out. The trouble with me was, Jim, I never could believe harm of anybody I loved."

While we were talking, Ántonia assured me that she could keep me for the night. "We've plenty of room. Two of the boys sleep in the haymow till cold weather comes, but there's no need for it. Leo always begs to sleep there, and Ambrosch goes along to look after him."

I told her I would like to sleep in the haymow, with the boys.

"You can do just as you want to. The chest is full of clean blankets, put away for winter. Now I must go, or my girls will be doing all the work, and I want to cook your supper myself."

As we went toward the house, we met Ambrosch and Anton, starting off with their milking-pails to hunt the cows. I joined them, and Leo accompanied us at some distance, running ahead and starting up at us out of clumps of ironweed, calling, "I'm a jack rabbit," or, "I'm a big bull-snake."

I walked between the two older boys—straight, well-made fellows, with good heads and clear eyes. They talked about their school and the new teacher, told me about the crops and the harvest, and how many steers they would feed that winter. They were easy and confidential with me, as if I were an old friend of the family—and not too old. I felt like a boy in their company, and all manner of forgotten interests revived in me. It seemed, after all, so natural to be walking along a barbed-wire fence beside the sunset, toward a red pond, and to see my shadow moving along at my right, over the close-cropped grass.

"Has mother shown you the pictures you sent her from the old country?" Ambrosch asked. "We've had them framed and they're hung up in the parlor. She was so glad to get them. I don't believe I ever saw her so pleased about anything." There was a note of simple gratitude in his voice that made me wish I had given more occasion for it.

I put my hand on his shoulder. "Your mother, you know, was very much loved by all of us. She was a beautiful girl."

"Oh, we know!" They both spoke together; seemed a little surprised that I should think it necessary to mention this. "Everybody liked her, didn't they? The Harlings and your grandmother, and all the town people."

"Sometimes," I ventured, "it doesn't occur to boys that their mother was ever young and pretty."

"Oh, we know!" they said again, warmly. "She's not very old now," Ambrosch added. "Not much older than you."

"Well," I said, "if you weren't nice to her, I think I'd take a club and go for the whole lot of you. I couldn't stand it if you boys were inconsiderate, or thought of her as if she were just somebody who looked after you. You see I was very much in love with your mother once, and I know there's nobody like her."

The boys laughed and seemed pleased and embarrassed. "She never told us that," said Anton. "But she's always talked lots about you, and about what good times you used to have. She has a picture of you that she cut out of the Chicago paper once, and Leo says he recognized you when you drove up to the windmill. You can't tell about Leo, though; sometimes he likes to be smart."

We brought the cows home to the corner nearest the barn, and the boys milked them while night came on. Everything was as it should be: the strong smell of sunflowers and ironweed in the dew, the clear blue and gold of the sky, the evening star, the purr of the milk into the pails, the grunts and squeals of the pigs fighting over their supper. I began to feel the loneliness of the farm-boy at evening, when the chores seem everlastingly the same, and the world so far away.

What a tableful we were at supper; two long rows of restless heads in the lamplight, and so many eyes fastened excitedly upon Ántonia as she sat at the head of the table, filling the plates and starting the dishes on their way. The children were seated according to a system; a little one next an older one, who was to watch over his behavior and to see that he got his food. Anna and Yulka left their chairs from time to time to bring fresh plates of *kolaches* and pitchers of milk.

After supper we went into the parlor, so that Yulka and Leo could play for me. Ántonia went first, carrying the lamp. There were not nearly chairs enough to go round, so the younger children sat down on the bare floor. Little Lucie whispered to me that they were going to have a parlor carpet if they got ninety cents for their wheat. Leo, with a good deal of fussing, got out his violin. It was old Mr. Shimerda's instrument, which Ántonia had always kept, and it was too big for him. But he played very well for a self-taught boy. Poor Yulka's efforts were not so successful. While they were playing, little Nina got up from her corner, came out into the middle of the floor, and began to do a pretty little dance on the boards with her bare feet. No one paid the least attention to her, and when she was through she stole back and sat down by her brother.

Ántonia spoke to Leo in Bohemian. He frowned and wrinkled up his face. He seemed to be trying to pout, but his attempt only brought out dimples in unusual places. After twisting and screwing the keys, he played some Bohemian airs, without the organ to hold him back, and that went better. The boy was so restless that I had not had a chance to look at his face before. My first impression was right; he really was faun-like. He hadn't much head behind his ears, and his tawny fleece grew down thick to the back of his neck. His eyes were not frank and wide apart like those of the other boys, but were deep-set, gold-green in color, and seemed sensitive to the light. His mother said he got hurt oftener than all the others put together. He was always trying to ride the colts before they were broken, teasing the turkey gobbler, seeing just how much red the bull would stand for, or how sharp the new axe was.

After the concert was over Ántonia brought out a big boxful of photographs; she and Anton in their wedding clothes, holding hands; her brother Ambrosch and his very fat wife, who had a farm of her own, and who bossed her husband, I was delighted to hear; the three Bohemian Marys and their large families.

"You wouldn't believe how steady those girls have turned out," Ántonia remarked. "Mary Svoboda's the best butter-maker in all this country, and a fine manager. Her children will have a grand chance."

As Ántonia turned over the pictures the young Cuzaks stood behind her chair, looking over her shoulder with interested faces. Nina and Jan, after trying to see round the taller ones, quietly brought a chair, climbed up on it, and stood close together, looking. The little boy forgot his shyness and grinned delightedly when familiar faces came into view. In the group about Ántonia I was conscious of a kind of physical harmony. They leaned this way and that, and were not afraid to touch each other. They contemplated the photographs with pleased recognition; looked at some admiringly, as if these characters in their mother's girlhood had been remarkable people. The little children, who could not speak English, murmured comments to each other in their rich old language.

Ántonia held out a photograph of Lena that had come from San Francisco last Christmas. "Does she still look like that? She hasn't been home for six years now." Yes, it was exactly like Lena, I told her; a comely woman, a trifle too plump, in a hat a trifle too large, but with the old lazy eyes, and the old dimpled ingenuousness still lurking at the corners of her mouth.

There was a picture of Frances Harling in a be-frogged riding

costume that I remembered well. "Isn't she fine!" the girls murmured. They all assented. One could see that Frances had come
down as a heroine in the family legend. Only Leo was unmoved.

"And there's Mr. Harling, in his grand fur coat. He was awfully
rich, wasn't he, mother?"

"He wasn't any Rockefeller," put in Master Leo, in a very low
tone, which reminded me of the way in which Mrs. Shimerda had
once said that my grandfather "wasn't Jesus." His habitual skepticism was like a direct inheritance from that old woman.

"None of your smart speeches," said Ambrosch severely.

Leo poked out a supple red tongue at him, but a moment later
broke into a giggle at a tintype of two men, uncomfortably seated,
with an awkward-looking boy in baggy clothes standing between
them; Jake and Otto and I! We had it taken, I remembered, when
we went to Black Hawk on the first Fourth of July I spent in
Nebraska. I was glad to see Jake's grin again, and Otto's ferocious
mustaches. The young Cuzaks knew all about them.

"He made grandfather's coffin, didn't he?" Anton asked.

"Wasn't they good fellows, Jim?" Ántonia's eyes filled. "To this
day I'm ashamed because I quarreled with Jake that way. I was
saucy and impertinent to him, Leo, like you are with people
sometimes, and I wish somebody had made me behave."

"We aren't through with you, yet," they warned me. They produced a photograph taken just before I went away to college; a
tall youth in striped trousers and a straw hat, trying to look easy
and jaunty.

"Tell us, Mr. Burden," said Charley, "about the rattler you
killed at the dog town. How long was he? Sometimes mother says
six feet and sometimes she says five."

These children seemed to be upon very much the same terms
with Ántonia as the Harling children had been so many years
before. They seemed to feel the same pride in her, and to look to
her for stories and entertainment as we used to do.

It was eleven o'clock when I at last took my bag and some blankets and started for the barn with the boys. Their mother came to

the door with us, and we tarried for a moment to look out at the white slope of the corral and the two ponds asleep in the moonlight, and the long sweep of the pasture under the star-sprinkled sky.

The boys told me to choose my own place in the haymow, and I lay down before a big window, left open in warm weather, that looked out into the stars. Ambrosch and Leo cuddled up in a hay-cave, back under the eaves, and lay giggling and whispering. They tickled each other and tossed and tumbled in the hay; and then, all at once, as if they had been shot, they were still. There was hardly a minute between giggles and bland slumber.

I lay awake for a long while, until the slow-moving moon passed my window on its way up the heavens. I was thinking about Ántonia and her children; about Anna's solicitude for her, Am-brosch's grave affection, Leo's jealous, animal little love. That moment, when they all came tumbling out of the cave into the light, was a sight any man might have come far to see. Ántonia had always been one to leave images in the mind that did not fade—that grew stronger with time. In my memory there was a succession of such pictures, fixed there like the old woodcuts of one's first primer: Ántonia kicking her bare legs against the sides of my pony when we came home in triumph with our snake; Ántonia in her black shawl and fur cap, as she stood by her father's grave in the snowstorm; Ántonia coming in with her work-team along the evening sky-line. She lent herself to immemorial human attitudes which we recog-nize by instinct as universal and true. I had not been mistaken. She was a battered woman now, not a lovely girl; but she still had that something which fires the imagination, could still stop one's breath for a moment by a look or gesture that somehow revealed the meaning in common things. She had only to stand in the orchard, to put her hand on a little crab tree and look up at the apples, to make you feel the goodness of planting and tending and harvesting at last. All the strong things of her heart came out in her body, that had been so tireless in serving generous emotions.

It was no wonder that her sons stood tall and straight. She was a rich mine of life, like the founders of early races.

II

When I awoke in the morning long bands of sunshine were coming in at the window and reaching back under the eaves where the two boys lay. Leo was wide awake and was tickling his brother's leg with a dried cone-flower he had pulled out of the hay. Ambrosch kicked at him and turned over. I closed my eyes and pretended to be asleep. Leo lay on his back, elevated one foot, and began exercising his toes. He picked up dried flowers with his toes and brandished them in the belt of sunlight. After he had amused himself thus for some time, he rose on one elbow and began to look at me, cautiously, then critically, blinking his eyes in the light. His expression was droll; it dismissed me lightly. "This old fellow is no different from other people. He doesn't know my secret." He seemed conscious of possessing a keener power of enjoyment than other people; his quick recognitions made him frantically impatient of deliberate judgments. He always knew what he wanted without thinking.

After dressing in the hay, I washed my face in cold water at the windmill. Breakfast was ready when I entered the kitchen, and Yulka was baking griddle-cakes. The three older boys set off for the fields early. Leo and Yulka were to drive to town to meet their father, who would return from Wilber on the noon train.

"We'll only have a lunch at noon," Ántonia said, "and cook the geese for supper, when our papa will be here. I wish my Martha could come down to see you. They have a Ford car now, and she don't seem so far away from me as she used to. But her husband's crazy about his farm and about having everything just right, and they almost never get away except on Sundays. He's a handsome boy, and he'll be rich some day. Everything he takes hold of turns out well. When they bring that baby in here, and unwrap him, he looks like a little prince; Martha takes care of him so beautiful. I'm reconciled to her being away from me now, but at first I cried like I was putting her into her coffin."

We were alone in the kitchen, except for Anna, who was

pouring cream into the churn. She looked up at me. "Yes, she did. We were just ashamed of mother. She went round crying, when Martha was so happy, and the rest of us were all glad. Joe certainly was patient with you, mother.

Ántonia nodded and smiled at herself. "I know it was silly, but I couldn't help it. I wanted her right here. She'd never been away from me a night since she was born. If Anton had made trouble about her when she was a baby, or wanted me to leave her with my mother, I wouldn't have married him. I couldn't. But he always loved her like she was his own."

"I didn't even know Martha wasn't my full sister until after she was engaged to Joe," Anna told me.

Toward the middle of the afternoon the wagon drove in, with the father and the eldest son. I was smoking in the orchard, and as I went out to meet them, Ántonia came running down from the house and hugged the two men as if they had been away for months.

"Papa" interested me, from my first glimpse of him. He was shorter than his older sons; a crumpled little man, with run-over boot heels, and he carried one shoulder higher than the other. But he moved very quickly, and there was an air of jaunty liveliness about him. He had a strong, ruddy color, thick black hair, a little grizzled, a curly mustache, and red lips. His smile showed the strong teeth of which his wife was so proud, and as he saw me his lively, quizzical eyes told me that he knew all about me. He looked like a humorous philosopher who had hitched up one shoulder under the burdens of life, and gone on his way having a good time when he could. He advanced to meet me and gave me a hard hand, burned red on the back and heavily coated with hair. He wore his Sunday clothes, very thick and hot for the weather, an unstarched white shirt, and a blue necktie with big white dots, like a little boy's, tied in a flowing bow. Cuzak began at once to talk about his holiday—from politeness he spoke in English.

"Mama, I wish you had see the lady dance on the slack-wire in the street at night. They throw a bright light on her and she float through the air something beautiful, like a bird! They have a dancing bear, like in the old country, and two three merry-go-around, and people in balloons, and what you call the big wheel, Rudolph?"

"A Ferris wheel," Rudolph entered the conversation in a deep baritone voice. He was six foot two, and had a chest like a young blacksmith. "We went to the big dance in the hall behind the saloon last night, mother, and I danced with all the girls, and so did father. I never saw so many pretty girls. It was a Bohunk crowd, for sure. We didn't hear a word of English on the street, except from the show people, did we, papa?"

Cuzak nodded. "And very many send word to you, Ántonia. You will excuse"—turning to me—"if I tell her." While we walked toward the house he related incidents and delivered messages in the tongue he spoke fluently, and I dropped a little behind, curious to know what their relations had become—or remained. The two seemed to be on terms of easy friendliness, touched with humor. Clearly, she was the impulse, and he the corrective. As they went up the hill he kept glancing at her sidewise, to see whether she got his point, or how she received it. I noticed later that he always looked at people sidewise, as a work-horse does at its yoke-mate. Even when he sat opposite me in the kitchen, talking, he would turn his head a little toward the clock or the stove and look at me from the side, but with frankness and good-nature. This trick did not suggest duplicity or secretiveness, but merely long habit, as with the horse.

He had brought a tintype of himself and Rudolph for Ántonia's collection, and several paper bags of candy for the children. He looked a little disappointed when his wife showed him a big box of candy I had got in Denver—she hadn't let the children touch it the night before. He put his candy away in the cupboard, "for when she rains," and glanced at the box, chuckling. "I guess you must have hear about how my family ain't so small," he said.

Cuzak sat down behind the stove and watched his women-folk and the little children with equal amusement. He thought they were nice, and he thought they were funny, evidently. He had been off dancing with the girls and forgetting that he was an old fellow, and now his family rather surprised him; he seemed to think it a joke that all these children should belong to him. As the younger ones slipped up to him in his retreat, he kept taking things out of his pockets; penny dolls, a wooden clown, a balloon pig that was inflated by a whistle. He beckoned to the little boy they called Jan, whispered to him, and presented him with a paper snake, gently, so as not to startle him. Looking over the boy's head he said to me, "This one is bashful. He gets left."

Cuzak had brought home with him a roll of illustrated Bohemian papers. He opened them and began to tell his wife the news, much of which seemed to relate to one person. I heard the name Vasakova, Vasakova, repeated several times with lively interest, and presently I asked him whether he were talking about the singer, Maria Vasak.

"You know? You have heard, maybe?" he asked incredulously. When I assured him that I had heard her, he pointed out her picture and told me that Vasak had broken her leg, climbing in the Austrian Alps, and would not be able to fill her engagements. He seemed delighted to find that I had heard her sing in London and in Vienna; got out his pipe and lit it to enjoy our talk the better. She came from his part of Prague. His father used to mend her shoes for her when she was a student. Cuzak questioned me about her looks, her popularity, her voice; but he particularly wanted to know whether I had noticed her tiny feet, and whether I thought she had saved much money. She was extravagant, of course, but he hoped she wouldn't squander everything, and have nothing left when she was old. As a young man, working in Wienn, he had seen a good many artists who were old and poor, making one glass of beer last all evening, and "it was not very nice, that."

When the boys came in from milking and feeding, the long table was laid, and two brown geese, stuffed with apples, were put down sizzling before Ántonia. She began to carve, and Rudolph, who sat next his mother, started the plates on their way. When everybody was served, he looked across the table at me.

"Have you been to Black Hawk lately, Mr. Burden? Then I wonder if you've heard about the Cutters?"

No, I had heard nothing at all about them.

"Then you must tell him, son, though it's a terrible thing to talk about at supper. Now, all you children be quiet, Rudolph is going to tell about the murder."

"Hurrah! The murder!" the children murmured, looking pleased and interested.

Rudolph told his story in great detail, with occasional promptings from his mother or father.

Wick Cutter and his wife had gone on living in the house that Ántonia and I knew so well, and in the way we knew so well. They grew to be very old people. He shriveled up, Ántonia said, until he looked like a little old yellow monkey, for his beard and his fringe of hair never changed color. Mrs. Cutter remained flushed and wild-eyed as we had known her, but as the years passed she became afflicted with a shaking palsy which made her nervous nod continuous instead of occasional. Her hands were so uncertain that she could no longer disfigure china, poor woman! As the couple grew older, they quarreled more and more about the ultimate disposition of their "property." A new law was passed in the State, securing the surviving wife a third of her husband's estate under all conditions. Cutter was tormented by the fear that Mrs. Cutter would live longer than he, and that eventually her "people," whom he had always hated so violently, would inherit. Their quarrels on this subject passed the boundary of the close-growing cedars, and were heard in the street by whoever wished to loiter and listen.

One morning, two years ago, Cutter went into the hardware store and bought a pistol, saying he was going to shoot a dog, and adding that he "thought he would take a shot at an old cat while he was about it." (Here the children interrupted Rudolph's narrative by smothered giggles.)

Cutter went out behind the hardware store, put up a target, practiced for an hour or so, and then went home. At six o'clock that evening, when several men were passing the Cutter house on their way home to supper, they heard a pistol shot. They paused and were looking doubtfully at one another, when another shot came crashing through an upstairs window. They ran into the house and found Wick Cutter lying on a sofa in his upstairs bed-room, with his throat torn open, bleeding on a roll of sheets he had placed beside his head.

"Walk in, gentlemen," he said weakly. "I am alive, you see, and competent. You are witnesses that I have survived my wife. You will find her in her own room. Please make your examination at once, so that there will be no mistake."

One of the neighbors telephoned for a doctor, while the others went into Mrs. Cutter's room. She was lying on her bed, in her nightgown and wrapper, shot through the heart. Her husband must have come in while she was taking her afternoon nap and shot her, holding the revolver near her breast. Her nightgown was burned from the powder.

The horrified neighbors rushed back to Cutter. He opened his eyes and said distinctly, "Mrs. Cutter is quite dead, gentlemen, and I am conscious. My affairs are in order." Then, Rudolph said, "he let go and died."

On his desk the coroner found a letter, dated at five o'clock that afternoon. It stated that he had just shot his wife; that any will she might secretly have made would be invalid, as he sur-vived her. He meant to shoot himself at six o'clock and would, if he had strength, fire a shot through the window in the hope that passers-by might come in and see him "before life was extinct," as he wrote.

"Now, would you have thought that man had such a cruel heart?" Ántonia turned to me after the story was told. "To go and do that poor woman out of any comfort she might have from his money after he was gone!"

"Did you ever hear of anybody else that killed himself for spite, Mr. Burden?" asked Rudolph.

I admitted that I hadn't. Every lawyer learns over and over

how strong a motive hate can be, but in my collection of legal anecdotes I had nothing to match this one. When I asked how much the estate amounted to, Rudolph said it was a little over a hundred thousand dollars.

Cuzak gave me a twinkling, sidelong glance. "The lawyers, they got a good deal of it, sure," he said merrily.

A hundred thousand dollars; so that was the fortune that had been scraped together by such hard dealing, and that Cutter himself had died for in the end!

After supper Cuzak and I took a stroll in the orchard and sat down by the windmill to smoke. He told me his story as if it were my business to know it.

His father was a shoemaker, his uncle a furrier, and he, being a younger son, was apprenticed to the latter's trade. You never got anywhere working for your relatives, he said, so when he was a journeyman he went to Vienna and worked in a big fur shop, earning good money. But a young fellow who liked a good time didn't save anything in Vienna; there were too many pleasant ways of spending every night what he'd made in the day. After three years there, he came to New York. He was badly advised and went to work on furs during a strike, when the factories were offering big wages. The strikers won, and Cuzak was blacklisted. As he had a few hundred dollars ahead, he decided to go to Florida and raise oranges. He had always thought he would like to raise oranges! The second year a hard frost killed his young grove, and he fell ill with malaria. He came to Nebraska to visit his cousin, Anton Jelinek, and to look about. When he began to look about, he saw Ántonia, and she was exactly the kind of girl he had always been hunting for. They were married at once, though he had to borrow money from his cousin to buy the wedding-ring.

"It was a pretty hard job, breaking up this place and making the first crops grow," he said, pushing back his hat and scratching his grizzled hair. "Sometimes I git awful sore on this place and want to quit, but my wife she always say we better stick it out.

The babies come along pretty fast, so it look like it be hard to move, anyhow. I guess she was right, all right. We got this place clear now. We pay only twenty dollars an acre then, and I been offered a hundred. We bought another quarter ten years ago, and we got it most paid for. We got plenty boys; we can work a lot of land. Yes, she is a good wife for a poor man. She ain't always so strict with me, neither. Sometimes maybe I drink a little too much beer in town, and when I come home she don't say nothing. She don't ask me no questions. We always get along fine, her and me, like at first. The children don't make trouble between us, like sometimes happens." He lit another pipe and pulled on it contentedly.

I found Cuzak a most companionable fellow. He asked me a great many questions about my trip through Bohemia, about Vienna and the Ringstrasse and the theaters.

"Gee! I like to go back there once, when the boys is big enough to farm the place. Sometimes when I read the papers from the old country, I pretty near run away," he confessed with a little laugh. "I never did think how I would be a settled man like this."

He was still, as Ántonia said, a city man. He liked theaters and lighted streets and music and a game of dominoes after the day's work was over. His sociability was stronger than his acquisitive instinct. He liked to live day by day and night by night, sharing in the excitement of the crowd.—Yet his wife had managed to hold him here on a farm, in one of the loneliest countries in the world.

I could see the little chap, sitting here every evening by the windmill, nursing his pipe and listening to the silence; the wheeze of the pump, the grunting of the pigs, an occasional squawking when the hens were disturbed by a rat. It did rather seem to me that Cuzak had been made the instrument of Ántonia's special mission. This was a fine life, certainly, but it wasn't the kind of life he had wanted to live. I wondered whether the life that was right for one was ever right for two!

I asked Cuzak if he didn't find it hard to do without the gay company he had always been used to. He knocked out his pipe against an upright, sighed, and dropped it into his pocket.

"At first I near go crazy with lonesomeness," he said frankly, "but my woman is got such a warm heart. She always make it as good for me as she could. Now it ain't so bad; I can begin to have some fun with my boys, already!"

As we walked toward the house, Cuzak cocked his hat jauntily over one ear and looked up at the moon. "Gee!" he said in a hushed voice, as if he had just wakened up, "it don't seem like I am away from there twenty-six year!"

III

After dinner the next day I said good-bye and drove back to Hastings to take the train for Black Hawk. Ántonia and her children gathered round my buggy before I started, and even the little ones looked up at me with friendly faces. Leo and Ambrosch ran ahead to open the lane gate. When I reached the bottom of the hill, I glanced back. The group was still there by the windmill. Ántonia was waving her apron.

At the gate Ambrosch lingered beside my buggy, resting his arm on the wheel-rim. Leo slipped through the fence and ran off into the pasture.

"That's like him," his brother said with a shrug. "He's a crazy kid. Maybe he's sorry to have you go, and maybe he's jealous. He's jealous of anybody mother makes a fuss over, even the priest."

I found I hated to leave this boy, with his pleasant voice and his fine head and eyes. He looked very manly as he stood there without a hat, the wind rippling his shirt about his brown neck and shoulders.

"Don't forget that you and Rudolph are going hunting with me up on the Niobrara next summer," I said. "Your father's agreed to let you off after harvest."

He smiled. "I won't likely forget. I've never had such a nice thing offered to me before. I don't know what makes you so nice to us boys," he added, blushing.

"Oh, yes you do!" I said, gathering up my reins.

He made no answer to this, except to smile at me with un-abashed pleasure and affection as I drove away.

My day in Black Hawk was disappointing. Most of my old friends were dead or had moved away. Strange children, who meant nothing to me, were playing in the Harlings' big yard when I passed; the mountain ash had been cut down, and only a sprout-ing stump was left of the tall Lombardy poplar that used to guard the gate. I hurried on. The rest of the morning I spent with Anton Jelinek, under a shady cottonwood tree in the yard behind his saloon. While I was having my mid-day dinner at the hotel, I met one of the old lawyers who was still in practice, and he took me up to his office and talked over the Cutter case with me. After that, I scarcely knew how to put in the time until the night express was due.

I took a long walk north of the town, out into the pastures where the land was so rough that it had never been ploughed up, and the long red grass of early times still grew shaggy over the draws and hillocks. Out there I felt at home again. Overhead the sky was that indescribable blue of autumn; bright and shadow-less, hard as enamel. To the south I could see the dun-shaded river bluffs that used to look so big to me, and all about stretched drying cornfields, of the pale-gold color I remembered so well. Russian thistles were blowing across the uplands and piling against the wire fences like barricades. Along the cattle paths the plumes of golden-rod were already fading into sun-warmed vel-vet, gray with gold threads in it. I had escaped from the curious depression that hangs over little towns, and my mind was full of pleasant things; trips I meant to take with the Cuzak boys, in the Bad Lands and up on the Stinking Water. There were enough Cuzaks to play with for a long while yet. Even after the boys grew up, there would always be Cuzak himself! I meant to tramp along a few miles of lighted streets with Cuzak.

As I wandered over those rough pastures, I had the good luck to stumble upon a bit of the first road that went from Black Hawk out to the north country; to my grandfather's farm, then on to the Shimerdas' and to the Norwegian settlement. Everywhere else it had been ploughed under when the highways were surveyed; this half-mile or so within the pasture fence was all that was left of that old road which used to run like a wild thing across the open prairie, clinging to the high places and circling and doubling like a rabbit before the hounds. On the level land the tracks had almost disappeared—were mere shadings in the grass, and a stranger would not have noticed them. But wherever the road had crossed a draw, it was easy to find. The rains had made channels of the wheel-ruts and washed them so deep that the sod had never healed over them. They looked like gashes torn by a grizzly's claws, on the slopes where the farm wagons used to lurch up out of the hollows with a pull that brought curling muscles on the smooth hips of the horses. I sat down and watched the haystacks turn rosy in the slanting sunlight.

This was the road over which Ántonia and I came on that night when we got off the train at Black Hawk and were bedded down in the straw, wondering children, being taken we knew not whither. I had only to close my eyes to hear the rumbling of the wagons in the dark, and to be again overcome by that obliterating strangeness. The feelings of that night were so near that I could reach out and touch them with my hand. I had the sense of coming home to myself, and of having found out what a little circle man's experience is. For Ántonia and for me, this had been the road of Destiny; had taken us to those early accidents of fortune which predetermined for us all that we can ever be. Now I understood that the same road was to bring us together again. Whatever we had missed, we possessed together the precious, the incommunicable past.

THE END

. . .

THE SCULPTOR'S FUNERAL

A group of the townspeople stood on the station siding of a little Kansas town, awaiting the coming of the night train, which was already twenty minutes overdue. The snow had fallen thick over everything; in the pale starlight the line of bluffs across the wide, white meadows south of the town made soft, smoke-coloured curves against the clear sky. The men on the siding stood first on one foot and then on the other, their hands thrust deep into their trousers pockets, their overcoats open, their shoulders screwed up with the cold; and they glanced from time to time toward the southeast, where the railroad track wound along the river shore. They conversed in low tones and moved about restlessly, seeming uncertain as to what was expected of them. There was but one of the company who looked as though he knew exactly why he was there; and he kept conspicuously apart; walking to the far end of the platform, returning to the station door, then pacing up the track again, his chin sunk in the high collar of his overcoat, his burly shoulders drooping forward, his gait heavy and dogged. Presently he was approached by a tall, spare, grizzled man clad in a faded Grand Army suit, who shuffled out from the group and advanced with a certain deference, craning his neck forward until his back made the angle of a jack-knife three-quarters open.

"I reckon she's a-goin' to be pretty late agin tonight, Jim," he remarked in a squeaky falsetto. "S'pose it's the snow?"

"I don't know," responded the other man with a shade of annoyance, speaking from out an astonishing cataract of red beard that grew fiercely and thickly in all directions.

The spare man shifted the quill toothpick he was chewing to the other side of his mouth. "It ain't likely that anybody from the

East will come with the corpse, I s'pose," he went on reflectively.

"I don't know," responded the other, more curtly than before.

"It's too bad he didn't belong to some lodge or other. I like an order funeral myself. They seem more appropriate for people of some repytation," the spare man continued, with an ingratiating concession in his shrill voice, as he carefully placed his toothpick in his vest pocket. He always carried the flag at the G.A.R. funerals in the town.

The heavy man turned on his heel, without replying, and walked up the siding. The spare man shuffled back to the uneasy group. "Jim's ez full ez a tick, ez ushel," he commented commiseratingly.

Just then a distant whistle sounded, and there was a shuffling of feet on the platform. A number of lanky boys of all ages appeared as suddenly and slimily as eels wakened by the crack of thunder; some came from the waiting-room, where they had been warming themselves by the red stove, or half asleep on the slat benches; others uncoiled themselves from baggage trucks or slid out of express wagons. Two clambered down from the driver's seat of a hearse that stood backed up against the siding. They straightened their stooping shoulders and lifted their heads, and a flash of momentary animation kindled their dull eyes at that cold, vibrant scream, the worldwide call for men. It stirred them like the note of a trumpet; just as it had often stirred the man who was coming home to-night, in his boyhood.

The night express shot, red as a rocket, from out the eastward marsh lands and wound along the river shore under the long lines of shivering poplars that sentinelled the meadows, the escaping steam hanging in grey masses against the pale sky and blotting out the Milky Way. In a moment the red glare from the headlight streamed up the snow-covered track before the siding and glittered on the wet, black rails. The burly man with the dishevelled red beard walked swiftly up the platform toward the approaching train, uncovering his head as he went. The group of men behind him hesitated, glanced questioningly at one another, and awkwardly followed his example. The train stopped, and the crowd shuffled up to the express car just as the door was thrown open, the spare man in the G.A.R. suit thrusting his head forward with curiosity. The express messenger appeared in the doorway, accompanied by a young man in a long ulster and travelling cap.

"Are Mr. Merrick's friends here?" inquired the young man.

The group on the platform swayed and shuffled uneasily. Philip Phelps, the banker, responded with dignity: "We have come to take charge of the body. Mr. Merrick's father is very feeble and can't be about."

"Send the agent out here," growled the express messenger, "and tell the operator to lend a hand."

The coffin was got out of its rough box and down on the snowy platform. The townspeople drew back enough to make room for it and then formed a close semicircle about it, looking curiously at the palm leaf which lay across the black cover. No one said anything. The baggage man stood by his truck, waiting to get at the trunks. The engine panted heavily, and the fireman dodged in and out among the wheels with his yellow torch and long oil-can, snapping the spindle boxes. The young Bostonian, one of the dead sculptor's pupils who had come with the body, looked about him helplessly. He turned to the banker, the only one of that black, uneasy, stoop-shouldered group who seemed enough of an individual to be addressed.

"None of Mr. Merrick's brothers are here?" he asked uncertainly.

The man with the red beard for the first time stepped up and joined the group. "No, they have not come yet; the family is scattered. The body will be taken directly to the house." He stooped and took hold of one of the handles of the coffin.

"Take the long hill road up, Thompson, it will be easier on the horses," called the liveryman as the undertaker snapped the door of the hearse and prepared to mount to the driver's seat.

Laird, the red-bearded lawyer, turned again to the stranger: "We didn't know whether there would be any one with him or not," he explained. "It's a long walk, so you'd better go up in the hack." He pointed to a single battered conveyance, but the young man replied stiffly: "Thank you, but I think I will go up with the hearse. If you don't object," turning to the undertaker, "I'll ride with you."

They clambered up over the wheels and drove off in the starlight up the long, white hill toward the town. The lamps in the still village were shining from under the low, snow-burdened roofs; and beyond, on every side, the plains reached out into emptiness, peaceful and wide as the soft sky itself, and wrapped in a tangible, white silence.

When the hearse backed up to a wooden sidewalk before a naked, weather-beaten frame house, the same composite, ill-defined group that had stood upon the station siding was huddled about the gate. The front yard was an icy swamp, and a couple of warped planks, extending from the sidewalk to the door, made a sort of rickety footbridge. The gate hung on one hinge, and was opened wide with difficulty. Steavens, the young stranger, noticed that something black was tied to the knob of the front door.

The grating sound made by the casket, as it was drawn from the hearse, was answered by a scream from the house; the front door was wrenched open, and a tall, corpulent woman rushed out bare-headed into the snow and flung herself upon the coffin, shrieking: "My boy, my boy! And this is how you've come home to me!"

As Steavens turned away and closed his eyes with a shudder of unutterable repulsion, another woman, also tall, but flat and angular, dressed entirely in black, darted out of the house and caught Mrs. Merrick by the shoulders, crying sharply: "Come, come, mother; you musn't go on like this!" Her tone changed to one of obsequious solemnity as she turned to the banker: "The parlour is ready, Mr. Phelps."

The bearers carried the coffin along the narrow boards, while the undertaker ran ahead with the coffin-rests. They bore it into a large, unheated room that smelled of dampness and disuse and fur-niture polish, and set it down under a hanging lamp ornamented with jingling glass prisms and before a "Rogers group" of John Alden and Priscilla, wreathed with smilax. Henry Steavens stared about him with the sickening conviction that there had been some horrible mistake, and that he had somehow arrived at the wrong destination. He looked painfully about over the clover-green Brussels, the fat plush upholstery; among the hand-painted china placques and panels, and vases, for some mark of identification, for something that might once conceivably have belonged to Harvey Merrick. It was not until he recognized his friend in the crayon portrait of a little boy in kilts and curls hanging above the piano, that he felt willing to let any of these people approach the coffin.

"Take the lid off, Mr. Thompson; let me see my boy's face," wailed the elder woman between her sobs. This time Steavens looked fearfully, almost beseechingly into her face, red and swollen under its masses of strong, black, shiny hair. He flushed, dropped his eyes, and then, almost incredulously, looked again. There was a kind of power about her face—a kind of brutal handsomeness, even, but it was scarred and furrowed by violence, and so coloured and coarsened by fiercer passions that grief seemed never to have laid a gentle finger there. The long nose was distended and knobbed at the end, and there were deep lines on either side of it; her heavy, black brows almost met across her forehead, her teeth were large and square, and set far apart—teeth that could tear. She filled the room; the men were obliterated, seemed tossed about like twigs in an angry water, and even Steavens felt himself being drawn into the whirlpool.

The daughter—the tall, raw-boned woman in crêpe, with a mourning comb in her hair which curiously lengthened her long face—sat stiffly upon the sofa, her hands, conspicuous for their large knuckles, folded in her lap, her mouth and eyes drawn down, solemnly awaiting the opening of the coffin. Near the door stood a mulatto woman, evidently a servant in the house, with a timid bearing and an emaciated face pitifully sad and gentle. She was weeping silently, the corner of her calico apron lifted to her eyes, occasionally suppressing a long, quivering sob. Steavens walked over and stood beside her.

Feeble steps were heard on the stairs, and an old man, tall and frail, odorous of pipe smoke, with shaggy, unkempt grey hair and a dingy beard, tobacco stained about the mouth, entered uncertainly. He went slowly up to the coffin and stood rolling a blue cotton handkerchief between his hands, seeming so pained and embarrassed by his wife's orgy of grief that he had no consciousness of anything else.

"There, there, Annie, dear, don't take on so," he quavered timidly, putting out a shaking hand and awkwardly patting her elbow. She turned with a cry, and sank upon his shoulder with such violence that he tottered a little. He did not even glance toward the coffin, but continued to look at her with a dull, frightened, appealing expression, as a spaniel looks at the whip. His sunken cheeks slowly reddened and burned with miserable shame. When his wife rushed from the room, her daughter strode after her with set lips. The servant stole up to the coffin, bent over it for a moment, and then slipped away to the kitchen, leaving Steavens, the lawyer and the father to themselves. The old man stood trembling and looking down at his dead son's face. The sculptor's splendid head seemed even more noble in its rigid stillness than in life. The dark hair had crept down upon the wide forehead; the face seemed strangely long, but in it there was not that beautiful and chaste repose which we expect to find in the faces of the dead. The brows were so drawn that there were two deep lines above the beaked nose, and the chin was thrust forward defiantly. It was as though the strain of life had been so sharp and bitter that death could not at once wholly relax the tension and smooth the countenance into perfect peace—as though he were still guarding something precious and holy, which might even yet be wrested from him.

The old man's lips were working under his stained beard. He turned to the lawyer with timid deference: "Phelps and the rest are comin' back to set up with Harve, ain't they?" he asked. "Thank 'ee, Jim, thank 'ee." He brushed the hair back gently from his son's forehead. "He was a good boy, Jim; always a good boy. He was ez gentle ez a child and the kindest of 'em all—only we didn't none of us ever onderstand him." The tears trickled slowly down his beard and dropped upon the sculptor's coat.

"Martin, Martin. Oh, Martin! come here," his wife wailed from the top of the stairs. The old man started timorously: "Yes, Annie, I'm coming." He turned away, hesitated, stood for a moment in miserable indecision; then reached back and patted the dead man's hair softly, and stumbled from the room.

"Poor old man, I didn't think he had any tears left. Seems as if his eyes would have gone dry long ago. At his age nothing cuts very deep," remarked the lawyer.

Something in his tone made Steavens glance up. While the mother had been in the room, the young man had scarcely seen any one else; but now, from the moment he first glanced into Jim Laird's florid face and blood-shot eyes, he knew that he had found what he had been heartsick at not finding before—the feeling, the understanding, that must exist in some one, even here.

The man was red as his beard, with features swollen and blurred by dissipation, and a hot, blazing blue eye. His face was strained—that of a man who is controlling himself with difficulty—and he kept plucking at his beard with a sort of fierce resentment. Steavens, sitting by the window, watched him turn down the glaring lamp, still its jangling pendants with an angry gesture, and then stand with his hands locked behind him, staring down into the master's face. He could not help wondering what link there could have been between the porcelain vessel and so sooty a lump of potter's clay.

From the kitchen an uproar was sounding; when the dining-room door opened, the import of it was clear. The mother was abusing the maid for having forgotten to make the dressing for the chicken salad which had been prepared for the watchers. Steavens had never heard anything in the least like it; it was injured, emotional, dramatic abuse, unique and masterly in its excruciating cruelty, as violent and unrestrained as had been her grief of twenty minutes before. With a shudder of disgust the lawyer went into the dining-room and closed the door into the kitchen.

"Poor Roxy's getting it now," he remarked when he came back. "The Merricks took her out of the poor-house years ago; and if her loyalty would let her, I guess the poor old thing could tell tales that would curdle your blood. She's the mulatto woman who was standing in here a while ago, with her apron to her eyes. The old woman is a fury; there never was anybody like her for demonstrative piety and ingenious cruelty. She made Harvey's life a hell for him when he lived at home; he was so sick ashamed of it. I never could see how he kept himself so sweet."

"He was wonderful," said Steavens slowly, "wonderful; but until to-night I have never known how wonderful."

"That is the true and eternal wonder of it, anyway; that it can come even from such a dung heap as this," the lawyer cried, with a sweeping gesture which seemed to indicate much more than the four walls within which they stood.

"I think I'll see whether I can get a little air. The room is so close I am beginning to feel rather faint," murmured Steavens, struggling with one of the windows. The sash was stuck, however, and would not yield, so he sat down dejectedly and began pulling at his collar. The lawyer came over, loosened the sash with one blow of his red fist and sent the window up a few inches. Steavens thanked him, but the nausea which had been gradually climbing into his throat for the last half hour left him with but one desire—a desperate feeling that he must get away from this place with what was left of Harvey Merrick. Oh, he comprehended well enough now the quiet bitterness of the smile that he had seen so often on his master's lips!

He remembered that once, when Merrick returned from a visit home, he brought with him a singularly feeling and suggestive bas-relief of a thin, faded old woman, sitting and sewing something pinned to her knee; while a full-lipped, full-blooded little urchin, his trousers held up by a single gallows, stood beside her, impatiently twitching her gown to call her attention to a butterfly he had caught. Steavens, impressed by the tender and delicate modelling of the thin, tired face, had asked him if it were his mother. He remembered the dull flush that had burned up in the sculptor's face.

The lawyer was sitting in a rocking-chair beside the coffin, his head thrown back and his eyes closed. Steavens looked at him earnestly, puzzled at the line of the chin, and wondering why a man should conceal a feature of such distinction under that disfiguring shock of beard. Suddenly, as though he felt the young sculptor's keen glance, he opened his eyes.

"Was he always a good deal of an oyster?" he asked abruptly. "He was terribly shy as a boy."

"Yes, he was an oyster, since you put it so," rejoined Steavens. "Although he could be very fond of people, he always gave one the impression of being detached. He disliked violent emotion; he was reflective, and rather distrustful of himself—except, of course, as regarded his work. He was sure-footed enough there. He distrusted men pretty thoroughly and women even more, yet somehow without believing ill of them. He was determined, indeed, to believe the best, but he seemed afraid to investigate."

"A burnt dog dreads the fire," said the lawyer grimly, and closed his eyes.

Steavens went on and on, reconstructing that whole miserable boyhood. All this raw, biting ugliness had been the portion of the man whose tastes were refined beyond the limits of the reasonable—whose mind was an exhaustless gallery of beautiful impressions, and so sensitive that the mere shadow of poplar leaf flickering against a sunny wall would be etched and held there forever. Surely, if ever a man had the magic word in his finger tips, it was Merrick. Whatever he touched, he revealed its holiest secret; liberated it from enchantment and restored it to its pristine loveliness, like the Arabian prince who fought the enchantress spell for spell. Upon whatever he had come in contact with, he had left a beautiful record of the experience—a sort of ethereal signature; a scent, a sound, a colour that was his own.

Steavens understood now the real tragedy of his master's life; neither love nor wine, as many had conjectured; but a blow which had fallen earlier and cut deeper than these could have done—a shame not his, and yet so unescapably his, to hide in his heart from his very boyhood. And without—the frontier warfare; the yearning of a boy, cast ashore upon a desert of newness and ugliness and sordidness, for all that is chastened and old, and noble with traditions.

At eleven o'clock the tall, flat woman in black crêpe entered and announced that the watchers were arriving, and asked them "to step into the dining-room." As Steavens rose, the lawyer said dryly: "You go on—it'll be a good experience for you, doubtless; as for me, I'm not equal to that crowd to-night; I've had twenty years of them."

As Steavens closed the door after him he glanced back at the lawyer, sitting by the coffin in the dim light, with his chin resting on his hand.

The same misty group that had stood before the door of the express car shuffled into the dining-room. In the light of the kerosene lamp they separated and became individuals. The minister, a pale, feeble-looking man with white hair and blond chin-whiskers, took his seat beside a small side table and placed his Bible upon it. The Grand Army man sat down behind the stove and tilted his chair back comfortably against the wall, fishing his quill toothpick from his waistcoat pocket. The two bankers, Phelps and Elder, sat off in a corner behind the dinner-table, where they could finish their discussion of the new usury law and its effect on chattel security loans. The real estate agent, an old man with a smiling, hypocritical face, soon joined them. The coal and lumber dealer and the cattle shipper sat on opposite sides of the hard coal-burner, their feet on the nickel-work. Steavens took a book from his pocket and began to read. The talk around him ranged through various topics of local interest while the house was quieting down. When it was clear that the members of the family were in bed, the Grand Army man hitched his shoulders and, untangling his long legs, caught his heels on the rounds of his chair.

"S'pose there'll be a will, Phelps?" he queried in his weak falsetto.

The banker laughed disagreeably, and began trimming his nails with a pearl-handled pocketknife.

"There'll scarcely be any need for one, will there?" he queried in his turn.

The restless Grand Army man shifted his position again, getting his knees still nearer his chin. "Why, the ole man says Harve's done right well lately," he chirped.

The other banker spoke up. "I reckon he means by that Harve ain't asked him to mortgage any more farms lately, so as he could go on with his education."

"Seems like my mind don't reach back to a time when Harve wasn't bein' edycated," tittered the Grand Army man.

There was a general chuckle. The minister took out his handkerchief and blew his nose sonorously. Banker Phelps closed his knife with a snap. "It's too bad the old man's sons didn't turn out better," he remarked with reflective authority. "They never hung together. He spent money enough on Harve to stock a dozen cattle-farms and he might as well have poured it into Sand Creek. If Harve had stayed at home and helped nurse what little they had, and gone into stock on the old man's bottom farm, they might all have been well fixed. But the old man had to trust everything to tenants and was cheated right and left."

"Harve never could have handled stock none," interposed the cattleman. "He hadn't it in him to be sharp. Do you remember when he bought Sander's mules for eight-year olds, when everybody in town knew that Sander's father-in-law give 'em to his wife for a wedding present eighteen years before, an' they was full-grown mules then."

Every one chuckled, and the Grand Army man rubbed his knees with a spasm of childish delight.

"Harve never was much account for anything practical, and he shore was never fond of work," began the coal and lumber dealer. "I mind the last time he was home; the day he left, when the old

man was out to the barn helpin' his hand hitch up to take Harve
to the train, and Cal Moots was patchin' up the fence, Harve, he
come out on the step and sings out, in his ladylike voice: "Cal
Moots, Cal Moots! please come cord my trunk."

"That's Harve for you," approved the Grand Army man gleefully. "I kin hear him howlin' yet when he was a big feller in long
pants and his mother used to whale him with a rawhide in the
barn for lettin' the cows git foundered in the cornfield when he
was drivin' 'em home from pasture. He killed a cow of mine that-
a-way onct—a pure Jersey and the best milker I had, an' the ole
man had to put up for her. Harve, he was watchin' the sun set
acrost the marshes when the anamile got away; he argued that
sunset was oncommon fine."

"Where the old man made his mistake was in sending the boy
East to school," said Phelps, stroking his goatee and speaking in
a deliberate, judicial tone. "There was where he got his head
full of trapseing to Paris and all such folly. What Harve needed,
of all people, was a course in some first-class Kansas City business college."

The letters were swimming before Steavens's eyes. Was it possible that these men did not understand, that the palm on the
coffin meant nothing to them? The very name of their town
would have remained forever buried in the postal guide had it not
been now and again mentioned in the world in connection with
Harvey Merrick's. He remembered what his master had said to
him on the day of his death, after the congestion of both lungs
had shut off any probability of recovery, and the sculptor had
asked his pupil to send his body home. "It's not a pleasant place
to be lying while the world is moving and doing and bettering,"
he had said with a feeble smile, "but it rather seems as though we
ought to go back to the place we came from in the end. The
townspeople will come in for a look at me; and after they have
had their say I shan't have much to fear from the judgment of
God. The wings of the Victory, in there"—with a weak gesture
toward his studio—"will not shelter me."

The cattleman took up the comment. "Forty's young for a Merrick to cash in; they usually hang on pretty well. Probably he helped it along with whisky."

"His mother's people were not long lived, and Harvey never had a robust constitution," said the minister mildly. He would have liked to say more. He had been the boy's Sunday-school teacher, and had been fond of him; but he felt that he was not in a position to speak. His own sons had turned out badly, and it was not a year since one of them had made his last trip home in the express car, shot in a gambling-house in the Black Hills.

"Nevertheless, there is no disputin' that Harve frequently looked upon the wine when it was red, also variegated, and it shore made an oncommon fool of him," moralized the cattleman.

Just then the door leading into the parlour rattled loudly and every one started involuntarily, looking relieved when only Jim Laird came out. His red face was convulsed with anger, and the Grand Army man ducked his head when he saw the spark in his blue, blood-shot eye. They were all afraid of Jim; he was a drunkard, but he could twist the law to suit his client's needs as no other man in all western Kansas could do; and there were many who tried. The lawyer closed the door gently behind him, leaned back against it and folded his arms, cocking his head a little to one side. When he assumed this attitude in the court-room, ears were always pricked up, as it usually foretold a flood of withering sarcasm.

"I've been with you gentlemen before," he began in a dry, even tone, "when you've sat by the coffins of boys born and raised in this town; and, if I remember rightly, you were never any too well satisfied when you checked them up. What's the matter, anyhow? Why is it that reputable young men are as scarce as millionaires in Sand City? It might almost seem to a stranger that there was some way something the matter with your progressive town. Why did Ruben Sayer, the brightest young lawyer you ever turned out, after he had come home from the university as straight as a die, take to drinking and forge a check and shoot himself? Why did

Bill Merrit's son die of the shakes in a saloon in Omaha? Why was Mr. Thomas's son, here, shot in a gambling-house? Why did young Adams burn his mill to beat the insurance companies and go to the pen?"

The lawyer paused and unfolded his arms, laying one clenched fist quietly on the table. "I'll tell you why. Because you drummed nothing but money and knavery into their ears from the time they wore knickerbockers; because you carped away at them as you've been carping here to-night, holding our friends Phelps and Elder up to them for their models, as our grandfathers held up George Washington and John Adams. But the boys, worse luck, were young, and raw at the business you put them to; and how could they match coppers with such artists as Phelps and Elder? You wanted them to be successful rascals; they were only unsuccessful ones—that's all the difference. There was only one boy ever raised in this borderland between ruffianism and civilization, who didn't come to grief, and you hated Harvey Merrick more for winning out than you hated all the other boys who got under the wheels. Lord, Lord, how you did hate him! Phelps, here, is fond of saying that he could buy and sell us all out any time he's a mind to; but he knew Harve wouldn't have given a tinker's damn for his bank and all his cattle-farms put together; and a lack of appreciation, that way, goes hard with Phelps.

"Old Nimrod, here, thinks Harve drank too much; and this from such as Nimrod and me!

"Brother Elder says Harve was too free with the old man's money—fell short in filial consideration, maybe. Well, we can all remember the very tone in which brother Elder swore his own father was a liar, in the county court; and we all know that the old man came out of that partnership with his son as bare as a sheared lamb. But maybe I'm getting personal, and I'd better be driving ahead at what I want to say."

The lawyer paused a moment, squared his heavy shoulders, and went on: "Harvey Merrick and I went to school together, back East. We were dead in earnest, and we wanted you all to be proud of us some day. We meant to be great men. Even I, and I haven't lost my sense of humour, gentlemen, I meant to be a great man. I came back here to practise, and I found you didn't in the least want me to be a great man. You wanted me to be a shrewd lawyer—oh, yes! Our veteran here wanted me to get him an increase of pension, because he had dyspepsia; Phelps wanted a new county survey that would put the widow Wilson's little bottom farm inside his south line; Elder wanted to lend money at 5 per cent a month, and get it collected; old Stark here wanted to wheedle old women up in Vermont into investing their annuities in real-estate mortgages that are not worth the paper they are written on. Oh, you needed me hard enough, and you'll go on needing me; and that's why I'm not afraid to plug the truth home to you this once.

"Well, I came back here and became the damned shyster you wanted me to be. You pretend to have some sort of respect for me; and yet you'll stand up and throw mud at Harvey Merrick, whose soul you couldn't dirty and whose hands you couldn't tie. Oh, you're a discriminating lot of Christians! There have been times when the sight of Harvey's name in some Eastern paper has made me hang my head like a whipped dog; and, again, times when I liked to think of him off there in the world, away from all this hog-wallow, doing his great work and climbing the big, clean upgrade he'd set for himself.

"And we? Now that we've fought and lied and sweated and stolen, and hated as only the disappointed strugglers in a bitter, dead little Western town know how to do, what have we got to show for it? Harvey Merrick wouldn't have given one sunset over your marshes for all you've got put together, and you know it. It's not for me to say why, in the inscrutable wisdom of God, a genius should ever have been called from his place of hatred and bitter waters; but I want this Boston man to know that the drivel he's been hearing here to-night is the only tribute any truly great man could ever have from such a lot of sick, side-tracked, burnt-dog, land-poor sharks as the here-present financiers of Sand City— upon which town may God have mercy!"

The lawyer thrust out his hand to Steavens as he passed him, caught up his overcoat in the hall, and had left the house before the Grand Army man had had time to lift his ducked head and crane his long neck about at his fellows.

Next day Jim Laird was drunk and unable to attend the funeral services. Steavens called twice at his office, but was compelled to start East without seeing him. He had a presentiment that he would hear from him again, and left his address on the lawyer's table; but if Laird found it, he never acknowledged it. The thing in him that Harvey Merrick had loved must have gone under ground with Harvey Merrick's coffin; for it never spoke again, and Jim got the cold he died of driving across the Colorado mountains to defend one of Phelps's sons who had got into trouble out there by cutting government timber.

· · ·

THE GARDEN LODGE

When Caroline Noble's friends learned that Raymond d'Esquerré was to spend a month at her place on the Sound before he sailed to fill his engagement for the London opera season, they considered it another striking instance of the perversity of things. That the month was May, and the most mild and florescent of all the blue-and-white Mays the middle coast had known in years, but added to their sense of wrong. D'Esquerré, they learned, was ensconced in the lodge in the apple orchard, just beyond Caroline's glorious garden, and report went that at almost any hour the sound of the tenor's voice and of Caroline's crashing accompaniment could be heard floating through the open windows, out among the snowy apple boughs. The Sound, steel-blue and dotted with white sails, was splendidly seen from the windows of the lodge. The garden to the left and the orchard to the right had never been so riotous with spring, and had burst into impassioned bloom, as if to accommodate Caroline, though she was certainly the last woman to whom the witchery of Freya could be attributed; the last woman, as her friends affirmed, to at all adequately appreciate and make the most of such a setting for the great tenor.

Of course, they admitted, Caroline was musical—well, she ought to be!—but in that as in everything she was paramountly cool-headed, slow of impulse, and disgustingly practical; in that, as in everything else, she had herself so provokingly well in hand. Of course it would be she, always mistress of herself in any situation, she who would never be lifted one inch from the ground by it, and who would go on superintending her gardeners and workmen as usual, it would be she who got him. Perhaps some of them suspected that this was exactly why she did get him, and it but nettled them the more.

Caroline's coolness, her capableness, her general success, especially exasperated people because they felt that, for the most part, she had made herself what she was; that she had cold-bloodedly set about complying with the demands of life and making her position comfortable and masterful. That was why, every one said, she had married Howard Noble. Women who did not get through life so well as Caroline, who could not make such good terms either with fortune or their husbands, who did not find their health so unfailingly good, or hold their looks so well, or manage their children so easily, or give such distinction to all they did, were fond of stamping Caroline as a materialist and called her hard.

The impression of cold calculation, of having a definite policy, which Caroline gave, was far from a false one; but there was this to be said for her, that there were extenuating circumstances which her friends could not know.

If Caroline held determinedly to the middle course, if she was apt to regard with distrust everything which inclined toward extravagance, it was not because she was unacquainted with other standards than her own, or had never seen another side of life. She had grown up in Brooklyn, in a shabby little house under the vacillating administration of her father, a music teacher who usually neglected his duties to write orchestral compositions for which the world seemed to have no especial need. His spirit was warped by bitter vindictiveness and puerile self-commiseration, and he spent his days in scorn of the labour that brought him bread and in pitiful devotion to the labour that brought him only disappointment, writing interminable scores which demanded of the orchestra everything under heaven except melody.

It was not a cheerful home for a girl to grow up in. The mother, who idolized her husband as the music lord of the future, was left to a life-long battle with broom and dust-pan, to never ending conciliatory overtures to the butcher and grocer, to the making of her own gowns and of Caroline's, and to the delicate task of mollifying Auguste's neglected pupils.

The son, Heinrich, a painter, Caroline's only brother, had inherited all his father's vindictive sensitiveness without his capacity for slavish application. His little studio on the third floor had been much frequented by young men as unsuccessful as himself, who met there to give themselves over to contemptuous derision of this or that artist whose industry and stupidity had won him recognition. Heinrich, when he worked at all, did newspaper sketches at twenty-five dollars a week. He was too indolent and vacillating to set himself seriously to his art, too irascible and poignantly self-conscious to make a living, too much addicted to lying late in bed, to the incontinent reading of poetry and to the use of chloral, to be anything very positive except painful. At twenty-six he shot himself in a frenzy, and the whole wretched affair had effectually shattered his mother's health and brought on the decline of which she died. Caroline had been fond of him, but she felt a certain relief when he no longer wandered about the little house, commenting ironically upon its shabbiness, a Turkish cap on his head and a cigarette hanging from between his long, tremulous fingers.

After her mother's death Caroline assumed the management of that bankrupt establishment. The funeral expenses were unpaid, and Auguste's pupils had been frightened away by the shock of successive disasters and the general atmosphere of wretchedness that pervaded the house. Auguste himself was writing a symphonic poem, Icarus, dedicated to the memory of his son. Caroline was barely twenty when she was called upon to face this tangle of difficulties, but she reviewed the situation candidly. The house had served its time at the shrine of idealism; vague, distressing, unsatisfied yearnings had brought it low enough. Her mother, thirty years before, had eloped and left Germany with her music teacher, to give herself over to life-long, drudging bondage at the kitchen range. Ever since Caroline could remember, the law in the house had been a sort of mystic worship of things distant, intangible and unattainable. The family had lived in successive ebulitions of generous enthusiasm, in talk of masters and masterpieces, only to come down to the cold facts in the case; to boiled mutton and to the necessity of turning the dining-room carpet. All these emotional pyrotechnics had ended in petty jealousies, in neglected duties and in cowardly fear of the little grocer on the corner.

From her childhood she had hated it, that humiliating and uncertain existence, with its glib tongue and empty pockets, its poetic ideals and sordid realities, its indolence and poverty tricked out in paper roses. Even as a little girl, when vague dreams beset her, when she wanted to lie late in bed and commune with visions, or to leap and sing because the sooty little trees along the street were putting out their first pale leaves in the sunshine, she would clench her hands and go to help her mother sponge the spots from her father's waistcoat or press Heinrich's trousers. Her mother never permitted the slightest question concerning anything Auguste or Heinrich saw fit to do, but from the time Caroline could reason at all she could not help thinking that many things went wrong at home. She knew, for example, that her father's pupils ought not to be kept waiting half an hour while he discussed Schopenhauer with some bearded socialist over a dish of herrings and a spotted table cloth. She knew that Heinrich ought not to give a dinner on Heine's birthday, when the laundress had not been paid for a month and when he frequently had to ask his mother for car fare. Certainly Caroline had served her apprenticeship to idealism and to all the embarrassing inconsistencies which it sometimes entails, and she decided to deny herself this diffuse, ineffectual answer to the sharp questions of life.

When she came into the control of herself and the house, she refused to proceed any further with her musical education. Her father, who had intended to make a concert pianist of her, set this down as another item in his long list of disappointments and his grievances against the world. She was young and pretty, and she had worn turned gowns and soiled gloves and improvised hats all her life. She wanted the luxury of being like other people, of being honest from her hat to her boots, of having nothing to hide, not even in the matter of stockings, and she was willing to work for it. She rented a little studio away from that house of misfortune, and began to give lessons. She managed well and was the sort of girl people liked to help. The bills were paid and Auguste went on composing, growing indignant only when she refused to insist that her pupils should study his compositions for the piano. She began to get engagements in New York to play accompaniments at song recitals. She dressed well, made herself agreeable, and gave herself a chance. She never permitted herself to look further than a step ahead, and set herself with all the strength of her will to see things as they are and meet them squarely in the broad day. There were two things she feared even more than poverty; the part of one that sets up an idol and the part of one that bows down and worships it.

When Caroline was twenty-four she married Howard Noble, then a widower of forty, who had been for ten years a power in Wall street. Then, for the first time, she had paused to take breath. It took a substantialness as unquestionable as his; his money, his position, his energy, the big vigour of his robust person, to satisfy her that she was entirely safe. Then she relaxed a little, feeling that there was a barrier to be counted upon between her and that world of visions and quagmires and failure.

Caroline had been married for six years when Raymond d'Esquerré came to stay with them. He came chiefly because Caroline was what she was; because he, too, felt occasionally the need of getting out of Klingsor's garden, of dropping down somewhere for a time near a quiet nature, a cool head, a strong hand. The hours he had spent in the garden lodge were hours of such concentrated study as, in his fevered life, he seldom got in anywhere. She had, as he told Noble, a fine appreciation of the seriousness of work.

One evening two weeks after d'Esquerré had sailed, Caroline was in the library giving her husband an account of the work she had laid out for the gardeners. She superintended the care of the grounds herself. Her garden, indeed, had become quite a part of her; a sort of beautiful adjunct, like gowns or jewels. It was a famous spot, and Noble was very proud of it.

"What do you think, Caroline, of having the garden lodge torn down and putting a new summer house there at the end of the arbour; a big rustic affair where you could have tea served in mid-summer?" he asked.

"The lodge?" repeated Caroline looking at him quickly. "Why, that seems almost a shame, doesn't it, after d'Esquerré has used it?"

Noble put down his book with a smile of amusement.

"Are you going to be sentimental about it? Why, I'd sacrifice the whole place to see that come to pass. But I don't believe you could do it for an hour together."

"I don't believe so, either," said his wife, smiling.

Noble took up his book again and Caroline went into the music-room to practise. She was not ready to have the lodge torn down. She had gone there for a quiet hour every day during the two weeks since d'Esquerré had left them. It was the sheerest sentiment she had ever permitted herself. She was ashamed of it, but she was childishly unwilling to let it go.

Caroline went to bed soon after her husband, but she was not able to sleep. The night was close and warm, presaging storm. The wind had fallen and the water slept, fixed and motionless as the sand. She rose and thrust her feet into slippers and putting a dressing-gown over her shoulders opened the door of her husband's room; he was sleeping soundly. She went into the hall and down the stairs; then, leaving the house through a side door, stepped into the vine covered arbour that led to the garden lodge. The scent of the June roses was heavy in the still air, and the stones that paved the path felt pleasantly cool through the thin soles of her slippers. Heat-lightning flashed continuously from the bank of clouds that had gathered over the sea, but the shore was flooded with moonlight and, beyond, the rim of the Sound lay smooth and shining. Caroline had the key of the lodge, and the door creaked as she opened it. She stepped into the long, low room radiant with the moonlight which streamed through the bow window and lay in a silvery pool along the waxed floor. Even that part of the room which lay in the shadow was vaguely illuminated; the piano, the tall candlesticks, the picture frames and white casts standing out as clearly in the half-light as did the sycamores and black poplars of the garden against the still, expectant night sky. Caroline sat down to think it all over. She had come here to do just that every day of the two weeks since d'Esquerré's departure, but, far from ever having reached a conclusion, she had succeeded only in losing her way in a maze of memories—sometimes bewilderingly confused, sometimes too acutely distinct—where there was neither path, nor clue, nor any hope of finality. She had, she realized, defeated a life-long regimen; completely confounded herself by falling unaware and incontinently into that luxury of revery which, even as a little girl, she had so determinedly denied herself; she had been developing with alarming celerity that part of one which sets up an idol and that part of one which bows down and worships it.

It was a mistake, she felt, ever to have asked d'Esquerré to come at all. She had an angry feeling that she had done it rather in self-defiance, to rid herself finally of that instinctive fear of him which had always troubled and perplexed her. She knew that she had reckoned with herself before he came; but she had been equal to so much that she had never really doubted she would be equal to this. She had come to believe, indeed, almost arrogantly in her own malleability and endurance; she had done so much with herself that she had come to think that there was nothing which she could not do; like swimmers, overbold, who reckon upon their strength and their power to hoard it, forgetting the ever changing moods of their adversary, the sea.

And d'Esquerré was a man to reckon with. Caroline did not deceive herself now upon that score. She admitted it humbly enough, and since she had said good-bye to him she had not been free for a moment from the sense of his formidable power. It formed the undercurrent of her consciousness; whatever she might be doing or thinking, it went on, involuntarily, like her breathing; sometimes welling up until suddenly she found herself suffocating. There was a moment of this to-night, and Caroline rose and stood shuddering, looking about her in the blue duskiness of the silent room. She had not been here at night before, and the spirit of the place seemed more troubled and insistent than ever it had been in the quiet of the afternoons. Caroline brushed her hair back from her damp forehead and went over to the bow window. After raising it she sat down upon the low seat. Leaning her head against the sill, and loosening her night-gown at the throat, she half closed her eyes and looked off into the troubled night, watching the play of the sheet-lightning upon the massing clouds between the pointed tops of the poplars.

Yes, she knew, she knew well enough, of what absurdities this spell was woven; she mocked, even while she winced. His power she knew, lay not so much in anything that he actually had—though he had so much—or in anything that he actually was; but in what he suggested, in what he seemed picturesque enough to have or be—and that was just anything that one chose to believe or to desire. His appeal was all the more persuasive and alluring that it was to the imagination alone, that it was as indefinite and impersonal as those cults of idealism which so have their way with women. What he had was that, in his mere personality, he quickened and in a measure gratified that something without which—to women—life is no better than sawdust, and to the desire for which most of their mistakes and tragedies and astonishingly poor bargains are due.

D'Esquerré had become the centre of a movement, and the Metropolitan had become the temple of a cult. When he could be induced to cross the Atlantic, the opera season in New York was successful; when he could not, the management lost money; so much every one knew. It was understood, too, that his superb art had disproportionately little to do with his peculiar position. Women swayed the balance this way or that; the opera, the orchestra, even his own glorious art, achieved at such a cost, were but the accessories of himself; like the scenery and costumes and even the soprano, they all went to produce atmosphere, were the mere mechanics of the beautiful illusion.

Caroline understood all this; to-night was not the first time that she had put it to herself so. She had seen the same feeling in other people; watched for it in her friends, studied it in the house night after night when he sang, candidly putting herself among a thousand others.

D'Esquerré's arrival in the early winter was the signal for a feminine hegira toward New York. On the nights when he sang, women flocked to the Metropolitan from mansions and hotels, from typewriter desks, school-rooms, shops and fitting-rooms. They were of all conditions and complexions. Women of the world who accepted him knowingly, as they sometimes took champagne for its agreeable effect; sisters of charity and over-worked shop-girls, who received him devoutly; withered women who had taken doctorate degrees and who worshipped furtively through prism spectacles; business women and women of affairs, the Amazons who dwelt afar from men in the stony fastnesses of apartment houses. They all entered into the same romance; dreamed, in terms as various as the hues of phantasy, the same dream; drew the same quick breath when he stepped upon the stage, and, at his exit, felt the same dull pain of shouldering the pack again.

There were the maimed, even; those who came on crutches, who were pitted by smallpox or grotesquely painted by cruel birth stains. These, too, entered with him into enchantment. Stout matrons became slender girls again; worn spinsters felt their cheeks flush with the tenderness of their lost youth. Young and old, however hideous, however fair, they yielded up their heat— whether quick or latent—sat hungering for the mystic bread wherewith he fed them at this eucharist of sentiment.

Sometimes when the house was crowded from the orchestra to the last row of the gallery, when the air was charged with this ecstasy of fancy, he himself was the victim of the burning reflection of his power. They acted upon him in turn; he felt their

fervent and despairing appeal to him; it stirred him as the spring
drives the sap up into an old tree; he, too, burst into bloom. For
the moment he, too, believed again, desired again, he knew not
what, but something.

But it was not in these exalted moments that Caroline had
learned to fear him most. It was in the quiet, tired reserve, the
dullness, even, that kept him company between these outbursts
that she found that exhausting drain upon her sympathies which
was the very pith and substance of their alliance. It was the tacit
admission of disappointment under all this glamour of success—
the helplessness of the enchanter to at all enchant himself—that
awoke in her an illogical, womanish desire to in some way com-
pensate, to make it up to him.

She had observed drastically to herself that it was her eighteenth year he awoke in her—those hard years she had spent in
turning gowns and placating tradesmen, and which she had never
had time to live. After all, she reflected, it was better to allow one's
self a little youth; to dance a little at the carnival and to live these
things when they are natural and lovely, not to have them coming
back on one and demanding arrears when they are humiliating
and impossible. She went over to-night all the catalogue of her
self-deprivations; recalled how, in the light of her father's example,
she had even refused to humour her innocent taste for improvis-
ing at the piano; how, when she began to teach, after her mother's
death, she had struck out one little indulgence after another,
reducing her life to a relentless routine, unvarying as clockwork.
It seemed to her that ever since d'Esquerré first came into the
house she had been haunted by an imploring little girlish ghost
that followed her about, wringing its hands and entreating for an
hour of life.

The storm had held off unconscionably long; the air within
the lodge was stifling, and without the garden waited, breathless.
Everything seemed pervaded by a poignant distress; the hush
of feverish, intolerable expectation. The still earth, the heavy
flowers, even the growing darkness, breathed the exhaustion of

protracted waiting. Caroline felt that she ought to go; that it was wrong to stay; that the hour and the place were as treacherous as her own reflections. She rose and began to pace the floor, stepping softly, as though in fear of awakening some one, her figure, in its thin drapery, diaphanously vague and white. Still unable to shake off the obsession of the intense stillness, she sat down at the piano and began to run over the first act of the *Walküre*, the last of his rôles they had practised together; playing listlessly and absently at first, but with gradually increasing seriousness. Perhaps it was the still heat of the summer night, perhaps it was the heavy odours from the garden that came in through the open windows; but as she played there grew and grew the feeling that he was there, beside her, standing in his accustomed place. In the duett at the end of the first act she heard him clearly: "*Thou art the Spring for which I sighed in Winter's cold embraces.*" Once as he sang it, he had put his arm about her, his one hand under her heart, while with the other he took her right from the keyboard, holding her as he always held *Sieglinde* when he drew her toward the window. She had been wonderfully the mistress of herself at the time; neither repellant nor acquiescent. She remembered that she had rather exulted, then, in her self-control—which he had seemed to take for granted, though there was perhaps the whisper of a question from the hand under her heart. "*Thou art the Spring for which I sighed in Winter's cold embraces.*" Caroline lifted her hands quickly from the keyboard, and she bowed her head in them, sobbing.

The storm broke and the rain beat in, spattering her nightdress until she rose and lowered the windows. She dropped upon the couch and began fighting over again the battles of other days, while the ghosts of the slain rose as from a sowing of dragon's teeth. The shadows of things, always so scorned and flouted, bore down upon her merciless and triumphant. It was not enough; this happy, useful, well-ordered life was not enough. It did not satisfy, it was not even real. No, the other things, the shadows—they were the realities. Her father, poor Heinrich, even her mother,

who had been able to sustain her poor romance and keep her little illusions amid the tasks of a scullion, were nearer happiness
than she. Her sure foundation was but made ground, after all, and
the people in Klingsor's garden were more fortunate, however
barren the sands from which they conjured their paradise.

The lodge was still and silent; her fit of weeping over, Caroline
made no sound, and within the room, as without in the garden,
was the blackness of storm. Only now and then a flash of lightning showed a woman's slender figure rigid on the couch, her face
buried in her hands.

Toward morning, when the occasional rumbling of thunder
was heard no more and the beat of the rain drops upon the
orchard leaves was steadier, she fell asleep and did not waken until
the first red streaks of dawn shone through the twisted boughs of
the apple trees. There was a moment between world and world,
when, neither asleep nor awake, she felt her dream grow thin,
melting away from her, felt the warmth under her heart growing
cold. Something seemed to slip from the clinging hold of her
arms, and she groaned protestingly through her parted lips, following it a little way with fluttering hands. Then her eyes opened
wide and she sprang up and sat holding dizzily to the cushions of
the couch, staring down at her bare, cold feet, at her labouring
breast, rising and falling under her open night-dress.

The dream was gone, but the feverish reality of it still pervaded her and she held it as the vibrating string holds a tone. In
the last hour the shadows had had their way with Caroline. They
had shown her the nothingness of time and space, of system and
discipline, of closed doors and broad waters. Shuddering, she
thought of the Arabian fairy tale in which the Genii brought the
princess of China to the sleeping prince of Damascus, and carried
her through the air back to her palace at dawn. Caroline closed
her eyes and dropped her elbows weakly upon her knees, her
shoulders sinking together. The horror was that it had not come
from without, but from within. The dream was no blind chance; it
was the expression of something she had kept so close a prisoner

that she had never seen it herself; it was the wail from the donjon deeps when the watch slept. Only as the outcome of such a night of sorcery could the thing have been loosed to straighten its limbs and measure itself with her; so heavy were the chains upon it, so many a fathom deep it was crushed down into darkness. The fact that d'Esquerré happened to be on the other side of the world meant nothing; had he been here, beside her, it could scarcely have hurt her self-respect so much. As it was, she was without even the extenuation of an outer impulse, and she could scarcely have despised herself more had she come to him here in the night three weeks ago and thrown herself down upon the stone slab at the door there.

Caroline rose unsteadily and crept guiltily from the lodge and along the path under the arbour, terrified lest the servants should be stirring, trembling with the chill air, while the wet shrubbery, brushing against her, drenched her night-dress until it clung about her limbs.

At breakfast her husband looked across the table at her with concern. "It seems to me that you are looking rather fagged, Caroline. It was a beastly night to sleep. Why don't you go up to the mountains until this hot weather is over? By the way, were you in earnest about letting the lodge stand?"

Caroline laughed quietly. "No, I find I was not very serious. I haven't sentiment enough to forego a summer-house. Will you tell Baker to come to-morrow to talk it over with me? If we are to have a house party, I should like to put him to work on it at once."

Noble gave her a glance, half humorous, half vexed. "Do you know I am rather disappointed?" he said. "I had almost hoped that, just for once, you know, you would be a little bit foolish."

"Not now that I've slept over it," replied Caroline, and they both rose from the table, laughing.

. . .

PAUL'S CASE

A STUDY IN TEMPERAMENT

It was Paul's afternoon to appear before the faculty of the Pittsburgh High School to account for his various misdemeanours. He had been suspended a week ago, and his father had called at the Principal's office and confessed his perplexity about his son. Paul entered the faculty room suave and smiling. His clothes were a trifle outgrown and the tan velvet on the collar of his open overcoat was frayed and worn; but for all that there was something of the dandy about him, and he wore an opal pin in his neatly knotted black four-in-hand, and a red carnation in his buttonhole. This latter adornment the faculty somehow felt was not properly significant of the contrite spirit befitting a boy under the ban of suspension.

Paul was tall for his age and very thin, with high, cramped shoulders and a narrow chest. His eyes were remarkable for a certain hysterical brilliancy and he continually used them in a conscious, theatrical sort of way, peculiarly offensive in a boy. The pupils were abnormally large, as though he were addicted to belladonna, but there was a glassy glitter about them which that drug does not produce.

When questioned by the Principal as to why he was there, Paul stated, politely enough, that he wanted to come back to school. This was a lie, but Paul was quite accustomed to lying; found it, indeed, indispensable for overcoming friction. His teachers were asked to state their respective charges against him, which they did with such a rancour and aggrievedness as evinced that this was not a usual case. Disorder and impertinence were among the offences named, yet each of his instructors felt that it was scarcely possible to put into words the real cause of the trouble, which lay in a sort of hysterically defiant manner of the boy's; in the contempt which they all knew he felt for them, and which he seemingly made not the least effort to conceal. Once, when he had been making a synopsis of a paragraph at the blackboard, his English teacher had stepped to his side and attempted to guide his hand. Paul had started back with a shudder and thrust his hands violently behind him. The astonished woman could scarcely have been more hurt and embarrassed had he struck at her. The insult was so involuntary and definitely personal as to be unforgettable. In one way and another, he had made all his teachers, men and women alike, conscious of the same feeling of physical aversion. In one class he habitually sat with his hand shading his eyes; in another he always looked out of the window during the recitation; in another he made a running commentary on the lecture, with humorous intention.

His teachers felt this afternoon that his whole attitude was symbolized by his shrug and his flippantly red carnation flower, and they fell upon him without mercy, his English teacher leading the pack. He stood through it smiling, his pale lips parted over his white teeth. (His lips were continually twitching, and he had a habit of raising his eyebrows that was contemptuous and irritating to the last degree.) Older boys than Paul had broken down and shed tears under that baptism of fire, but his set smile did not once desert him, and his only sign of discomfort was the nervous trembling of the fingers that toyed with the buttons of his overcoat, and an occasional jerking of the other hand that held his hat. Paul was always smiling, always glancing about him, seeming to feel that people might be watching him and trying to detect something. This conscious expression, since it was as far as possible from boyish mirthfulness, was usually attributed to insolence or "smartness."

As the inquisition proceeded, one of his instructors repeated an impertinent remark of the boy's, and the Principal asked him whether he thought that a courteous speech to have made a woman. Paul shrugged his shoulders slightly and his eyebrows twitched.

"I don't know," he replied. "I didn't mean to be polite or

impolite, either. I guess it's a sort of way I have of saying things regardless."

The Principal, who was a sympathetic man, asked him whether he didn't think that a way it would be well to get rid of. Paul grinned and said he guessed so. When he was told that he could go, he bowed gracefully and went out. His bow was but a repetition of the scandalous red carnation.

His teachers were in despair, and his drawing master voiced the feeling of them all when he declared there was something about the boy which none of them understood. He added: "I don't really believe that smile of his comes altogether from insolence; there's something sort of haunted about it. The boy is not strong, for one thing. I happen to know that he was born in Colorado, only a few months before his mother died out there of a long illness. There is something wrong about the fellow."

The drawing master had come to realize that, in looking at Paul, one saw only his white teeth and the forced animation of his eyes. One warm afternoon the boy had gone to sleep at his drawing-board, and his master had noted with amazement what a white, blue-veined face it was; drawn and wrinkled like an old man's about the eyes, the lips twitching even in his sleep, and stiff with a nervous tension that drew them back from his teeth.

His teachers left the building dissatisfied and unhappy; humiliated to have felt so vindictive toward a mere boy, to have uttered this feeling in cutting terms, and to have set each other on, as it were, in the grewsome game of intemperate reproach. Some of them remembered having seen a miserable street cat set at bay by a ring of tormentors.

As for Paul, he ran down the hill whistling the Soldiers' Chorus from *Faust* looking wildly behind him now and then to see whether some of his teachers were not there to writhe under his light-heartedness. As it was now late in the afternoon and Paul was on duty that evening as usher at Carnegie Hall, he decided that he would not go home to supper. When he reached the concert hall the doors were not yet open and, as it was chilly

outside, he decided to go up into the picture gallery—always
deserted at this hour—where there were some of Raffelli's gay
studies of Paris streets and an airy blue Venetian scene or two that
always exhilarated him. He was delighted to find no one in the
gallery but the old guard, who sat in one corner, a newspaper on
his knee, a black patch over one eye and the other closed. Paul
possessed himself of the place and walked confidently up and
down, whistling under his breath. After a while he sat down
before a blue Rico and lost himself. When he bethought him to
look at his watch, it was after seven o'clock, and he rose with a
start and ran downstairs, making a face at Augustus, peering out
from the cast-room, and an evil gesture at the Venus of Milo as he
passed her on the stairway.

When Paul reached the ushers' dressing-room half-a-dozen
boys were there already, and he began excitedly to tumble into his
uniform. It was one of the few that at all approached fitting, and
Paul thought it very becoming—though he knew that the tight,
straight coat accentuated his narrow chest, about which he was
exceedingly sensitive. He was always considerably excited while
he dressed, twanging all over to the tuning of the strings and the
preliminary flourishes of the horns in the music-room; but to-
night he seemed quite beside himself, and he teased and plagued
the boys until, telling him that he was crazy, they put him down
on the floor and sat on him.

Somewhat calmed by his suppression, Paul dashed out to the
front of the house to seat the early comers. He was a model usher;
gracious and smiling he ran up and down the aisles; nothing was
too much trouble for him; he carried messages and brought pro-
grammes as though it were his greatest pleasure in life, and all the
people in his section thought him a charming boy, feeling that he
remembered and admired them. As the house filled, he grew
more and more vivacious and animated, and the colour came to
his cheeks and lips. It was very much as though this were a great
reception and Paul were the host. Just as the musicians came out
to take their places, his English teacher arrived with checks for

the seats which a prominent manufacturer had taken for the season. She betrayed some embarrassment when she handed Paul the tickets, and a *hauteur* which subsequently made her feel very foolish. Paul was startled for a moment, and had the feeling of wanting to put her out; what business had she here among all these fine people and gay colours? He looked her over and decided that she was not appropriately dressed and must be a fool to sit downstairs in such togs. The tickets had probably been sent her out of kindness, he reflected as he put down a seat for her, and she had about as much right to sit there as he had.

When the symphony began Paul sank into one of the rear seats with a long sigh of relief, and lost himself as he had done before the Rico. It was not that symphonies, as such, meant anything in particular to Paul, but the first sigh of the instruments seemed to free some hilarious and potent spirit within him; something that struggled there like the Genius in the bottle found by the Arab fisherman. He felt a sudden zest of life; the lights danced before his eyes and the concert hall blazed into unimaginable splendour. When the soprano soloist came on, Paul forgot even the nastiness of his teacher's being there and gave himself up to the peculiar stimulus such personages always had for him. The soloist chanced to be a German woman, by no means in her first youth, and the mother of many children; but she wore an elaborate gown and a tiara, and above all she had that indefinable air of achievement, that world-shine upon her, which, in Paul's eyes, made her a veritable queen of Romance.

After a concert was over Paul was always irritable and wretched until he got to sleep, and to-night he was even more than usually restless. He had the feeling of not being able to let down, of its being impossible to give up this delicious excitement which was the only thing that could be called living at all. During the last number he withdrew and, after hastily changing his clothes in the dressing-room, slipped out to the side door where the soprano's carriage stood. Here he began pacing rapidly up and down the walk, waiting to see her come out.

Over yonder the Schenley, in its vacant stretch, loomed big and square through the fine rain, the windows of its twelve stories glowing like those of a lighted card-board house under a Christmas tree. All the actors and singers of the better class stayed there when they were in the city, and a number of the big manufacturers of the place lived there in the winter. Paul had often hung about the hotel, watching the people go in and out, longing to enter and leave schoolmasters and dull care behind him forever.

At last the singer came out, accompanied by the conductor, who helped her into her carriage and closed the door with a cordial *auf wiedersehen* which set Paul to wondering whether she were not an old sweetheart of his. Paul followed the carriage over to the hotel, walking so rapidly as not to be far from the entrance when the singer alighted and disappeared behind the swinging glass doors that were opened by a negro in a tall hat and a long coat. In the moment that the door was ajar, it seemed to Paul that he, too, entered. He seemed to feel himself go after her up the steps, into the warm, lighted building, into an exotic, a tropical world of shiny, glistening surfaces and basking ease. He reflected upon the mysterious dishes that were brought into the dining-room, the green bottles in buckets of ice, as he had seen them in the supper party pictures of the *Sunday World* supplement. A quick gust of wind brought the rain down with sudden vehemence, and Paul was startled to find that he was still outside in the slush of the gravel driveway; that his boots were letting in the water and his scanty overcoat was clinging wet about him; that the lights in front of the concert hall were out, and that the rain was driving in sheets between him and the orange glow of the windows above him. There it was, what he wanted—tangibly before him, like the fairy world of a Christmas pantomime, but mocking spirits stood guard at the doors, and, as the rain beat in his face, Paul wondered whether he were destined always to shiver in the black night outside, looking up at it.

He turned and walked reluctantly toward the car tracks. The end had to come sometime; his father in his night-clothes at the top of the stairs, explanations that did not explain, hastily impro-vised fictions that were forever tripping him up, his upstairs room and its horrible yellow wall-paper, the creaking bureau with the greasy plush collar-box, and over his painted wooden bed the pic-tures of George Washington and John Calvin, and the framed motto, "Feed my Lambs," which had been worked in red worsted by his mother.

Half an hour later, Paul alighted from his car and went slowly down one of the side streets off the main thoroughfare. It was a highly respectable street, where all the houses were exactly alike, and where business men of moderate means begot and reared large families of children, all of whom went to Sabbath-school and learned the shorter catechism, and were interested in arithmetic; all of whom were as exactly alike as their homes, and of a piece with the monotony in which they lived. Paul never went up Cordelia Street without a shudder of loathing. His home was next the house of the Cumberland minister. He approached it to-night with the nerveless sense of defeat, the hopeless feeling of sinking back forever into ugliness and commonness that he had always had when he came home. The moment he turned into Cordelia Street he felt the waters close above his head. After each of these orgies of living, he experienced all the physical depression which follows a debauch; the loathing of respectable beds, of common food, of a house penetrated by kitchen odours; a shuddering repul-sion for the flavourless, colourless mass of every-day existence; a morbid desire for cool things and soft lights and fresh flowers.

The nearer he approached the house, the more absolutely unequal Paul felt to the sight of it all; his ugly sleeping chamber; the cold bath-room with the grimy zinc tub, the cracked mirror, the dripping spiggots; his father, at the top of the stairs, his hairy legs sticking out from his nightshirt, his feet thrust into carpet slippers. He was so much later than usual that there would cer-tainly be inquiries and reproaches. Paul stopped short before the door. He felt that he could not be accosted by his father to-night; that he could not toss again on that miserable bed. He would not go in. He would tell his father that he had no car fare, and it was raining so hard he had gone home with one of the boys and stayed all night.

Meanwhile, he was wet and cold. He went around to the back of the house and tried one of the basement windows, found it open, raised it cautiously, and scrambled down the cellar wall to the floor. There he stood, holding his breath, terrified by the noise he had made, but the floor above him was silent, and there was no creak on the stairs. He found a soap-box, and carried it over to the soft ring of light that streamed from the furnace door, and sat down. He was horribly afraid of rats, so he did not try to sleep, but sat looking distrustfully at the dark, still terrified least he might have awakened his father. In such reactions, after one of the experiences which made days and nights out of the dreary blanks of the calendar, when his senses were deadened, Paul's head was always singularly clear. Suppose his father had heard him getting in at the window and had come down and shot him for a burglar? Then, again, suppose his father had come down, pistol in hand, and he had cried out in time to save himself, and his father had been horrified to think how nearly he had killed him? Then, again, suppose a day should come when his father would remember that night, and wish there had been no warning cry to stay his hand? With this last supposition Paul entertained himself until daybreak.

The following Sunday was fine; the sudden November chill was broken by the last flash of autumnal summer. In the morning Paul had to go to church and Sabbath-school, as always. On seasonable Sunday afternoons the burghers of Cordelia Street always sat out on their front "stoops," and talked to their neighbours on the next stoop, or called to those across the street in neighbourly fashion. The men usually sat on gay cushions placed upon the steps that led down to the sidewalk, while the women, in their Sunday "waists," sat in rockers on the cramped porches, pretending to be greatly at their ease. The children played in the streets; there were so many of them that the place resembled the recreation grounds of a kindergarten. The men on the steps—all in their shirt sleeves, their vests unbuttoned—sat with their legs well apart, their stomachs comfortably protruding, and talked of the prices of things, or told anecdotes of the sagacity of their various chiefs and overlords. They occasionally looked over the multitude of squabbling children, listened affectionately to their high-pitched, nasal voices, smiling to see their own proclivities reproduced in their offspring, and interspersed their legends of the iron kings with remarks about their sons' progress at school, their grades in arithmetic, and the amounts they had saved in their toy banks.

On this last Sunday of November, Paul sat all the afternoon on the lowest step of his "stoop," staring into the street, while his sisters, in their rockers, were talking to the minister's daughters next door about how many shirt-waists they had made in the last week, and how many waffles some one had eaten at the last church supper. When the weather was warm, and his father was in a particularly jovial frame of mind, the girls made lemonade, which was always brought out in a red-glass pitcher, ornamented with forget-me-nots in blue enamel. This the girls thought very fine, and the neighbours always joked about the suspicious colour of the pitcher.

To-day Paul's father sat on the top step, talking to a young man who shifted a restless baby from knee to knee. He happened to be the young man who was daily held up to Paul as a model, and after whom it was his father's dearest hope that he would pattern. This young man was of a ruddy complexion, with a compressed, red mouth, and faded, near-sighted eyes, over which he wore thick spectacles, with gold bows that curved about his ears. He was clerk to one of the magnates of a great steel corporation, and was looked upon in Cordelia Street as a young man with a future. There was a story that, some five years ago—he was now barely twenty-six—he had been a trifle dissipated but in order to curb his appetites and save the loss of time and strength that a sowing of wild oats might have entailed, he had taken his chief's advice, oft reiterated to his employees, and at twenty-one had married the first woman whom he could persuade to share his fortunes. She happened to be an angular school-mistress, much older than he, who also wore thick glasses, and who had now borne him four children, all near-sighted, like herself.

The young man was relating how his chief, now cruising in the Mediterranean, kept in touch with all the details of the business, arranging his office hours on his yacht just as though he were at home, and "knocking off work enough to keep two stenographers busy." His father told, in turn, the plan his corporation was considering, of putting in an electric railway plant at Cairo. Paul snapped his teeth; he had an awful apprehension that they might spoil it all before he got there. Yet he rather liked to hear these legends of the iron kings, that were told and retold on Sundays and holidays; these stories of palaces in Venice, yachts on the Mediterranean, and high play at Monte Carlo appealed to his fancy, and he was interested in the triumphs of these cash boys who had become famous, though he had no mind for the cash-boy stage.

After supper was over, and he had helped to dry the dishes, Paul nervously asked his father whether he could go to George's to get some help in his geometry, and still more nervously asked for car fare. This latter request he had to repeat, as his father, on principle, did not like to hear requests for money, whether much or little. He asked Paul whether he could not go to some boy who lived nearer, and told him that he ought not to leave his school work until Sunday; but he gave him the dime. He was not a poor man, but he had a worthy ambition to come up in the world. His only reason for allowing Paul to usher was, that he thought a boy ought to be earning a little.

Paul bounded upstairs, scrubbed the greasy odour of the dish-water from his hands with the ill-smelling soap he hated, and then shook over his fingers a few drops of violet water from the bottle he kept hidden in his drawer. He left the house with his geometry conspicuously under his arm, and the moment he got out of Cordelia Street and boarded a downtown car, he shook off the lethargy of two deadening days, and began to live again.

The leading juvenile of the permanent stock company which played at one of the downtown theatres was an acquaintance of Paul's, and the boy had been invited to drop in at the Sunday-night rehearsals whenever he could. For more than a year Paul had spent every available moment loitering about Charley Edwards's dressing-room. He had won a place among Edwards's following not only because the young actor, who could not afford to employ a dresser, often found him useful, but because he recognized in Paul something akin to what churchmen term "vocation."

It was at the theatre and at Carnegie Hall that Paul really lived; the rest was but a sleep and a forgetting. This was Paul's fairy tale, and it had for him all the allurement of a secret love. The moment he inhaled the gassy, painty, dusty odour behind the scenes, he breathed like a prisoner set free, and felt within him the possibility of doing or saying splendid, brilliant, poetic things. The moment the cracked orchestra beat out the overture from *Martha*, or jerked at the serenade from *Rigoletto*, all stupid and ugly things slid from him, and his senses were deliciously, yet delicately fired.

Perhaps it was because, in Paul's world, the natural nearly always wore the guise of ugliness, that a certain element of artificiality seemed to him necessary in beauty. Perhaps it was because his experience of life elsewhere was so full of Sabbath-school picnics, petty economies, wholesome advice as to how to succeed in life, and the unescapable odours of cooking, that he found this existence so alluring, these smartly-clad men and women so attractive, that he was so moved by these starry apple orchards that bloomed perennially under the lime-light.

It would be difficult to put it strongly enough how convincingly the stage entrance of that theatre was for Paul the actual portal of Romance. Certainly none of the company ever suspected it, least of all Charley Edwards. It was very like the old stories that used to float about London of fabulously rich Jews, who had subterranean halls there, with palms, and fountains, and soft

lamps and richly apparelled women who never saw the dis-
enchanting light of London day. So, in the midst of that
smoke-palled city, enamoured of figures and grimy toil, Paul had
his secret temple, his wishing carpet, his bit of blue-and-white
Mediterranean shore bathed in perpetual sunshine.

Several of Paul's teachers had a theory that his imagination had
been perverted by garish fiction, but the truth was that he scarcely
ever read at all. The books at home were not such as would either
tempt or corrupt a youthful mind, and as for reading the novels
that some of his friends urged upon him—well, he got what he
wanted much more quickly from music; any sort of music, from
an orchestra to a barrel organ. He needed only the spark, the indescribable thrill that made his imagination master of his senses,
and he could make plots and pictures enough of his own. It was
equally true that he was not stage struck—not, at any rate, in the
usual acceptation of that expression. He had no desire to become
an actor, any more than he had to become a musician. He felt no
necessity to do any of these things; what he wanted was to see, to
be in the atmosphere, float on the wave of it, to be carried out,
blue league after blue league, away from everything.

After a night behind the scenes, Paul found the school-room
more than ever repulsive; the bare floors and naked walls; the
prosy men who never wore frock coats, or violets in their button-
holes; the women with their dull gowns, shrill voices, and pitiful
seriousness about prepositions that govern the dative. He could
not bear to have the other pupils think, for a moment, that he
took these people seriously; he must convey to them that he
considered it all trivial, and was there only by way of a jest, anyway. He had autograph pictures of all the members of the stock
company which he showed his classmates, telling them the most
incredible stories of his familiarity with these people, of his
acquaintance with the soloists who came to Carnegie Hall, his
suppers with them and the flowers he sent them. When these stories lost their effect, and his audience grew listless, he became
desperate and would bid all the boys good-bye, announcing that

he was going to travel for awhile; going to Naples, to Venice, to Egypt. Then, next Monday, he would slip back, conscious and nervously smiling; his sister was ill, and he should have to defer his voyage until spring.

Matters went steadily worse with Paul at school. In the itch to let his instructors know how heartily he despised them and their homilies, and how thoroughly he was appreciated elsewhere, he mentioned once or twice that he had no time to fool with theorems; adding—with a twitch of the eyebrows and a touch of that nervous bravado which so perplexed them—that he was helping the people down at the stock company; they were old friends of his.

The upshot of the matter was, that the Principal went to Paul's father, and Paul was taken out of school and put to work. The manager at Carnegie Hall was told to get another usher in his stead; the doorkeeper at the theatre was warned not to admit him to the house; and Charley Edwards remorsefully promised the boy's father not to see him again.

The members of the stock company were vastly amused when some of Paul's stories reached them—especially the women. They were hard-working women, most of them supporting indigent husbands or brothers, and they laughed rather bitterly at having stirred the boy to such fervid and florid inventions. They agreed with the faculty and with his father that Paul's was a bad case.

The east-bound train was ploughing through a January snow-storm; the dull dawn was beginning to show grey when the engine whistled a mile out of Newark. Paul started up from the seat where he had lain curled in uneasy slumber, rubbed the breath-misted window glass with his hand, and peered out. The snow was whirling in curling eddies above the white bottom lands, and the drifts lay already deep in the fields and along the fences, while here and there the long dead grass and dried weed stalks protruded black above it. Lights shone from the scattered houses, and a gang of labourers who stood beside the track waved their lanterns.

Paul had slept very little, and he felt grimy and uncomfortable. He had made the all-night journey in a day coach, partly because he was ashamed, dressed as he was, to go into a Pullman, and partly because he was afraid of being seen there by some Pittsburgh business man, who might have noticed him in Denny & Carson's office. When the whistle awoke him, he clutched quickly at his breast pocket, glancing about him with an uncertain smile. But the little, clay-bespattered Italians were still sleeping, the slatternly women across the aisle were in open-mouthed oblivion, and even the crumby, crying babies were for the nonce stilled. Paul settled back to struggle with his impatience as best he could.

When he arrived at the Jersey City station, he hurried through his breakfast, manifestly ill at ease and keeping a sharp eye about him. After he reached the Twenty-third Street station, he consulted a cabman, and had himself driven to a men's furnishing establishment that was just opening for the day. He spent upward of two hours there, buying with endless reconsidering and great care. His new street suit he put on in the fitting-room; the frock coat and dress clothes he had bundled into the cab with his linen. Then he drove to a hatter's and a shoe house. His next errand was at Tiffany's, where he selected his silver and a new scarf-pin. He would not wait to have his silver marked, he said. Lastly, he stopped at a trunk shop on Broadway, and had his purchases packed into various travelling bags.

It was a little after one o'clock when he drove up to the Waldorf, and after settling with the cabman, went into the office. He registered from Washington; said his mother and father had been abroad, and that he had come down to await the arrival of their steamer. He told his story plausibly and had no trouble, since he volunteered to pay for them in advance, in engaging his rooms; a sleeping-room, sitting-room and bath.

Not once, but a hundred times Paul had planned this entry into New York. He had gone over every detail of it with Charley Edwards, and in his scrap book at home there were pages of description about New York hotels, cut from the Sunday papers.

When he was shown to his sitting-room on the eighth floor, he saw at a glance that everything was as it should be; there was but one detail in his mental picture that the place did not realize, so he rang for the bell boy and sent him down for flowers. He moved about nervously until the boy returned, putting away his new linen and fingering it delightedly as he did so. When the flowers came, he put them hastily into water, and then tumbled into a hot bath. Presently he came out of his white bath-room, resplendent in his new silk underwear, and playing with the tassels of his red robe. The snow was whirling so fiercely outside his windows that he could scarcely see across the street, but within the air was deliciously soft and fragrant. He put the violets and jonquils on the taboret beside the couch, and threw himself down, with a long sigh, covering himself with a Roman blanket. He was thoroughly tired; he had been in such haste, he had stood up to such a strain, covered so much ground in the last twenty-four hours, that he wanted to think how it had all come about. Lulled by the sound of the wind, the warm air, and the cool fragrance of the flowers, he sank into deep, drowsy retrospection.

It had been wonderfully simple; when they had shut him out of the theatre and concert hall, when they had taken away his bone, the whole thing was virtually determined. The rest was a mere matter of opportunity. The only thing that at all surprised him was his own courage—for he realized well enough that he had always been tormented by fear, a sort of apprehensive dread that, of late years, as the meshes of the lies he had told closed about him, had been pulling the muscles of his body tighter and tighter. Until now, he could not remember the time when he had not been dreading something. Even when he was a little boy, it was always there—behind him, or before, or on either side. There had always been the shadowed corner, the dark place into which he dared not look, but from which something seemed always to be watching him—and Paul had done things that were not pretty to watch, he knew.

But now he had a curious sense of relief, as though he had at last thrown down the gauntlet to the thing in the corner.

Yet it was but a day since he had been sulking in the traces; but yesterday afternoon that he had been sent to the bank with Denny & Carson's deposit, as usual—but this time he was instructed to leave the book to be balanced. There was above two thousand dollars in checks, and nearly a thousand in the bank notes which he had taken from the book and quietly transferred to his pocket. At the bank he had made out a new deposit slip. His nerves had been steady enough to permit of his returning to the office, where he had finished his work and asked for a full day's holiday to-morrow, Saturday, giving a perfectly reasonable pretext. The bank book, he knew, would not be returned before Monday or Tuesday, and his father would be out of town for the next week. From the time he slipped the bank notes into his pocket until he boarded the night train for New York, he had not known a moment's hesitation. It was not the first time Paul had steered through treacherous waters.

How astonishingly easy it had all been; here he was, the thing done; and this time there would be no awakening, no figure at the top of the stairs. He watched the snow flakes whirling by his window until he fell asleep.

When he awoke, it was three o'clock in the afternoon. He bounded up with a start; half of one of his precious days gone already! He spent more than an hour in dressing, watching every stage of his toilet carefully in the mirror. Everything was quite perfect; he was exactly the kind of boy he had always wanted to be.

When he went downstairs, Paul took a carriage and drove up Fifth Avenue toward the Park. The snow had somewhat abated; carriages and tradesmen's wagons were hurrying soundlessly to and fro in the winter twilight; boys in woollen mufflers were shovelling off the doorsteps; the avenue stages made fine spots of colour against the white street. Here and there on the corners were stands, with whole flower gardens blooming under glass cases, against the sides of which the snow flakes stuck and melted; violets, roses, carnations, lilies of the valley—somehow vastly more lovely and alluring that they blossomed thus unnaturally in the snow. The Park itself was a wonderful stage winter-piece.

When he returned, the pause of the twilight had ceased, and the tune of the streets had changed. The snow was falling faster, lights streamed from the hotels that reared their dozen stories fearlessly up into the storm, defying the raging Atlantic winds. A long, black stream of carriages poured down the avenue, intersected here and there by other streams, tending horizontally. There were a score of cabs about the entrance of his hotel, and his driver had to wait. Boys in livery were running in and out of the awning stretched across the sidewalk, up and down the red velvet carpet laid from the door to the street. Above, about, within it all was the rumble and roar, the hurry and toss of thousands of human beings as hot for pleasure as himself, and on every side of him towered the glaring affirmation of the omnipotence of wealth.

The boy set his teeth and drew his shoulders together in a spasm of realization; the plot of all dramas, the text of all romances, the nerve-stuff of all sensations was whirling about him like the snow flakes. He burnt like a faggot in a tempest.

When Paul went down to dinner, the music of the orchestra came floating up the elevator shaft to greet him. His head whirled as he stepped into the thronged corridor, and he sank back into one of the chairs against the wall to get his breath. The lights, the chatter, the perfumes, the bewildering medley of colour—he had, for a moment, the feeling of not being able to stand it. But only for a moment; these were his own people, he told himself. He went slowly about the corridors, through the writing-rooms, smoking-rooms, reception-rooms, as though he were exploring the chambers of an enchanted palace, built and peopled for him alone.

When he reached the dining-room he sat down at a table near a window. The flowers, the white linen, the many-coloured wine glasses, the gay toilettes of the women, the low popping of corks, the undulating repetitions of the *Blue Danube* from the orchestra, all flooded Paul's dream with bewildering radiance. When the roseate tinge of his champagne was added—that cold, precious,

bubbling stuff that creamed and foamed in his glass—Paul wondered that there were honest men in the world at all. This was
what all the world was fighting for, he reflected; this was what
all the struggle was about. He doubted the reality of his past.
Had he ever known a place called Cordelia Street, a place where
fagged-looking business men got on the early car; mere rivets in a
machine they seemed to Paul,—sickening men, with combings of
children's hair always hanging to their coats, and the smell of
cooking in their clothes. Cordelia Street—Ah! that belonged to
another time and country; had he not always been thus, had he
not sat here night after night, from as far back as he could remember, looking pensively over just such shimmering textures, and
slowly twirling the stem of a glass like this one between his
thumb and middle finger? He rather thought he had.

He was not in the least abashed or lonely. He had no especial
desire to meet or to know any of these people; all he demanded
was the right to look on and conjecture, to watch the pageant.
The mere stage properties were all he contended for. Nor was he
lonely later in the evening, in his lodge at the Metropolitan. He
was now entirely rid of his nervous misgivings, of his forced
aggressiveness, of the imperative desire to show himself different
from his surroundings. He felt now that his surroundings
explained him. Nobody questioned the purple; he had only to
wear it passively. He had only to glance down at his attire to reas-
sure himself that here it would be impossible for any one to
humiliate him.

He found it hard to leave his beautiful sitting-room to go to
bed that night, and sat long watching the raging storm from his
turret window. When he went to sleep it was with the lights
turned on in his bedroom; partly because of his old timidity, and
partly so that, if he should wake in the night, there would be no
wretched moment of doubt, no horrible suspicion of yellow wall-
paper, or of Washington and Calvin above his bed.

Sunday morning the city was practically snow-bound. Paul
breakfasted late, and in the afternoon he fell in with a wild San

Francisco boy, a freshman at Yale, who said he had run down for a "little flyer" over Sunday. The young man offered to show Paul the night side of the town, and the two boys went out together after dinner, not returning to the hotel until seven o'clock the next morning. They had started out in the confiding warmth of a champagne friendship, but their parting in the elevator was singularly cool. The freshman pulled himself together to make his train, and Paul went to bed. He awoke at two o'clock in the afternoon, very thirsty and dizzy, and rang for ice-water, coffee, and the Pittsburgh papers.

On the part of the hotel management, Paul excited no suspicion. There was this to be said for him, that he wore his spoils with dignity and in no way made himself conspicuous. Even under the glow of his wine he was never boisterous, though he found the stuff like a magician's wand for wonder-building. His chief greediness lay in his ears and eyes, and his excesses were not offencive ones. His dearest pleasures were the grey winter twilights in his sitting-room; his quiet enjoyment of his flowers, his clothes, his wide divan, his cigarette and his sense of power. He could not remember a time when he had felt so at peace with himself. The mere release from the necessity of petty lying, lying every day and every day, restored his self-respect. He had never lied for pleasure, even at school; but to be noticed and admired, to assert his difference from other Cordelia Street boys; and he felt a good deal more manly, more honest, even, now that he had no need for boastful pretensions, now that he could, as his actor friends used to say, "dress the part." It was characteristic that remorse did not occur to him. His golden days went by without a shadow, and he made each as perfect as he could.

On the eighth day after his arrival in New York, he found the whole affair exploited in the Pittsburgh papers, exploited with a wealth of detail which indicated that local news of a sensational nature was at a low ebb. The firm of Denny & Carson announced that the boy's father had refunded the full amount of the theft, and that they had no intention of prosecuting. The Cumberland minister had been interviewed, and expressed his hope of yet reclaiming the motherless lad, and his Sabbath-school teacher declared that she would spare no effort to that end. The rumour had reached Pittsburgh that the boy had been seen in a New York hotel, and his father had gone East to find him and bring him home.

Paul had just come in to dress for dinner; he sank into a chair, weak to the knees, and clasped his head in his hands. It was to be worse than jail, even; the tepid waters of Cordelia Street were to close over him finally and forever. The grey monotony stretched before him in hopeless, unrelieved years; Sabbath-school, Young People's Meeting, the yellow-papered room, the damp dish-towels; it all rushed back upon him with a sickening vividness. He had the old feeling that the orchestra had suddenly stopped, the sinking sensation that the play was over. The sweat broke out on his face, and he sprang to his feet, looked about him with his white, conscious smile, and winked at himself in the mirror. With something of the old childish belief in miracles with which he had so often gone to class, all his lessons unlearned, Paul dressed and dashed whistling down the corridor to the elevator.

He had no sooner entered the dining-room and caught the measure of the music than his remembrance was lightened by his old elastic power of claiming the moment, mounting with it, and finding it all sufficient. The glare and glitter about him, the mere scenic accessories had again, and for the last time, their old potency. He would show himself that he was game, he would finish the thing splendidly. He doubted, more than ever, the existence of Cordelia Street, and for the first time he drank his wine recklessly. Was he not, after all, one of those fortunate beings born to the purple, was he not still himself and in his own place? He drummed a nervous accompaniment to the Pagliacci music and looked about him, telling himself over and over that it had paid.

He reflected drowsily, to the swell of the music and the chill sweetness of his wine, that he might have done it more wisely. He might have caught an outbound steamer and been well out of their clutches before now. But the other side of the world had seemed too far away and too uncertain then; he could not have waited for it; his need had been too sharp. If he had to choose over again, he would do the same thing to-morrow. He looked affectionately about the dining-room, now gilded with a soft mist. Ah, it had paid indeed!

Paul was awakened next morning by a painful throbbing in his head and feet. He had thrown himself across the bed without undressing, and had slept with his shoes on. His limbs and hands were lead heavy, and his tongue and throat were parched and burnt. There came upon him one of those fateful attacks of clear-headedness that never occurred except when he was physically exhausted and his nerves hung loose. He lay still and closed his eyes and let the tide of things wash over him.

His father was in New York; "stopping at some joint or other," he told himself. The memory of successive summers on the front stoop fell upon him like a weight of black water. He had not a hundred dollars left; and he knew now, more than ever, that money was everything, the wall that stood between all he loathed and all he wanted. The thing was winding itself up; he had thought of that on his first glorious day in New York, and had even provided a way to snap the thread. It lay on his dressing-table now; he had got it out last night when he came blindly up from dinner, but the shiny metal hurt his eyes, and he disliked the looks of it.

He rose and moved about with a painful effort, succumbing now and again to attacks of nausea. It was the old depression exaggerated; all the world had become Cordelia Street. Yet somehow he was not afraid of anything, was absolutely calm; perhaps because he had looked into the dark corner at last and knew. It was bad enough, what he saw there, but somehow not so bad as his long fear of it had been. He saw everything clearly now. He had a feeling that he had made the best of it, that he had lived the sort of life he was meant to live, and for half an hour he sat staring at the revolver. But he told himself that was not the way, so he went downstairs and took a cab to the ferry.

When Paul arrived at Newark, he got off the train and took another cab, directing the driver to follow the Pennsylvania tracks out of the town. The snow lay heavy on the roadways and had drifted deep in the open fields. Only here and there the dead grass or dried weed stalks projected, singularly black, above it. Once well into the country, Paul dismissed the carriage and walked, floundering along the tracks, his mind a medley of irrelevant things. He seemed to hold in his brain an actual picture of everything he had seen that morning. He remembered every feature of both his drivers, of the toothless old woman from whom he had bought the red flowers in his coat, the agent from whom he had got his ticket, and all of his fellow-passengers on the ferry. His mind, unable to cope with vital matters near at hand, worked feverishly and deftly at sorting and grouping these images. They made for him a part of the ugliness of the world, of the ache in his head, and the bitter burning on his tongue. He stooped and put a handful of snow into his mouth as he walked, but that, too, seemed hot. When he reached a little hillside, where the tracks ran through a cut some twenty feet below him, he stopped and sat down.

The carnations in his coat were drooping with the cold, he noticed; their red glory all over. It occurred to him that all the flowers he had seen in the glass cases that first night must have gone the same way, long before this. It was only one splendid breath they had, in spite of their brave mockery at the winter outside the glass; and it was a losing game in the end, it seemed, this revolt against the homilies by which the world is run. Paul took one of the blossoms carefully from his coat and scooped a little hole in the snow, where he covered it up. Then he dozed a while, from his weak condition, seeming insensible to the cold.

The sound of an approaching train awoke him, and he started to his feet, remembering only his resolution, and afraid least he should be too late. He stood watching the approaching locomotive, his teeth chattering, his lips drawn away from them in a frightened smile; once or twice he glanced nervously sidewise, as though he were being watched. When the right moment came, he jumped. As he fell, the folly of his haste occurred to him with merciless clearness, the vastness of what he had left undone. There flashed through his brain, clearer than ever before, the blue of Adriatic water, the yellow of Algerian sands.

He felt something strike his chest, and that his body was being thrown swiftly through the air, on and on, immeasurably far and fast, while his limbs were gently relaxed. Then, because the picture making mechanism was crushed, the disturbing visions flashed into black, and Paul dropped back into the immense design of things.

THE END

. . .

INTERVIEW

Willa Sibert Cather

BY

ARCHER LATROBE CARROLL

On the Nebraska prairie some years ago, a little girl rode about on her pony, among settlements of Scandinavians and Bohemians, listening to their conversation, fascinated by their personalities. She was Willa Sibert Cather, who, as a woman, was to give in her novels the story of their struggle with the soil. Ever since those early years, she has been studying people, until she is today one of that small group of American writers who tell of life with beauty and entire earnestness. She has won the praise of those critics whose standards are highest, whose condemnation of insincerity and distortion is severest. Listen to Randolph Bourne: "She has outgrown provincialism and can now be reckoned among those who are richly interpreting youth all over the world." And to H. L. Mencken: "There is no other American author of her sex, now in view, whose future promises so much."

Miss Cather's reputation is of recent growth. Though her first novel, "Alexander's Bridge", was published in 1912, she remained comparatively unknown until about five years ago. Then critics realized that every successive book of hers had shown an advance, and began to look forward with interest to her future work. She is, however, still unknown to large sections of the American reading public.

Not long ago, she sat in her New York apartment in Greenwich Village, and talked to me about her books. She seems just the one to have written them. She is sincere, vigorous, self-controlled. There is no flippancy about her. She has not made herself the heroine of any of her novels, but she is akin to her own heroines. In "The Song of the Lark", one of the characters remarks that Thea Kronborg, the central figure, "doesn't sigh every time the wind blows". Miss Cather herself is that sort. She has a mental sturdiness.

She spoke of the beginnings of her impulse to write.

"When I was about nine," she said, "father took me from our place near Winchester, Virginia, to a ranch in Nebraska. Few of our neighbors were Americans—most of them were Danes, Swedes, Norwegians, and Bohemians. I grew fond of some of these immigrants—particularly the old women, who used to tell me of their home country. I used to think them underrated, and wanted to explain them to their neighbors. Their stories used to go round and round in my head at night. This was, with me, the initial impulse. I didn't know any writing people. I had an enthusiasm for a kind of country and a kind of people, rather than ambition.

"I've always had a habit of remembering mannerisms, turns of speech," she explained. "The phraseology of those people stuck in my mind. If I had made notes, or should make them now, the material collected would be dead. No, it's memory—the memory that goes with the vocation. When I sit down to write, turns of phrase I've forgotten for years come back like white ink before fire. I think that most of the basic material a writer works with is acquired before the age of fifteen. That's the important period: when one's not writing. Those years determine whether one's work will be poor and thin or rich and fine."

After a high school preparation, Miss Cather entered the University of Nebraska. She said, of this time:

"Back in the files of the college magazine, there were once several of my perfectly honest but very clumsy attempts to give the story of some of the Scandinavian and Bohemian settlers who lived not far from my father's farm. In these sketches, I simply tried to tell about the people, without much regard for style. These early stories were bald, clumsy, and emotional. As I got toward my senior year, I began to admire, for the first time, writing for writing's sake. In those days, no one seemed so wonderful as Henry James; for me, he was the perfect writer."

When Willa Cather graduated at nineteen, her instructors and friends expected her to become a "writer" in a few months, and achieve popular success. But they were disappointed. For almost nine years she wrote little besides a volume of verse, the experimental "April Twilights", and a dozen stories for magazines. Most of these stories she now dismisses as "affected" and "bad".

"It wasn't that I didn't want to write," she said of this period. "But I was too interested in trying to find out something about the world and about people. I worked on the Pittsburgh 'Leader', taught English in the Allegheny High School, went abroad for long periods, and traveled in the west. I couldn't have got as much out of those nine years if I'd been writing."

In 1905 there was published a collection of her stories, "The Troll Garden". Largely by reason of these, she was offered a position on "McClure's Magazine", of which she was managing editor from 1908 until 1912.

"I took a salaried position," she said, "because I didn't want to write directly to sell. I didn't want to compromise. Not that the magazine demands were wrong. But they were definite. I had a delightful sense of freedom when I'd saved up enough to take a house in Cherry Valley, New York, and could begin work on my first novel, 'Alexander's Bridge'.

"In 'Alexander's Bridge' I was still more preoccupied with trying to write well than with anything else. It takes a great deal of experience to become natural. People grow in honesty as they grow in anything else. A painter or writer must learn to distinguish what is his *own* from that which he admires. I never abandoned trying to make a compromise between the kind of matter that my experience had given me and the manner of writing which I admired, until I began my second novel, 'O Pioneers!' And from the first chapter, I decided not to 'write' at all—simply to give myself up to the pleasure of recapturing in memory people and places I had believed forgotten. This was what my friend Sarah Orne Jewett had advised me to do. She said to me that if my life had lain in a part of the world that was without a literature, and I couldn't tell about it truthfully in the form I most admired, I'd have to make a kind of writing that would tell it, no matter what I lost in the process."

"O Pioneers!" placed Miss Cather definitely among the writers who count. It is an epic of the early struggles of Swedish and Bohemian settlers in Nebraska—a book of beauty and power. In taking a for a title the name of one of Walt Whitman's poems, the author drew attention to his influence upon the mood of her narrative.

In "The Song of the Lark", Willa Cather chose a less impressionistic method. It is longer than "O Pioneers!", less concentrated, resembling more closely the conventional psychological novel. It is the story of Thea Kronborg, a Swedish-American singer, who wrenches herself away from an environment antagonistic to art, and becomes an opera "star". Critics took widely divergent attitudes toward the book. To many, it has not the same *aliveness* as "O Pioneers!" Randolph Bourne found it a digression into a field for which Miss Cather was not really fitted, either by her style, or her enthusiasm. But Edward Everett Hale discovered in it "a sense of something less common than life: namely, art as it exists in life—a very curious and elusive thing, but so beautiful, when one gets it, that one forgets all else."

Miss Cather's most recent novel, "My Antonia", is a fuller evocation of the "old, old west" than was "O Pioneers!" The descriptions of the western prairie, brief, poignant, lift us from our easy chairs and set us down on those high plains. The book is ruthless, poetical, tremendously alive. It is the finest thing Miss Cather has written. H. L. Mencken laid it down with the conviction that it is the best piece of fiction done by any woman in America. The portrayal of Antonia is masterly.

"She was a Bohemian girl," Miss Cather said, "who was good to me when I was a child. I saw a great deal of her from the time I was eight until I was twelve. She was big-hearted and essentially romantic."

Willa Cather's foreigners are true to type. August Brunius, after noting that the Swede, as presented by writers outside his own country, usually seems absurd to a Swedish reader, goes on to say that in "O Pioneers!"and "The Song of the Lark," Swedes are presented with true insight and art. Small wonder that all Miss Cather's books have been translated into the Scandinavian and are to be translated into French.

Her latest volume, "Youth and the Bright Medusa", is a collection of eight short stories. Simply and vividly told, they are studies of the artistic temperament. In them, there is none of the usual sentimentalizing about the artist. They are widely recognized as work of distinction. An anonymous critic in "The Nation" slyly remarks that the collection "represents the triumph of mind over Nebraska".

Willa Cather's best work is satisfying because it is sincere. In her books, there is none of the sweet reek that pervades the pages of so many "lady novelists". Love, to her, is "not a simple state, like measles". Her treatment of sex is without either squeamishness or sensuality. She loves the west, and the arts, particularly music, and she has sought to express feelings and convictions on these subjects. She tried, failed, and kept on trying until she succeeded. For example, we have her word for it that at college she attempted to tell about immigrants in rough sketches. She drew them more skilfully in "The Bohemian Girl", a short story which appeared in "McClure's Magazine" in 1912. Then came "O Pioneers!", a work of art. In "My Antonia", she reached what she had been advancing toward for many years. Similarly in her exploration of the minds and emotions of artists, she has striven to tell the truth—the truth stripped of sentimentality. She experimented in "The Troll Garden", succeeded partially in "Youth and the Bright Medusa", grasped fully what she had sought in "The Song of the Lark". It would, of course, be unfair to speak of the books and stories that led up to this novel and to "My Antonia" as preliminary studies, for there is too much in them not touched upon in the two later novels. But there is a certain summing up, in these books, of two subjects which have interested Miss Cather profoundly: the life of foreigners in the west, and the mind and heart of the artist. Of the books, the author herself said: "I think 'My Antonia' is the most successfully done. 'The Song of the Lark' was the most interesting to write."

"I work from two and a half to three hours a day," Miss Cather went on to say. "I don't hold myself to longer hours; if I did, I wouldn't gain by it. The only reason I write is because it interests me more than any other activity I've ever found. I like riding, going to operas and concerts, travel in the west; but on the whole writing interests me more than anything else. If I made a chore of it, my enthusiasm would die. I make it an adventure every day. I get more entertainment from it than any I could buy, except the privilege of hearing a few great musicians and singers. To listen to them interests me as much as a good morning's work.

"For me, the morning is the best time to write. During the other hours of the day I attend to my housekeeping, take walks in Central Park, go to concerts, and see something of my friends. I try to keep myself fit, fresh: one has to be in as good form to write as to sing. When not working, I shut work from my mind."

At present, Miss Cather is writing a new novel—she says of it:

"What I always want to do is to make the 'writing' count for less and less and the people for more. In this new novel I'm trying to cut out all analysis, observation, description, even the picture-making quality, in order to make things and people tell their own story simply by juxtaposition, without any persuasion or explanation on my part.

"Just as if I put here on the table a green vase, and beside it a yellow orange. Now, those two things affect each other. Side by side, they produce a reaction which neither of them will produce alone. Why should I try to say anything clever, or by any colorful rhetoric detract attention from those two objects, the relation they have to each other and the effect they have upon each other? I want the reader to see the orange and the vase—beyond that, I am out of it. Mere cleverness must go. I'd like the writing to be so lost in the object, that it doesn't exist for the reader—except for the reader who knows how difficult it is to lose writing in the object. One must choose one's audience, and the audience I try to write for is the one interested in the effect the green vase brings out in the orange, and the orange in the green vase."

Miss Cather has never sought publicity, or quick success. It took her three years to write "The Song of the Lark", and three to write "My Antonia". Of the two paths of art—give the public what it wants, or make your work so fine that the public will want it—she has consistently chosen the path of fine work. She is moving unhurriedly toward a richer self-expression.

Archer Latrobe Carroll (1894–1996) was born in Washington, D.C. Following his graduation from Harvard University he became a journalist, with a career spanning more than fifteen years, until he began a career as freelance writer. He and his wife, Ruth Robinson Carroll, co-authored a number of children's books, including the award-winning *Peanut* written in 1951, and *Digby the Only Dog* written in 1955.